JODENE WEBER

THE BALD-FACED DECEPTION

Author's Note:

This is a work of fiction but partially inspired by the author's own experience as a 9/11 responder.

Publicly available information from the National Alopecia Areata Foundation was researched, but any mistakes regarding alopecia are entirely my own.

The drug Wozilfin is a fictitious creation and any similarities to existing pharmaceuticals are purely coincidental.

Part I
The Cover-Up

1
LINDSAY
June 2

It's been twenty-four hours and thirty-seven minutes since my husband kissed me goodbye, drove off to work, and disappeared.

Nick didn't come home last night. At first, I thought he was running late, stuck in traffic, or changing a flat tire. Any of those reasonable explanations a wife considers when her husband isn't where he is supposed to be.

When I called him initially, Nick's phone went straight to voicemail. A tinge of worry colored my curiosity. Thirty minutes later, I gave him another jingle, hoping he had grabbed a beer after work with a buddy and would apologize for having lost track of time. But when Nick didn't pick up then, or on my third attempt, I slumped against the kitchen counter with a sick sensation in my gut.

The sad truth is I've searched for my husband before, and when I did, I didn't like what I found.

But this is different than the last time I played detective. After forty-seven unanswered phone calls, umpteen ghosted texts, fruitless drives through random streets while contacting area hospitals and everybody else I can think of, *I can't find Nick.*

The one thing I do have that I didn't have before is the knowledge I gained from my previous hunt. Names, faces, places—the all-important details plotting an unsettling connect-the-dots picture of what is afoot.

I've watched enough *Dateline* to know the cops won't do anything until a person has been missing for at least twenty-four hours, and then, you need to bypass the crusty deputy out front and demand to speak to a real detective—so here I am, at the police station, sitting in a musty, square room with oatmeal-colored walls, ready to spill my guts about my missing husband and who might want to harm him.

The door opens and a burly man enters the room. He walks to the other side of the small table from where I sit and places his notebook down. Pulling out a chair, he says, "I'm Detective Bob Klink. Heard you insisted on speaking with a detective?"

I straighten from a slouch as he settles into his seat.

"Yes, I'm Lindsey Sutton. Nick Sutton is my husband. He never came home last night," I say, getting right to the meat of the matter. "He's not answering his phone. I called his friends and checked the local hospitals, but no one knew where he was or what happened to him. And Oliver, Nick's brother... I called him, too. He runs the family business."

Detective Klink doesn't blink or mutter a word when I pause to take a breath, which is somewhat unnerving. I gesture to the left with my thumb, like a hitchhiker, coughing up what little information I have about Nick's last-known whereabouts.

"Do you know Sutton's Apothecary on Old Winston Road?" I ask, not waiting for him to answer. "Nick works there, but Ollie said he left his truck in the parking lot. He drove off in one of the company cars yesterday..."

"Whoa, okay, let's slow down," Detective Klink barks, halting my story while opening his notebook and clicking his pen. He scribbles a few notations and says, "What's your husband's full name and age?"

"Nicholas Isaac Sutton. He's thirty-four," I say, fidgeting on my chair.

"Height, weight, hair and eye color?"

"Um, he's six-two, maybe 185 pounds, with brown hair and blue eyes."

"Any distinguishing marks, scars, or tattoos?"

"He had knee surgery. There's a nasty scar."

"Which knee?"

"His left knee."

"When was the last time you saw your husband, and what was he wearing?"

"Yesterday morning around eight, when he left for work. He had a golf shirt on, a red one with a Nike logo, and tan pants. And, ah, brown loafers and a leather belt. His truck..."

"Make and model?"

I swipe a stray tendril of hair off my face, frustrated by the pace of this conversation.

"He drives a Ford F150, but the truck isn't missing. It's still parked at the apothecary. Nick took a delivery car…"

Detective Klink raises his index finger, like he's pressing an imaginary pause button.

"What's the make and model of the delivery vehicle?"

"Um, it's a smaller Chevy, I think. Oliver will know. He, ah, he didn't want me coming here."

Detective Klink glances up from his notebook with a quizzical expression that scrunches his bushy eyebrows together, as he ponders my statement.

"Why not?" he asks, his pen perched, ready to jot down my response. "Isn't he worried about his brother?"

Shaking my head, a beat passes, and I say, "He doesn't want me to tell you that Nick is cheating on me."

The admission is humiliating and my eyelids flutter, as I fend off tears. Detective Klink inhales a long, raspy breath, taking a pause of his own. When I glance at him again, he grumbles, "Mrs. Sutton, the police don't track down cheating spouses."

"He's not with her!" I snap at him, unwilling to be turned away. "I drove by her house last night. It was the first place I checked when Oliver said Nick's truck was still at the apothecary. I thought, maybe, he found the slap-on tracker and switched to a delivery car…"

Detective Klink interrupts me again.

"You have a tracking device on your husband's truck?"

Nodding, I'm still jolted by the memory of how I discovered the affair. Three weeks ago, I went to visit my mother-in-law, Fran, at Willow Bend Long-Term Care Home. Out of nowhere, she muttered, with a twinkle in her eye, that Nick was in love with her physician, Dr. Diane Desmond. Under normal circumstances, I wouldn't have given Fran's remark a second thought, especially given her early-stage dementia. People use the word love colloquially all the time… they love their doctors, their plumbers, their hairdressers. No big deal. But Nick *did* visit Willow Bend a lot, and I was super hormonal from the never-ending IVF shots that have yet to produce a baby. One little comment, mixed with an eye twinkle, ignited a spark in me that fear set ablaze.

As a child of philandering parents, I know the lengths people go to when hiding affairs. It took me less than a hot minute with a slap-on tracking device to figure out Fran was right. Nick's truck tracked to a remote rental cabin on a Saturday afternoon when he was supposed to be at work. From the thick woods, I watched with binoculars, biting my knuckles when dishy Dr. Desmond showed up in mile-high stilettos and a trench coat, with God-knows-what on underneath. She flitted into the cabin with a bottle of wine in her hand and a way-too-confident smirk painted on her face.

"You and your husband are having marital issues," Detective Klink says, flipping his notebook shut. "But it's not a crime for a guy to take off for a day or two to get some space. He'll come home when he's ready."

My fists pound the table, pent-up dismay over Nick's betrayal fusing with my current level of fear.

"You don't understand! I *never* confronted Nick about the affair. He's still hiding it from me, so not showing up at home last night makes no sense, especially because his mistress was at home with *her* husband," I say, leaning forward. "They live on a corner lot, and I drove by several times while they were outside, barbecuing in the back yard. They had friends join them for a late dinner. Nick *wasn't* there," I stress, frustration lacing my tone.

"So what?" Detective Klink shrugs, stroking his goatee. "Your husband could be holed up at a motel or staying with a friend. Maybe when you were calling his pals trying to find him, one of them lied to you—guys will do that for their buddies. Or, for all you know, he could be having affairs with multiple women."

Detective Klink's implication that Nick is more likely a serial cheater than a potential crime victim infuriates me. Doubling down, my protests become louder and more insistent.

"Don't you *see*?" I counter, disgust peppering my pitch. "Her husband was making sure other people were around! People who can say he acted normally at a casual barbeque, that last night was just like any other night. But *something* happened to Nick yesterday, sometime during the day. That's why he never returned to work…"

Dubious, Detective Klink cuts me off. His tone is curt.

"Mrs. Sutton, you have the right to file a missing persons report. However, I warn you, you sound a bit paranoid. There is no evidence of a crime, and as I said, your husband might be taking a little time away to sort himself out. He'll probably show up today."

Paranoid? Not after what I saw two Saturdays ago.

"Or perhaps," I hiss, folding my arms across my chest, "Mayor Roger Desmond did something to my husband to *punish* Nick for sleeping with his wife!"

The accusation is a verbal sucker punch rendering Detective Klink speechless. He glances down at his notebook, avoiding eye contact with me.

My mouth twists into a tight pucker, determined to make Detective Klink understand the threat Nick poses to Romulus Mayor Roger Desmond.

"I assume, given your line of work, you know Mayor Desmond. Have you met his wife? Dr. Diane Desmond?" I ask.

Detective Klink scoffs, as he recovers from his initial shock.

"That's enough, Mrs. Sutton. The mayor and Dr. Desmond are an upstanding couple, both very well respected in this community. Just because your husband didn't come home last night is no reason to impugn their reputations. I'm not including your allegation in my report. We'll file the paperwork that Nick is missing, but like I said, I'm sure your husband will turn up in a day or two."

"And if he doesn't?" I press, incensed that he characterized Nick's mistress as respectable. "Then what?"

"If necessary, we will try to determine if a crime has occurred or if your husband took off on his own accord. We'll issue a press release to the local television stations and to the online news site *The Finger Lakes Flash*—most people get their news on their cell phones these days," he adds. "For now, go home. Try not to worry."

It's my turn to scoff, which irks Detective Klink. He pushes his chair back and stands to leave. Gathering his notebook, he scowls at me, slinging a final insult.

"One more thing, Mrs. Sutton. If your husband is the victim of a crime, rest assured I will investigate all avenues necessary… to include *you.*"

THE FINGER LAKES FLASH

Your online snapshot capturing the local news you need to know.
June 5

LOCAL VETERAN REPORTED MISSING

Nicholas "Nick" Sutton, age 34, a lifelong resident of Romulus, is missing. Sutton, a member of the United States Army Reserve and a combat veteran with two tours in Afghanistan, was reported missing by his wife, Lindsay Sutton, on June 2.

Sutton was last seen on June 1, when he reported to work at Sutton's Apothecary, an independent pharmacy founded by his father, Theodore Sutton, in 1985. The Romulus Police Department says Sutton was delivering prescription pharmaceuticals in a maroon, Chevrolet Malibu at the time of his disappearance. This vehicle has a removable placard containing the Sutton's Apothecary logo on the driver's side door, and a "SUTTON 3" personalized New York license plate.

Oliver Sutton, a licensed pharmacist and the current owner of Sutton's Apothecary, declined to provide a statement about his brother's disappearance to *The Finger Lakes Flash.*

Sutton is described as a white male, 6'2" tall, 185 pounds, with brown hair, blue eyes, and a surgical scar on his left knee. He was last seen wearing a red Nike golf shirt, tan pants, and brown loafers.

The Romulus Police Department urges anyone with information about Nicholas Sutton's whereabouts to contact their tip line, at 1-800-543-TIPS. Callers may remain anonymous.

2
CLAUDIA
June 6

The missing veteran story is piquing interest. Among readers, and with me.

Nick Sutton's disappearance is a headline maker and I'm thirsty for details—eager to seek the truth, all while camouflaging my own.

My room of disguises sits at the end of the hallway underneath the spiral staircase leading to the attic office, where the scuffed wood floor slopes to the left. The door is nondescript, a simple portal leading into what one would assume is a normal spare bedroom, with a sturdy bed frame hiding dust bunnies and an odd spare sock forgotten by last year's guest. Only there isn't a bed. And no guests are welcome.

This room serves as my secret weapon, the heart of my safe zone. A compilation of all things necessary to camouflage the *damage*. It's a convalescence cave, equipped with the essential things, like darkening shades, specialty LED lights, and the all-important swivel chair, the maneuvering mechanism able to whirl me away from my enemy, the mirror.

This room makes the new life I created for myself possible. Rubbing topical foam solution on my bald head to stimulate my hair follicles, I'm ready to begin my rituals.

By day, I am the owner and operator of the online news and events sensation, *The Finger Lakes Flash*. Covering the local communities surrounding Seneca, Cayuga, and Keuka Lakes in north-central New York's wine country, my website consumes most of my time, which helps, because late at night, without the distraction of work, I remember.

I don't look the same anymore, and I don't like to talk about my appearance much because it triggers my anxiety. In simple terms, not everyone harmed at the scene of a mass murder dies right away. Some people, like me, may die later from their injuries and/or corresponding illnesses. If I do, my death will be added to the official fatality count, which is growing all the time. And in the meantime, I live my life cringing at the site of my true reflection.

Wigs rest atop an army of porcelain mannequin heads, postured like protective soldiers reinforcing my bunker. The shorter styles sit on the highest shelf, with my longer human hair and synthetic tresses mounted below. Most people don't know that wigs are named, and for today, I'm picking Chloe. The most natural look I sport, but also a masterpiece of construction, with a lace front, giving the appearance of scalp and a hairline. Chloe's tawny bob-cut camouflages my head, and all the insecurities festering inside of it.

My attackers struck on 9/11 by hijacking an airplane and crashing it in a remote Pennsylvania field, killing all onboard. I was a television journalist then, and I inhaled toxic jet fuel for days covering the crash of Flight 93. Inasmuch as, I am classified as a 9/11 responder, with an unprecedented, *"probably, but we need more data"* condition, where strange things are happening, something none of the brightest ego-God physicians can explain. My hair started falling out four years ago. The doctors call it alopecia. I call it an ominous first sign of trouble.

Reaching up to the top shelf, I snatch Chloe from her perch, whispering to her like a pet.

"Your turn this afternoon. Lucky you, Chloe. This could be *big*."

My yearning for information about Nick Sutton's disappearance is tempered only by the realization I need to leave my house. Since Oliver Sutton wouldn't speak to me on the phone about his missing brother, I've decided to venture out and pay a visit to Sutton's Apothecary. Most of the content for my online news site is generated through telephone interviews, text messages, or email press releases. In the digital age, it's amazing how much I can do from home. But sometimes, face-to-face contact is necessary. I don't relish it, but it's a lot like my bald head—I need to come to terms with it.

Slouching in my rolling swivel chair, my bare feet push along the cold, wood floor toward the mirror. Not a day goes by that I don't miss my hair and the curtain of protection it fostered—not just for my head, but for my heart. Staring in the mirror at the vast, patchy bald ovals that dot the landscape of my scalp, my daily lens is routinely fogged by an internal storm of resentment and sadness. Wigs cover my baldness, but I can't bandage my wounded spirit. Four years after my hair started falling out, I am a virtual hermit.

I place Chloe on my left hand, like a softball player donning a field glove. By rote memory, my hands position the hair piece over the mesh cap atop my skull, allowing my skin to breathe while preventing the wig from slipping. An elastic band encircles the back of my head, and with a final tug, I turn to face my image.

The person I am today stares back at me. Not bad, all things considered. Eyebrow and eyelash application are next. As I'm reaching for a tube of glue, my cell phone vibrates atop my vanity. I hit the speaker button on my phone.

"*The Finger Lakes Flash*. Claudia Marton speaking. How can I help you?"

A woman clears her throat and says, "This is Lindsay, Nick Sutton's wife. You ran a story about him yesterday."

The missing veteran. Oliver Sutton's brother. *His wife is calling me.*

"Yes, hello," I say, fumbling out of my rolling chair and heading to the spiral staircase in the hallway. "The police press release came in late yesterday afternoon. I tried to get a comment from your brother-in-law, Oliver—he advertises the apothecary on my site, but he didn't want to speak to me about your husband. Would you be willing to talk with me?"

"That's why I'm calling," Lindsay says, in a clipped tone. "I want to speak with you."

Excitement pulses through me. "Great. Let me get to my computer so I can take notes."

Ascending the spiral staircase in short order, I step inside my office and open my laptop as Lindsay Sutton starts babbling.

"Oliver doesn't know I am contacting you. In fact, he told me to keep my trap shut and *not* talk to you," she says, with emphasis. "But there's a bigger story here. My husband has been missing for days. I think someone may have killed him."

Taken aback, I start typing as fast as I can.

"Okay, um, why do you think your husband is dead and who would want to kill him?"

Lindsay's voice drops to a hushed whisper. "Can I stay anonymous?"

The request intrigues me, but I need to be transparent. "Ideally, I would like to use you as a named source. But for now, if you feel more comfortable, you can tell me what you know, and I won't attribute the information to you," I say, hoping this will satisfy her.

She sighs into the phone but doesn't answer me, and I fear she'll hang up.

"This must be very stressful for you," I add, glancing at the photo of her husband contained in the police press release. Nick Sutton is a very handsome man. It's not surprising to me that his vanishment story, accompanied by this picture, is generating buzz on *The Finger Lakes Flash*.

"Oliver doesn't want me talking to you," Lindsay repeats. "He's mad that I went to the police." Her delivery accelerates, growing anxious. "Nick's family doesn't want me sharing what I know, especially my sister-in-law, Brenda. She's afraid this will hurt business at the apothecary."

My forehead furrows, confused by the family division. I was disappointed Oliver wouldn't speak with me yesterday, but my years as a journalist have taught me that a multitude of factors can be at play when people refuse to comment. I don't know what type of relationship Oliver Sutton has with his younger sibling. Are they close, or do they barely speak? Does he believe Nick's in danger? Or is he angry and annoyed, thinking his missing brother simply took off for a few days and this is a fuss about nothing?

Lindsay Sutton's sister-in-law may have valid concerns, too. Chitter-chatter could hurt their family business. The Finger Lakes region is full of tiny lakeside communities where everybody knows everyone else. A place where small town gossip blossoms faster than a giant hogweed plant but is equally poisonous.

"Tell me about Nick," I say, uncertain if my attempt to redirect the conversation will further unsettle Lindsay. To my relief, her guard relaxes, and she pipes up.

"We met when we were fifteen, at Lakeview High. Nick was a jock, and I was a cheerleader. He's always been athletic, so none of us were surprised when he joined the military. He's in the Army Reserve now and works at the apothecary with Oliver. We married ten years ago and he's—well, my everything. We have this magnetic connection, like the moon tugging at the ocean. I never wanted to be with anyone else."

Lindsay pauses, and I'm flummoxed. Perhaps she's sleep deprived and sick with worry, but I was expecting her to describe her husband's behavior. What does he like to do, and where should people look for him? Does he have a favorite fishing spot, or hike specific nature trails? Is he friendly, someone who strikes up conversations with total strangers? Or is he more sullen, apt to fall off the grid and camp in the wilderness by himself? And most importantly, who are his enemies? *Why does she think someone killed her husband?*

Scribbling verbatim notes of her comments, I am about to ask another question when she lets out a startled gasp.

"Someone's here," she cries. "They're banging at my front door. Stay on the line with me. Please!"

"Of course," I reply, alarmed by the fear radiating in her voice. I tuck a strand of wig hair behind my ear, listening for clues. Sharp thuds pound in succession, but Lindsay is as silent as a stone, making me wonder if she is holding her breath as she approaches her door. A few more seconds pass, and suddenly, a plaintive wail emits from the telephone.

"Oh, no," she moans. "No, no, no!"

Clenching my cell phone, my anxiety level spikes. Her cry is haunting, equal measures pain and dread, and I fear the worst.

"What's happening, Lindsay?"

She chokes back a sob and says, "The police are here."

THE FINGER LAKES FLASH

Your online snapshot capturing the local news you need to know.
June 8

MISSING VETERAN CONFIRMED DEAD

Breaking News: The Seneca County medical examiner confirms the human remains found in Buttermilk Creek on June 6 belonged to Nicholas "Nick" Sutton, age 34, a lifelong resident of Romulus. The cause of Sutton's death is listed as blunt force trauma, but manner of death is undetermined. The Romulus Police Department reports no sign of foul play in connection to Sutton's death.

Sutton, a member of the United States Army Reserve and a combat veteran with two tours in Afghanistan, was reported missing on June 2. His remains were discovered in Buttermilk Creek by local teens. At the time of his death, Sutton worked for his brother at Sutton's Apothecary, an independent pharmacy serving residents in the Finger Lakes.

Sutton is survived by his wife, Lindsay Sutton, his mother Francine Sutton, his brother Oliver (Brenda) Sutton, and his niece Delaney Sutton, all of Romulus. He is preceded in death by his father, Theodore Sutton, the founder of Sutton's Apothecary.

Condolence messages may be posted on the In Memoriam-Nicholas Sutton Page under *The Finger Lakes Flash* obituary tab. All postings are publicly available.

THE FINGER LAKES FLASH

Your online snapshot capturing the local news you need to know.
June 9

In Memoriam: Nicholas Sutton

~Nick was a delightful young man. Always had a smile on his face.
Heaven gained an angel.
Rosemary Dixon, former neighbor

~Nicholas was a wonderful asset to the local community.
Heartfelt condolences to the Sutton family and the entire team
at Sutton's Apothecary during this most difficult time.
Roger Desmond, mayor of Romulus

~No one made me laugh harder. My brother from another
mother. Luv ya buddy!
John Corry, lifelong friend,
employee at Sutton's Apothecary

~Nick made enemies. He didn't kill himself.
The cops don't want you to know.
They won't say who wanted him dead and WHY!
Lindsay Sutton, widow of Nick Sutton

ELEVEN WEEKS LATER

3
LINDSAY
August 26

My husband was murdered. Nick isn't coming back. Not ever. And my mother-in-law knows more about it than she is saying.

Fran Sutton lives in room 319 at Willow Bend Long-Term Care Home. It's a small, cramped space—larger than a broom closet but smaller than an efficiency apartment. She rocks in her chair, with a crocheted blanket tossed across her lap. In her hand, a pen idles over a Sudoku puzzle in a game book. As I lean in, she eyes me with suspicion.

"Let's talk about what you said, Fran. The truth about Nick."

Her eyes glance toward a small table holding photographs of the family, including one of my late husband Nick, her youngest son. There's not much to see in this room. The hospital bed is tidy, and a few novels are pinched between shiny brass bookends atop a four-drawer dresser. The door to the adjoining bathroom is ajar and I detect the faint odor of bleach. Fran cocks her head to the side before answering me.

"He's not here."

"That's right. Do you know why?"

Hitting the recording button on my cell phone, I swipe to my screen saver and hoist the phone up to chin level, about six inches from her mouth and six inches from mine. Nick's picture is displayed on the glass face. Fran swipes at it with her hand.

"No, no. No hitting. Say it again. Tell me about Nick," I say, pointing at the photo.

Her face contorts, folds creasing her forehead. A small tremor quivers her upper lip, while the Sudoku book and pen fall to the floor, as she grabs for my phone.

"Stop it, Fran. Come on, it's me—Lindsay. Remember? Your favorite daughter-in-law. Let's talk about Nick," I say again, placing her hand gently back in her lap.

17

She rebels, reaching for my neck. Blue and purple veins bulge beneath paper-thin dry skin and her jagged nails scratch and pierce like a feral cat. She squeezes. Hard. I gag, dropping my phone as I yank her hands off my neck and jerk away before she crushes my windpipe. Fran still thinks Nick is alive, despite crying heavy tears on three separate occasions after I reminded her of the truth. Nick's death is a daily nightmare for me, too.

Fran moans, wringing her hands. I scoop the Sudoku book and pen from the floor, along with my phone. By some miracle, the glass face didn't shatter.

"You can't strangle me, Fran," I sigh with exasperation, shaken by her sudden aggression. "You *will* remember telling me Nick was in love with your doctor. Today's just not the day."

She stares at me, her face an empty chalkboard, dusty white and blank.

I give up, placing her game book on the table as I head for the door. My hand twists the knob, and I glance over my shoulder at the once vibrant woman slouched in her chair. A thought occurs to me, and I gulp.

Show time.

"She's trying to kill me!"

My scream bounces off the tile floor, echoing down the drab hallway where a fluorescent light blinks with sporadic bursts amid water-stained ceiling panels. I peer to the left, and then to the right. My neck aches from the tight pressure applied by my mother-in-law's liver-spotted hands a moment ago. Silence. Where is everybody? Why isn't there an army of medical saviors in crisp white coats running toward me with stethoscopes? I sigh again.

Maybe because I cry murder a lot.

I am the one everyone is whispering about, the old-lady gossips, the nosy neighbors, the news junkies, and the Karens. The *delusional* one in their midst. A sad, pretty widow in denial, drinking wine from the bottle while crumpled on the closet floor, surrounded by scattered pictures of me and Nick and all the big and little moments that built our love story. The snaps taken at our high school prom, with my carnation corsage and his bubble-gum pink bow tie, or the shutter clicks capturing lazy summer afternoons in our fishing boat, with a cooler of beer, matching smiles, and sun-kissed shoulders. There's a bunch of merry shots of our flannel pajama Christmas mornings, and even more of our flannel shirt campfire nights. *Plenty* of photographs showing how *happy* we were.

But I am also the wretch who passes out on the same closet floor only to rise at eleven in the morning, with a lion's mane hairdo and mucous crust in the corners of her eyes, repeating the same nasty, two syllable word. The word no one believes or wants to hear.

Murder.

I blame *The Finger Lakes Flash*. Nick's photograph headlined under the *Flash's* website banner for several days, his toothy grin and dimples a magnet for the online gawkers and the whisperers. The missing hometown hero, an Army Reservist with two tours in Afghanistan, movie star looks, and the beautiful but oh-so-delicate *barren* wife.

Me. I'm the barren wife. That's what the whisperers say.

Nick was found dead eleven weeks ago in a creek bed beneath a high bluff, without his cell phone, which remains missing. The medical examiner's office listed the cause of his death as blunt force trauma, but the manner of death was undetermined, which is loosey-goosey dead body lingo meaning they couldn't tell if he fell, jumped, or was pushed. Everyone's favorite online news source printed this little tidbit, followed by the official police statement: *No sign of foul play.* But worst of all, *The Finger Lakes Flash* trashed my post on Nick's In-Memoriam page, erasing any suggestion that something sinister happened to my husband.

It's time someone listens to me.

My feet start the long, slow march down the hallway, following a blue stripe painted on the floor. Fran knew Nick's secret. Maybe if we adjust her medicine, she'll remember it. It's essential. My survival depends on it.

If a husband fails to make passionate pleas for his missing wife's safe return, he is suspect number one, a mid-life crisis kind of guy with a piece of ass on the side and a hefty life insurance policy. But then, there's me. My gut-punch suspicions about Nick's disappearance and death didn't land with even a blip of credibility on *The Finger Lakes Flash's* radar. Talk about cyber-bullying. After the police said *No sign of foul play*, erasing my post from Nick's memorial page sent a subliminal news vibe out to the masses… my athletic husband most likely didn't fall, and he wasn't pushed. He bailed out, and I'm not facing it.

Here's the true headline: Police departments don't want homicides. Neither do lakefront resorts, souvenir shops, or the Friday fish fry hotspots. Dead bodies are bad for business. They stop visitors in their tracks, spooking them off the hiking trails and away from the local wineries with bottles of Riesling for sale. The regional economy depends upon tourists getting hammered on sweet white wine while soaking up the fall foliage with drunken kaleidoscope goggles. Murders make the local fizz flat, corking any reasonable person's desire to spend time in a breathtaking but lethal locale. Shutting me up is a mutually beneficial, double backscratching agreement between the police and the business crowd. Their muzzle of choice is a false narrative:

Lindsay Sutton is unhinged.

Only I'm not. What I am is *pissed,* and for a good reason.

I went to the police. I sat in their stuffy interview room across from Detective Klink and I tried laying it all out. But Detective Klink shut me down, hard and fast. *Too fast.*

Nick deserves justice, even if he was a cheater. If Fran can remember what she said about Dr. Desmond, it will help establish two important things: I'm not crazy, and a motive existed for killing Nick. The last part is crucial since a murderer is on the loose, and because life insurance doesn't pay for potential suicidal jumps into shallow creeks within a year of opening the policy.

People are gathered at the nurse's station at the end of the hall. An elderly woman in a wheelchair waves her arms in animated fashion, her right leg elevated and encased in a fiberglass cast. She points in my direction while speaking with Ken Preston, a male nurse, and a former high school classmate of mine. He glances over his shoulder, his forehead creasing.

"Lindsay, what's wrong?"

My vague memories of teenage Ken consist of acne, awkwardness, and little else.

"My mother-in-law is getting worse, Ken. She's spiraling. She lunged at me and put her hands around my throat."

Trembling, I tug at the collar of my tight shirt, exposing the swollen, bloody track marks her fingernails raked across the left side of my neck.

The woman in the wheelchair responds first, a sharp tone zinging her words.

"Honey, when Franny goes zombie-like silent is when you worry. There's a spark left. Don't kill it. Be patient with her."

Don't kill it.

Rage bubbles in my throat. *Be patient.* My husband cheated on me, but I said nothing, because a stocked designer nursery awaited the baby I wanted, but still didn't have. I am the poster child for patience.

"You know Fran?" I ask, in the flattest tone one can muster.

"Yes, dear, we went to primary school together. I'm Marlene Flynn, but my maiden name is Wyatt. Fran and I reconnected here. She still experiences many good days. All is not lost yet."

Bingo. I'm counting on the synapses firing in my favor.

"I'm Lindsay, her daughter-in-law. My husband Nick…"

"Yes, dear. My condolences. We all know what happened, ah, with your husband."

The hell you do.

Dr. Diane Desmond forgot the Hippocratic Oath while using her feverish bedside manner on Nick. "First do no harm" didn't extend to me, or to her husband, Roger.

"Ken, will you walk with me outside so I can speak with you about Fran's medication? I don't like her agitation, but as Mrs. Flynn points out, there are still good days when she's cogent. I want to help her focus."

Ken nods, and my plan is in motion. Tweaking the meds will calm my mother-in-law down, allowing her to focus and remember what she told me. *She still has good days.* As a long-standing pillar of Romulus society, people *will* believe her when she says it again, helping to expose her son's murderer… an admission sure to rock everyone's boat.

Romulus Mayor Roger Desmond had motive. His glamorous wife two-timed him with the corpse found in the creek. The police were told, and they did *nothing.*

The Finger Lakes Flash followed in locked step, publishing the false narrative the cops spoon fed the media, while also torpedoing my post on Nick's memorial page.

Eleven long weeks later, I am increasingly anxious, my grief ping-ponging between walls of frustration and towers of sadness. My husband's death warrants justice, and I am entitled to his life insurance money.

And as for the old-lady gossips, the nosy neighbors, the news junkies, and the Karens… those busybodies fell for a phony cover-up story. Shame on them for labeling me as crazy, delusional, and unhinged. My husband *was* murdered, and I am determined to prove it. If Fran can't remember what she said, I'll come up with another strategy. I'll search. I'll dig.

Someone must know something.

4
CLAUDIA
August 26

Glancing at the printed words on the page, endorphins surge within me. An anonymous message arrived a few moments ago in the tipster email box for *The Finger Lakes Flash*, and it oozes with a stronghold squeeze, hinting at a blockbuster news story.

Listen up!

I think they are on to me.

Go to Lakeview Cemetery. Section E. Find Seymour Ghent. He holds the clue.

Hurry! People are dying, only their deaths are masked with a clever veil.

It's not natural.

This is murder.

Since I'm both a journalist and a living victim of the deadliest murder plot ever carried out on American soil, the tipster got my attention. I'm fascinated, wondering what clue I will find at Seymour Ghent's grave.

Pulling open a drawer in my vanity, I grab a plastic case with dividers, anxious to finish my grooming routine so I can go. Enclosed in the case are Angelina, Sandra, Brooke, Reese, Kim, and Julia, the celebrity-name-inspired stars of my paste-on eyebrow wig collection. The Brooke brows are fantastic, with a natural, thick shape. The Angelina arches compliment my longer wigs, and my Sandra set is the all-around winner for looking nice with everything. Today, I'm going with Julia eyebrows and my Wendy wig, a light-brown shag cut with caramel highlights. Painting a thin coat of glue on the lace backing of the brow wigs, I position them and examine my work. Pleased, the corners of my mouth perk, and I tell my reflection, "Wendy and Julia, you are a killer combination."

Time for eyelashes.

I debate applying individual lashes or strips. Today's snoop mission is outdoors, with the double-trouble possibility of rain and human interaction, so presentable but forgettable is the look I'm going for. The magnetic type won't cling without any real eyelashes anchoring them, so a self-adhesive false lash-line pair is my best bet. Less time consuming than individual lash application, and no sticky glue fuss. In the game of hairlessness, I celebrate minor victories.

Patting the lashes into place, I survey the results.

Not bad. A quick dusting of blending powder at the edge of my wig, a touch of blush and a dab of lip gloss. All set. Transformed into an anonymous entity, normal in appearance, able to walk among the masses without a care in the world.

I sigh.

Little do they know.

5
LINDSAY
August 26

Ken Preston follows me into the parking lot like an overeager puppy, blabbering away about a bunch of dementia-related stuff I will never remember. Why isn't he zoning in on Fran's tiger claw attack on my neck and her fading memory? He doesn't get it. She is the character witness, the one who can tell the snooty sauvignon sisters gathering for monthly mahjong meetups that despite popular opinion, I am not headed for the loony bin.

"…which is why geriatric care is so rewarding. Your mother-in-law's comfort is paramount, and it is my duty to ensure she receives the best care in the world. I found my calling."

Ken shoots me one of those know-it-all end-of-lecture gazes, which is ridiculous. Willow Bend reeks of menthol liniment mixed with bleach and pee, and given the mauling my neck took, "the best care in the world" doesn't include mani-pedis. Ken's male ego wants stroking, but that's not on my takeout menu.

"I can buy Fran comfort with high thread count sheets, Ken. She needs action and activity. Something to keep her in the zone. Tell me, how come Dr. Desmond is never here during any of my visits?"

His eyes cast downward—an avoidance mechanism anybody who watches *Dateline* knows is an admission of guilt.

"I don't know. She may be with other patients when you visit or at the hospital, making rounds. I'm sure it is a bit awkward…"

"Awkward, why?"

"Um, since Nick's death, his mother doesn't always remember he's not coming back. Dr. Desmond and I do our best to be honest with Fran while caring for her cognitive issues." Ken flounders for something else to say, but his word tank is not deep. Flustered, he turns, pointing left to a row of cars. "Hey, let me show you my new wheels."

My mental playbook shuffles. Ken's goofy awkwardness is annoying, but I need him if my plan is going to work. We sidestep a few jagged ruts in the parking lot, walking toward a shiny BMW sedan.

"Oh, how beautiful, Ken… a Beamer! You did well, my friend. Working with Dr. Desmond is paying off."

He beams with pride, clueless to the name drop. "Maybe, sometime, um, we can take a drive?"

Leverage, finally. My teeth bite at the back of my tongue, triggering my tear ducts to produce the perfect watery eye.

"That's nice… But I can't. Despite what everyone is saying, it is still too soon."

Boom. Bait dangled. Come on sucker. Bite.

Ken stares at me with a look of disappointment.

"Um, sure. I… I get it. Maybe some other time?" His tone drops an octave lower, in the caliber range where suggestion and understanding mesh.

"Do me a favor? Talk to Dr. Desmond. Ask her to tweak Fran's medication. As Mrs. Flynn said, there are still many good days. Nick would want me to do what I can to help her focus." I lower my voice to a whisper. "Dr. Desmond's bedside manner went outside the walls of Willow Bend, Ken. I can't ask her myself."

My zing lands, pooling in the nearby cement pockmarks dotting the parking lot. Turning toward my practical sport utility vehicle with my chin held high, Ken and his mid-life-crisis luxury car are left in my wake. My mind imagines him staring, mouth agape, watching the sway of my hips.

Sliding behind the steering console, my hands grip the wheel as my eyelids shut. My obsession with Nick's betrayal is not without purpose. He wouldn't jump to his death while living every hot-blooded guy's mid-life fantasy. No way. The hotter the affair, the easier it is to convince myself that the jealous mayor murdered him in a secluded spot deep in the woods. A place with no surveillance cameras, no Wi-Fi, and no witnesses to a crime in commission. The *perfect* place for a heated confrontation and a hefty push. Nick's death was no simple *Humpty Dumpty* tumble. *The Finger Lakes Flash* erased my post for a reason. Rejected and dismissed. Like me, the forgotten wife.

My purse rests on the passenger seat, and I rifle through crumpled tissues and unpaid bills, hunting for my flask and anxiety medication.

The vial contains one solitary pill, which would depress me if I wasn't confident about scoring more medication. Unscrewing the cap on the flask, the alcohol oozes down my throat with a lazy river burn. It washes the anti-anxiety pill down, draining the last droplets in the flask. A little crutch until I can get home.

Starting the ignition, I flip open the visor mirror. The parallel scratches on my neck resemble red licorice sticks. Of all of us, Nick spent the most time with Fran, and now the rest of the family needs to figure out a visitation schedule. Maybe these catlike claw markings can work to my advantage. I hit the button on the dash screen and say, "Call Brenda."

Amped with purpose and a plan, my car eases out of the parking lot as my sister-in-law picks up her phone on the third ring.

"Lindsay Kelly Sutton, what took you so long?"

Brenda Hawthorne Sutton speaks with brazenness, which syncs with her poppy red hair color. A plump counterpart to my waif figure, Brenda is six years my senior and an only child, like me. Her social status places her in wide acquaintance circles, but I can't name a single woman she considers a close friend, which I can relate to. I don't have girlfriends, by choice. My mother warned me long ago how dangerous other women can be, and Diane Desmond is a perfect example. Brenda's the beta to my alpha, although I let her think she's the alpha. It helps me manipulate her into doing what I need. Like getting Oliver, Nick's pharmacist brother and Brenda's husband, to refill my prescriptions before the allowable fill date.

"Your mother-in-law tried to strangle me. Show me some sympathy."

"Oh, good God in heaven, *your* mother-in-law needs her meds adjusted. I'll talk to Ollie. He mentioned he wanted Fran's prescriptions reviewed. She's been cranky. Are you okay?"

"I will be in about ten minutes, when I'm home with a vodka tonic in my hand. Bren, I don't want us to lose her so soon after…"

I let my words dangle. Brenda doesn't like it when I talk about the slap-on tracking device I put on Nick's truck. She hates it when I talk about the affair, and she's forbidden the word murder. She's still in step with Oliver—afraid my insinuations will hurt business at the apothecary.

"Do you want me to come over tomorrow? Oliver's at work and I am shuttling Delaney to the movies later with her girlfriends, otherwise I would come tonight."

My niece Delaney. The best added perk of marrying into the Sutton family is getting to spoil this sweet child. Aunt Lindsay always managed to find the toys Santa's elves were too lazy to get their asses out of bed to buy on Black Fridays, and now that Delaney's a teen, I indulge her with all the trendy labels. Brenda's never threatened by how fabulous I am with her daughter, which is a bonus.

"Can you ask Oliver to refill my script? Fran took a lot out of me. Please? You can bring it over tomorrow."

Brenda's sigh echoes in my eardrum, signaling either concern for me or disappointment. I suspect the latter.

"One last time. No more. This is starting to become a pattern. Hey, pull some smoked trout from the freezer so it has time to thaw. I'll bring cheese and crackers. We can figure out what to do about Fran over a bottle of Pinot."

My shoulders start to relax as I pull into my driveway, the automatic garage door sliding upward on its track. Brenda's bringing me more pills in twenty-four hours, and she's talking to Oliver about Fran's meds—a double dose of encouragement. Shifting the gear, I park in the garage. Home, alone again.

"Sounds good. I'll pull the trout out now before I forget. See you tomorrow."

The call disconnects as I turn the ignition off, hitting one of two buttons on a tandem garage door opener clipped to the passenger seat visor. My garage is equipped with both front and back door entrances, a quirky asset. The front door slides down, closing me in for another night.

Entering the mud room, I set my keys and purse on a nearby bench. The basement door is on the right and I descend, navigating down the stairwell into the recreation room. Illumination from the sun filters in through the window well openings, casting a shimmer off the glossy taxidermy trophies lining the walls of Nick's man cave. Our basement is a waterless aquarium of dead fish, with Nick's poker table and wide screen television substituting as decorative tank accessories. During the years of non-reproductivity, Nick sequestered himself down here, secluded from my infertility gripes. The aquarium of the dead gave him a place to drown his sorrows.

Until Dr. Desmond came along.

Pushing the panel door open, the unfinished section of our basement is exposed. I haven't been back here since Nick died. Fishing rods are propped against the far side cinder block wall, near a work bench outfitted with crafting tools for constructing artificial lures. Various tackle boxes are scattered about the cement floor, intermixed with ice augers, tip-ups, and portable shanties. Single and two-seat kayaks nestle side by side, their paddles tossed across their bows. I walk around the vessels, stepping over Nick's fishing items and passing in front of the gas furnace. The aluminum chest freezer sits in the left corner, next to the sump pump.

Opening the lid, my pupils adjust to the brightness of the glowing interior light and the frosty chill emanating from the appliance. The steel baskets are crowded with maroon freezer paper packages, each mummy-wrapped with masking tape. Tossing several packages of perch to the side, I search for Brenda's appetizer request. The packages are colder and heavier than I anticipated. My mind struggles to calculate how there are so many uneaten fish, and why some of them contain the catch date of May eighteenth.

My birthday.

Nick didn't go fishing on my birthday. He was with me at the infertility specialist in New York City, sitting in the waiting room next to optimistically placed copies of *Parents Magazine*. We ate final slices of burnt almond torte cake at *Magnolia's* afterward, signaling to the universe we were transitioning to cakes with sprinkles, glittery princesses, and buttercream superheroes from now on. Cakes that parents eat with their children.

My pace quickens, noting package after package with the midnight black markings of 5/18. Distracted and confused, my haste causes a sharp edge of wrapping paper to flex against my thumb, slicing a quick and shallow cut. The stinging pain makes me cry out. Bright red droplets of blood discolor the packages beneath my hand, each one unique, like individual crime scene snowflakes. I jam my thumb to my lips.

"Damn!" I fling the bloodstained packages out of the freezer in frustration, hearing the loud thump as they land and skid across the basement floor. Using my good hand, I toss additional packages to the right side of the freezer, more than ready to score the stupid smoked trout and return upstairs where I can unwind with some vodka. About to accept defeat, I spot an elongated package near the bottom of the chest, labeled "Trout-Smoked 4/17." My hands clutch the bundle with a vice-like grip, pulling it out. The lid to the freezer slams shut and I turn, having forgotten about the bloodstained packages still littering the floor.

The masking tape on one of the packages tore open from the force of my toss, fanning the contents across the darkened cement. A thick stack of green currency lies face up. A chilling ache runs through my body, a new hurt on top of the old pain.

My husband hid much more from me than a hot-to-trot mistress. Our freezer contains cold, hard cash. Enough in this single package of fake fish alone to indicate whatever he was netted in was fishy.

The eyes of Benjamin Franklin lock with mine, jolting me with a kite string and a key electric shock possibility.

What if it wasn't an illicit affair that got Nick killed? What if he cheated someone out of a boatload of money?

6
CLAUDIA
August 26

The debonair, deep voice of Rod Serling, host of the 1960's television show, *The Twilight Zone*, resonates in my memory. Heavy on attitude, lighter than evil, with a lit cigarette aglow. Every episode contained a spooky greeting, an invitation to enter a new world, where the expectant norms go wonky, twisting logic and reason inside out, stoking fear as unspoken truths are slowly revealed. I stare at his gravestone, remembering a line from the anonymous tip I received:

People are dying, only their deaths are masked with a clever veil.

No wonder the tipster sent me here.

Born in nearby Syracuse and raised in Binghamton, Serling rests in Interlaken's Lakeview Cemetery, with a simple rectangular granite marker commemorating his service in the United States Army during World War II. Cable television reruns of his weekly suspense show classic still generate goosebumps. As I stand above his grave, I wonder if the anonymous tip I received would have had the same effect on him.

A chuckle escapes my lips, an outburst of spirit a casual observer could misconstrue as disrespect. My cell phone chimes in, blurting out a shrill tone capable of waking the dead, all but cementing my lack of cemetery etiquette. Felicia's name is displayed in capital letters on the glass face of my phone.

There are no coincidences with my sister. Our relationship is hinged by unspoken truths, too, much like an episode of *The Twilight Zone*. Maybe Rod Serling is sending me a message now.

Felicia's a pattern person, set in her ways with structured routines, and never deviating. Windows are washed on the first Saturday in April unless it rains, and if it does, the baseboards are wiped down to smooth, glossy perfection instead. Tacos are always served on Tuesday nights, and her social media platitudes tout familiar refrains every time the calendar page flips from August to September. My rigid, eighteen-month older sister, with her "God doesn't give us more than we can handle" and "We'll never forget" annual rally cries, is unbendable, and stuck in a twilight zone of her own making.

"Right on schedule, Felicia."

"How are you?"

"Good. How are the girls? Bruce?"

"We're fine. Busy school shopping and spending days at the pool before the end of summer break. Anything new?"

Ouch. Loaded question.

"Yes, but I'm working now, following up on a story. Can I call you back?"

"Oh, okay… So, you're getting out more? Not just working from home, behind the screen?" Her question carries an accusatory tone.

"Yes. I've got my wigs, my eyebrow appliances. I'm not a total recluse."

"Good. That's so good! You need to get out. I worry about you up there, alone…"

Here we go.

"No, business is hopping, and I'm researching a new story I'm excited about."

"Are you still seeing the therapist?"

Subtle. Or not.

"Yes. I'm *still* going to the therapist."

"Well, don't get pissy. Bruce and I worry, you know? We all do."

Her words trigger the jellybean effect, a big glob of half-chewed candy gelling-together sensation which parks in my throat and alerts me that my anxiety level is spiking.

"I gotta go. I'm working.

"Claudia…"

"I'll call you later. Say hi to Bruce and the girls."

There. Her Google calendar check-in call is completed. I have work to do.

Glancing over my shoulder, I scan the panoramic view of this vast burial ground. Tall obelisk-shaped monuments tower above a multitude of sunburst-style stones, all relics from the 1800s. Next to them, four-sided markers with elaborate stone masonry stand along the historic walking avenues. Mourners and landscapers are visible in the distance, animated characters amid the greenery and gray stones.

The wig camouflages me, a synthetic armor enabling me to nod at strangers I pass or return a smile at an unsuspecting and chivalrous man watering flowers near a stone bench. The everyday nothings. The blink-and-you-miss-it nuggets. The normal, simple actions I stopped taking for granted when the loss of my hair equated to the erosion of my sense of self.

The library and local bookstores don't stock a self-help section for my special category as a 9/11 responder. Words can't capture what evil smelled like anyway, at least not words I know. The pungent, indiscriminate jet fuel blanket suspended in the air, a malevolent cloud of toxicity attacking me and thousands of others while we tried to help.

An all-in, full-on pernicious exposure killing us now.

Toxic poisoning doesn't follow taco Tuesday timetables.

My gaze shifts to the right, past the small, one-room chapel near the entrance gate. Symbolic cedar trees flank the structure, their evergreen presence signifying eternal life. The first burials occurred here more than a century ago and were coordinated through the sexton, who assigned the lots and dug the graves. The wonders of the internet informed me of the rest, including a handy map to use as my guide. Reaching into the side pocket of my hiking vest, I pull out my research. Unfolding the paper, my finger traces the heart-shaped loops encircling the chapel. A vault sits in the upper right chamber of "the heart" and to the east, lie sections B, E, and G. An ornate wrought iron fence borders the property line amid more cedar trees. The advent of autumn is mere weeks away, yet the lush greenery shows no signs of imminent death.

It's not natural. This is murder.

The cyber tip is laser printed on my mind. I swipe a tendril of artificial hair out of my face and turn in the direction of the vault.

No one is in section E, or in the adjacent sections B and G. The consequence of acid rain mixed with time is evident on the scattering of stone steles. The eroded carvings cause a jolt of concern. What if I can't find Seymour Ghent? My pace quickens, dismissing the possibility. The tipster wouldn't send me to an unreadable headstone.

Nearing the end of a row of markers and turning to my left, a shocking burst of color catches my eye. From the new vantage point, another grouping of monuments is visible, some jutting this way and that, no longer obstructed by the vault. At the base of a grave marker, is the signal I was sent here to find.

Blood red roses. At least a dozen, by a Victorian monument. Something is underneath the flowers, propping them at a curious angle. My feet outpace my heart, a thumping sprint of body and mind. I forget I am wearing a wig, and that my problems outnumber the solutions. In the few exhilarating steps to the gravestone, I live in the moment.

Seymour Humphrey Ghent
A Patriot of the Revolution
Died December 8, 1842
Age 87 years

My fingers tremble as I remove my cell phone from the back pocket of my jeans and begin snapping photographs. Walking in a circle around the stone, I search for any sign of who my snitch may be. No footprints. Stashing the phone in my pocket again, I pull a plastic garbage bag and latex gloves from my vest.

I gather the long stem roses, placing one after another in the garbage bag. Is the tipster a florist? My mind debates the endless possibilities until I see it. My breath catches, like it did when I lost the first lock of hair, a symbol screaming so much more than words ever could. Pinching my gloved index finger and thumb together, I raise a plastic bag up to my face. A small, pharmaceutical pill vial rattles within, topped with a stamped "Sutton's Apothecary" cap.

The pill vial is a transparent tannish color, reminiscent of weak coffee. I shake it, confirming it is empty. Flipping the bag over and jostling the vial, one word is visible on what remains of the torn prescription label. It doesn't contain the name of the prescription recipient or the prescribing physician. Instead, only a drug name appears:

Wozilfin.

With my free left hand, I grab my cell phone from the pocket of my jeans. Unlocking the screen, I type "Wozilfin" into the search bar. The first result piques my interest.

New wonder drug offers a cheaper alternative for managing schizophrenia, bipolar disorder, and depression.

My mind swirls, staring at the pill vial cap, with the "Sutton's Apothecary" stamp. Nick Sutton was found dead several weeks ago. The image of his dimpled face etches in my memory bank, as does the brief telephone conversation I had with his wife, Lindsay. She suspected someone killed him. Is this connected to his death, or is this something else?

The police said there was no sign of foul play in connection to Nick Sutton's death. It is believed he fell or jumped from a high bluff above Buttermilk Creek, although his wife won't accept it. I removed Lindsay's inflammatory post from her husband's memorial page as a favor to Nick's brother, Oliver. Still, many people read her comment, insinuating someone wanted her husband dead. Did the tipster see Lindsay Sutton's post? If so, how does that connect with Wozilfin?

Placing the pill bottle package into my bag and tying a quick, tidy knot, I turn toward the vault. My baldness forgotten, my imagination dancing at the possibility of what this find means. As I pass Rod Serling's burial marker, his distinctive voice chirps in my memory again, nudging a gentle reminder that everything may not be as it appears.

Take me, for example…

"…their deaths are masked with a clever veil."

…and the evidence in my hand.

7
LINDSAY
August 26

Stacks of cash surround me, towering above crumpled freezer paper wrappings littered across the cold, cement floor. My legs are cramping, slouched in a less-than-comfortable folding lawn chair, and I clutch a glass of vodka with my bandaged right hand. The room-temperature alcohol sooths my initial shock, but the bottle is in the freezer for my next pour and the ones to follow. A hysterical convenience considering the circumstances, only I'm not laughing.

Nick. Who was my husband? Did I ever know the real him? Are all my pictures of us a lie?

The greenback piles are numerous. This is a boatload of big money, the sneak-away-to-an-island-under-an-assumed-name kind of money you don't hoard without an illegitimate purpose and a plan. My husband, who pouted over the escalating cost of our infertility treatments, hid this secret stash of cash underneath my nose and never said a word about it.

If he wasn't already dead, I'd kill him myself.

The yellow rubber kitchen gloves I wore to unwrap the phony fish decoys lay at my feet. Staring at them, I'm lost in thought. There's no wiggle room for any wrong moves now. No more mixing benzos with booze and doubling up on my pills. I've been blurring the line between use and abuse, and I can't keep slipping. Especially now that I know *I was right.*

Mayor Roger Desmond murdered my husband. Nick stole his wife, and she stole her husband's money to run off with my spouse. Detective Klink was wrong not to listen to me.

Looking at the cash defrosting at my feet, my guard melts, because the prize for my non-delusional accuracy is still widowhood and a wealth of loneliness.

Since I can't count on a life insurance payout, maybe I'll use Nick and Diane's currency popsicles to fund my get-out-of-Dodge plan instead. Take the money and run, blowing off my employer and my paltry salary. The bereavement period from my job at Pattycake Childcare ends in a few weeks, unceremoniously extended after I showed up four weeks ago slurring my words, loopy from double-dosing on my meds and tequila with lemon-lime soda. The Nick-isn't-coming-back reality show of my life was starting to set in, and I needed a baby-fix. My boss, Nancy, pulled me into her office, away from the snooty tennis-skirted moms depositing their offspring, afraid they would see the effects of my gloom and doom intoxication.

"Lindsay, maybe it is too soon, honey. Let me call a ride service. It's not safe for you to drive."

Protests slathered out across my tongue, heavy and thick. "What about the babies? I wanna take care of the babies!" My words puffed, jumbo tears spilling down my cheeks. Nancy's sympathy for my inebriated grief lasted about three seconds and contained a no-nonsense, bottom-line warning: Take two more months off, cry some tears, put your affairs in order, and don't ever show up wasted and jeopardize my state business license again.

Swallowing another sip of vodka, I wonder if hiding a fortune disguised as frozen fish qualifies under the category of putting my affairs in order?

I pitched the miscellaneous fishing gear into a large heap, making space on the floor for unwrapping the money. Glow-in-the-dark fishing bobbers and worms decorate the growing darkness, the colorful orbs and bait cheery highlights among the cluttered mess. One of the kayaks lay on its side, overturned in my earlier haste, now perpendicular to its two-seater twin. A thin white string dangles above it, suspended from the lightbulb switch anchored on the exposed wooden frame ceiling.

I don't dare turn on the light.

What if the mayor is watching the house, waiting for a chance to find all this cash? My drain-the-bottle, self-soothing stay-in has provided few opportunities for an unwanted intruder to launch a treasure hunt.

Until today. My unbandaged hand slaps over my mouth. While I was at Willow Bend, trying to drum up proof of Nick's affair from Fran's foggy memory, Dr. Desmond was away and off-duty. What if someone was in my house? Nick's cell phone was never found, presumably because it contains evidence of the affair. Would Roger Desmond hunt in my home for further corroboration of the dalliance between Nick and Diane? I think he would, especially if he was looking for the missing money, too.

My gaze darts to the panel door, before shifting to the furnace. What if someone is hiding here now?

Holding my breath, my memory strains, trying to remember if anything was out of place when I ran upstairs to grab kitchen gloves and the vodka. Nothing stands out, but I have brain-freeze from the shock of this. I wish I had a cigarette. And a plan. A careful, methodical, strategic, thought-out, I-win plan.

The smarty-pants of this operation must be Diane. She's probably been squirreling this money away from her bigwig mayor hubby for a while now, swiping funds out of the joint checking account, and sneaking miscellaneous twenties from his wallet while he lingered in the shower on snowy mornings. She straddled my husband while strapping her own for cold, hard cash.

I blink, trying to focus on the fuzzy little dust mites floating above the money piles, visible in the rays of moonlight seeping in through the dirty windows. A chill seizes my body, and as my eyes gaze down at the vodka swishing in my glass, a new idea occurs to me.

What if Diane nixed her affair with Nick, pulling an unpredictable pivot and deciding she couldn't leave her prominent politician husband after all? What if Nick *was* despondent? Not about me and our childless marriage, but about the finality of his fairytale fling?

I stomp my foot on the rubber gloves. No. *I am right.* Nick was murdered. Even if he was falling out of love with me, he worshipped and adored his mother and Delaney. He would never put them through this on purpose.

"Mr. Jilted Mayor is going to want his money back," I say aloud, which helps make sense of all the variables I'm calculating in my head. "And if not him, then devious Diane."

Unless…

My eyes narrow, trying to recount the piles. Reaching thirty-two, I get confused, so I start again. With a growing sense of panic, my new grandiose total of fifty-one greenback mini towers shocks me. Nick and I spent his overseas danger pay on fertility treatments. We/he didn't have thousands upon thousands of dollars in cash laying around. Stockpiling this type of stash is a stretch, even with Diane pitching in, which means one thing.

This money represents something else, something dirtier and filthier than an affair.

What if Nick was leaking classified military information to the enemy? He did have a top-secret government clearance. Spies play on weaknesses. What if our infertility became Nick's weakness? Would he trade insider information to pay for another round of IVF?

After I discovered Nick's affair, it was easier to spot his efforts at sneakiness—like using encrypted technology on his cell phone. One night during the Stanley Cup playoffs, Nick was down in the basement man cave watching the game, while I was upstairs. I reached for my phone to text Mother, who was in Mexico on a four-day vacay with her latest conquest. Tapping the What's App icon, I saw Nick's profile picture had the word *online* underneath it, which was odd. When he was overseas, we used What's App to communicate due to its encrypted technology feature. But at home, if Nick wanted to text his buddies or check on other game scores, he could use his regular browser and texting account. Instead, he stayed online using What's App during the entire game. I assumed he was communicating with his mistress, but what if he was texting with someone else?

I wish I had his phone. I wish I had confronted him. I wish he was still alive, and we were pregnant. I wish, I wish, I wish…

The memory of him holding my hand in the doctor's office two weeks before his disappearance flashes in my mind. A firm clutch, which told me he still had love for me, and he wanted us to have a baby. It was enough to convince myself I could forgive his affair, ignoring my knowledge of it like an ugly too-big number on the bathroom scale and pretend I never suspected a thing.

I'm good at pretending. For years, I was an accomplice to Mother's infidelity, complicit in her secret, and I studied how she leveraged knowledge for power. If I kept quiet about Nick's affair, it could pay off, and as he squeezed my hand, I promised myself I could and would do all the bullshit pretenses necessary if it resulted in a chubby baby bouncing on my lap.

Oh, God.

What if giving me a baby was supposed to be a parting gift, a way to not feel guilty for wanting a future with someone else? Nick wasn't aware that I knew about his affair. Is that why he continued to support IVF treatment, thinking a baby was a get-out-of-jail-free card, where a child would prevent me from having a bankrupt belief in love and loyalty?

It doesn't jive. Any of it. Not the affair, or his disappearance, and certainly not his death. And now, this smells fishy, too, because it is.

I sop up my runny nose with the edge of my sleeve and stifle a yawn. This money is mine now. Do I run with it, leaving town under the big ball glow of sleepy orange moonlight and start fresh, somewhere with sperm donation centers and fertility clinics? Paper bills soak up oil from fingertips, or so they say on *Dateline*. One lousy fingerprint and no one will believe I am not the mastermind who put this fortune on ice. I'll be blamed for whatever unlawful crime caused this treasure trove to accumulate. If I do take off, loaded down with dirty proceeds, the talk about me will escalate. And it won't be good.

I'll never achieve justice for Nick if I leave town. And there's the possibility more false narratives will spring up. Mr. Big-Shot Mayor or his police buddies will say *I* stole this money and killed my husband to stop him from reporting it. I'll be framed for Nick's death, and every move of mine the past few months will be put under the microscope. Nancy will say my sadness didn't cause me to show up for work drunk as a skunk, but rather the guilt of shutting up my husband for good. *The Finger Lakes Flash* will pony up the records of my online comments, noting the day and time I suggested someone else was responsible for the casualty in the creek. And eyewitness Ken Preston will stack the deck with testimony about my paranoia over an affair with the esteemed Dr. Desmond.

No one will believe me.

Again.

The bones of my house creak and I gasp. My eyes glance at a window well, watching for feet passing on the other side of the glass, anticipating a bulky figure dressed in black crouching to stare at me. My current fear of the dark pales compared to the truth alighting before me.

Someone will come for this money eventually, I suspect, and if Nick was worth killing for it, so am I. Trembling at the thought, the glass of vodka slips from my hand, shattering into tiny shards upon hitting the cement floor. My shriek is loud and shrill, bouncing off the cinder block walls with taunting effectiveness.

If I call the police, they'll serve me with a search warrant. What if more money is hidden in the house? It will take days for me to scour every inch of this place.

Bile rises in my throat as I remember I won't be alone for long.

Brenda is bringing my prescription over tomorrow, with cheese and crackers and a bottle of wine. I'm supposed to bring her up to speed on Franny's flip-out today.

All she wanted from me was the smoked fish…

From the freezer.

Turning my head, the coffin-shaped appliance hums, like it's mocking me.

I can't put Brenda off. If I don't come to the door, it won't matter.

She'll open her purse and pull out her key.

8
CLAUDIA
August 26

Bounding up the twisty steps of the spiral staircase to my office, I grip the plastic bag containing the pill vial, curiosity burning within me like an inferno.

What does the Wozilfin container mean?

I scurry into the desk chair, my gaze focused downward on the laptop keyboard. A deliberate don't look, don't peek, which I do out of habit. A blank computer screen is a cousin of the enemy, able to mirror my image back at me. Sometimes, like now, I work with a wig on, but my office is designed as an above-ground bunker of safety for when I am not covered up. It's free of photographs encased in glass and equipped with plastic spoons for adding sugar to my coffee. No chance at glimpsing a reflection or a stainless-steel distortion of my bald truth.

The computer comes alive, and I navigate to my search engine, typing in Wozilfin. A drug reference guide tops the list of matching results.

Antipsychotic: Prescription required; Used to treat schizophrenia, bipolar disorder, and depression.

Side Effects: Nausea, drowsiness, negative interactions if combined with alcohol.

A bunch of medical jargon-infused paragraphs follow, with chemical descriptions and mumbo jumbo explanations about inhibitors, substrates, and inducers. My forehead scrunches. I doubt the tipster would leave me a pill bottle clue if the solution required a pharmaceutical or medical degree.

Scrolling down, an article entitled *Drinks & Rape Drugs: A Chilling Cocktail* catches my eye. Enlarging the link full screen, the report documents the danger existing in bars around the world. *Both* women and men can be targeted by perpetrators slipping sedation pills in unattended drinks—easily done while a distracted woman fidgets with her purse or a man excuses himself to use the restroom. Colorless, odorless, and tasteless, the drug can dull a victim's ability to recognize incapacitation and further weaken the ability to fend off unwanted sexual advances. A list of pharmaceuticals utilized for drug-assisted sexual assaults includes Wozilfin.

Shuttling my mouse, I click on the crime blotter file. A string of stories I published on *The Finger Lakes Flash* alights. I search for reports about drug-related sexual assaults or rapes. Finding none, I am not discouraged. Victims of rape and sexual assault often fear embarrassment, shame, and stigma for reporting attacks. I close the file, pondering what to do next.

The possibility of Wozilfin-assisted assaults is a question for a law enforcement professional, someone familiar with current criminal trends. Someone like Peter, the police officer I interview when I need clarification on legal jargon for the court reports and arrests featured on the *Flash's* crime blotter. Asking Peter is a sticky situation, and not because of the leftover adhesive residue from my paste-on eyebrows.

Peter is *Peter*, Stella's boyfriend—my best friend who died four months ago. Stella was a 9/11 responder at the Pentagon. The toxins made her sick, too.

Following Stella's death, Peter joined the local police force to fill his days, and I use the *Flash* as a reason to contact him, more often than necessary. My feigned work questions are bald-faced lies. I miss him. I miss his tall frame and rugged face, his hands, exploring the curves of my smooth body, each of us acquiescing, desperate for comfort, craving touch. Our passion ignited in awkward haste a month after Stella's funeral, both of us clumsy but willing, ignoring the cliché of mourners who bond, substituting lust for grief. It was good until it wasn't. Until I jolted. Not out of guilt, but shame. I pushed his hands away from my wig, terrified my patchy baldness would repulse him.

"I can't do this," I lied. "You still belong to my best friend."

My conflicted feelings about Peter are another knotty situation I'm entangled in, involving both unspoken truths and blatant falsehoods I'm not facing. The thought of unspoken truths reminds me that I promised I'd call my sister back, something I cannot put off indefinitely.

I'm not ready to talk to Felicia about Peter yet, or about why I weaponize my alopecia. My disguises arm me with pseudo-confidence, allowing re-entry into the curated world of airbrushing and photographic filters. But the paradox of protecting my condition from human cruelty is the unintentional creation of a shield, a built-in excuse for self-isolation and mourning the person I used to be. And, with the 9/11 anniversary right around the corner, I'm sure Felicia will mention it.

Again.

Calling her number, my head aches a bit anticipating how this chat will play out after the abrupt way I ended our last conversation.

"Are you mad at me, Claudia?"

Mad? No. Frustrated? Yes.

"Sorry, I was working and distracted. So, what's up?"

"We want you to come to Pittsburgh for Labor Day weekend. The girls would love to see you, and the Pirates are in town."

I miss my nieces. Nadia is eleven, a mini-me version of my brother-in-law, Bruce. She's the performer in the family, wicked on the violin, in a modern Lindsey Stirling kind of way. Portia, my other niece, is seven, and our athlete. The one always moving, turning a cartwheel, or taking jump shots at an imaginary hoop in the center of the family room under the ceiling fan. Their innate differences are familiar, a next generation version of me and Felicia.

"…so, we could tailgate before the game, and there's the walking light exhibit down by the river…"

And it'll be the week before the 9/11 anniversary, I think to myself. Boxing a holiday weekend visit into a carefully constructed veneer is so Felicia. She doesn't grasp if I had hair, I'd pull it out in chunks if I had to live or spend extended time in her overly scheduled, suburban minivan utopia. And she exacerbates my guilt, because I know she's well-intentioned, imagining eating bloated, sweaty hot dogs at the ballpark with my nieces will bring me the same joy it does for her.

She doesn't see the triggers.

Her eyes won't track the jumbo jets with a flight path above the stadium. She'll be watching the laser throw from shortstop to first base, not the flying death traps in the sky approaching at five hundred knots while I sit paralyzed in a twenty-inch-wide seat. Her ears will tune for a call from the ballpark peanut vendor, not the whir of a plane suddenly nosediving. She'll rise during the seventh inning stretch, place her hand on her heart and sing, staring at the same stars and stripes I do, absent the flashbacks. Her eyes won't see three firefighters standing on a pile of steel rubble raising a flag, or uniformed officers draping the shiny copper casket of a fallen responder. For Felicia, it's another routine. Time to stand, time to sing, time to sit.

"I can't. I'm working on a new story lead, something with potential. And that's regatta weekend. For the business, I need to schmooze."

"Oh. The girls will be disappointed."

The pressure in my ears is the signal. The inflating air pocket balloons in my head, dominating the delicate space where the equilibrium meter lives. Breathing in slow, steady breaths is the only way to stave off dizziness and hyperventilation, before a full-on anxiety attack kicks in.

"Claudia, you shouldn't be alone now, with the anniversary…"

"Stop, okay? You don't understand. I'm a responder case. My bad days can happen any time of the year, not just around the anniversary."

"I meant…"

"No, stop, Felicia. Please! My condition is not going away. I am learning how to deal with it the best I can. Business is good, I'm getting out more, but I'm not a project you can check off on your master schedule."

"I never said you were a project."

The pressure spreads into my nasal passages, a throbbing pain I massage with my fingertips.

"I can't do this now. I'm getting upset."

I terminate the call before she can protest, taking slow, deep breaths. One, then another. Why did I call her back and give her an opening? I was having a good day. A day dawning with the thrill of a new story. The pursuit of the unknown. A building block, a plastic bag next to a gravestone. Felicia meant well. She did. And I know it. Our languages just don't translate.

Focus on the research. Figure out the clue. Breathe.

What secret is the Wozilfin prescription hiding? The label was torn to remove the name of the prescription recipient. Why?

It's not natural.

Sutton's Apothecary.

My client.

I think they are on to me.

Oliver Sutton complained to me about his sister-in-law's posting on the *Flash* following his brother's death. Is Nick Sutton's wife my tipster? A grieving widow in denial, wasting my time on a fruitless chase, searching for an alternate explanation for her husband's death plunge? Or does an employee at Sutton's Apothecary know something? What about the unknown Wozilfin prescription recipient? The tip stated the deaths are *not natural*. Is the wording in the tipster's message a symbolic clue, too?

Breathe. Slow and steady. In through the nose, out through the mouth.

Why didn't the tipster pick up the telephone and call 911? Police departments receive anonymous tips. Why choose *The Finger Lakes Flash* if this is murder?

The police. Peter. His hands. Breathe.

What if the tipster is a killer, some rage obsessed monster using me and my media platform for their own twisted notoriety purposes? The Zodiac Killer sent coded letters to San Francisco newspapers. Or maybe the tipster isn't a serial killer, but a garden-variety revenge seeker, someone wanting to destroy another for past slights, wrongdoings, and/or inflicted damage?

Regulating my breath intake, I remind myself to schedule another therapy appointment with Greta. A building blocks check. I need her. Especially now, on the cusp of September, when my psyche is annually taxed. Peter is a possible island oasis in my sea of self-imposed loneliness, but I need Greta's help dissecting my motivations and intentions.

The anxiety is ebbing. This is working. Focus on strategy.

Options pop in my mind, a honey-do list version of a snooping agenda. I'll call Peter about drug-related assaults and missing persons in the Finger Lakes region. Who's better to ask than my friend working on the police force? The perfect camouflage for contacting the subject of my fantasies. The perfect subject, with perfect hands, with the perfect touch. The perfect everything, except for my less-than-perfect journalistic integrity.

Perhaps an impromptu stop at Sutton's Apothecary, too, under the guise of an advertising promotion for valued clients of *The Finger Lakes Flash*. Boots on the ground. A small grin pinches dimples into my cheeks. My mojo likes my honey-do list. I'm breathing normally again.

I click the "X" in the upper righthand corner of my computer screen, forgetting my monitor will reflect the broad smile spreading across my face. The image catches me off guard, but I continue staring, savoring the enthusiasm mirrored back at me.

9
LINDSAY
August 27

Scanning the woods for anything out of the norm, I am met with the sight of wet trees drooping from falling rain. If someone is hiding out there and watching the house from under the soggy blanket of dense foliage, this is their chance. It's almost six, the time when fingers fumble in the darkness to stop shrilling alarms, and when the aroma of fresh brewed coffee first tickles the nose. It's also the moment my hide-the-cash-in-a-new-spot plan revs into action, as I sneak out the back door of the garage.

Marrying a man who likes to fish can be a pain in the ass, with early morning wakeups and the smelly fish guts. But in my case, I did achieve one beautiful bonus: a garage with front *and* back door entrances. I'll never forget Nick's joy when our realtor showed us this property nine years ago, with a rear entrance splicing off from a utility service road. Its winding path ended near the garage, next to multiple parking slabs, ideal for snowmobiles and fishing boat trailers. Nick lit up faster than a slot machine hitting the jackpot when he pressed the tandem buttons on the garage door opener. The left button opened the front garage door, while the right button opened the rear.

"Babe, this is *perfect*." My heart melted watching his giddy delight. *Nick loves it*, I thought to myself. He sees this as our destiny, our first real home. It didn't click at the time that his happiness was more about avoiding three-quarter turns with a boat trailer than about me.

As my car worms down the muddy utility road behind our house, the wiper on the back hatch sweeps across the glass. My fingers clutch the steering wheel, and I hold my breath as my eyes sneak a peek into the rearview mirror.

One swipe. Trees. Two swipes. More trees. Rain drops and trees. I half-expected the sight of a shadowy figure lumbering from the forest on

46

a hunt for cash, like a black bear tracing the scent of food, but no one emerges from the trees. Maybe I'm paranoid about a watcher in the woods. The whisperers would say I am, but I've watched a lot of *Dateline*. Guys like Nick don't just disappear and die while a small fortune sits chilling in the freezer.

The utility road runs about a half mile beyond our property line, ending near the Tifton's hunting cabin. They visit twice a year, at most, and the thick forest between our properties creates a buffer of isolation. We rarely saw anyone on this utility road, so in a way, Nick and I considered it our own second driveway.

As the gloomy day does battle with the leftover darkness of night, plump raindrops splatter on my windshield during the quick drive. Thank God for the Grocery Galleria and its ass-crack of dawn operating hours. I took my last swallow of vodka at or near the witching hour of midnight, so waiting until now for shopping gave me enough time to dry out and devise a save-my-neck plan. The trip so far is a nonevent—no cops, traffic, or deer springing out of nowhere like jackrabbits in heat. As I scoot into the discount store, shaking water off my umbrella and zeroing in on a flatbed cart, a loud voice halts my forward motion.

"Grocery Galleria greetings!"

I gasp, spinning around like a ninja, pointing my umbrella sword at an elderly Grocery Galleria greeter with buck-tooth dentures and kind eyes.

"Sorry, dear, didn't mean to startle you. I'm Melvin."

A slim man dressed in a flannel shirt and polyester pants waves at me, his blue smock dangling at his sides, with a walkie-talkie clipped to the front pocket. Large Woody Allen-style glasses hide half his face and his mouth slacks, like an eager golden retriever puppy. With a sweeping once-over, I put a lid on the pissed-off profanity popping within, sticking to one of Mother's golden rules: *Smile and fake it when you need to.*

"Well, aren't you cheery this rainy morning!" My painted-on grin charms the knee socks off Melvin the Grocery Galleria greeter, and with pleading eyes, I tell him I *urgently* need his help before the mob of daily shoppers arrive. Marvelous Melvin obliges. A half-hour later, with a quick call on his handy-dandy walkie-talkie and under Melvin's watchful eye, three stock boys help load the cash camouflage components into my car. They smirk, with shifty side glances at one another, questioning how bad my period must be if I'm buying a carload full of tampons and menstrual pads. Shooting them a look, I thank Melvin for helping me aid "so many poor souls in storm ravaged Florida," and he smiles again, winking at me.

"My pleasure, beautiful."

Sure thing, old man.

Hopping into the car for the trip home, I'm pleased with myself. My mother once told me valuable jewelry kept in a satin-lined box atop the bedroom dresser is "a magnet for thieves with sticky fingers." My fifth-grade brain didn't compute the wisdom behind her grin as she took my hand and led me to the vanity in the bathroom. She opened the lower cabinet door and grabbed a box of panty liners, padding her lecture about the birds and the bees under the guise of home security.

"See honey, Grandma's pearls are here at the bottom of this box, with one hundred dollars in case I need emergency gas or grocery money. No burglar is going to find this," she beamed with pride, while handing me a panty liner. "Now, do you know what these are for?"

The memory of Mother's squirreled away cash stashed in sanitary napkin boxes wiped away my internal SOS of what to do about my WTF discovery. And, as a bonus, it helped me chill a bit. Nick's not the champion secret-keeper in my life—Mother won that title long ago. As her co-conspirator, the facts of life were explained to me with an added footnote: Not all marriages, including hers, involve only two people. She trained me and I did her dirty work without any hormonal-teenager-being-an-asshole complaints, because she was more than just my mother. She was my closest friend. Despite her deviousness, she still is.

Now I'm the one who needs to be devious. Fifty-one thousand dollars is a lot of cash. All those true crime fans who watch *Dateline* would agree: Nick's killer will come for the money. It's not a matter of if, but when.

And I will be ready.

10
CLAUDIA
August 27

An overhead bell rings, more robotic than cheery, signaling my entry into Sutton's Apothecary and my escape from the misty rain blowing sideways. My journalistic juices are pumping, curious to learn more about the mysterious Wozlifin clue buried under blood red roses.

Outfitted in my standard businesswoman get-up, the "appearance" my clients recognize, my Pamela wig is a no-nonsense shoulder-length blunt cut, very Tina Fey-esque, only a dishwater blond hue instead of chocolate brown. It remains shrouded under my hooded windbreaker, as I survey the store before unveiling myself.

The pharmacy counter is strategically located at the end of the beauty aisle, ensuring customers navigate an orchestrated path amid bottles of hydrating shampoo and volumizing mascara. Walking toward the counter, I rehearse in my head what I plan to say. An elderly couple is listening to instructions given by a twenty-something male pharmacy technician I have not met before. Pulling the hood off my head, I wait for my turn.

The nametag on the technician's smock says Matthew, and as the elderly couple turns to leave, I step forward.

"Hello, Matthew. I'm Claudia, from *The Finger Lakes Flash*. Is Oliver in? I need to speak with him about a promotional discount for my most-valued advertisers."

Matthew nods, while raising his right thumb and gesturing over his shoulder.

"He's in the supply room doin' inventory. Would you like to wait in his office? I'll go get him for you."

"Great. Thank you."

I trail the young man to a door centered on the back wall. He opens it, exposing a short hallway with bare, chalk-colored walls. An entrance marked "Supply Room" faces me. Matthew points to an open door on the right.

"Take a seat. I'll tell the boss you're waitin' for him."

Stepping into a cluttered square of a room, five-drawer filing cabinets occupy all four corners, with an ox of an aluminum desk plopped in the center of the office, its surface covered with heaping stacks of paperwork and a half-empty coffee cup. Cardboard boxes litter the floor like discarded presents on Christmas morning, some with lids askew, exposing laminated punch card sample pill packets. Seating myself, I unzip my bag, as Matthew pokes his head back into the room.

"Mr. Sutton said he'll be with you in a couple of minutes."

Thanking him again, I pluck a promotional folder from my bag, filled with one-month, three-month, and six-month advertising plans, and glance around the room while I wait. Framed pharmaceutical licenses and certifications hang on the wall behind Oliver Sutton's desk. A bulletin board flanks the frames, displaying thumbtacked delivery schedules and an employee roster, complete with contact telephone numbers. I rise to my feet, the advertising folder falling to the ground. Stepping over a box spilling its contents and moving around the desk, I scan the employee roster.

To my surprise, muffled, angry voices are audible on the other side of the wall displaying the bulletin board. A man and a woman are bickering, their words a fluid mix of exasperation and accusation.

"Lindsay can talk to me from now on, Brenda. Filling her script early is asking for trouble."

"Come on, Oliver, she went to visit *your* mother and was attacked!"

Tapping the code into my phone, I open the camera application, as the argument on the other side of the drywall escalates.

"Lindsay isn't our family anymore—Nick's dead. Her insinuations on *The Finger Lakes Flash* almost cost us valuable clients! Why would anyone feel safe coming to our apothecary to have a prescription filled if someone was trying to kill us? Nick's death was a tragedy, but *not* murder. I resent having to correct her ridiculous remarks. And I don't want her around my mother."

"Lindsay is Delaney's aunt. Maybe if you came home and spent some time with your daughter instead of pretending to work late, you would understand the bond they share."

Seizing the opportunity, my thumb presses the perfect white circle on the glass face of my phone, snapping photographs of the delivery schedules and the employee roster with deliberateness, ignoring the sinful stabs in my gut questioning my journalistic integrity.

A faint black line stretching horizontally through a column catches my eye. Leaning forward, I see a listing of delivery personnel, with a name crossed out but still distinguishable: Nick Sutton.

The callousness Oliver Sutton displays by brushing over his brother's name with a dismissive ink stroke shocks me, as his tone snarls on the other side of the wall. The argument percolates at a nasty temperature level, way beyond heated at this point, and I sense my snooping time is dwindling.

Raising my phone again, I snap another quick succession of photographs, capturing images of the pharmacy licenses and the overall layout of the room, plus the paper-covered desktop. As I glance at what appears to be a supply order, I see the word Wozilfin written in bold letters. Snapping another photograph, the supply room door slams shut and heavy footsteps stomp down the hallway, growing louder as they approach. I slither across the room into my seat, grabbing the advertising folder from the floor, awaiting Oliver Sutton's greeting.

The footsteps clomp behind me but don't stop, punctuating Brenda Sutton's hasty exit. My previous interactions with her are limited, but her red hair is memorable. At a charity luncheon, she stuck out like a circus flame thrower. Her hairdo and caustic personality made for a fiery combination, much more conspicuous than any of my wigs.

Brenda's watchable, in a juicy nail-biter way, a mix of everything you might think but don't say. And when she circulates, she slices the crowd, slinging passive-aggressive comments like mud pies at the county fair. "Trish, you skipped Bunco. Everything all right on the home front?" Or worse, "Betty, your roots qualify for AARP. Call my girl, Tracey, at Snappy Snip. I'll make sure she fits you in."

My sensitivity to the hair comments notwithstanding, the wallflower observer in me questioned her bold confidence, although having money often blurs the line between confidence and arrogance. She and Oliver *were* generous, often buying charity tables for four on behalf of Sutton's Apothecary, supporting veterans' programs or another cause of the day. Her brother-in-law, Nick, coupled with his wife, Lindsay, often completed the foursome. Considering what I overheard, a lingering frostiness remains between Oliver Sutton and his sister-in-law, Lindsay.

I vividly remember how Lindsay told me that Oliver didn't want her to speak with me while Nick Sutton was missing. If Lindsay Sutton is my anonymous tipster, her remarks could be a crossword clue putting the Wozilfin vial in context.

The supply room door squeaks open, footsteps echoing in the hallway again, this version more plodding than stomping. Oliver Sutton beelines to his desk, not bothering with a handshake.

"Claudia, what a pleasant surprise. How can I help you today?"

He stands a few inches over six feet tall, a towering reed of a man, with a receding hairline and a greasy wisp of hair combed across his shiny dome. His inherent desperation to cling to what little hair remains stirs my empathy, as I thrust the advertising folder toward him. He glances at the materials, settling into the chair behind the desk.

"Thank you for seeing me. Thought I'd stop by before next weekend's Finger Lakes Regatta and offer my priority clients a special on new advertising plans. A little discount might come in handy now, with all the premier wine packages to bid on come Saturday."

Oliver Sutton chuckles, understanding the truth of my statement. The Finger Lakes Regatta is the toast of the town, an annual fundraiser that the local wineries combine with the last big boat race of the year. The gathering draws wine lovers and a who's who of the Finger Lakes community. The proceeds benefit the local food pantry and homeless shelter. As a business owner, schmoozing with potential advertisers is a boon for me, too.

"Yes, of course. We always buy a table, although this year will be rather different." Oliver Sutton looks away and clears his throat, shuffling papers around the desktop.

"Please accept my condolences again for your loss," I say, surprised he threw me such an easy ground ball to field. "How is Lindsay doing? She hasn't contacted the *Flash* since I took down her post on the In Memoriam page."

The heated words Oliver spewed a few minutes ago about refilling Lindsay's prescription ring in my head. What prescription is she taking? Wozilfin?

"Yes, thank you for helping me with her, um, unfortunate behavior."

My Angelina eyebrows perk, conveying understanding. Oliver takes my gesture as a cue and continues venting.

"Lindsay is so dramatic," he laments, rubbing the palms of his hands along his cheeks. "Very hyperbolic and fantastical—everything is a fairytale or a soap opera, or in Nick's case, a disappearance worthy of a *Dateline* episode."

I don't mention my phone call with Lindsay back in June. I promised her anonymity, and it's clear Oliver will be upset if he learns she tried contacting me. A pang of guilt washes over me, because I know I crossed an ethical line snapping the photographs of the Wozilfin supply order and the employee roster. Better get down to business and get out of here.

Pitching him the thumbnail highlights of the various advertising packages available with the discounted rates, Oliver appears relieved to refocus on work, choosing a one-month flu shot promotion as well as the standard three-month fall package. Short. Concise. Decisive. And dismissive. Sensing his eagerness for me to leave, I tell him to expect an email invoice, reflecting the discounted rate.

"Good luck with your auction bids next weekend, and thank you again, Oliver. I can show myself out."

He says a polite goodbye, rubbing one hand over the greasy combover strand of hair. Perhaps a subconscious tic, but exiting from the apothecary, my hunch is his mind is still entrenched in battle mode with Brenda.

The rain douses me as I run to my car, the wind whipping my wig. Settling into the front seat, I start the ignition. The defroster kicks in, eating away at the window fog as I scroll through the photographs of Oliver Sutton's office on my phone.

The bulletin board pictures of the work schedules and delivery routes are focused and clear, but the font is too small to read on my iPhone display. Swiping left, the same is true for the desktop paperwork images, so I swipe again, studying the wide-angle room shots—pictures of the corner filing cabinets, the hodgepodge of pharmaceutical sample boxes littering the floor, and the licenses hanging in crooked frames on the back wall. On the glass front of Oliver Sutton's pharmaceutical degree from Cornell University, a tiny object reflects amid the cylinder and conical measuring tools crowding the top of a filing cabinet in the corner of the room.

And there it is.

The jellybean clog in my throat returns, as I struggle to enlarge a blurry image in the last photograph. My thumb and forefinger click together, zooming in on the object.

Cursing myself, I scroll back to the wide-angle photographs of the filing cabinets. There it sits with a peacock glow, almost mocking me for missing it while sneaking snaps of the room. Mounted on the wall above the cabinet and hidden among the various pharmaceutical measuring devices is a security camera, with its lens pointing at Oliver Sutton's desk.

Sinking in my seat, rain droplets continue pelting my windshield, a cascade of hard, sharp pings trumpeting a symbolic forecast. My carelessness is a prescription for disaster.

11
LINDSAY
August 27

Sitting cross-legged on a boat cushion over the cold, cement floor, my purchased props and freezer funds surround me. I glance at the window wells, which serve as watery, two-way eyes. The rain on the glass blocks a clear view in or out, which is a trick bag. If Nick's killer is lingering outside, the proximity of imminent danger is cloaked.

Boxes of feminine hygiene pads, panty liners, and super-absorbent tampons are everywhere, along with the cash. Part one of my master game plan is well underway, a sobering strategy, despite the throbbing ache in my temple. First up: hide the money in a new location and make decoy packages for the freezer. My free hand sweats inside a latex glove while I grab a fistful of jumbo tampons from a petal-pink box. Each wad of Nick's freezer-wrapped cash totaled an even grand, so hiding fifty-one thousand dollars in a grab-and-go spot takes creativity. I wrap another money pack with an elastic band and toss it in a tampon box, piling some of the wrapped cotton hygiene plugs on top. Closing the lid, I chuck the box into a plastic storage crate, my shoulders slumping as the process begins again.

My gaze shifts to a window well, the dreariness of the day a somber reminder that sleep escaped me. The broken vodka glass shards lay shattered about four feet to my right. My escalating inebriation stopped after the glass broke. Preparing to duck and dodge requires focus. And my head is crowded, with a tangled web of thoughts and questions.

Where did Nick get all the money he stashed in the freezer? Were he and his mistress going to run off, start a new life in a quaint small town somewhere in the Adirondack Mountains, far across the state and away from me? Or does another secret exist, something that drew him to a meeting at the edge of a stony bluff? Was someone hammering him for

55

answers, demanding to know where he hid this money, pressing all his insecurity buttons so he suffered an acute case of diarrhea of the mouth? Did that get him killed? Or, when he didn't cough up an answer, when he stalled and zipped it like a tight-lipped clam protecting a shiny pearl, did that trigger a fatal shove?

I was Nick's pearl.

At least until Diane came along.

Stifling a yawn, I grab three of the thick, overnight pads and rip the peel-off coverings, exposing the sticky adhesive strips on each and bond them together. A fourth pad is flipped upside down on top of the others. With great care, I slap a one-hundred-dollar bill over the adhesive strip, which sticks, covering the menstrual pads beneath it. Placing another bill underneath my phony stack, I add rubber bands and twist, choking the ends. Grabbing one of the original freezer-paper wrappings, I fold along the crease lines, mummy wrapping the decoy with fresh masking tape, and survey my creation. "Perch-5/4". The package is lighter than the original but looks the same. Enough to fool any intruder, either one with advance knowledge of Nick's cash hideaway, or one searching for it.

Peering around the basement, I study the mess I created. I'm hiding the cash in every type of menstrual product box ever manufactured, and stockpiling it in nearby plastic crates, labeled as "Hurricane Relief" supplies. I'll store them in my car, which has an alarm system. The real fish are rewrapped in white paper, distinguishable from the phony-baloney maxi pad money packs filling the freezer. Nick's fishing gear clutters the floor, shambles to tackle another day.

Glancing at the window wells again, a nervous preoccupation lingers. Maybe I'm suffering from an anxiety medication withdrawal—my yawns becoming harder and harder to suppress.

My medication.

Oh, God.

Pulling up Brenda's number on my text feed, my gloved fingers tap away on my phone, clumsy and slow.

"Not feeling good. Probably picked something up at Fran's yester-day. Her place is full of germs. Don't want you or 'Laney to catch this. Call me."

I hit send.

Less than a minute later, my telephone jingles, the caller display showing Brenda's name.

"Hey, Bren."

"What's wrong? Are you sick?"

"Stomach bug or something. Feelin' pukey. I don't want you to catch this."

Brenda pauses before answering, but when she speaks, I notice a slight slur.

"Nah, it's okay. I kinda got some bad news. Oliver is being Mr. By-the-Book. I asked him, but he said no more pills."

No pills? Not even a few? Unbelievable. Why is Oliver pulling a choir boy act, *now*? Is this retaliation or karma for my post on *The Finger Lakes Flash*? I need this medicine for my mental health. Damn. I shouldn't have gotten sloppy with it. I can't call my doctor, either, because that would set off alarms.

"*Why?* Why won't he help me anymore?" I sniffle, ripples of emotion causing my gloved hand to shake.

"Damned if I understand him." Brenda's voice rises, her tone angry and spiteful. "I can try asking him again but… He's hiding more than pills, Lindsay."

A slurp follows her slam.

"What are you drinking?"

"Mimosa. Second one. Day drinking is highly underrated, but you understand."

Understand is an understatement.

"It's happy hour somewhere."

"Do I sound happy?!" Brenda shrills the rhetorical question, before dropping a bomb.

"Oliver has a lover. He says he's working late, but I've driven by the apothecary three times in the last month when he's supposed to be there, and he's not. The store was locked up."

The idea of Oliver and his comb-over getting hot and heavy beneath the sheets with someone would normally make me laugh, but I can't. Not now. Oliver and his dearly departed brother are suddenly two of a kind. Is that why Brenda didn't want to hear another peep about Nick having an affair? Did she muzzle me because she was afraid people would talk about Oliver's indiscretions, too?

"What? Are you sure?" I mumble.

She slurs again, a tonal cocktail laced with disgust.

"He stopped touching me years ago, you know that."

"Who is she?"

"You won't believe… wait, oh hell, Delaney's school is calling. I hope she didn't catch whatever you did. Maybe she's sick, too. I gotta go. Feel better. We've got the regatta this weekend. You need to get out of the house."

A shiver runs up my spine as Brenda ends the call.

You need to get out of the house.

My head turns toward the freezer, my thoughts on replay, scene by scene, like a DVD player on slow rewind. Her comment startles me, making me question if it was an offhand remark fueled by alcohol, or something more? Yesterday, Brenda offered to bring me my medicine along with a good bottle of wine, so we could "talk" while nibbling on crackers topped with smoked trout.

Only she's not bringing the pills, and I want my fix. Now. Just one. Two tops.

I stand, glancing at the window wells again. This is a doozy. I'm questioning everything and anyone, suspecting the worst, like Audrey Hepburn's blind character in the movie *Wait Until Dark*. Bad guys with black shoes are probably lurking outside my windows, wanting what is hidden in my house! *Waiting for their chance.* Pretty soon, scary feet and pants legs will start showing up in my basement windows, signaling danger! Only I'm not blind. *I will see them.*

The window wells gloss, rain trickling down the smooth, glass panes. No feet. No dark, scary shoes. My mind torques, a slow panic gripping my chest.

Maybe the threat isn't from the outside.

What if someone is already in the house?

The yellow kitchen glove covers my mouth, the rubber sticking to my cheek, stifling my cry.

Is Brenda messing with my mind, playing with my grief and insecurity over Nick's affair and death? Oliver isn't at the apothecary when he's supposed to be. Or so Brenda says. Nick wasn't where he was supposed to be either.

Brenda sent me to the freezer. My sister-in-law, my only quasi-friend, besides Mother. *My only quasi-friend…* I blink, four times in quick succession, with Mother's voice ringing in my head: *Don't trust other women.*

I back away, putting more distance between myself and the window wells. My foot lands on the glass fragments and the crunching sound startles me, sending me tumbling backward. My arms swing wildly, hitting an angled fishing rod propped against the wall next to the freezer. Crashing on my back, pain radiates up my side. The pole lands inches from my face, a jagged hook dangling over my right eye. The image triggers a piercing realization, both literal and terrifying.

My sister-in-law wants me to take the bait.

Why didn't I think of this sooner? Brenda handles the accounting records for the apothecary. If there's money missing, she would notice—especially a five-digit deficit. But how would she know the missing money was in *my* freezer?

Biting my lip, I mentally piece this together. Initially, I assumed Nick squirreled away the money with Diane so they could run off together. But what if the funds represent *Oliver's* get-away cache? If Brenda is correct about my brother-in-law having an affair, is it possible he siphoned operational funds with Nick's help? Technically, that's employee theft. The thought triggers a memory of a counter clerk who stole pills from the apothecary years ago, despite the security cameras.

"That's it!" I cry, thrilled by my Eureka moment of revelation.

Brenda must be checking the security cameras at the apothecary through an app on her phone. She's hunting, like I did when I first suspected Nick was cheating on me with Diane. But if Brenda knew about the money, why wouldn't she come and take it?

I've been reclusive since Nick died, so there weren't many opportunities for Brenda to swipe the cash. On the flip side, if my sister-in-law overheard Oliver and Nick talking about hiding money in our freezer, it could explain why she *wants* me to find the stockpile of Benjamins. She'd rather split it with me than have Oliver run off with it.

Unless I have this backwards? Maybe Nick and Oliver weren't stealing funds from the apothecary, but were hooked up in a shady moneymaking deal? Hiding secret loot from Brenda makes sense, because she would also recognize if *too much* money was in the apothecary till!

Or, what if I'm being paranoid like the whisperers say, and this has nothing to do with Brenda and Oliver?

Stop. Don't think like that. Being tired and anxious does not equal delusion. Hunky, athletic guys like Nick don't just disappear and die. He put fifty-one grand on ice. His phone is *missing*!

My mind circles back to thoughts about Roger Desmond and the possibility of revenge. If Nick was saving up to leave me for Diane, would his family help to finance his deception? It would explain how Brenda knows about the money in the freezer, but then why would she want me to find it? Trying to find logic in this illogical situation hurts my head.

Don't trust other women.

An eerie intuition tells me that my sister-in-law knows something she hasn't shared with me…

Something that requires I get out of the house.

12
CLAUDIA
August 27

My cell phone lets out a stifled sing-song chirp, and I'm anxious it might be Oliver Sutton calling to interrogate me. I glance at the display showing Peter's name, which doesn't bring relief. What if Oliver called the police?

"Hi, Peter."

"Hey, stranger."

My brain battles, at war with itself—the left side analyzing what I want to say, while the right side marinates in the memory of Peter's body pressed against mine. Do I talk shop by asking about Wozilfin and copping to my snooping session in Oliver's office? Or do I keep it light and let Peter lead? Maybe *he's* thinking about our make-out session and this call has nothing to do with work. It's a lopsided tussle. Right side brain wins. At least, for now.

"How are you?"

"Good. Thinking about you."

Tingles. Serious tingles. And by the sound of it, this isn't a business call, which is comforting.

"Good thoughts or bad thoughts?"

"Um, good. No bad ones, maybe a bit naughty."

He can't forget either. Now's my chance.

"Got any plans for the regatta?"

An endless pause lasting mere seconds elapses before a soft chuckle emanates from the receiver and he says, "Are you inviting me?"

"*The Finger Lakes Flash* bought a table for two. Help me celebrate my charitable tax deduction."

"Deal. What time should I pick you up?"

The question floats, filled with assumption, insinuation, and an air of establishment, a combustible mix for a (non)couple planning our (first) next date. Glancing at the rearview mirror, I catch sight of the business uniform Pamela wig. My right brain fantasies don't include Pamela. When Peter and I caved, surrendering under the weight of our phero-mones, I wore my Nicole wig. On purpose. Premeditatively selected, morphing me into the woman I used to be. An assumption, on my part, that if I mimicked the old me, the result would be the same.

Nicole's long auburn tresses more than compliment my green eyes—they transform me, from workday normal into a pin-me-against-the-wall kind of hot. An insinuation by appearance. I embraced my disguise, ignoring the established fact the woman underneath it was no longer the same. And, as Peter's hands navigated my body, a slow, painful truth was revealed. I haven't accepted that the new me is here to stay.

I'll be business Claudia in the plain Pamela wig for the regatta, and despite every flirty fiber in my body screaming at me to redo the do-me hairdo, I need to tell him the truth, establishing a boundary for expect-ations. Building block. Breathe.

"I'll be working the room, so I'll be dressed like people know me…" My voice trails off, not saying all the things he is smart enough to figure out. "But I want you as my table guest. Meet me there?"

"Deal."

Another deal. Twice now. Short, succinct, and definitive. No hesitation. Right brain in overdrive. Breathe. Don't ruin the mood. Wozilfin questions can wait until after I study the photographs from Oliver's office. In the meantime, I'll dangle a suggestion and see if I get a nibble.

"I may want your help on a story I'm working on."

"I'm here for you. What's it about?"

"Ah, a few lingering questions concerning the missing veteran, Nick Sutton."

Peter clears his throat. "Really? Why?"

I didn't tell Oliver Sutton about Lindsay's phone call to me because of their family tension and my promise that I would keep what she reported anonymous, but I never published anything she told me. Legally, I don't have an obligation to hold up my end of the deal, but I recognize that would stretch ethical boundaries. Peter doesn't need to know that Lindsay herself is my source. I'll be vague.

"A source called me right after Lindsay reported him missing. The source said that Lindsay was convinced someone killed her husband. As we were talking, your colleagues showed up at Lindsay's house—they were making the death notification. She didn't get the chance to tell my source who she thinks killed Nick."

"And you believe her? I thought you took the comments she posted down…"

"I did!" I say with haste, not wanting him to think I mistrust the police. "It's touchy. I want to reach out to her, but Oliver Sutton is my client. He was furious by what she wrote."

Peter lets a beat pass and says, "Between you and me, a couple things were odd about his disappearance."

Plump rain drops splash on the windshield as I sit up straight in the driver's side seat, Peter's tantalizing comment spurring my curiosity.

"Care to share?" I ask.

"His cell phone wasn't located. We found the business placard for the car in Taughannock Falls State Park, but his work vehicle was abandoned at Buttermilk State Park—twelve miles away."

Peter's right. This is an odd detail.

"Do the police think someone took his phone and discarded the placard? Was he mugged?"

Peter speaks slowly, choosing his words with care. "His cause of death is undetermined, but he was found in the creek beneath a high bluff, well over a mile from where his car was parked. If he was considering self-harm, he may have gotten rid of the placard on his own and left his phone somewhere else, so he couldn't be tracked."

Or, if someone harmed him, they may have planted the placard in Taughannock Falls State Park to throw searchers off in the wrong direction, I muse to myself.

"Was the phone traced?" I ask.

"It wasn't found with his body. That's all I can say," Peter says, changing topic. "I'm excited to see you this weekend, Claudia."

A wave of exhilaration washes over me, and a slow grin spreads across my face.

"Me too. Cocktails start at six thirty."

"I'll meet you there," he says, and the call disconnects.

Amid the drumming beat of raindrops tap-tapping on my windshield, my body celebrates our date with a mini happy dance in my seat. The giddy rush pulses, over the subtlety of his "deal" with me. All those years fighting to be "seen" for my talents, my intelligence, but outshined by my looks. And now, the situation is inverted, but still the same. My hairless head only defines who I am if I let it. My therapist Greta will be proud that I owned my truth, and Peter doesn't care if this is a Pamela event or a Nicole upgrade night. The choice is up to me.

There's only one problem.

What if the security camera recorded me photographing Oliver Sutton's office? He'll be at the regatta, too. The perfect place to make a scene.

13
LINDSAY
August 28

I'm crashing today. Hiding all the money in the tampon boxes and creating decoy packages for the freezer was exhausting, and my anxiety is kicking into rocket propulsion mode—I am edgier than the Grand Canyon without my prescription. Double dosing on meds the past few weeks screwed up my system. I'm pooped out, overtired but jittery at the same time. I need to finish searching in the house, but I'm afraid of what else I might find. I wish I could sleep.

Curling up in the fetal position under a fuzzy throw on my couch, I grab the remote, checking the menu on my streaming service. Shuffle, shuffle. There it is.

Wait Until Dark.

Selecting the movie, I hit the play button.

Pay attention. Watch how Audrey Hepburn's character is tricked by people she thinks she can trust.

Can I trust Brenda?

She made me shut up after Nick's death. *"You're hurting the family, Lindsay."* Was I? Or were they hurting me, and I was too zonked out with grief to catch on? My angry comments on *The Finger Lakes Flash* following Nick's death cut both ways. The post got tongues wagging, but not about police incompetence or extramarital affairs. I became the buzz—the one swallowed up by sorrow, in need of a good long rest and a few hearty sandwiches with extra mayonnaise to put some meat on my bones, or so Brenda told me over heavy-handed pours of my favorite cabernet.

My words were the straw stirring a poisonous drink, and my sister-in-law said it had to stop. Nick worshipped me. Period. His suicide was a result of battle demons, a permanent mistake caused by temporary mental illness, she said. Oliver was irate, worried about the impact Nick's death and my public posting would have on his mother, the family business, and on Delaney. Brenda's voice quivered when she mentioned my niece's name. I never stopped to think about how Nick's death was affecting her young life. Not only was her fun-loving uncle dead, but now her favorite (and only) aunt thought he was a liar, too.

Refocusing my attention on the television, tiny Audrey Hepburn lights up the screen. She plays a plucky blind woman, who counts steps and knows exactly where everything belongs and what's out of place.

I sink further into my couch cushions. I'm the one who doesn't see. My husband kept big secrets from me. And now, Brenda says Oliver is doing the same thing to her.

Oliver never liked me. He and Nick, opposite as two brothers could be, so I'm not sure he would have liked anyone Nick chose to date or marry. Brenda acted shellshocked when Nick went missing, which meshed with how I felt. And Nick knew how much we all worried about him when he was in Afghanistan. He never wanted anyone to worry. Not me, or his mom. He wouldn't deliberately disappear.

The step count doesn't add up. Everything around me, off-kilter.

Gazing back at the screen, Audrey Hepburn's acting chops amaze me—her delicate face projects unease, her wispy frame tensing with rigidity. Her instincts are spot-on.

My mind swirls. Fran said Nick loved Dr. Desmond. I could have called bullshit or chalked it up to dementia-related confusion, but I didn't. My hunch was right, too.

Watching the remainder of the film, a thought occurs to me. I'm smart enough to hide the money I found, but there's one big difference between me and this fictional suspense caper unfolding on my television screen:

I believe my husband cheated on me and lied.

The slap-on tracker traced Nick's truck to the cabin in the woods. The data is recorded in the GPS system. My binoculars focused on Diane's bouncy curls blowing in the breeze as she arrived, and I watched her skip up the porch steps in her fancy heels. I told Brenda *all* of this, both while Nick was missing and again, after his death. Why is she acting like it didn't happen?

My brow furrows, watching fear radiate across Audrey Hepburn's face as the movie reaches its climax. Danger is lurking in the dark.

I tug the blanket up to my chin, frustrated by the figurative darkness enveloping me, too. So many unanswered questions. Who killed Nick? Why did he go to the bluff above Buttermilk Creek? What happened to his phone? Where did the money come from?

Audrey is outsmarting the killer. Her strategy is brilliant. An idea comes to me.

I'll booby trap my house.

I can't stay in the shadows any longer. My comments on *The Finger Lakes Flash* were a start. But now, it's time to turn on the floodlights and expose all the strange circumstances surrounding Nick's suspicious death.

And I know just the place to start.

THE FINGER LAKES FLASH

Your online snapshot capturing the local news you need to know.
August 28

THE FINGER LAKES REGATTA
Saturday, September 1
Seneca Yacht Club

Sailboat races begin at 10:00 a.m.
Scull races begin at 2:00 p.m.

Raffle tickets $5.00 each
Dinner at 7:00 p.m. $50.00 per person
Auction at 8:30 p.m.
Twenty-five local wine packages to bid on!

Master of Ceremonies: Romulus Mayor Roger Desmond

For questions or to sponsor a charity table,
contact the Finger Lakes Regatta Coordinator
Dr. Diane Desmond, 315-555-9683

All proceeds benefit The Finger Lakes Food Pantry and
Homeless Shelter

14
CLAUDIA
August 28

The latest edition of *The Finger Lakes Flash* is posted, and I'm consumed, analyzing every minute detail in the photographs from Sutton's Apothecary. The camera mounted above the left-corner filing cabinet in Oliver Sutton's office is magnified to wide screen prominence on my computer monitor. I zoom on the image, trying to spot any small, illuminated red lights or power buttons. Not noticing the most crucial element in the room annihilates my investigative integrity. On the business front, my sloppiness could curse my career.

Only something in my gut tells me otherwise, which lessens my worry.

I stare at the Wozilfin bottle with its Sutton's Apothecary cap, pondering my vulnerability. My snooping may cost me a paying client, but Oliver Sutton won't trash-talk me around town. Not eleven weeks after he begged me to remove Lindsay Sutton's statements, suggesting her husband's death involved a cover-up. No, quite the opposite. Oliver Sutton wants silence.

My tipster thinks so, too. Sutton's Apothecary is part of the mix. *The clever veil.*

My fingertip clicks on the mouse button, closing the photograph with a perfect view of the security camera. I can understand security measures in the supply room and in the retail area of the apothecary, but why a hawk-eye camera focused on Oliver's desk?

Next to his half-empty coffee cup rests a small stack of pharmaceutical supply purchase orders. Magnifying the image, the supplier's name and address, and last month's order date come into sharp focus. Near the bottom of the photographed page is my second clue.

One thousand Wozilfin pills in variable milligram dosages are listed, ranging from the low-end dosage of twenty-five milligrams to a high of seven-hundred-fifty milligrams. The higher potency pills are the bulk of the shipment, with both standard and extended-release versions listed. My cursor jostles to the web browser, my fingers typing "Wozilfin dosages" into the search engine. Protocols for treatment of schizophrenia and bipolar disorder are listed, followed by the recommended application for managing depression. I bookmark the page, vowing to study it in more detail later in the week, after I tackle a mountain of business obligations for the *Flash,* and before my therapy appointment next week with Greta.

She'll ask if I am still taking my anti-anxiety prescription.

I smile. My bottle of medication sits untouched in the medicine cabinet. I'm managing the clammy sweats, the loss of breath, and the panicky carnival ride sensations where the room spins around me while I struggle to stand. I controlled my breathing after the call with Felicia. And I'm doing it now, sitting without a head covering, staring at a photograph exposing my bald intrusion into Oliver Sutton's business affairs. My smile widens, thinking how pleased Greta will be with my progress. Building blocks.

I rub my palm over the itchy stubble sprouting at the back of my skull and debate about sending Peter a text. One quick text, a simple flirt disguised as a work question. My fingers type faster than the tiny shrieks ringing out in my head, warning me to slow my roll, to stay *in control.*

Nineteen years after 9/11, the out-of-control hair loss began, and I felt like a disoriented pilot who loses sight of the horizon, my fate sealed before the enormity of the problem is realized or diagnosed. Amid the uncertainty of potential doom, I cling to what I can still control… the physical disguises, the online business operated from a windowless attic. My haste at Sutton's Apothecary caused me to miss the security camera, yet my thirst for discovery quenched a drought deep within my soul. I didn't think about alopecia while snapping the office pictures, or any of the "maybe-I'm-dying-I-just-don't-know-it-yet" thoughts festering in my mind like weedy dandelions. While clicking away, snapping photos of Oliver Sutton's office, I lived in the moment. And now, when I should panic, when I should worry my snoopiness may destroy my livelihood and ruin my reputation, I am invigorated.

Staring at the text message, my index finger hovers over the send button.

"Working on a story I need your legal expertise on... call me."

Not quite right. Too bossy and impersonal, but I don't want cutesy. No emojis. I want flirty—not silly. I add one more word. *"Deal?"*

The phone rings in my hand, startling me. The screen says "Peter" is calling and I scramble to see if I pushed send. Nope. The message sits in the text box. My heart thumps as I accept the call, giddy and nervous, with a "he's-thinking-of-me-while-I'm-thinking-of-him" thrill mixed in.

I don't bother with hello.

"I was just thinking about you."

He exhales, with a wide smile forming, at least that's how I envision it in my head.

"Lucky me. Whatcha thinking about? Saturday?"

His tone is happy. Flirty.

My invigoration is knocking on the door to exhilaration. I think this is *on*.

"Um, well, yesss…" I wonder if he senses I am smiling. "Looking forward to it."

"What are you going to wear?"

Wow. I imagine him undressing me. God, this is fun.

"Black dress, heels. Big smile."

He chuckles. "Good. I thought maybe my tie should match with your outfit, for all those pictures you are going to post on the 'Hot Happenings' page of the *Flash*."

You are my hot happening, Peter. No doubt.

"Yes, I might sneak a picture or two of you into the mix. Say, speaking of pictures…"

I pause, as the image of the Wozilfin purchase order catches my attention again.

"I'm working on a new story lead. Something big. I reviewed the blotter reports for the last year or so, but I didn't find what I was looking for. Have you heard about a drug called Wozilfin?"

A few seconds pass before he says, "The date rape drug?"

"You know it? I didn't find reports of sexual assaults, but that doesn't mean they aren't happening. Maybe they're not being reported."

"Wait… slow down… You think someone is drugging women and assaulting them with Woozies? Are you okay? Did something happen to you?" His voice rises as he slips into the street lingo, concern erasing the smile I imagined on his face a moment ago.

"No, no. I'm good." I let my reassurance float for a few seconds, not sure how to launch my test probe. "Um, could Wozilfin be used for more than incapacitation? Like, ah, to murder people?"

"*What*? Claudia… come clean. What are you talking about?"

"Like I said… a possible story lead. I'm checking a few things out. Any rise in missing persons reports? I mean, besides Nick Sutton. He was the story of the summer."

Peter's silence is the weighty kind, a heavy measure registering on the "I can't talk about this" scale. My years of interviewing people have taught me to differentiate silences. Sometimes quiet means nothing more than a simple second of thought or reflection, but often, unspoken words spread over time mean *everything*. Silence holds true value, like the heavy burden of professional confidentiality, when a guy like Peter can't say there *is* more to Nick Sutton's death, because saying so contradicts the official statement released by his department.

"The manner of Nick's Sutton's death was undetermined," he says, enunciating each word. "And the medical examiner's report didn't indicate drug usage, not illicit or pharmaceutical."

The clever veil.

"Could it be a homicide?"

Silence again. Only this time, Peter uses it as deflection.

"How did you become interested in Wozilfin?"

"Like I said, following a lead," I respond, somewhat dismayed at how our flirtation faceplanted in a matter of minutes.

Another heavy silence. I wait for what feels like eons, but when he speaks, his voice is soft and sad.

"You know, the thing about Woozie assaults—they rob a person of trust. The perp gets the pills ahead of time. There's premeditation… a deliberate plan to hurt someone."

I listen, blinking fast.

"And when people are victimized, they are afraid to be vulnerable again—they build up walls. They shut people out, even people who don't want to hurt them."

His words land softly, cloaked with gentle intent, and while I know he's trying so hard not to upset me, I find myself getting emotional. I never imagined when I covered the crash of Flight 93 that I could become a victim, too. I've put up walls out of fear, even for someone like Peter, who doesn't have any intention of harming me. If someone is drugging women with Wozilfin and assaulting them, they may be hiding in a prison of their own making, too. The candy clog in my throat returns, along with the thumping pressure in my ears. I can't speak, because I might cry.

Peter knows how to read silences, too.

"As hard as it is, walls aren't good. They let the bad guys win."

Closing my eyes tight, I try not to sniffle. Peter's telling me not to let the 9/11 terrorists win. Sequestration and hyper-independence are the bricks and mortar that built my self-imposed entrapment castle. I've taken baby steps and started getting out more. I am doing better. But his words are a prompt, a caring nudge. It's time to lower the drawbridge and get on with living a full life.

"If you develop more details, run it by me. Maybe, I can help," he says, evenly. "I'll see you on Saturday, Claudia."

The call ends before I can say goodbye. Sucking in a deep breath, I blink back tears, replaying his words and their double meaning in my head. Wow. I wasn't expecting this.

Breathe. We made a date and he's telling me it's going to be okay. I don't need to be scared. I can trust *him*. I smile, a tiny tear sliding down my cheek.

The old me never hesitated. I was a confident on-air reporter, with a fast-paced life. Always curious. I chased the new, the unknown. People, stories, answers. I wasn't afraid to trust.

I grab a tissue and blow my nose. Breathe.

He's right. I spent my first year here hunkered in my cabin setting up the *Flash*, sending email promotions to every local business in the Chamber of Commerce registry. I worked the phones, building connections for press releases, court reports, and death notices. In the digital age, after initial introductions, very rarely did I venture out in my Pamela wig to meet with clients or do face-to-face business. The local wineries helped spread the word about my website, eager to see if my discounted advertising rates would translate to better sales. It worked. All of it. I launched a successful business while building a cocoon around the bald shell of the old me.

I was safe. I could hide my patchy head and all the pain going on inside of it.

The terrorists and their toxic dust clouds won.

Breathe.

Don't let them win now. Fight.

I've got a date and a real story, something with teeth, like in the old days on television. Focus on the story. What else does Peter know or suspect about Nick Sutton's death?

My breath catches, causing me to hiccup.

Why can't I shake the feeling that I'm missing something?

15
LINDSAY
August 30

Back for round two with Melvin the Grocery Galleria greeter.

Parking my car, I sneak a peek in the rearview mirror. Good God. The first rays of sunshine highlight the sharpness of the cheekbones jutting from my face, their bony ridges framing the skeletal craters containing my bloodshot eyeballs. I look like a walking cadaver.

Weeks of hangovers and hibernation have taken a toll. Now, night after night, when the shades are drawn, I hunt, armed with a nearby baseball bat to fend off any middle-of-the-night intruders. Danger will come in the dark, so I stay awake, like last night, searching for answers about Nick's frozen fortune and any other squirreled-away secrets he stashed in our home.

The contents of Nick's dresser lay on the floor, like every piece of clothing from his closet. I turned the pockets inside out, flipped the mattress off the box spring, unscrewed electrical socket plates, threw books off shelves, checked the chimney for loose bricks, and even opened a sealed box of diapers in the finished nursery, just in case Nick hid something there and glued it shut again.

The hunt hurts, and since I'm stiff-arming Brenda with the fake flu until I can figure out if she is friend or foe, I'm still operating in a prescription-free zone.

Birdsong welcomes me as I step out of my car. It won't be long now, and the birds will disappear, heading south to warmer weather. Like Mother. She came back and stayed for two weeks after Nick's body was found, but she grew restless, took flight, and flew the coop. For the first time in my life, my mother was speechless. She didn't have a roster of rules to guide me with, and I think she thought I would go with her down to Florida, where we'd mourn Nick together over a pitcher or twelve of margaritas. I couldn't leave with her. I needed answers.

Unlike me, the leaves on the deciduous trees are adjusting well to less sunlight, as shades of fresh green morph into rich gold and bright orange. The Finger Lakes Regatta is the last bash before the fall foliage hits its peak and the swanky Manhattanite wine swillers return for weekend escapes. It also marks my grand return to society, part two of my plan, when the paranoid, grieving widow with the zombie-like appearance sits at the prominent Sutton's Apothecary table and lets everyone see she's not at home.

The automatic doors slide open. Melvin smiles at me with a mixture of delight and surprise.

"Look who's back!"

My dimples pop. I'm prepped to poison him with fake details, spinning a yarn like Mother used to do with Daddy. The key to making men believe what you need them to believe is all in the delivery, she would say, and I believed her. *Make every man feel like he is the most important person in the world.*

Kooky Ken at Willow Bend and his ridiculous BMW received the benefit of Mother's wisdom. And now, Melvin gets a turn, too.

"Hello, my friend. Yes, I am back and in need of your *extraordinary* assistance."

Melvin bows, treating me like a queen. Despite my baggy sweatpants and bed-head hair, a healthy dose of royal treatment does wonders for the state of my emotional kingdom.

"Getting ready to ship the relief supplies to Florida, Melvin, but I need packaging tape, labels, moving boxes, and lots of trash bags. Cleaned the house, top to bottom… sending a lot of stuff I no longer use." Melvin nods his head, soaking in every word like it is earth-shattering news. "And, as you can see, I've been working myself to the bone and am out of everything… shampoo, soap, toothpaste, groceries. Can the stock boys help load my car again?"

Spry Melvin pushes a jumbo cart in my direction, before reaching for his walkie-talkie with one hand and shooting me a thumbs-up signal with the other. As he barks orders into his hand-held device, I beeline it to the office supply aisle. Clear packaging tape is an ordinary purchase for a hurricane relief donor sending supplies—it's also a fantastic way to seal my door and window frames. A simple trap, so I'll know if any intruders break into my house while I'm the buzz of the Finger Lakes Regatta.

A queen's crown jewels can't compete with the wealth of attention I will get, since Nick's funeral was for family only. Oliver insisted, after *The Finger Lakes Flash* removed my post.

"Everyone will show up for the wake and ask what you meant," Brenda had said, delivering Oliver's command while swiping my alpha tiara and abdicating my marital right to reign over the procession of mourners. So ridiculous. Let's stick Nick in the ground and pretend everyone isn't trampling all over his memory with questions about why the local Prince Charming died at Buttermilk Creek.

Brenda led the stiff upper lip shushing campaign against me.

Hmm…

People don't ask questions they already know the answers to.

I've got to find out what Brenda knows and I'm going to do it in style. Pushing my cart into the cosmetics aisle, I catch sight of a shimmery tube of lip gloss, the same kind Mother used to buy me all those years ago. I toss the lip gloss into my cart.

Saturday is my day to accept condolences while captivating the masses in a simple but stylish black sheath dress. I'll tie a scarf around my neck, covering the tiger claw marks Fran inflicted the other day, and twist my blond hair in a tidy updo, nailing the Grace Kelly effect.

Talk about fanfare and a royal spectacle.

The frail, barren widow reemerging as a comeback queen, at the same place the mayor and his cheating wife, Dr. Diane Desmond, hold court.

If Roger Desmond killed Nick, it's time for *his* reign of power to end.

16
CLAUDIA
August 30

There's a clue here I'm missing. But now, three days later, I still can't find it.

Toggling through the photographs of Oliver Sutton's office, my eyes linger again on the employee roster and delivery schedules. Oliver Sutton is the only licensed pharmacist on the list, followed by the names of numerous pharmacy technicians. My cursory review pauses at the name Matthew Weathers, remembering the young man who escorted me to Oliver's office. Cordial, but I didn't get a good enough read to pitch him as an informant. At least, not yet. Recruitment of sources with access takes time, a slow and steady development, with deliberate rapport building while wooing. And based on my last phone call with Peter, my wooing ability is woeful, considering I couldn't keep him and his coordinating tie on the phone.

Adjacent to the employee roster is the list of delivery drivers and route locations. The one with the ominous black line. My mind grapples with the insensitivity shown by Oliver Sutton toward his deceased sibling. My sister Felicia and I go together like fine china and canned tuna, but I would never obliterate her name and *display* it. Was Nick Sutton delivering Wozilfin when he disappeared?

The coarse black line extends to a grouping of his delivery routes and locations. The Finger Lakes Center for Youth in Crisis, the state correctional facility in Romulus, and Willow Bend Long-Term Care Home. Nick Sutton supplemented his military income by assisting with the family business prior to his death. Did helping with the day-to-day operations at the apothecary contribute to his demise? I peer again at the roster of delivery drivers, wondering who acquired Nick's delivery route following his disappearance. I don't recognize any of the other names on

78

the list. The discarded vehicle placard with Sutton's Apothecary's logo was an interesting tidbit from Peter—did the police investigate what pharmaceuticals Nick Sutton was delivering at the time of his disappearance? What if Nick's cell phone isn't the only thing missing? What if prescription drugs vanished, too?

Sipping strong black coffee, my hands encircle the warm cup as I wonder about Wozilfin treatment for bipolar disorder and schizophrenia. Patients at all three of Nick Sutton's former delivery locations could require antipsychotic medication. But what about Nick himself? He deployed abroad with the military and post death, the whisperers around town suggested he suffered from post-traumatic stress disorder. The thought jogs my memory. Opening the archive In Memoriam file, I scroll to the accusation posted by Nick Sutton's widow.

Nick made enemies. He didn't kill himself. The cops don't want you to know. The cops. Cops like Peter? What enemies? Other officers or detectives? Is she implying police corruption, a cover-up, *a clever veil?*

As a business owner, I can understand why Oliver Sutton wanted the post taken down. The police said this wasn't a crime. *No sign of foul play.* A false accusation against the police department, in writing no less, could constitute defamation. Lindsay Sutton's next line of commentary, both insidious and damning, shuffles the deck, playing a fresh accusatory card.

They won't say who wanted him dead and WHY!

Who is she talking about?

I return to the photographs of Oliver Sutton's office, zooming in on the image of the security camera. What is he protecting? The room is in disarray, a cluttered mess of boxes, trash, and paperwork—a contradiction of sloppiness, compared to the precision his job requires. As pharmacist in charge, he alone verifies each prescription dispensed for accuracy, confirming the recipient, the dosage, and the total amount of pills. He also reviews the prescribing physician's orders for medication incompatibility.

I sit up straight in my chair, nearly knocking my coffee cup off its coaster and spilling the liquid contents on my keyboard. Peter's words echo in my mind: *"If you develop more details, run it by me."* Sutton's Apothecary is one part of a triangular equation, fulfilling the pharmaceutical need or needs for the recipient of the prescription.

But the power, the true power, belongs to the holder of the prescription pen.

"That's it!" I shout.

I know what I missed before. The pill vial only contained a partial label, with the drug name Wozilfin. I don't know who received this prescription, but I'm *also* missing the name of the prescribing physician.

Time to tickle the wire.

With a few keystrokes, my page layout for *The Finger Lakes Flash* fills the screen. I jockey to the classified ad section, dragging and clicking a few yard sale advertisements, for-sale-by-owner posts, and lakefront real estate listings around the perimeter, until a nice empty gap opens in the center of the page.

Perfect. My fingers dance across the keyboard, typing a question to my mysterious graveyard snitch in a one-line want ad.

A want ad that I want answered.

THE FINGER LAKES FLASH

Your online snapshot capturing the local news you need to know.
August 31

Classified Advertisements

For Sale:
Wood Clarinet
Mint Condition.
Accepting Best Offer
Call Libby: 315-555-2431

Seymour:

Where should I go to the doctor?

Rummage Sale:
Saturday, September 15
7:00 AM -3PM
Baby clothes/equipment
Kids clothing
Toys
122 Wicker Street
Romulus

17
LINDSAY
September 1

The gloss shimmers on my lips, a delicate shade of pink. I stare at my reflection in the mirror, pleased as punch. Grace Kelly perfection. Mother would approve.

I zip the lip gloss into my purse like it's a lucky penny. In some ways, it feels like it. A little piece of Mother and all her devious tricks will be with me tonight.

Mother always placed my pink suitcase on my bed, along with a new reward of some kind, usually a palate of eyeshadows or glittery lip gloss. This signaled we were going again. Another weekend in Buffalo, or Niagara Falls, or Canton, Ohio. Any of those cities close enough to drive to but far enough away to facilitate Mother's secret life. The one she crafted for herself when she realized the perfect little home and daughter that she gave my Daddy wasn't enough to keep his pants zipped while he went away on business trips week after week as a regional distribution manager for Castle Cola.

Mother called our weekend trips "away games," and I was her teammate. All I had to do was cartwheel and backflip my way through gymnastics workshops and weekend camps, toning my scrawny nine-year-old legs and firming my ass. Pretty simple, other than the keeping-my-mouth-shut part around Daddy. Mother saw it as a win-win situation.

And we did have bucket loads of fun. I liked our road trips along the sleepy state highways. Sometimes, Mother let me read the latest issue of *Cosmopolitan* magazine, with articles about the eleven secrets of world class lovers and the nine that could work for me, which was much more interesting than the boring pimple zapping stuff in teen magazines. And I loved, loved, loved when she filled me in on *Days of Our Lives*, telling me all about the scheming girl who got in the way of the couple everybody wanted to be together.

The entire process of checking in to our adjoining rooms at the various hotels was a trip within a trip. The ladies behind the counters always smelled nice and wore fancy red lipstick, and as they handed Mother shiny keys with numbers attached and told her the rooms were prepaid, they added that another key would be at the desk for when "Daddy" arrived. Mother flashed her biggest smile, snapping her purse shut and thanking them, while winking at me to "come along." As Mother's teammate, my job was to play by the rules to keep our secret safe, so we could do it again and again. I never said "Daddy's not coming" or called out Mother's lie. The truth was my mother placed ads in newspapers lonely men Daddy's age read, and they called the house phone during the day when I was stuck at school learning about igneous rocks and multiplying fractions. She had a knack for finding men with names like Gordon, Victor, and Stanley, and they visited her at the hotels while I was at day camp. And somehow, Sylvia Elaine Kelly always finagled these men to pay for our adjoining rooms *and* buy us dinner at fancy steakhouses, the kind with white linen tablecloths and red votive candles. Back in the days when metal hotel room keys and newspapers dominated, Mother was a sneaky genius.

Daddy didn't complain that he never saw us. He left Mother a stack of cash for groceries and necessities when he was gone during the week, which Mother said included enough to buy her silence. When I was eleven, I asked her what this meant. She rolled down the car window and lit a long cigarette before answering.

"Lindsay, some men have pants problems." She glanced at me with a smirk, before taking another puff on her cigarette and blowing the smoke out the window. "And by some men, I mean your father. Do you know what a pants problem is?"

I shook my head.

"Men roam. With their eyes, their minds, their hearts, their hands. And eventually, with their dicks."

"Oh," I said, shocked at her crudeness.

"So, a pants problem is when they can't keep their pants on around other women… women who aren't their wives."

"Like the guys on *Jerry Springer*?"

"Yes, but normal men, too. The kind like your Daddy."

My spirit deflated, her words hitting me like a sucker punch while I sat smushed in my bucket seat, the seatbelt tugging at my side. I expected Mother to drop the word divorce at any second, but I was wrong.

"Now, there are a few things you need to understand, Lindsay. Little gems you can thank me for some day, because if you listen, it will save you a lot of pain." Mother tossed the stub of her cigarette out the window, her voice steady and convincing.

"Don't complain. I don't. I let Daddy do what Daddy's going to do and I make it work for me. Adults call it 'an arrangement.' And arrangements work if both people agree not to ask questions and don't complain."

I wanted to ask Mother what would happen if someone did complain or ask a question, but she didn't give me the chance.

"Next, and this is important… Are you listening? Women are not your friends! Don't trust them. They want what you have, and they will steal it if you let them. They *will* lie. You have me. You can trust *me*."

I chewed my lip, confused. While I did trust her, I also heard Mother lie to the women behind the hotel check-in counters. And one time, Gordon forgot he left his wedding ring in Mother's room, and we had to go back and get it after we were done eating an enormous tower of fancy seafood at a restaurant with dark corner booths hidden behind velvet drapes. I asked Gordon why he took his ring off in Mother's room, and he said he washed his hands after using the bathroom, which would have been a fine answer except the ring was next to the phone and the King James Bible on the table by the bed. Mother swiped it up in her hand and slipped it back on Gordon's finger as his right hand rested on her ass cheek.

If Mother lied and she helped Gordon lie, would following her rules make me a liar too? She didn't have friends, so how would she know this gem?

On some sad kids-know-more-than-adults-think-they-know level, Mother tried to do a lot to make up for Daddy's disappointment at having a daughter. I wasn't the weekend fishing or hunting buddy he wanted, his archaic mindset about gender roles unbreakable, so Mother made me her best friend instead. But by the age of twelve, I was also wise enough to know that Mother and Daddy's "arrangement" wasn't what she wanted either. And I heard sly whispers at school, too—little digs suggesting some of the other kids had mothers who didn't want their husbands anywhere near "that floosy" Sylvia Kelly. I started to suspect Mother slipped in a few "home games" between the "away game" trips.

This realization swirled within me, cutting a path for the future I envisioned. I wanted my own *Days of Our Lives* epic love story, one without a scheming girl, or any other women for that matter. I would do what Mother said to do and follow her rules but add my own twist. I'd be cautious around other girls, the lying-and-stealing schemers of the world, and I could learn from watching Mother with the hotel guys because she had that down pat.

But I would not settle for an arrangement. I wanted a real beau, not a guy like Daddy or Gordon, but one who loved me. Only me. And I wanted to give him a baby so we could be a family, a solid, loving family where daddies liked having daughters and didn't take their wedding rings off in hotel rooms with other men's wives. It was a big dream. My dream, and I almost got it.

Only Nick had a pants problem, too.

Tonight, I'm going to face the people who killed my dream.

18
CLAUDIA
September 1

My black dress hangs from the hook on the back of my bedroom door, sheathed in a plastic cape.

I haven't worn this cocktail dress since the regional Emmy awards four years ago. I won that night in the best breaking news reporting category, for my coverage of a train derailment and hazardous chemical spill.

More toxins. Go figure.

Four years have come and gone since I wore this fancy dress and celebrated something. I have pictures of me from that event. Smiling, happy, with a full head of hair. On top of my game.

I don't take pictures like that anymore. The picture with Stella on my mantle, and my driver's license photo, are the only two pictures I've taken since I moved here, now that I think about it.

Stella. We met two and a half years ago in a drafty church basement, sitting on folding chairs, sipping diluted coffee. Angela and Patrice were there too, but Stella started attending meetings only three months before I joined the survivor's guilt group, so she was happy to cede her title as resident newcomer. We clicked, like tweens with nervous giggles, discovering new friends on the first day of the school year. On that rainy Tuesday night, when the dampness of the approaching spring battled with the lingering chill of fading winter, Stella's face, or what remained of it, drew me to her.

In the circle of folding chairs, I settled in next to her, transfixed at how she smiled with the one side of her face that wasn't paralyzed. Her eyes studied me, unguarded and keen. She handed me a name tag label and a marker and said with slurring speech, "Welcome to Surviving Survivor's Guilt, or as I call it, round two."

Such few words said so much.

While I stood in the Pennsylvania countryside on September 11, 2001, as a thirsty twenty-something television journalist reporting near the edge of a chemical crater containing what little remained of Flight 93, federal police officer Stella Morgan was simultaneously experiencing a toxic tsunami at the Pentagon. The Flight 77 airstrike ignited a raging fire, scorching through two solid rings of the world's largest office building, rendering it defenseless despite the military strength contained within it. Neither of us considered not responding, a basic sense of humanity far outranking our occupational titles and duties. We didn't think about turning away from the indelible carnage or the river of darkening fumes drowning out the sunny sky. And what we didn't fathom on an unprecedented day when nearly three thousand people died, was that a subsequent attack would strike in quiet clusters years later, as an ever-growing number of 9/11 first responders began dying.

My alopecia and Stella's parotid tumor were early indications, the biological warning lights signaling an alarming message: Your sickness is coming. We grappled with the guilt of surviving a national crisis for a second time while our colleagues started dying. And the toxins robbed the remainder of our lives in a most superficial way. Surgeons sliced Stella's facial nerve while removing her glandular mass, causing numbness and drooping on the left side of her face. Unlike me, she couldn't camouflage her disfigurement with a room full of clever disguises. But it didn't matter. She had the greatest accessory possible in Peter.

Stella used to invite me over for dinner at the home she shared with him, her later-in-life boyfriend and protector. They met more than thirty years prior at the police academy, both denying their attraction while married to others, but life and time and Facebook rectified the situation. A cabin in the woods funded by their mutual pensions made for a comfortable life, until the discovery of Stella's tumor and her eventual brain cancer. Our meals together took on an unspoken urgency, despite our diminished appetites. Tears well in my eyes, reminiscing about one of my last visits with Stella.

"When life gives you lemons, spike the lemonade, Claudia." Our glasses clinked midair, the pucker factor of our circumstance a sour ending to our bittersweet beginning. Two great friends, meeting at what should have been middle age, only our responses on 9/11 altered our expectant midlife point.

"Cheers. To us, to finding each other." It was the hardest toast I've ever had to make, because we both knew the days of cocktails on the cabin deck underneath the redwood canopy were running out. Happy hour toasts aren't supposed to sound like a eulogy.

"See. Something good came out of this mess."

Peter snapped a picture of us in our matching purple head scarves, the closest glimpse of my true appearance given to anyone outside of my medical team. The photograph sits centered on my fireplace mantle. Stella died thirteen days later, four months ago next Wednesday.

Estate planning brochures, advanced life care directives, and a mishmash of all the loose ends preparing for my eventual demise requires are stacked on top of a filing cabinet in my office. Other than mirrors, it's the thing I avoid the most. Death is a nagging adversary—a looming opponent we all lose to, some sooner than others. With my odds falling in the sooner column, I promised Stella I'd meet with her attorney.

"Get it done, Claudia. Get it done so you can get on with living."

I look at the dress again.

Four years is a long time without any fancy cocktail dresses, happy pictures, or celebrations. It's a long time letting the bad guys win.

I'm ready to take some new pictures.

An hour later, I glance at my reflection in the full-length mirror, my fingers struggling to connect the hook and eye closure at the top of the zipper. It doesn't matter, since the long, auburn tendrils of my Nicole wig skim the middle of my back, covering the clasp. I'm doing it. Living on the edge. Ditching my sensible Pamela topper for the seductiveness of Nicole.

Living in the now.

Following my brief, blink-and-you-missed-it marriage after college, I immersed myself in the fly-by-the-seat-of-your-pants lifestyle of television journalism, and it suited me well. Ready to jump at any assignment, at any time, without shackles or impending guilt-trips. Content with breezy, non-committal coupledom, a see-ya when I see-ya kind of thing, with no meet-my-mother strings attached. I could do that when I had hair.

Confidence existed, assuming there would always be another guy, somewhere, sometime. I didn't worry about feeling sexy again, because it never occurred to me sexy was an emotional sensation I could lose.

Alopecia did more than flush my hair down the shower drain—it swallowed my pride.

My hair falling out was breaking news. High-definition television doesn't allow for a sunshiny morning beat reporter to lose her hair without a public outcry. Viewer questions about my sudden change of hairdo ignited wig whispers. I became the story for the exact thing I craved viewers would ignore. My looks. A mic drop moment in every sense.

Relocating to the Finger Lakes allowed me to hide. But tonight, I'm ready to step out.

I turn, facing my reflection in the enemy, staring at the slim woman in the sleeveless black dress and stiletto heels. It's like the old me, or at least what the old me looked like before the alopecia. But, instead of rushing away from the image, my body stands still, mesmerized. The corners of my mouth turn up, a pulse of excitement radiating through me. It beats steadily, free of panic and breathlessness.

"I missed you," I say aloud.

Tonight, Claudia Marton returns.

19
LINDSAY
September 1

In the distance, the lake water shimmers under the late afternoon sun, beads of silver reflecting the rich beauty of the day that was, with near-perfect conditions for boat racing. A gentle wind ripples the water ever-so-slightly, almost in synchronized harmony with the rustle of dry, late-summer leaves clinging to the trees. Closer in, the lane buoys bob up and down, a hypnotic rhythm left in the wake of the last heat of scullers. A scattering of people, lounging on the lawn below the redwood deck, stare out at the impressive gathering of bright sailboat masts, a collage of kaleidoscope colors mirrored on the surface of the water. Laughter filters up from the slips where pontoon boats anchor, interspersed among the festive clinks of champagne glasses.

Show time.

Stepping out of my car, my hands smooth my dress, and I look around. I scored a great parking spot, waiting as a family of five packed up their picnic basket and blanket and loaded their weary, sun-kissed children into car seats. The youngest boy, his eyelids droopy, sucked on his right thumb as he turned to wave a last goodbye at the boats.

I hit the button on my key fob, alarming my SUV and its cash cargo. The clapboard white clubhouse with its periwinkle blue trim offers panoramic views of the lake, and perfect eyeshot of my parked car. No one will dare mess with it here, I think, stepping on a cobblestone paver and approaching the entrance to the yacht club. Nick's killer may be here tonight, but no one will risk breaking into an alarmed SUV with a who's who of witnesses in plain sight. All those busybodies will be watching *my* every move, curious to see how the widow Sutton is holding up.

Wondering if I'm unhinged.

My gut clenches at the thought, a precursor to the seismic stress toll

I anticipate inside. God, I want an anxiety pill. I silently curse Oliver for denying me a wink-wink early refill. I'm wobbly in my stilettos—not from heel height or the pebbled paver stones, but from the lack of my pharmaceutical crutch.

I tuck my car keys into my purse, willing myself to breathe as I reach the steps to the redwood deck at the back of the clubhouse. The din of the crowd assaults my spirit, with boisterous laughs coming from a group of men gathered at the bar on the far side of the deck. How many times did Nick gravitate to that same spot, happy to talk to his hometown buddies about the latest Yankees game, or the upcoming golf tournament? Anything to avoid Oliver's mind-numbing droning about business and the state of the economy. The scene looks identical to previous gatherings here, with the guys' navy blazers tossed over the backs of chairs at nearby cocktail tables where their girlfriends and wives sit, nursing tall flutes of sparkling wine while protecting their wrinkle-free faces under sun umbrellas.

A few heads turn my way, inquisitive eyes boring through me like a corkscrew, twisting my insides. Act like you own this place, I tell myself, nodding my head at a mother I recognize from Pattycake Childcare. She raises her hand in a cautious wave. A large table sporting The Finger Lakes Regatta welcome banner extends to my right, manned by teens about Delaney's age.

"Raffle tickets, miss?"

The teen smacks her gum, handing me an event program.

"Yes, twenty tickets please," I say, forking over my payment.

Behind the ticket table, the raffle items are propped, their crisp cellophane wrappers reflecting the twinkling light from the crystal chandeliers. Most of the raffle donations are gift baskets from the local wineries, containing bottles of Riesling and the premium dessert ice wines made from rare frozen fall grapes. The items are numbered, resting next to boxes with wide slots for depositing the raffle tickets. After dinner, when everyone is slightly sauced and the blowhard welcome speeches and the kissy-kissy thank you's are done, the winning numbers will be drawn. I'll save depositing my tickets for now, in case Oliver nettles my nerves at the dinner table. Dropping tickets in raffle boxes is a convenient escape.

Glancing down, my program lists the sponsored dinner tables with a corresponding seat map. Sutton's Apothecary is number nine, catty-corner from table eleven in the center of the room. My breath catches in my throat. Willow Bend Long-Term Care Home is table eleven. A glossy photograph of Diane and her husband adorns the back of the program, listing her as the event coordinator and Roger Desmond as Master of Ceremonies.

Stepping into the dining room, I spot Mayor Desmond almost instantly, up front, near a microphone. He's involved in an animated conversation with a man in a blue suit, and as he gestures with his hand holding a wine goblet, he catches me eyeing him. He pauses, but he doesn't look away.

It takes everything in my power not to flinch.

The mayor continues to hold my gaze, locking me in a stare-down. My knees wobble like jelly on a butter knife, but his laser focus on my entrance speaks volumes. The comments I put on *The Finger Lakes Flash* are about him. And he knows it.

"Aunt Lindsay!"

My niece's voice interrupts my dither. A welcome relief, as the weight of both the mayor's stare and community indifference strain my nervous system. No one rushed over offering condolences or said in passing, "Oh, hey." The ghost of Nick is palpable everywhere I look, but Mother's aura pinches at my frayed nerves, too. How silly of me to forget. Without Nick, I revert to being nothing more than Sylvia Kelly's daughter now. A woman everyone in town thinks is a slut. I turn away from facing Roger Desmond and greet my niece.

"Hi, honey! You look pretty!"

Delaney grins and does a slow twirl for me in a bubble gum pink flare dress, oblivious to my unease.

"Mom sent me over to get you. FYI. She's pissed at Dad." She rolls her eyes.

"How come?"

"Don't know the deets." She grabs my hand and says, "Come on."

We walk to the table. The one without a seat for Nick or Fran. I hadn't considered this. Nothing is ever going to be the same. Every event, every gathering, every everything will be like this, with Fran at Willow Bend and Nick gone. Gone for good.

Anxiety grips me with a wringing fist. I let go of Delaney's hand, not wanting to hurt her, certain she's disgusted by the damp sponge feeling of mine. Brenda sits next to the wine chiller bucket, helping herself with a generous pour.

"There you are. God, you're pale. Pass me your wine glass. Are you feeling better? I'm glad we got you out of the house."

She said it again! This isn't some fluky comment she's making by accident.

My sister-in-law pours some wine, and motions at Delaney.

"Aunt Lindsay and I need to talk. Go mingle."

"K."

And like a lake frog, my niece bounces, from the grown-ups' table to a better pad. My eyes shift from Delaney to Brenda, not sure how bad things are with Oliver. Is this what she wants to talk about?

My brain has "Brenda is the reason I went to the freezer" on loop, and I'm afraid to speak. She *must* know about the cash—why else would she keep making comments about getting me out of the house? Or am I paranoid? Sipping wine, I crave my medication.

"Bren, can I bum a pill? I thought I was ready for this, but everywhere I look, I see Nick, or where Nick is supposed to be…"

My breath accelerates, catching me off guard, as my hand reaches again for the wine glass. I slug the vino, desperate to stop the shallow breaths and the onset of a panic attack. Half the wine goes up my nose, causing me to spasm, with choking coughs. I grab a cloth napkin from the table and cover my mouth, while Brenda puts all two hundred and ten pounds of her weight into slaps on my back. My eyes shut, imagining all the whispers around the room.

"Psst… wait for it. Lindsay Sutton's hyperventilating, and she's been here a whopping five minutes."

"Are you okay?" Brenda asks, sounding concerned.

My eyes open, spotting Oliver standing in front of me across the table. His arms are folded, wrinkling the sleeves of his seersucker suit, the scowl on his face transmitting more than minor irritation at my choking fit commotion. I cough again. Oliver pulls out his chair as a gentle tap on my shoulder registers, and I imagine some stranger's arms, seconds away from encircling my waist and yanking my internal organs with the life-saving Heimlich maneuver. Turning, I stifle another cough. The sight in front of me makes me want to sink into the floor.

Melvin the Grocery Galleria greeter stands behind me, grinning ear to ear at his favorite customer. He's dressed in a plaid sports coat, with a blue bow tie matching his eye color.

"Are you okay, my dear?"

Nodding my head, my body summons every bit of resolve. If Melvin mentions my early-bird visits to the Grocery Galleria, I'll be chicken on a stick for Brenda and Oliver. They'll pepper me with questions, and, if they *are* involved with the deposits in my deep freezer, they'll get salty when my answers are vague.

"Hi, Melvin! That bow tie is divine."

Melvin's eyebrows shoot up and his cheeks dimple. He's about to respond, but I cut him off at the pass.

"Thank you for helping me load my groceries this morning. Let me introduce you to my family, and then, I'd like to buy you a drink."

Turning toward Brenda to make the introduction, she sits, glaring across the table with unspoken disgust written all over her face.

I swivel in my seat, nearly choking again. Dr. Diane Desmond's arm drapes around Oliver's shoulders and the back of his chair, her curvaceous body pressed against him, in a way-too-chummy side hug.

With a broad smile, she purrs, "Hello, Lindsay."

20
CLAUDIA
September 1

The Finger Lakes Flash table flanks the left side of the banquet room, with breathtaking views of the lake, and a perfect perch for people watching. My inquisitiveness activates, scanning the room for people I want to spy on.

The Sutton family tops the list.

The table Sutton's Apothecary sponsored sits in the middle of the room, sandwiched between the donors from Willow Bend Long-Term Care Home and Kipling's Tire Center. Kipling's is a client of mine. Without knowing if Oliver Sutton caught me snooping around his office on his security camera, I'm hedging my bets on public humiliation. He might confront me tonight in front of my other clients.

The string quartet up front plays a medley of Sinatra classics. The hubbub of lively conversation and laughter in the room drowns them out, an expected consequence when free samples of Riesling flow faster than the Hudson River. I'm abstaining for now, wanting to be on my game for my clients. Putting Pamela out to pasture in favor of my Nicole wig has my advertisers doing double takes. If they didn't realize that I wear wigs, they do now. Still, along with the second glances, my clients are dropping compliments in equal measure.

"Claudia, I didn't recognize you," a voice from behind me says. "You are stunning!"

Spinning on my heels, the manager of Shilman's Winery thanks me for the promotional support I provided for tonight's event. We make small talk for a few minutes, which includes a play-by-play recap over a contested scull race from earlier in the day. Despite my self-imposed hermit social life over the past few years, the conversation flows with ease, and we agree to chat about fall advertising spots next week. "Enjoy

95

your evening, Claudia," my business associate says, before adding, "Again, you look great!"

The truth is I feel great. Confident. Assured. *Attractive.* A few more clients stop by, and we talk before posing for joint selfies, and wishing each other well. A waitress arrives with a tray of appetizers, and my fingers snag a coconut-crusted shrimp as my cell phone vibrates. Looking down, there's a picture of me, taken a few moments ago with the owner of a local coffee house. I text a quick thank you to him for sending me the shot. Photographs don't lie. My wide smile and dimpled cheeks convey happiness. I forward the image to Felicia as proof I'm out among the living on a Saturday night, not locked in a dark room. The picture marks progress in my recovery, especially on the cusp of the anniversary of the 9/11 attacks.

Scanning the room again, I search for Peter. He's up front, engrossed in conversation with Mayor Roger Desmond, who along with his physician wife, Diane, achieved prominent seat assignments at the head table next to the owners of the yacht club. Peter is listening to whatever the mayor is saying, while Dr. Desmond hobnobs around the room. She approaches the table sponsored by Sutton's Apothecary, where Oliver Sutton is now sitting. She wraps her arm around him, causing Brenda Sutton's face to turn as red as her hair. Lindsay Sutton speaks with an elderly gentleman dressed in a polyester sport coat and bow tie, but as she turns in her seat toward her sister-in-law, I observe a horrified reaction as she glances at Oliver.

Her face pales in an instant, a stunning contrast to Brenda's flushed appearance.

A rush of concern for Lindsay Sutton floods my psyche. Her face projects terror and I can't help but remember our phone conversation, when she was afraid to go on the record about who she believes killed her husband. As a favor to Oliver, I removed her comments from Nick Sutton's memorial page, but now, I wonder if I am supporting the wrong person. I can't shake the conversation I heard between Oliver and Brenda Sutton, and the black line scratched through Nick's name on the delivery route schedule. Does Lindsay Sutton have a reason to fear her brother-in-law?

My anonymous tipster didn't indicate if the Wozilfin clue has anything to do with Nicholas Sutton's death—admittedly, the tip I received could be referring to something else. But, watching Lindsay Sutton now, I want so badly to speak with her. She may still be upset because I took down her remarks, but it's worth a try.

As I debate approaching their table, a low whistle, soft but shrill, rings out behind me.

Turning, I find Peter towering over me, smiling.

"Hi, pretty lady."

Our eyes connect, speaking with a flirtatious language of their own. I return his smile, and say, "Thank you. Hi yourself."

"You were studying something." Peter's gaze shifts to the center of the room, and then back to me. "Do I have competition?"

Raising my Brooke eyebrows and shaking my head, I glance again at Lindsay Sutton's tense face. Oliver's back is to me, still draped by Dr. Diane Desmond's arm, and by the looks of things, my snoop session in his office isn't his most pressing problem. Turning my full attention to Peter, I brush off his concern with a smile, hoping Oliver Sutton is too busy with family drama to confront me.

"No, silly, no competition. Just keeping my eye out for one of my clients."

21
LINDSAY
September 1

Nick's mistress stands a few feet from me, bedecked in a sparkling white dress and silver jewelry. Her hair cascades in soft, loose waves, her makeup flawless. She smiles at me, feigning kindness, but I know the silent message she's sending—it's not her fault my husband wanted her more than me. That's *my* character flaw, and her fake smile hammers it home in the most patronizing way.

"And Melvin, darling Melvin, how are you?" Diane drawls, as Melvin chuckles behind me.

"Happy to be here with all the pretty ladies!"

His comment elicits a scoff from Brenda. She sets her wine glass down on the table with too much force, seething, "Why are you hanging on my husband?"

A jolt of unbridled appreciation for my sister-in-law stokes my confidence, enough for me to hop on the insinuation train.

"Dr. Desmond, you're never at Willow Bend when I stop by to visit Fran. People are going to wonder what you're up to."

Diane's eyes flicker, but she doesn't break. Like a fighter, she deflects.

"Lindsay, are you all right? I came over when I saw you coughing. Anything I can do?" She places her right hand on her hip seductively, while her left arm remains draped around Oliver.

Before I can respond, Brenda interjects, "Yeah, let go of my husband!"

Her voice carries, causing a few people at nearby tables to look our way. Ken Preston saunters up to the Willow Bend table with a glass of wine in his hand, followed by Marlene Flynn in a motorized wheelchair. A few other elderly guests are seated there, with one giving a tiny wave to Melvin.

98

Ken wears an impeccable custom-fitted suit and silk tie. He adjusts a diamond encrusted cufflink, glancing at our table with curiosity. Melvin scoots from behind me, forgetting my drink offer, and approaches Marlene. He pulls a chair out at the Willow Bend table, making room for the wheelchair, and then plops himself down in the seat next to her. Ken walks over to Melvin, extending his hand. The moving pieces of the scene muddle, a standard backdrop to the showstopper unraveling in front of me.

Oliver snarls at Brenda through gritted teeth.

"Stop it."

His command does nothing but enrage my sister-in-law.

"Why should I?" Brenda tosses back at him, unwilling to cede her position.

Diane squeezes Oliver's arm and demurs, "Obviously, this is still a difficult time for your family. Lindsay, my condolences for your loss."

The bottled-up hatred festering in me bubbles, but before I can respond, her husband floats her a verbal rescue raft.

"Ladies and gentlemen, if I can have your attention, please." Mayor Roger Desmond's voice booms into a microphone at the front of the room. "If we can all take our seats, I would like to begin our program for this evening."

Diane takes her cue. "Enjoy the party, everyone."

Her arm falls from Oliver's body, and she glides on her stiletto heels to the front table, taking her seat of prominence. Brenda and I sit like twin hawks watching her every move, until Delaney returns to the table, pulls out her chair and says, "What gives?"

Brenda wastes no time responding.

"Ask your father."

Oliver shoots back a look of pure agitation and says, "We'll talk about it later."

Delaney rolls her eyes at me, picks up her cell phone, and begins texting a friend. Brenda empties the bottle of wine into her glass and says, "You bet we will."

The murmur of the crowd dwindles as the mayor launches into his welcome speech. Roger Desmond radiates confidence. He isn't unattractive, but his personality doesn't float my boat. Considering Diane cut anchor and went adrift with my husband, she doesn't think he's a prize catch, either. But you would never know it by watching her now.

She beams at the mayor like a lighthouse beacon, and I'm hit with the sinking realization that everyone else is in the dark about her, too.

"Folks, on behalf of the Finger Lakes Regatta committee, I would like to welcome you tonight to our annual fundraising dinner."

As Roger Desmond commands center stage, the slow creep of my anxiety accelerates. He's polished, with hubris suggesting he wouldn't tolerate another man touching his wife. This man doesn't share, I think to myself, eliminating the possibility of an open marriage. If he discovered Nick and Diane's affair, he would retaliate. I'm certain of it.

Brenda motions to a waiter, requesting another bottle of wine for the table.

"Slow down, *dear,*" Oliver hisses, loud enough for the Willow Bend crowd to overhear. Ken Preston shoots me a sympathetic glance and a quick wave. My hand brushes empty air, a lazy return greeting resembling a bored swipe at a nagging fly.

"Oh, pipe down, Oliver, this is for charity, remember?" Brenda's voice thunders. The mayor pauses his introduction, shooting her a look of consternation before continuing.

"As I was saying, make sure you have your raffle ticket stubs handy. We will announce the winning numbers after the trophy presentations. We had some great races today, and Mother Nature blessed us with beautiful weather."

Polite applause fills the room. Diane Desmond claps, as her husband pauses his speech. How dare she sit here, acting like nothing happened? Pretending her car wasn't parked at the rental cabin next to Nick's truck on a Saturday afternoon last spring? My breath catches, a sickening thought settling in and taking hold, the kind of thought I've tried to ignore, hoping it wouldn't resurface.

I should have confronted them, exposing their dirty, ugly affair, calling her out for the cheater she is. But I didn't. I dropped my binoculars and ran to my car, doing exactly what Mother told me most wives do when they discover their husbands are cheating. I denied it to myself, not ready to give up on us. On the subconscious level, I pretended my increasing bitchiness didn't matter all those childless years, minimizing how the hormones made me feel bloated and ugly, and how I resisted sex except when I ovulated. If I had spoken up about the affair, maybe Nick would be alive today. But *I didn't.* My mouth swallowed the words, choking them back into the dark recesses of denial. We were a few weeks away from another embryo transfer, and I wanted that baby, the way other cheated-on wives want their mansions behind wrought-iron gates or their invite-only country club memberships. All the reasons we justify pretense. And now, Nick is dead, the embryo transfer was cancelled, and she's *clapping*.

The bile in my throat curdles as the mayor continues speaking, but my ears are no longer listening. His words sound hollow, like echoes in a tunnel, and a basketball-sized pressure swells in my chest, restricting the free flow of oxygen to my lungs. The room starts spinning. The owner of the yacht club gets up from his seat, walks over to Roger Desmond, and shakes his hand. They're saying something, something I can't understand.

Focus. Don't give in to it. Breathe.

My throat struggles to swallow. Air dies in my nose, with empty exhales coming quicker through my mouth. What is he saying?

"And thank you to Claudia Marton for the publicity about tonight's fundraiser on *The Finger Lakes Flash*."

Through my daze, a woman across the room rises from her seat, giving a small wave of acknowledgement. She's the one! The editor I called, the one who nixed my comments, muzzling me as a favor to Oliver. A tingling sensation radiates along my jawline. The woman nods, before glancing over her shoulder, looking out the big plate glass window her table flanks. As my eyes fixate on her every move, she turns back to the room at-large and says to no one in particular, "Someone's car alarm is going off."

22
CLAUDIA
September 1

Peter claps for me as I retake my seat, amid the deafening sound of a car alarm shrilling from the other side of the giant glass window overlooking the lake. A waiter arrives with a bottle of wine. He presents the bottle to Peter for his inspection and then pours a sample for him to taste. Peter nods his head in agreement, and we wait as our glasses are filled. The waiter turns to leave, and I raise my glass in a toast to my dinner companion.

"*The Finger Lakes Flash* thanks you for being my guest tonight."

He smiles, clinking his glass with mine. "My pleasure. And, if this is your 'I'm working' look, I'll have dinner with you, anytime."

I blush, enjoying the moment, soaking up the ambiance of the room and Peter's inference. Nothing, not the mayor's rambling or the bleating of the car horn, can drown out the underlining suggestion his comment implies. "Mixing business with pleasure won't kill me," I say with a wink, before regretting my poor word choice.

We both know what will kill me. The same thing that killed Stella. Maybe not the exact same cancer, but some malignant menace born from the 9/11 toxins. The number of responders dying from illnesses related to their exposure will soon surpass the number of victims murdered by the plane crashes. An infinite crime, decades in the making. Peter's face registers the remark, but he deflects it, refusing to quash the good vibe between us.

"No talk about Stella tonight. I may have a scoop for you."

"I love scoops."

He chuckles and leans in, whispering over the scentless candle flickering between us.

"Mayor Desmond is going to drop some big news tonight."

My Brooke eyebrows arch, my interest piqued.

"What news?"

"We should listen to him. It's a headline you'll want for the *Flash*," he says, as he reaches across the table for my hand. "I don't want to distract you from a major story."

Too late.

My hand accepts his, giving it an appreciative squeeze. Maybe distraction is *good*, I think, looking around the room at the other attendees. My business is solid, and the Wozilfin clue revived my investigative journalism motor, with its blockbuster story potential. And as I sneak a peek at Peter, I realize we have potential, too. Dating could be the spark that my personal life needs.

Whatever the mayor's announcement is about, it pales in comparison to the all-points bulletin Peter's touch sends to my brain. I scan the crowd, wondering if people are watching us, taking in our cozy flirtation amid candlelight. Do they see what's happening? Can they see the twinkle in my eyes, the carefree comfort I exude, the obliviousness to my mirror image reflection in the plate glass window at my side? I crave confirmation that someone, anyone, notices what my soul is screaming. I'm not concentrating on what I've lost and I'm not fearing what's ahead. I'm honest-to-goodness savoring *the now*.

To my disappointment, all eyes are focused on the mayor. Glancing at Lindsay Sutton, she looks sick to her stomach.

"Now, I know everyone is hungry, so I'm going to make this quick. This beautiful evening would not be possible without the extraordinary efforts of my lovely wife." Roger Desmond cracks an adoring smile at his spouse, allowing the spattering of applause to continue as waiters hasten to refill glasses before the first course is served. "Honey, please stand, and take a bow. Ladies and gentlemen, please give a hand for our Finger Lakes Regatta coordinator, Dr. Diane Desmond!"

The doctor projects an air of sophistication as she rises, kissing her husband on the cheek before turning to smile at the crowd. She nods her head at the hearty applause, her sparkling white sequined dress glistening under the chandelier lights.

From a table in the center of the room, at the precise second when the handclapping ends but the first words of dinner conversation lay idle on the tongue, a caustic voice rings out, causing a ripple current through the crowd.

"At least she's focused on *her* husband now."

23
LINDSAY
September 1

The thumping of my heart syncs with the repetitive horn siren blaring outside, alerting me of simultaneous attacks. My car. The alarm going off must be mine. No one else came to this shindig with a car loaded with loot. I glance around the room, taking inventory of my suspects while trying to ignore the squeezing pain in my chest. If I stand up now, fleeing to my car, everyone will see. More whispers and stares.

The Finger Lakes Flash lady sits back in her seat, and the mayor is blabbering away again while shaking hands with some puffed-up wine guy, but their words don't resonate with me, not amid the incessant horn beeps. Whatever Roger Desmond says sounds muffled and groggy, like an old cassette tape played at the wrong speed. Diane sparkles nearby in her sequin number, playing the supportive wife's role so well she deserves a participation trophy. Brenda sits hunched next to me, her elbow grazing mine, well on her way to full-on sloshed. Oliver twists in his seat, his back to us, as he pretends to be fascinated by the mayor's dog-and-pony show.

Think. All my suspects are accounted for. Maybe someone set off an alarm on another car, or an old geezer couple forgot their cheater reading glasses and are hitting the wrong key fob button, making us all suffer in the process. Although, if they can't see, maybe they can't hear either.

Should I ask someone to go with me to my car? My gaze roams to Melvin at the next table. He's happy, soaking up all the bubbles and fizz the mayor is floating, and as Diane rises from her seat and kisses her husband on the cheek, Melvin claps, joining another round of applause erupting in the room. My fists tense, watching Diane dazzle in her one-shoulder dress. The clapping peters out and my hunched over sister-in-

104

law croaks out a line of sarcasm betraying both her thoughts and her inebriation level.

"At least she's focused on *her* husband now."

A few audible gasps slip out of pencil-lined lips, and the weight of collective stares coming from all directions sucks my breath away. Oliver spins in his seat, his eyes beady and incensed. Brenda gulps her wine, relishing the attention. I clutch my purse in my lap, rocking back and forth, because darkness will overtake me if I sit still—I might faint. My insinuations on *The Finger Lakes Flash* about Nick's affair seem feeble now compared to the intoxicated implication Brenda put on blast. A sea of murmurs rocks the room.

"Stop. It. Now!" Oliver seethes, through a clenched jaw.

"Ugh, *Mom*!" Delany tosses her cloth napkin on her plate and pushes back her seat. "I'm bouncing. This is *so* uncool. Like, not Gucci, Mom."

My niece stomps over to her group of friends at the back of the room. They flock around her like protective hens, clucking about the mean rooster crowing gossip. Why is Brenda changing her mind? She made me shut up about Nick's affair, claiming my words would hurt Delaney, the business, the family. I swallow, trying to breathe. Why is she spewing like this now, and why didn't she give me a heads-up? Or is that the point? To make me come unglued by pushing all the necessary buttons, ensuring a public meltdown? A seventy-two-hour psychiatric hold is a great way to guarantee I'll be sequestered and monitored, leaving my car and home vulnerable to whomever wants their money back.

My car. Did Brenda *time* her comment to distract from the car alarm? I grip the edge of the table, preparing to stand. As I do, the mayor and Dr. Desmond are rescued from the awkwardness of Brenda's outburst by a waiter, who hands the mayor a piece of paper. Roger Desmond skims it and raises his microphone again.

"Ladies and gentlemen, will the owner of a black Durango, license plate number TRF-6574 please report to your vehicle? Your car alarm is going off."

His words pump oxygen into my lungs. It's not my car. Letting out a sigh, I barely have time to savor the relief, before Brenda makes another shocking statement.

"Why don't *you* stop using other people's cars for your secret meetings with her, Oliver?"

Brenda swirls the wine in her glass, landing her accusation with the forceful jab of a champion prize fighter, only I'm the one seeing stars. Oliver sits ramrod still, his hatred for my sister-in-law plastered all over his face. He's a frightening sight, which is made scarier by the added implications her statement has for me. My mind flutters again to the image of Nick's truck parked at a remote fishing cabin on a Saturday afternoon four months ago, nestled under budding poplar trees aside Diane's vehicle, still bearing the murky remnants of late winter slush dissolved by sodium chloride. What if Nick wasn't there? What if what Brenda says is true? Did *Oliver* use decoy cars to camouflage an adulterous affair with the mayor's wife?

The hubbub in the room simmers, but Brenda's not done. Her voice cuts through the muckety-muck like a sculling paddle, swift and quick, as she points toward Dr. Desmond at the front of the room.

"If she comes near you again, she'll pay for it."

The startled gasps around the room cause me to tremble, with strong heart palpitations pounding in my chest. The internal beating hurts, like successive sharp kicks to a bruised body. My breathing accelerates and my stomach lurches with a nauseating warning. I'm verging on a panic attack. Brenda's admission confirms what I suspected. She has been keeping a secret from me. *The woman Oliver is having an affair with is Diane Desmond!*

No wonder my brother-in-law wanted my comments removed from *The Finger Lakes Flash*. Oliver feared exposure of his own deception! For that matter, Brenda let me believe Nick was a cheater, too. But the most glaring revelation from this deceit is that my initial hunch is probably right: Roger Desmond made the same mistake I did. He assumed Diane was having an affair with Nick. *He killed the wrong brother!*

My body isn't mine, but it moves somehow. I stand at the table, amid the watchful eyes of the other diners, who whisper in muffled tones about my sister-in-law's outburst. Turning toward the front of the room, I stare directly at Roger Desmond and wait until he notices me. He's speaking quietly to his wife, and glances in the direction of our table. For the second time tonight, he catches sight of me and does not look away. The guests at the nearby tables take note of our silent face-off, and suddenly, a quiet hush settles over the dining room.

Clutching my purse to my belly, my voice quivers as I proclaim, "You got the wrong guy!"

The mayor recoils, setting his jaw while standing speechless, staring at both my sister-in-law and me as spectators bristle over my announcement. My nausea escalates, and on some level, it registers I'm not strong enough to make it to my car. I move away from my seat, my body maneuvering around the hodgepodge pattern of scattered dinner tables. A voice in my head tells me I'm going to vomit. I stagger into the small, knotted pine restroom, and pummel through a stall doorway, collapsing on the floor in front of a commode base. A lingering scent of evergreen assaults my nostrils.

I regurgitate into the toilet, a violent sickness, making it hard to catch my breath. Nick loved me! He was faithful! He wanted me, he wanted our baby, our family…

Grasping the toilet tank, the room won't stop spinning. As my body trembles, I hear the gentle slide of the bathroom door opening. Someone enters, walking with slow, steady steps.

The back of my hand drags across my lips, the putrid taste in my mouth inciting a fresh wave of gut-churning agitation, made worse by the sickening realization the footsteps directly behind me are there to rest. I torque my body, clinging to the commode base for support, not understanding why my unwelcome stall visitor isn't talking. A surprising set of eyes peer down at me, but they don't offer me solace.

Instead, a new shiver of panic radiates through me.

24
CLAUDIA
September 1

Peter drops my hand the minute Brenda Sutton's verbal threat rings out, his body tensing like an Irish setter on point, trained to focus on the offending quarry. Unexpectedly, Lindsay Sutton stands, glaring at the mayor and his wife.

"You got the wrong guy!" she seethes, her body trembling. The clamoring in the room bubbles, as more than one jaw drops open, and heads turn. The wait staff pretends not to notice, wine continuing to flow into goblets and flutes, intensifying the pucker factor reaction to both Brenda Sutton's insult and Lindsay's outcry.

Roger Desmond's face blanches an ashen white, which matches his wife's dress, only without the sparkles. Whatever his planned announcement, this aspersion dimmed the glimmer of it, but you would never know it by watching Dr. Desmond. She stands tall and proud, unfazed, caressing her husband's back with her hand, a pitying grimace on her face.

My date rises, scuttling toward Sutton's Apothecary's table. As he approaches, Lindsay Sutton shrinks away from her sister-in-law, clutching her purse to her stomach. She walks toward the restroom, her angst expression laced with disgust and anger.

Lindsay's actions trigger me. *"You got the wrong guy!"* She still believes someone killed her husband! Was her declaration an accusation of murder? *Against the mayor?* My body is pulled by the tug of invisible puppet strings, my mind recognizing the mirror image of my own struggles with anxiety. Voyeurism makes Brenda and Oliver Sutton fascinating targets, and my romantic fantasies yearn for Peter's return to our table, but the reporter within me screams above all the other voices in my head, sending me on a quest of my own.

108

My feet trail Peter's by a stride or two, my body slithering between dinner seats at the center of the room. As Peter approaches Brenda Sutton, Oliver extends his hand, gripping my wrist and barking out a question in the form of a command.

"A word with you, *please*?"

I resist, jerking from his clutch. The movement elicits more audible shock from nearby diners, and Peter turns around. Oliver's anger flares his nostrils, a temper boiling at the surface, ready to explode.

"Leave her alone!"

Peter's demand silences everyone in the room, except Brenda Sutton, who points at me and slurs.

"She's another one—*way* too interested in my husband. I caught *her* on the camera."

Brenda's comment refocuses her husband's attention, allowing me to skirt away, but my worst fear is realized: Brenda Sutton knows I was snooping in her husband's office, and now the entire town thinks I might have a romantic interest in him, too. Her voice bellows again against Peter's firm tone, with Oliver beseeching his wife to calm down.

I find Lindsay Sutton crumpled in the first stall, sprawled on the floor like a marathon runner seizing in pain, a body exhausted by the combined physical and emotional toll of the day. She wipes at her mouth and turns, fixating on my face for a long second before registering my identity. Her eyes grow wide, and I witness a painful expression I know all too well. *Fear.* Lindsay scrutinizes me the same way I did the ominous bald patch on my scalp the first time it reflected in my bathroom mirror.

Dropping to the floor, my hands touch her arms, which are riddled with goosebumps. Watching Lindsay struggle for breath, her forehead beading with perspiration, I see a woman in the throes of my secret struggle.

"Breathe, Lindsay. I'm here. It's going to be all right. Breathe."

Her eyes hold mine, her body trembling, as she inhales and tries to regain her composure. Sitting on the floor in our black sleeveless dresses, I rub her arms, encouraging her to keep pacing her breaths. "That's right. You got this."

A questioning fog clouds her face, the pupils of her eyes enlarged and still frenzied. Her head shakes as she forms a meek reply.

"I can't go back out there."

Her breath catches again, a precursor to a new round of hyperventilation. Her gaze pleads for an answer.

"Okay. Um, let me think," I say, pausing for lack of a plan. She nods, releasing long, slow breaths out of her mouth, her shoulders drooping.

"I'm going to peek out there and see what's happening, okay? I'm not leaving. I'll be right back."

She blinks in rapid succession.

"I'm right here. Keep breathing." I step backward toward the bathroom door, pulling the handle and opening it a crack. Peter, Roger Desmond, and a few other men encircle the Sutton's Apothecary table, where Brenda Sutton now stands, brushing away attempts to escort her out. A teenage girl tugs at Oliver Sutton's arm, her face tear stained. The regatta revelers are transfixed by the sight. An opportunity for escape exists.

Turning back to face Lindsay, the image of her striking blond hair set against a similar black dress spurs me, a plan of action formulating. A plan benefiting both her and me. The comment I made to Peter moments ago echoes in my head, strong and pronounced.

"Mixing business with pleasure won't kill me."

Every fiber of my being knows what I must do.

"Give me your scarf."

Her mouth gapes, a renewed flicker of fear haunting her eyes.

There's only one way to make her understand. Reaching up, my fingers grasp at the thick Nicole tresses, tugging at the wig lace, the hair piece slipping off my head, revealing the patchy lot of uneven bristles interspersed among the bald patches. Lindsay recoils in shock, her body colliding with the toilet. She lets out a small cry of pain, never taking her eyes off me.

She doesn't understand that my cover-up is up for grabs.

"Here. Take this. Put it on. I'll help you. If you hurry, you can sneak out of here and get to the parking lot. Don't look at your family's table. Walk straight out and let people think you are me."

She sits motionless, too stunned to speak.

"Give me your scarf so I can cover my head. After you walk out, I'll go to the front and ask to make an announcement. The anniversary of 9/11 is next week. People will listen to what I have to say once I take off the scarf." I pause, painfully aware of the rest. "Let my appearance be the distraction you need."

I pull a business card out from my purse, and hand it to Lindsay.

"My name and contact information are on my card, in case you've lost my number. We'll talk next week—we never finished our conversation in June. I'd like to circle back when you're feeling better. Are you okay to drive?"

Lindsay Sutton's hands move to the scarf draped around her neck. She pulls it off, exposing faint red marks around her neck. She gulps, extending the cloth to me, bobbing her head up and down.

"Here."

Wrapping the scarf on my head, I help Lindsay tuck a few loose tendrils of blonde hair under my Nicole wig. Extending my hand to her, I help her to her feet.

"You can do this. Remember to breathe. Okay?"

She nods, somewhat tranced, but squeezes my hand.

"*Thank you,*" she whispers.

I squeeze back, unsure if I've made a tragic mistake or a profound rescue, not only for her, but for me. I can't risk turning back now. If I stall, I'll lose my nerve and she'll miss her chance to escape, so I say the only word that matters.

"Go."

25
LINDSAY
September 1

The car door slams behind me. I glance at the plastic bins, resting undisturbed on the rear passenger seat. I need to bail. Fast. Slouching in my seat, my hand fumbles, reaching for the seat belt. My escape flight took mere seconds, with a stride quick and purposeful. I did what my unlikely savior told me to do—looking at no one, unaware of any specific noises, conversations, or background music. A flight of fear, shellshocked by the secrets unveiled to me in the dining room and on the nasty bathroom floor.

The Finger Lakes Flash lady and I have something in common: anxiety, bolstered by secrets we're both hiding. Only her secret lies buried under fake hair, not phony fish wrappings. My accusation against Mayor Desmond got her attention! She gave me the wig off her head. Is that why she is helping me now, after she sliced and diced my comments from Nick's memorial page? Oliver is her client! *Think.*

I lock my car door and refocus on the rearview mirror. The sun is setting, its orange, balmy glow reflecting off the smooth, glassy surface of the lake.

No one followed me. All I need to do is start the car and drive. Not too fast. Not too slow. Drive like a person without a boat load of money stashed in tampon boxes and someone else's wig on my head.

Damn. I look like a criminal. But maybe my husband didn't have a pants problem after all! *Breathe.* I can't pass out behind the wheel and risk an accident. I need to check my booby-trapped house, with packaging tape on every window crack and door seam. If the tape is busted, I'll know someone came looking for the money while I was here.

And if not…

My enemy or enemies were here with me tonight.

Looking in the rearview mirror again, I spot a new reason for concern, in between the locks of phony hair cascading in front of my face. My stomach flips like a fresh-caught fish still hooked to a line. The door of the yacht club is closing. A man walks out, taking a few steps in my direction before stopping. He puts his hands in his pockets, staring at my car.

It's *him.* The car alarm started going off… the *Flash* lady turned around to look out the window… everyone was clapping for her. *He was sitting at her table.* Why is he standing there, looking at me in my car? Can he see me? What does he want?

The money.

If I back out now with the wig on, he's going to think I'm the biggest loon on the lake taking off with the *Flash* lady's wig. But, if I slide it off, and he or anyone else sees me do it, I'm screwed. Why is he standing there looking at my car?

She has my scarf. On her head. On top of those patchy spots. The *Flash* lady took my scarf.

He knows I am in her disguise.

My hand trembles starting the car and shifting the gear into reverse. Oliver or Brenda may come looking for me next. Or Delaney. Good God, what do I do if Delaney catches me like this?

Breathe. Back out slowly. Now turn to the left. Steady, don't look. Don't look. Gentle on the gas. *Breathe.*

My car rounds the end of a parking row and backtracks through the lot, heading to the wrought iron gate entranceway decorated with a large anchor emblem. I pass underneath the ornate structure, exiting on the roadway. My mouth releases an exhale causing a hiccup.

This is all wrong. My eyes blink as tears start to well. Mother's rules. I broke them with Brenda. *Don't trust other women.* It doesn't matter if I am the alpha and she's the beta. She has a daughter, and I don't, and I want what I was for Mother. My own little partner, my own mini-me secret keeper, my own genetic best friend. And spending time with Delaney was the closest I got to it because the pee sticks never showed the plus sign. Brenda gave me a taste of what I am missing out on, but now I'm scared. What if she's mind-fucking me and lying about Oliver?

Brenda says she'll make Diane Desmond pay if she gets near him again. A full-out threat, the I'm-not-screwing-around kind. And Brenda sent me to the freezer! What if Nick and Oliver had a handshake pact? We needed the money for IVF and the embryo transfer. What if Brenda knew about the money in the freezer and *she* killed Nick?

Oh, God, *that makes sense.* Except I just called out Mayor Roger Desmond, in front of everyone in town. *"You got the wrong guy!"*

What if *I* got the wrong guy?

My hand swipes at the tears running down my face, as my eyes peek at the speedometer. Keep it steady. Don't get pulled over now. Checking the rearview mirror again, my cheeks resemble the rinsing cups the Pattycake kids use for their watercolor paint brushes, with my runny mascara streaked all over them. And I'm still wearing the *Flash* lady's hair! I gave her my scarf. I took her wig. I *thanked* her.

My breath catches thinking how disappointed Mother would be with me. I broke another rule. *Don't complain.* The *Flash* lady rubbed my goose flesh while I wiped spittle from my mouth while sprawled on the disgusting bathroom floor. Why did she help me escape? And what the hell happened to her hair?

I sniffle, the memory of her shoving her card at me clicks in my brain. She said we would talk next week. Does she believe me now? Who is the man she was sitting with and why was he watching me in the parking lot? *Did the mayor send him after me?* Is he the reason the *Flash* lady is helping me now, when she didn't help me after Nick died?

My car turns on a darkened side street about a mile from my home. I'm not strong enough to go in now. What if one of the tape strips is broken? *Think.* If Roger Desmond spotted Nick's truck at the cabin and made the same assumption I did, Nick's death could be the result of mistaken identity.

After hearing Brenda's slurs tonight, I'm not sure Nick was the Sutton brother Diane was screwing. Oliver made it clear he still hates me… did he hate Nick too? Did he switch his car with Nick's truck to be with Diane at the cabin? Was he setting Nick up?

"You need to get out of the house." If I find broken tape, the threat is stickier. Maybe Nick had enemies I don't know about, or got messed up in some get-rich-quick scheme to fund IVF? What if someone *is* in the house?

A soft wail escapes my lips as my hands jerk the steering wheel, guiding the car to the side of the road. Only one person can help me now. The same person I aided for years.

Town pariah Sylvia Kelly can help me figure out if a home game or an away game strategy is best. My voice activation system kicks in as I place the call, my tone croaky and weak. She answers on the second ring.

"Mother? It's payback time."

26
CLAUDIA
September 1

I wait a few minutes, locked in the bathroom stall, preparing myself for what I'm about to do. There's no turning back. I can nail this, like I used to do every day on live television. Speak off-the-cuff, laying out the facts and the concerns.

Lindsay's scarf is wrapped tightly around my head. She must be out of the building by now.

Here I go.

My fingers snap open the lock on the bathroom stall and as I step out, I glance in the mirror mounted above the sink basin.

An elegant woman stares back at me, looking chic in her black cocktail dress and silk head scarf. A modern-day Grace Kelly.

I can do this.

Clutching the bathroom door handle, I pull it, exiting back into the banquet room. The excitement at the center of the room has ceased, and the table sponsored by Sutton's Apothecary is now empty. I don't see Peter anywhere. Mayor Desmond is back at the microphone, giving props to the local musicians playing the Sinatra classics. As he concludes his remarks, I hasten up front, smiling at the mayor while asking if I can make an announcement. He nods at me curiously, staring at the head scarf, but hands me the microphone.

The dinner guests are impatient, hungry for food to be served.

"Hey everybody, um, I'll make this quick. It's me, Claudia Marton, from *The Finger Lakes Flash*. With the anniversary of 9/11 next week, I am publishing profiles about the 9/11 responders living among us here in the Finger Lakes, and those we have recently lost."

A low current of dinner table chatter hums, and a few of my clients strain their necks, staring at the scarf on my head. Other tables ignore me while passing the bread baskets, wondering aloud when the first course will be served.

"A growing number of 9/11 responders are dying. Cancers, pulmonary issues, respiratory diseases…"

The hum intensifies. I'm losing them. My audience is growing impatient, hunger eclipsing any desire to hear about another cause of the day. They want the crab bisque and the Caesar salad starters, not a speech about ugly sickness and deadly endings. My hand trembles as I touch the edge of the scarf near my temple. It's now or never.

With a quick tug, I bare my head. A few gasps ring out, as well as a somewhat loud "Holy shit" from the back of the room. Suddenly, everyone refocuses their eyes on me. A hush fills the air.

"And a growing number of us are *living* with toxic poisoning. This…" I rub my patchy scalp and turn in a slow, full circle, "this is what toxic poisoning has done to me."

The stares are heavy but fixed.

"Please read the profiles on *The Finger Lakes Flash* next week. Together, we must do more for our ailing first responders."

I have their attention. They're listening. *I'm back.* There's only one thing bothering me.

Peter is missing. He's gone. Ditching me, right when I ditched my wig.

He said I should trust people again. Tear down the walls. Don't let the bad guys win.

I am tearing down my walls of protection—I'm here, without a disguise, baring my vulnerability in public and not letting the bad guys win. And yet, he's gone. Apprehension washes over me, ebbing my surge in confidence.

Why would Peter run?

Why would he hide?

What doesn't he want to say?

Brenda Sutton's slur resonates in my memory. Does Peter think I am romantically involved with Oliver Sutton? Did Brenda tell him what she saw on the security camera video while I was in the bathroom comforting Lindsay?

Peter wanted me to trust him, but does he trust me?

Maybe not, but I don't deserve an Irish goodbye.

Walking out on our date without explanation is a bad guy move.

27
LINDSAY
September 1

The house is dark.

Mother calmed me down for a bit, telling me to go home, take the wig off my head, and pack my things to come to Florida. Her reassurance that the house would be okay soothed me temporarily, but now that I'm pulling into my driveway, I'm jittery again.

What if someone is in the house?

Driving into the garage, my hands are clammy on the steering wheel. Shifting the gear into park, I turn, looking at the crates of cash in the back seat. The money is safe for now. The question is, am I?

Mother said I sounded like a hysterical cuckoo bird for tape-sealing the doors and windows, but she wants me in Florida.

"Darling, pack your bags. We'll figure this all out *down here*."

I can't go to Florida and leave without answers. Not after finding out Oliver may have switched cars with Nick. Brenda was inebriated, but sometimes, alcohol is the best truth serum.

My key slides into the lock of the door leading into the mudroom. The door opens, and as quietly as I can, I enter the house. Holding my breath, I am greeted with an eerie silence.

Talk to yourself, I say in my head.

Mother is sniffing glue. I am not a cuckoo bird.

Lindsay Sutton is coming unhinged.

The whisperers are wrong, too.

The money in the freezer didn't fall out of the sky. Nick is dead. Those are real things.

I am not a cuckoo bird.

The door from the garage leading into the mudroom is the only door I couldn't seal. The front and back doors have packaging tape around

117

them. Same with the windows. Did my enemy come to the house while I was out, or was he or she at the regatta keeping a watchful eye on me?

The man sitting with *The Finger Lakes Flash* lady… *He watched me.*

I tiptoe across the kitchen to the back door, not daring to turn on the light. What if there *is* a watcher in the woods? My fingers trail the seam of the doorframe. The tape is in place, but I'm afraid to breathe. There are other ways in.

Pivoting on my heel and straining my eyes, a pool of blackness envelopes me.

Checking the front door is next.

I enter the hallway, leading to the foyer. My arms stretch forward, zombie-like, feeling for the door. My hand brushes the handle and with my fingertips, I determine the latch is still locked. I pat the seam of the door frame. Tape seals are in place.

With haste, I check the windows in the bedrooms and bathrooms next. Nothing is disturbed.

Only the basement remains.

I suddenly feel nauseated again. The only way to get into the basement from down there is through a window well. It's an unlikely entry point, but I can't stay here tonight not knowing if the fish fund decoys are still in place.

Do it. Walk down the stairs. Go through the man-cave aquarium of dead fish mounts. Pull the panel door. Check the freezer…

Wait!

Get a knife. Something to protect yourself with in case Nick's killer is down there. Grab a knife. Any one of them. Don't be stupid.

I cross back through the kitchen to the utensil drawer. It slides open with a tug, and my fingers grasp the handle of a utility knife. The sensation gives me pause. On some level, holding the knife as a potential weapon feels strangely different than holding it as a cooking utensil.

Do I have what it takes to use this knife to defend myself if I need to?

I wish Nick was here. I wish he never kept secrets from me and never went missing. I wish this was just another annual night at the regatta, where we drink too much sweet wine and come home happily buzzed, swapping sloppy kisses while tearing off our clothes for a round of kinky sex on the kitchen floor.

If Nick leant Oliver his truck, he kept it a secret from me. Just like Oliver did. And Brenda, too, until tonight. Hell, even the *Flash* lady has secrets.

Everyone is covering up something. My fingers tighten around the knife.

Go.

The basement door in the mudroom is closed. I open it a crack, slithering my body onto the first step, my hand grasping in the dark for the railing.

One step. And another. Careful. Don't make any noise.

Listen.

All I hear is my heart thumping in my chest.

Keep talking to yourself. Check the freezer and call Mother back. Let her know if anything is out of place.

I reach the bottom of the stairwell. Light illuminating from Nick's Yuengling beer sign is accompanied by moonlight streaming in from the nearby window well. The windowpane is intact.

Watch for movement on the other side of the glass. Think about who might be lingering outside.

Barely blinking, I stare at the window well. Eternal minutes pass. No one appears.

The folding door to the back room is on my right. I clutch the knife handle and jerk the accordion panel open, crying out, stabbing at dead air. The blade hits empty space, surprising me. My body swivels in the direction of the freezer.

Run.

Scurrying across the cement floor and bypassing the kayaks and the furnace, I fling the freezer lid open, light bathing my face.

The packages are aligned just as I arranged them the other day. Nothing has moved. Nothing is out of place.

No one has been here.

Lindsay Sutton is coming unhinged.

Stop it. Don't think that way. Breathe.

Slumping against the appliance with relief, I take a deep breath, glancing up at another window well. Moonlight streams in through the square glass, and in a matter of seconds, a seismic panic numbs my body. A piece of packaging tape bends at an awkward angle, no longer seamlessly adhered to the edge of the window frame.

A scream emits from my mouth with a force I don't recognize. My hand clenches the knife tighter, and I raise it, ready to strike.

The light emanating from the freezer illuminates Nick's fishing gear, the kayaks, and the furnace. No one is hiding in this section of the basement, and I turn again, making sure I didn't imagine that the phony decoy packages were still in place. They remain untouched, neatly stacked in the wire freezer bins. Gazing at the tape again, I am sickened, wondering if humidity or a simple draft caused the adhesive to loosen.

Nausea overcomes me and I sprint to the finished man-cave, fearful I will vomit for the second time tonight.

Barreling into the small powder room near the poker table, I collapse in front of the commode, lifting the toilet seat. My body writhes from dry heaves, and I spit bile into the bowl.

As I try to regroup, my phone suddenly emits a shrilling chirp, causing me to yelp. The knife falls to the floor with a clatter, barely missing my feet.

Mother is probably texting me, checking to see if I survived the boogey-man I was convinced I'd find hiding in my house.

I am not a cuckoo bird. I am not a cuckoo bird. I am not a cuckoo bird.

Letting out a long exhale, I glance at my phone.

This message is from *Brenda.*

"Are you home?"

A new wave of nausea hits and I regurgitate into the toilet, my body surrendering to the unending emotional turmoil of the last few months. Leaning against the porcelain toilet bowl, I softly weep. Salty tears flow down my cheeks, each one representing a moment, an hour, or a day robbed from the future I had envisioned with Nick. Our beautiful love story, rocked by his untimely death. But maybe it wasn't compromised by adultery, after all.

Minutes pass. I don't respond to Brenda's text, and I don't have the energy for Mother's "told you so's." All I want to do now is to pull my covers up to my chin and go to sleep. Gripping the knife, I prepare to stand. My fingers hit the toilet handle. The tension is slack, and the bowl doesn't flush. I try again, staring at my own vomit. Nothing happens.

Setting the knife in the pedestal sink basin, I tug at the lid of the tank, hoping this is a simple fix, like the lever arm chain has disengaged from the flapper. The rectangular porcelain lid slides off the tank base, and I peer within.

The flapper and the chain are disconnected, but that's not my primary concern.

Three months to the day since my husband vanished, I finally have an answer for why my forty-seven phone calls to him went unanswered.

Encased in a plastic bag, Nick's cell phone nestles next to the fill valve in our basement toilet tank.

Part II
The Unveiling

28

CLAUDIA

September 4

Greta's fingers tap the laptop keys at warp speed, capturing each monumental detail of my public unveiling. My legs cramp sitting cross-legged on her couch, with a throw pillow nesting on my lap, the perfect tabletop for my jumbo box of hot cinnamon candy. She leads our discussion, but somehow, I need to find a way to ask her about Wozilfin.

"Quite a breakthrough."

"Yes, I think so, too."

She pauses, allowing a beat to pass, her hands resting on the upper corners of the laptop screen. "How are you processing this?"

The answer isn't simple. I spent twenty-one days standing on a rural state highway in a big toxic cloud of somberness, broadcasting live, day after day, grateful for life while a crater of death smoldered behind me, a ghastly sight among the otherwise relative emptiness of the debris field. The incessant hum of bulldozers moving hallowed earth swallowed the stridulating chirp of crickets, and at night, the backlighting of the moon made the specter of the fumes appear menacing, like eerie phantoms. The image haunts me, like a murder victim able to dream with precognition, watching my eventual killer in three-dimensional vividness, with the terrifying uncertainty of not knowing when death will come.

"Good and bad."

"Why?"

"I think I deal with my guilt by creating a new situation to feel guilty about."

Greta cocks her head to the side, prompting me with her silence for further explanation.

"I remember sitting at the table with Peter, and I was in the moment, you know? I was proud! Not thinking about the alopecia, or my guilt over

123

wanting to sleep with my best friend's boyfriend, or overanalyzing the cliché…"

"Why do you say cliché?"

I blink, thinking the answer is obvious.

"I'm a journalist. I don't like clichés," I say, my fingers punctuating my statement with air quotes. "I never thought of myself as someone who would fall into the arms of a guy who's mourning the same loss I am. That stuff happens in the movies…"

"Only, it is happening. To you."

I toss another handful of candy in my mouth, pondering how to express my angst without sounding pessimistic about my progress.

"Well, yes, on one hand, I am making strides. Sitting at the table with him, I was living the *now*." I puff air with my mouth closed, creating a purposeful lip trill. "But, taking my wig off in public and doing an impromptu public service announcement about the wave of maladies attacking 9/11 responders…" I shrug and glance at the ceiling, frustrated with myself. "I'm going from zero to sixty way too fast, which is the easiest way to make a date crash and burn."

Greta's face scrunches with curiosity.

"Are you implying you unveiled your condition because you felt guilty about enjoying an evening with Peter?"

"Part of me thinks so, yeah."

"Part of you?"

Watching Lindsay Sutton hyperventilate on the floor of the bathroom stall did remind me of myself. But now, in the aftermath, I flash back to my on-the-spot decision to help her and wonder if subconscious motivators were at play. Focusing on Lindsay's anxiety, her outburst, and her husband's possible connection to the Wozilfin clue made it easy for me to deflect attention from Peter.

"He was flirting and part of me thinks he's great, the right kind of guy who can be sympathetic to my situation, but hot too…"

"Part of you?" Greta repeats.

"I don't want careful sex. Wait, that came out wrong." I cover my face with my palms, spreading my fingers so I can still talk. "I want sex to be like before. Where I don't analyze or overthink, and I just go with it. I want to be *in the now* then, too."

"What's wrong with that?"

"It bleeds over into the alopecia, laying on the guilt… complaining about my condition and whining about how I want sex to be again when so many responders are dying. And, above all else, the guy I want to do it with was Stella's lover."

Greta's fingertips tap the keyboard again. She reads the words on her screen, before voicing her next thought.

"You mentioned feeling 'in the moment' with Peter while you sat at the table you shared. Not thinking about yesterdays or tomorrows. This, by itself, was a huge step for you."

I agree with Greta. My thoughts jump to recent memories of the Lakeview Cemetery scavenger hunt and the photos I snapped in Oliver Sutton's cluttered office, two other live-in-the-moment experiences. I'm not ready to tell her specifics about why I engaged in these activities, which is making it difficult for me to transition the conversation and ask her about the Wozilfin.

"Yes," I say, "And I'm not sure either of us have fully dealt with our grief over Stella. I'm wondering if we're gravitating together with deliberate blinders on."

"That's a legitimate concern. Would you consider going back to the group meeting on Tuesday night? What about asking the woman you helped to join you? She's grieving too."

The Tuesday night survivor's guilt group was my space with Stella, although Angela and Patrice became friends, too. I'm hesitant about taking Lindsay Sutton, a potential informant, with me.

"Lindsay's situation is different."

"Grief is grief. You're both missing someone you cared deeply for. Maybe you are meant to help Lindsay Sutton the way Stella helped you."

Pay it forward. Stella's probably applauding Greta now.

"Have you spoken to Peter about your conflicted emotions?"

"No, not since I stopped him the first time when we… we… lost control. And now, tossing the idea around, maybe I unveiled my condition the other night as a way of *forcing* us to have the conversation. To make sure, like, we're *sure*."

"Why didn't you have the conversation?"

"He said, 'No talking about Stella tonight,' and I was enjoying myself, living in the moment, but now I'm second-guessing why he didn't want to talk about her. And later, he followed Lindsay outside, because he thought she was me, taking off and ditching him! When he figured out it was Lindsay, he came back inside, and I was at the microphone."

"What was his reaction to your speech?"

I shake my head. "*He* left!"

Greta's eyebrows rise. "He left?"

"Yep. At first, I thought it was because Brenda Sutton made a comment about me and her husband—Oliver is my client. I was afraid Peter misinterpreted what she meant. But he texted me and said the mayor had pulled him aside—Roger Desmond wanted to press charges against Brenda for making a terroristic threat toward his wife. Peter said he had to handle the matter and brief his chief."

"Do you believe him?"

"He did leave for work, but the room also got quiet when I removed the scarf. I'm not sure if he caught a glimpse before he left."

"And after you spoke? What was the reaction in the room?"

I hesitate before answering, the memory surreal.

"Standing ovation."

Greta's mouth turns up at the edges and she looks at her notes while typing away.

"Do you plan to see Peter again anytime soon?"

"Good question. The mayor was supposed to announce his candidacy for the State Senate at the regatta but decided to postpone it after his wife was threatened. And, since our evening was nixed when he asked Peter to help him, he wants to make it up to us with dinner at his home Saturday night."

"So, Peter agreed?"

"Yes, but I can't since I want to run a story about the mayor's candidacy on the *Flash*."

Her eyebrows rise again, denying me the opportunity to squirm away from the meatier subject.

"Okay, Peter deserves an explanation, so he can understand why I took my wig off and caught everyone by surprise."

"Including yourself," Greta adds.

I stare at the box of candy, grasping her words.

"You don't think I was subconsciously sabotaging our date?"

Greta shakes her head. "The first time you rebuffed Peter, you told him it was because of guilt over Stella. But that wasn't true. You were insecure about your alopecia. You sabotaged your first tryst because you feared being truthful," Greta says, eyeing me. "Now, you made a choice, a conscious choice, because you recognized your strength."

My mind absorbs her words, processing them, the look of terror in Lindsay's eyes fresh in my memory.

"Living in the moment is a major milestone. You can celebrate milestones," Greta says.

"I'm owning my truth."

"Yes, you are. And missing Stella is different. You can miss her, and you can grieve her loss. But here's the distinction: You can't hurt her by living in your truth."

I haven't thought much about my triggers. Other than the telephone call with Felicia, my busy schedule precluded obsessing about all the things the eleventh of September makes me fear. The sight of planes in view of a city skyline still takes my breath away. I can't eat eggs. The smell of the egg salad sandwiches donated by the sweet ladies from the Presbyterian church didn't mix well with the jet fuel-saturated air. If I think about it, I gag. And I will not go into a building taller than the longest firefighter's ladder. Not ever.

"This will be a good test for me, making another date with Peter. Felicia will be thrilled when I tell her." I swipe at my nose with a tissue, and add, "I'm working on a new lead from the tipster line. Might be a good story."

"What kind of story?"

"It involves the drug Wozilfin. I searched on the web and saw indications for treating schizophrenia, bipolar disorder, and depression. Do you think my grief and sadness about Stella makes me a good candidate to try it?"

Greta's head snaps up and shakes again from side to side. "No, no. Wozilfin is a potent antipsychotic medication. Have you discontinued taking your anxiety meds?"

"Yes, but I have some, just in case. I read about the dangers of predators using Wozilfin as a date-rape drug, so I figured it was strong. I suppose, in the wrong hands, it could be lethal, right?"

Greta nods. "Any antipsychotic pharmaceutical misused or diverted has the potential to be lethal. Woozie bombs, or Wozilfin mixed with cocaine, can kill you. But, using Wozilfin specifically for sedative purposes is alarming. Whether it's for sexual assault purposes, or if you're talking about an angel of death situation."

"I'm not tracking…"

"Right-to-die laws are in effect in some states, so physician assisted death or medical aid in dying is not illegal everywhere. But, when a physician is making the decision by him or herself, without patient knowledge or concurrence, there's one word for that—homicide."

People are dying, only their deaths are masked with a clever veil.

I gulp. The triangular equation.

Seymour, where should I go to the doctor? It fits.

It's not natural. Nope. It's a bald-faced deception.

Greta is saying the same thing the tipster did.

This is murder.

29
LINDSAY
September 4

I'm stumped trying to unlock Nick's phone. I don't know his code, and I only get nine chances to be wrong before the device is disabled after the tenth try. I've entered our birthdays, our anniversary, the date of our first kiss, Fran's birthday, his father's birthday, the day his dad passed away, and Delaney's birthday. None of them worked. Two more attempts are left, but I'm at a complete loss. Good thing Mother is coming.

Our reunion is inevitable in a way. Mother thought I was crazy to stick it out here "in the sticks" after Nick's death, urging me to put a fork in this cold, gristle of a life and migrate to the cocoa butter warmth and ease down south near her. Somehow, I resisted the sugar-coated bait she dangled about moving to Florida. When Mother doesn't get her way, she sometimes gives me the silent treatment until I cave.

My call for help after the regatta cemented her latest stonewalling victory.

"Mother, I'm freaking out!"

She didn't understand me at first, but she clued in when I rambled on about the *Flash* lady giving me her wig so I could escape to my car, full of tampon boxes plugged with wads of cash. Thinking back on it now, it did sound like I was coming apart at the seams.

Since I won't go to her, she's coming to me. It *is* payback time, and I'm hoping she'll help me crack the code to Nick's phone.

Sitting on a square boat cushion, I'm back on the basement floor, underneath the bright glow of the exposed lightbulb mounted on the rafter. The freezer paper splays out next to a gallon-size box of plastic bags. I'm in prep mode. Mother is flying in later this week to help me navigate the current turbulence in my life, but until she arrives, I am under strict instructions to self-isolate, pull my shit together, and act like stashing someone else's wig in the freezer is normal.

Mother told me to hide the wig in a safe place until she gets here. At first, I thought about stuffing it in a tampon box and adding it to the crates in the car. But, when I searched online about how to store a human hair wig, it said to avoid sunlight and hot temperatures, so here I am, again. I reach for the masking tape, tugging a big chunk off with my thumb, securing the freezer-paper wrapping.

For the past ten days, I have unwrapped and rewrapped secrets, and yet, the biggest mysteries remain. Who killed my husband? Where did this money come from? Why did Nick hide his phone in the toilet tank? Are there more secrets hidden in this house? I still have all the paperwork in the filing cabinets to go through.

Rising from the padded boat cushion, my legs cramp. Stretching my hamstrings, I think about how Mother said my panic attack on the bathroom floor at the yacht club may score me leverage. Claudia Marton will want her wig back, the perfect chip to play for the sympathy mulligan. According to Mother, a woman like that always has an agenda—we just need to figure out what it is.

Brenda is another story.

Stepping toward the freezer, my foot tingles from lack of circulation. As I open the lid, cool air slaps me in the face. Talking to Brenda is clutch. What does she know, or what does she *want* me to know, and what is the truth? Mother craves a front row seat for it. We're going to get Brenda toasted Friday night, while Delaney's off with her high school friends at the first football game of the season. Oliver will be at the game, too, since he's treasurer of the Booster Club and in damage control mode. This is our chance, with the script flipped.

Mother will be my accomplice now. She'll play along, watching, listening. She can help separate truth from fiction. It's a role reversal from our hotel days when I helped provide cover for Mother's secret life.

I lift some of the fake fish packages, making room for the wrapped wig. I've been thinking a lot about Mother's infidelity the last few days, since I'm still uncertain about Nick and if he cheated on me. Let's say Oliver *is* sleeping with Diane… he's hurting Brenda the same way Daddy hurt Mother. That's wrong. But Mother went on to cheat while married, too, and two wrongs don't make a right. She was my whole world as a child, and I obeyed out of loyalty. But how can I be mad at Diane for sleeping with either my husband or Delaney's father, and not feel the same way about Mother?

I stare at the wig package amid the menstrual pad fish decoys and ponder my own deception. Following Mother's rules wasn't only about allegiance. I believed her tactics would land me a guy who adored me and provide a replacement for the void created by Daddy. But selfishly, adhering to her rule about not trusting other females allowed me to dodge the one thing I didn't want to admit: I was envious of the girls who had fathers who twirled them at the annual father/daughter dance and who clapped for them at their piano recitals and ballet competitions. My father never took me to a dance, and he never saw me cheer. Clinging to Mother and her rules was my safety net, a way to hide from the pain caused by my father's neglect.

Closing the freezer, I slump against the appliance. Am I wrong to ask for Mother's help with this? When she switched from away-games to home-games while I was in high school, Seamus O'Reilly became her favorite pastime. They carried on for years, even though Seamus had six kids and a wife… well, until his wife killed herself.

The whispers about Mother ratcheted up then, with many around town labeling her as a homewrecker. Nick and I were engaged at the time. Sweet Fran told me I shouldn't have to bear the brunt of Mother's reputation, and she championed me when most would have shunned the daughter of the local pariah.

"Don't you worry, Lindsay. You're going to break the cycle. You and Nick have real love," she said, as she patted my hand.

And I believed with all my heart she was right. I ignored Mother's behavior and focused instead on the promising new role I would soon assume as Nick's bride. It's only now, with my happily-ever-after fairy-tale wiped out, that the damsel in distress recognizes her mother is sometimes a villain, too.

I grab the boat cushion off the floor, my thoughts shifting from Mother to Fran. Did she mix up names when she said Nick was in love with Dr. Desmond? It's possible, given her early-stage dementia. And, if Oliver was switching vehicles, that would explain Nick's truck at the remote rental cabin, too. My spontaneous outburst at Mayor Desmond accused him of making the same mistake that I did. But did he?

The vehicle swap doesn't spell out why Nick hid money in the freezer, where it came from, or why his cell phone was in the toilet tank.

As I lay the boat cushion next to Nick's tackle boxes along the wall, my attention is drawn to a sudden, unfamiliar sound.

What am I hearing?

There's some type of mechanical hum. It's not coming from the freezer, and the furnace wouldn't run now. I haven't touched the thermosstat.

Oh, God.

I look up at the small, square glass pane in the window well. I hear a car motor, accelerating up the angled slope of the rear driveway behind the house.

Mother's plane doesn't get in until Thursday night. Brenda texted me yesterday and said she's excited to come over on Friday. The Tiftons won't visit their cabin at the end of the utility road until hunting season, which is still weeks away.

Glancing at the freezer, an uncomfortable recognition settles in.

Audrey Hepburn! The whites of her eyes telegraphed her terror about unknown visitors. What unknown danger lurks on the other side of *my* window?

Pea gravel crunches under tires, biting and raw. This is real, not a figment of my imagination or paranoia. Visitors come to the front door, wiping their feet on the pineapple welcome mat while leaving a traceable fingerprint on the doorbell. Only danger parks in the back. My eyes scan the room, spotting Nick's polar shanty, the ice tip-ups, the portable heater, and the fishing rods. As a car door slams, I lunge for Nick's ice axe, gripping the weapon with my shaking hands.

Facing the window, I stifle a cry, as dark pant legs skim over the top of black leather shoes, the feet coming to rest in the center of the glass pane of the window well.

Mother was wrong.

This is a pants problem.

30
CLAUDIA
September 4

The advertising orders for space on the *Flash* are at an all-time high, a symbolic and reaffirming afterglow arising from my bald revelation at the regatta. The editorial email box is also at capacity, maxed out with a mix of laudatory comments, heartfelt condolences, and a checkerboard of contradictory emojis. For every dozen or so thumbs-up signals or hands folded in prayer, a few tears and a couple of turd symbols drop, too. Some readers want me to chronicle my story to raise awareness about the ongoing health struggles of living 9/11 responders, putting a familiar face on the public problem circling the community drain. Greta has suggested it, too, as a quasi-therapeutic journaling exercise. Maybe I will, in time. But now, all I can think about is exposing the angel of death living among us.

As a statistically probable murder victim, the idea of a devious killer lurking, stealing time, choices, and lives from the unsuspecting is a temple blow, the kind that knocks you from your feet, sucking the air from your lungs and ringing your bell. The tipster's message reads with greater urgency for me now, stoking a thirst for new information, and resuscitating my own personal quest for a small dose of vengeance.

There. I said it. The dirty little secret I shelter, invisible to watchful eyes, yet noticeable, nonetheless. Along with the fear and sadness within me is an anger, a dark peppery flavor speckling my thoughts, and spiking emotions. It sneaks up on me, and sometimes, I don't recognize my own voice. My sister Felicia stokes it the most, questioning my progress, never grasping this isn't something that will ever go away. Topical creams can stimulate my hair follicles, but nothing can regenerate the innocence I lost. It's gone, and sometimes, I grieve the loss. More so as time passes and the person I was fades from memory.

My sessions with Greta help, but the biggest challenge remains. In my core, a raw, meaty, anger hemorrhages. And it haunts me.

I crave a form of retribution, a payback for my pain. All my nights, crying into my pillow, my hands traveling over the coarse bristles of hair interspersed among glossy ovals of emptiness. I yearn for vengeance now, some way to channel the unfairness of Stella's drooping face, her scars and disfigurement, the chemo-ravaged frailness of her body near the end. I want to take all the anger locked inside and channel it into some massive hatred ball, hurling it hard at the person or persons using Wozilfin to sedate and kill.

There is no avenging the 9/11 terrorists who drove my psyche to the edge of a cliff, where I teeter-tottered for minutes or hours at a time, the struggle of living in the balding shell of my former self suffocating my optimism. But now, my long journey back is a literal blessing in disguise. *The Finger Lakes Flash* is more than my meal ticket. It's another secret weapon, like my room of disguises. I can use it to salve my inner wounds and quell my anger while clipping the wings of our local angel of death.

And I know where to start.

Dragging and dropping different advertisements around my format page, I create a wide-open space in the center, typing a few coded words to convey I understand the meaning behind the graveyard clue.

Answer me, Seymour.

Tell me which doctor is murdering patients under the guise of mercy killing. The image of Nick Sutton's name crossed out with a thick black line on the work schedule comes to mind. What if Lindsay Sutton was right? Did someone murder her husband? Maybe Nick stumbled across something at Sutton's Apothecary, and he knew too much? Oliver urged me to take Lindsay's post down from Nick's In Memoriam page, and the deliberate aim of his security camera indicates he's guarding something. What is *he* hiding? Brenda Sutton vowed to make Dr. Diane Desmond "pay" if she goes near Oliver again. What are *they* hiding?

My false eyelashes flutter as my mind absorbs what I witnessed.

Dr. Diane Desmond, a specialist in geriatric medicine, the wife of the mayor, and the lovely coordinator of the community regatta. Philanthropic, beautiful, and smart.

A living angel.

My fingers clip the keyboard keys with intensity, populating the search engine bar with the word combination "Wozilfin" and "elderly." Hitting the enter key, my suspicions are confirmed with an official government warning:

"Wozilfin is not approved for the treatment of patients with dementia-related psychosis. Elderly patients are at an increased risk of death."

Rereading the words, I am too stunned to move, as a gut-wrenching thought gnaws away at my conscience. If Dr. Desmond is using Wozilfin to mercy kill her patients, it may not be safe for Peter to eat dinner at her home on Saturday night.

Seymour needs to answer me.

THE FINGER LAKES FLASH

Your online snapshot capturing the local news you need to know.
September 4

Classified Advertisements

Harley Davidson
For Sale
Call Mickey: 315-555-7964
Price Negotiable

Seymour:
You are not like the others.
Give me a dose of mercy.
Answer me.

SWF seeking male companion for
hiking, biking, coffee drinking,
and watching Netflix. Friends first.
Must have job.
Call Beth: 315-555-0908

31
LINDSAY
September 4

My hands tremble around the wooden handle of the ice axe. Stretched out in front of my face, inches below the exposed light bulb, the shiny metal blade splices my view of the window well. It casts a menacing, elongated shadow across the cement floor, a dark projection of my fear.

The feet are at a standstill, plotting their next move.

Think.

My cell phone is cradled in my pocket. If I reach for it, am I strong enough to hold this axe with one hand? What if the feet start moving? Should I call Mother? I can't trust Brenda yet, not until she spills the tea. I could call 911 and report a stranger lurking in my backyard outside my window. A potential peeping Tom. I'm a single woman now, living alone. The tire tread from the stranger's car undoubtedly left clear, indelible patterns in the pea gravel, proof I'm not imagining this. Evidence, certifying I am not certifiable. A patrol officer won't investigate the menstrual pads stashed in my freezer or the-bank-on-wheels parked in my garage. He or she will mosey on up and sweep a flashlight beam across my yard, telling me what kind of skunk is scaring the smell out of me.

And knocking out my breath.

Don't fall apart now. No regatta repeats. A stitch in my chest tugs, constricting my lungs. Concentrate. Focus on the feet.

The feet aren't moving.

Letting my left hand go from around the grainy handle of the axe, my right arm protests with an achy strain, causing the weapon to pitch forward. A soft wail escapes my lips, and I scramble to regain control. The axe falls, creating a loud clatter against the basement floor, inches from my feet.

I freeze, my gaze held captive by the scene on the other side of the glass window.

The feet turn. Not away, in the direction they came from, but toward me, spurred by the clunking crash of the ice axe on the concrete.

What do they want? Shit. I know what they want. The money. And I'm in the way.

My hand snakes into the pocket of my jeans, grasping for my cell phone. With my thumbprint, I unlock the device, croaking out a desperate instruction.

"Call 911."

The feet move again, stepping inches closer to the window well.

My eyes are hypnotized by the sway of the black pant legs covering the shins and shoe tops of the unknown presence in my yard.

"911, what's your emergency?"

"Someone, a man I think, is outside my window!"

"Your name?"

"Lindsay Sutton."

"Address?"

"745 Hemlock Street. Romulus. Please! He's in the back."

"Are you alone?"

"Aren't you listening? There are feet outside my window!"

Lunging for the axe, my cell phone drops in the process, shattering the glass. Stumbling, I scurry behind the furnace. The 911 operator speaks to me again.

"Lindsay? Are you there? Lindsay, can you hear me?"

"Sssh… please! Send someone!"

"A patrol unit in your area is on the way. Lindsay, stay on the line with me. Is anyone else besides you in the house?"

"No, my tape seals aren't broken. But someone is out there!"

"Your what?"

Oh, shit. The thread in my chest tugs harder, the stitch expanding to a clench.

"Tell me what's happening, Lindsay."

"I'm afraid to look."

"Where are you in the house?"

"In my basement. Behind the furnace."

"And you saw someone outside your basement window?"

"Yes! Dark pants. Dark shoes. And a car! I heard a car. On the back driveway, off the utility road."

"Stay on the line with me. Do you see or hear anything else?"

I listen.

It's quiet, except for the soft hum of the freezer. Glancing at the appliance, it glistens white under the incandescent glow of the light bulb. Damn. No wonder the feet came to the window. Whoever it is, knows I'm down here. By the freezer. The tomb where Nick buried his unexplained treasure.

"I don't hear anything."

"Can you see anything?"

A rap of knuckles against the glass shatters the silence, causing me to yelp.

"He's knocking on the glass. He's going to break in!"

"Stay away from the window. The patrol car is almost there. Can you see who it is?"

Hunkering down, in the darkest part of the furnace shadow with the axe resting at my side, my head tilts, the hoop earring in my lobe grazing my shoulder. Clutching the axe, I peek at the window.

A surprising sight meets my eyes.

The face framed in the window well has a clownish smile, with apple cheeks, ruby lips, and arched brows over a prying set of eyes.

My mouth lets out a gasp, more pissed than relieved. Staring at my unwelcome visitor, my breaths start to regulate as the sensational equivalent of waking from a nightmare lessens, my anxiety ebbing as anger takes hold.

"I know who this is. I don't need the police."

"Are you sure, Lindsay?"

I'm annoyed out of my gourd sure.

"Yep. Thanks."

Rising from the cement floor, I vow to unscrew the lightbulb from the ceiling rafter after dealing with the nuisance at the back door. My cell phone screen is smashed, out-splintered only by my nerves. Damn. Raising my finger, indicating I'll be upstairs in a minute, the face in the window smiles and gives me a nod.

My feet stomp on the stairs, one louder than the next, until I reach the landing in the mudroom. After this inconvenience, I'm texting Brenda and demanding some pills. She's miffed at Oliver, but if she misses me like she says she does, she can cough up some of her anxiety medication and float me a loan. A little litmus loyalty test before Mother arrives—before we overpour Brenda into giving up the goods on Oliver's switcheroo scheme.

Crossing the kitchen to the back door, I peel off the shipping tape draping the framework. The adhesive sticks to my fingertips as I unsnap the bolt lock. A soft groan creaks from the hinges as the door opens. He stands on the cement porch, hunched at the shoulders, holding a brown paper bag in his hands.

My words tumble out, fast and terse, intentionally breaking Mother's golden rule about making every man feel important.

"What the hell are you doing here?"

32
CLAUDIA
September 4

My research into the first couple of Romulus reeks with type-A over-achievement, community prominence, and an unsettling record of near perfection. Dr. Desmond and her mayor husband Roger are cookie-cutter citizens, movers and shakers in elite social circles. They hang with the highly educated medical crowd, a sprinkling of physicians, researchers, and academics from Cornell, Dr. Desmond's alma mater, along with Roger Desmond's political cronies, a liberal-based composite of social justice champions and dedicated public servants. My own archives hold a bevy of photographs of the couple from my "Hot Happenings" page, grinning and posing at various philanthropic events with manicured sublimity.

A cursory review of their social media accounts reveals the same curated refinement. Swallowing a sip of coffee spiked with Kahlua while scanning the photospreads, my eyes search for one bad angle, blemish, or slouch. No such luck.

My online research also snagged a postcard worthy snap of the Desmond residence, where the American flag hangs from a post mounted above a "We support our troops" yard sign. No dandelions pox the thick, green lawn. The windows sparkle in glistening sunshine, trimmed with boxes of blooming petunias and marigolds. The welcome mat on the front porch lays centered between pineapple finials and decorative lights, and the driveway is free of any cracks, dips, or oil spots. I bet the birds know not to poop there, too.

Where is their blind spot, the weakness in their united armor? Despite the nobleness of their professions, Diane Desmond is a poster-child Karen, and he's a stereotypical Chad. A Karen and Chad combination is a mixture of rigidity, destined for fissure.

"If she comes near you again, she'll pay for it."

Brenda Sutton's outburst sings like a clue now, a not-so-subtle inference Diane Desmond's marriage may not be so ideal. Two career-oriented overachievers, both accustomed to the driver's seat, most comfortable taking the lead ahead of a pack of worshipping followers. Diane's father, Dr. Bennett Russell, preceded her as an esteemed local physician, and he bequeathed his medical practice to her following his death ten years ago. Her mother passed during childbirth, and her baby brother died three days later. She's an orphan married to a prominent man. A one-two punch kind of couple.

Or are they? Roger Desmond married well, no doubt. His campaign press packet promoting his run for the State Senate rests on my desk next to my coffee cup, summarizing a working-class upbringing in Scranton, Pennsylvania. It's filled with a mention of Sunday services at the local Methodist church and a "No dream is too big to dream" slogan. Graduating from the Wharton School of Business at the University of Pennsylvania, Desmond headed north with his Ivy League degree to a biotechnology upstart company in Rochester. His business accomplishments are listed in the campaign brochure, as well as a glossy head-shot portrait of Roger and Diane Desmond on their wedding day. Another photograph depicts his elderly parents and two brothers, positioned on a wrap-around porch with their extended families, outfitted in coordinating white shirts and dark denim under the stars and stripes flag, painting an almost too-perfect portrait of the All-American family.

Cookie-cutter, I think again, relishing the candid shots I've seen in other campaign packets over the years, where family members are laughing at a picnic table with half-eaten ears of corn, or throwing snowballs around a lopsided snowman decorated with apples in place of buttons and a New York Giants wool hat.

Did the mayor and his wife want kids? Many women are having children in their early to mid-forties with medical assistance, but for people like me, it's a conscious choice not to parent. A deliberate, well-thought-out self-actualization, which brings me full circle back to my suspicions about the Desmonds. Can two overachievers coexist without competition, without one surrendering or at least taking a step back, so the other person can shine? Can a couple with equal measures of hubris and drive not become resentful of each other?

"At least she's focused on her husband now."

Brenda Sutton's not-so-subtle implication isn't idle gossip when I put it in context with the Wozilfin clue. Diane Desmond sidled up next to Oliver Sutton at the regatta and I witnessed the horrified reactions of both Brenda *and* Lindsay Sutton. There's something there. I heard the words. I saw the emotion. And if Dr. Desmond is the prescribing physician for the Wozilfin dosages filled by Sutton's Apothecary, Oliver Sutton is complicit.

I think they are on to me.

C'mon Seymour. Answer me.

My tipster email box will trigger a VIP ding-dong alert on my cell phone if a message arrives. The current level of silence is maddening. If Lindsay Sutton is my Seymour, she's not in a rush to answer me or return my wig. And I want Nicole back before I see Peter again.

We need to talk, so he understands why I'm bailing out on dinner with the Desmonds. I worry about him going to their home, but I can't share my concerns about Dr. Desmond, not until I shore up some evidence with a source on the record. Lindsay Sutton is the logical place to start. Grabbing my cell phone, I debate whom to contact first.

Peter wins.

"Got time for a quick call?"

My fingers hit send, launching my text into cyberspace while searching my computer directory for Lindsay Sutton's email address. She sent the In Memoriam comments from her personal email account. As I begin composing my message to her, my text alert chirps.

"Responding to possible trespass. Call later."

Hitting the thumbs up emoji as a response to Peter, my attention returns to the email draft, punching out a few more words, before stopping to proof my message.

Hi Lindsay,

I hope you are feeling better. As someone who understands how crippling anxiety and panic attacks can be, I am glad I could help you the other night at the regatta. Can we meet for a cup of coffee or a drink? In case you misplaced my card, you can reach me at this email address.

Warm regards,

Claudia Marton

Too pushy? Maybe not. I didn't ask for my wig back. And if she is my secret cemetery clue-dropper, she'll respond. The hard part is on me now.

Journalists don't like to wait. They keep digging.

The sleek promotional materials the mayor's office forwarded to me sit next to the estate planning materials from Stella's attorney. Reaching for my phone, a receptionist answers on the second ring. After introducing myself, I am rewarded with the words I want to hear:

"The mayor will be delighted to meet with you for an interview. Does tomorrow afternoon work?"

I say that it does and end the conversation. My next task is setting up a meeting with Stella's attorney. Placing the call, I arrange for an appointment on Thursday morning. As I update my calendar and begin jotting down questions to ask the mayor, my telephone shrills an alarm, making me jump.

Something dropped in the tipster email account!

I yank the keyboard tray toward me, typing in my username and password. The message inbox alights on my screen.

There is an email with a video attachment. The sender's username, HeadsUp, is different from the previous email sent by the graveyard tipster. That email came from Anonymous123. Scrunching my forehead, I contemplate what this means. Has Seymour changed accounts or is this something different altogether? The subject line is blank.

I click on the email, my eyes growing wide reading the few words written in the message.

DO NOT TRUST LINDSAY SUTTON.

An uneasiness washes over me, making me question everything I've done in the last five minutes. I just sent Lindsay Sutton an email. What are the odds I would get a warning about her right after I attempted to contact her? Did someone hack into my computer, watching what I search and who I contact?

Shuttling my mouse, I click on the video attachment. Blood drains from my face as the video message plays on my monitor. At a slow, deliberate pace, the recording pans across a row of identical blank faces, emotionless, and stark. It's not the faces I recognize, but the wigs mounted on top of them. The video captures Chloe, Pamela, and all my other hair pieces, except for one.

Nicole.

The recording zooms when it reaches the topless mount where Nicole usually rests, lingering with eerie stillness on the wigless mannequin head.

Whoever made this video knows why that bust is empty.

Lindsay Sutton still has my Nicole wig.

I recoil from my computer, my body trembling.

Someone *is* watching me.

DO NOT TRUST LINDSAY SUTTON.

A frost of fear coats my thoughts and slows my movements, as I turn toward the office entrance and the spiral staircase leading downstairs. Someone knows about my room of disguises. Someone came here recently, trespassed on my property, and made this video.

And the terrifying part is that whoever did this, may still be in my house.

33
LINDSAY
September 4

"Brought you some ice cream."

He thrusts the brown paper bag at me, his smile outstretching his bow tie. Taking the crumpled sack from his hands, I peek inside. Mint chocolate chip. Winner-winner chicken dinner.

"You scared me to death, Melvin," I say, stepping aside and gesturing him in with my free hand.

He enters my kitchen, spry and curious, but pauses a second later, as the mess in the room greets his inquisitive eyes. Wine glasses and coffee cups clutter the kitchen sink, begging for a rinse and shine cycle in the dishwasher. The windowsill planter of herbs thirsts for water, the rosemary and thyme stalks resembling dry, brittle kindling. Piles of unread mail, some stamped with bright red "Second Notice" alerts scatter across my table, dislodging the saltshaker from its perch atop the center lazy Susan. It lay on its side, a casualty of a mindless toss from yesterday, or the day before, or the day before that. With Mother arriving later this week, tidying up the mail on the table is a project. Her ashtray will need space.

Grabbing bowls from a cabinet, I point at a chair.

"Make yourself comfy."

Melvin removes his jacket and sits, clearing a swath of mail from his placemat with the swipe of his forearm. I set a bowl and spoon for each of us, returning to the utensil drawer in search of an ice cream scooper.

"Thought you could use some cheering up," he says, while eyeing the strips of packaging tape surrounding my kitchen window.

Swiveling on my sneakered covered feet, ice cream scooper in hand, the utensil drawer closes with a bump from my hip as I ask, "How'd you find me?"

He watches as I remove the ice cream lid and spoon him a generous portion, which suddenly makes me tired. More emotionally weary than physically tired but too worn out to waste energy scooping my own bowl. Plunging my spoon into the container, I slump in my seat and begin eating, not caring if he thinks I'm gross.

He swallows his own spoonful of ice cream before answering.

"I didn't know my favorite early bird shopper had something in common with me until the regatta."

My spoon stops short of my mouth, his comment interrupting the unexpected contentment of the moment.

"My wife died earlier this year. And, until I saw you with your family, it didn't connect, you know, who you are... I was in the Army too... like your husband."

My eyebrows rise in silent acknowledgment, but I say nothing and resume shoveling ice cream into my mouth.

"Phone book helped me with the rest."

"You still use a phone book?"

"'Fraid so. Still works."

"You scared me coming in the back. Don't do it again."

Melvin smiles, grabbing a paper napkin from the holder at the center of the table and righting the fallen saltshaker.

"I'll take that as an invitation to come back."

Despite my annoyance with him, I can't stay mad. This ice cream is divine. And because I'm so tired, I use the easiest trick in Mother's proverbial book, the one requiring the least amount of work. The one that works best. Every time.

Always let a man talk about himself.

"Tell me about your wife."

His spoon drops slightly, a gentle nod to the impact her memory stirs within him. Melvin's face morphs before me, the age wrinkles around his eyes replaced with crinkles of delight.

"She liked ice cream, too," he says with a wink, before leaning back in his chair. "Met her when I was stationed overseas during the Korean War. She was a nurse, posted in Germany. Had a layover there. Seventy-two hours changed my life."

My memory flashes to high school geometry class and my prime seat next to Nick. We gave each other the once-over, both keenly aware of the other's blessings in the looks department. By the end of the first week, he folded a note into a triangular football and punt kicked it with his index finger, aiming at my breasts. It hit its mark. I unfolded it, careful not to let Mr. Slinger see, because he would scoop the paper up and announce its contents like a breaking-news bulletin to the class. I read the three little words contained in the note, and they packed a punch.

You are hot.

Seventy-two hours is all it took for us, too.

"What was her name?"

"Gwendolyn. Isn't that the most beautiful name?"

I smile.

"Yes, very pretty."

"So was she. And smart. Great with people. Nursing was her calling. Such a sad irony how it all slipped away in the end."

Melvin swipes his nose with his napkin. I swirl the ice cream around in my mouth, waiting a beat, and ask, "Do you and Gwendolyn have kids?"

He winces, and I want to reel the question back in, hooking it with a latch to the back of my throat so it never comes out. Instead, it's seeded in the common ground between us, an ugly pesky weed threatening to spread. Mowing over his grief cuts both ways, as I think back to all the times that I became defensive when the Pattycake mothers asked if I had children of my own. The ice cream man is a party of one, and part of me is melting inside.

"I'm alone, too, Melvin. Nick's family is here, but you saw what a train wreck they are."

He nods his head, his hand trembling as it lingers by the rim of the bowl.

"My Mother is coming to visit from Florida… soon… but she's… my father died my junior year of high school. He worked for Castle Cola and traveled a lot. Bit it in bed with some other woman in a hotel room in Cleveland. Massive heart attack. His death was sort of a release for my mother, in many ways."

The arch of Mother's back, leaning against the kitchen counter with the long curly cord of the wall phone wrapped around her body, listening as Daddy's boss called to give her the news is charred in my memory. She blinked at first, inhaling a long breath which she held while clutching a dish rag. When she spoke, her voice was firm. "Castle Cola sent him. Castle Cola can pay to bring him back." I watched as she listened halfheartedly to whatever the man on the other end of the phone was saying, checking her cuticles with exasperated boredom before cutting the call short. "You can send his final paycheck to the house. I don't care about what's in his desk." Mother hung up the wall phone, turned to me, and said, "We don't have to travel on the weekends anymore." And we didn't. Mother switched from "away games" to "home games" after that call.

"She cut loose. Big time. And, um, she wasn't the kind of mother the other mothers invited over for book club meetings, and not just because she wouldn't read the book, ya know? She got around and, ah, conquered the territory."

Melvin stirs his dessert until it resembles a green pond with chocolate chip lily pads. I don't sense his silence equates to judgment, and as he slurps, it hits me that I never spoke with my own father about anything over a bowl of ice cream.

"I'm sorry I snapped at you before, Melvin."

He rests the spoon at the side of the bowl and wipes his mouth again with the napkin, before waving his hand, dismissing the thought. "Next time, I will park in front and ring the doorbell. Do you have all the windows and doors sealed off there, too?"

A sheepish droop tugs at my face as I nod my head.

"Looks like the hurricane hit here."

Shrugging, I can't disagree with him.

"Not all the shipping tape was for relief supplies, was it?"

I shake my head, shifting my body to put my feet on the seat of my chair, peeking at him over my knobby knees.

"Someone killed my husband."

The words come out fast, surprising me. Melvin readjusts his bow tie, absorbing my accusation with a nervous twitch, pondering what to say. His hesitation is comforting. Finally, someone who doesn't immediately blow off my belief.

"Someone killed my wife, too."

My body registers shock as I gape at his face, a masking serum of seriousness toning his pallor.

"How? When?"

"Eight months ago. Gwendolyn was on the same floor as your mother-in-law, Fran. They were friends at Willow Bend."

No wonder Melvin was chummy with Marlene Flynn at the regatta. She is friendly with Fran, and so was Gwendolyn before her death. This makes sense now, why he sat at her table, next to kooky Ken and his diamond-encrusted cuff links. I'm overflowing with questions, but the chime of the front doorbell accompanied by a pounding fist knock, interrupts my inquiry.

Startled, our conversation hits a pause. Rising from my seat, I nervously glance at the back door, free of its sticky tape seal. Melvin pushes back his chair and says, "I'm coming with you."

I want to hug him.

He follows me out of the kitchen, past the powder room and around the corner by the dining room where I idle, eyeing the front door.

The two four-inch strips of clear shipping tape remain in place, above and below the handle and lock. I'll need to pull them off if I open the door. If, being the key word, since opening my door is not a constitutional requirement.

A fist pounds against the door again, thumping hard, interrupting all the mental excuses I'm making for not answering it.

"Police!"

Oh, shit.

I told them to stand down. Rolling my eyes at Melvin, I walk to the door and peel back the shipping tape. I ball it in my fist, as another loud rapping of knuckles hits my door.

"Okay, already, okay."

I unlock the door and swing it open, unprepared for what I see.

Him.

The *Flash* lady's boyfriend stands in front of me on my front step. The same guy sitting with her at the regatta when the car horn went off, almost giving me a coronary. He's the one who followed me out of the yacht club, watching me as I pulled away, driving out of the parking lot with my cash cargo *and* his girlfriend's wig. *He's the police.*

No wonder *The Finger Lakes Flash* lady took my comments about Nick's death down.

She's sleeping with the enemy.

34

CLAUDIA

September 4

I'm trapped.

Standing at the top rung of my spiral staircase, I stare below me, at the closed door to my room of disguises.

There's no way out without passing the doorway. Peter is working on a trespass call. Should I call him and tell him I've got a trespasser of my own?

If the video snoop is also my graveyard tipster, it means it's someone other than Lindsay Sutton. Someone who does not trust her, or someone who doesn't want *me* to trust her. The video suggests it was sent by someone who knows I gave Lindsay my wig at the regatta. The banquet room was at capacity. Anyone there could have sent this message.

Did my client, Oliver Sutton, send me a warning? Lindsay told me back in June that he didn't want her to talk with me about Nick's disappearance. She also mentioned that her sister-in-law, Brenda, was worried about disclosing information because it might have a negative impact on business at the apothecary.

Or is this retaliation for the snooping I did in Oliver's office? He grabbed my arm at the regatta wanting to talk, but Brenda Sutton specifically mentioned the camera system. If she saw the security footage and wanted to discuss it, why sneak around my property and send me a video?

I also can't forget Lindsay Sutton yelling, "You got the wrong guy!" at Roger Desmond, while he stood flummoxed at the microphone. What did she mean? Was she referring to her husband's death? It's unlikely the mayor of Romulus would risk sending me a threatening email or kill a local citizen! Or is that "the bigger story" Lindsay referred to on her telephone call to me back in June?

151

And what about his wife, Dr. Diane Desmond? Is she writing the Wozilfin prescriptions for mercy killing purposes? I need to check and see how many obituaries I've published for residents at Willow Bend Long-Term Care Home in the past year. I'll also study my research about the Wozilfin dosage levels listed on the purchase orders I photographed in Oliver's office.

Lending my wig to Lindsay Sutton has someone worried we will talk, *and* that I will believe what she says.

Another chill runs through me.

What if Lindsay Sutton is having a mental break? Something way beyond general anxiety and panic disorder? A split personality or paranoid schizophrenia… could *she* have done this? I just sent her an email invite. Is this a warning from an alternate personality, one at odds with the desperate woman I found on the bathroom floor at the yacht club?

Wozilfin is used to treat paranoid schizophrenia.

Anyone could send me an anonymous email. They didn't need to trespass on my property. Someone *wants* to scare me.

Peter is busy, but if I call the police, I'll have to tell them everything. They'll ask if I've received other anonymous tips recently. I'm not a good liar. I don't want to compromise the graveyard clue if it is completely unrelated to this. I slip my cell phone into my pocket and stare at the doorway.

Breathe.

Stepping to the next riser on the spiral staircase, the door to my room of disguises is mere feet from the bottom rung. I move silently, listening for any unexplained noises. The quiet does not reassure me. It's like all those interviews I've done where the pause that comes before the response is as telling as the words spoken.

I *know* silences, and I know this isn't good. Someone might be in the room.

Reaching for the door handle, I fling the door open and flip on the light switch.

The only faces greeting me are the head busts lining the back wall. The floor-length curtains surrounding my window sway in the gentle breeze, the screen popped from the frame.

Someone entered my most sacred space through the window.

I turn my attention to the closet door.

More silence.

A large can of hairspray sits on my vanity and I lunge for it. I snap the cap off, stepping toward the closet, my index finger set on the aerosol trigger nozzle. With my free hand, I swing the closet door open and spray the hair product into the void, hoping to stun anyone hiding among my spare winter coats and suitcases. The mist of hair spray dissipates as my unwanted intruder fails to appear.

Walking to the window, I close it, snapping the lock and yanking my darkening shades. Anger fuels me as I stomp to the front door. It's secured. I march through the kitchen to the back door in the rear hallway. It's bolted shut, too. Someone got too close, and I don't like it. Not one bit.

My adrenaline spikes as I think about what to do. The video was sent to unnerve me. If someone wanted to warn me about Lindsay Sutton, a simple email would do. The video was a scare tactic, designed to redirect my attention. Someone doesn't want me to trust Lindsay Sutton, and based on the video, lending her my wig crossed a battleground line.

Preparing my interview questions for Roger Desmond tomorrow is more important than ever, but I must craft how to bow out of our Saturday evening dinner. No respectable journalist would accept a dinner invitation from a political candidate. Especially when the candidate's wife may be the bigger headline grabber.

I wish Peter would call me. Breaking our Saturday night date presents a quandary for us, too. If there is an "us." We haven't talked in depth about my public unveiling, and there's only so long we can dance around an elephant before the elephant clones itself and becomes a herd, and our unspoken issues grow into a thundering stampede we can't outrun.

We need to talk. Today. Lay it out and take a chance with each other or commit to the friendzone. In the meantime, I need my wig back. Pronto, in case option one wins.

Lindsay Sutton hasn't responded to my email message yet, either. Her posts on the *Flash and* her outburst at the regatta suggest she's capable of unpredictable behavior. My hand rubs my scalp, scratching at an irritated hair follicle behind my left ear. It's not my only itch. I haven't shared the news of my big reveal with my sister yet, either.

Felicia is desperate for regatta details, but I've avoided telling her, presuming she won't understand, which is unfair from the jump, and I know it. And now, I can't tell her about the creepy video. She'd insist I call the police, which I'm not ready to do. I'll stall again, and text her a few more of the regatta selfie-shots with my clients. We'll speak this weekend, I'll say. Stall, stall, stall.

I missed dinner, but I'm not hungry. My fridge and pantry are replenished with an array of Rieslings and snack items, thanks to my double fortune of raffle basket wins at the regatta. I grab a bottle, unscrew the cork, and pour a glass of wine to settle my nerves. A notebook rests on the kitchen island where I perch, preparing interview questions for Roger Desmond.

Scanning my list, I toss my pen to the side, frustrated. The biggest questions I need answers to surround the events that unfolded at the regatta. Lindsay's accusation about "the wrong guy" and Brenda's threat aimed at the mayor's wife. What will he say about Dr. Desmond?

Reaching for my glass of vino, my phone alerts, causing me to jump.

The tipster email account alarm. *It's ringing again.*

My locked doors and empty coat closet are not enough to quell the trepidation the signal triggers within me.

What if the video sender is lingering outside?

I type my username and password. Another message sits in the tipster email box with a special VIP flag. There's no video attachment. This email was sent by Anonymous123.

Seymour. My original graveyard tipster. Hopefully, he or she answered my want ad, telling me where I should go to the doctor. I open the email.

A one-line sentence appears on the glass face of my phone:
You know where to find my answer.

35
LINDSAY
September 4

"I'm fine. False alarm."

Standing in the door frame, my body shelters Melvin from his sight. The cop strains like a curious cat, trying to gaze behind me to see what's happening in my house. I wave my hand in front of his face, breaking his eye-spy trance.

"Did you hear me? I'm good. You can leave."

"Are you Lindsay Sutton?"

You know who I am, hotshot. You watched me sail out of the yacht club in your girlfriend's wig.

"Yep."

"We had a 911 call from this residence, reporting a possible trespasser."

"I *told* you, false alarm."

"I'm required to make sure you are making this statement of your own free will. Mind if I come in and look around?"

Yes, I do mind.

"Can I have your name, Officer?"

"Officer Peter Graham," he says, pointing to a shiny gold badge. "Let me check out the property for you. You said on the call it was a prowler out back?"

Oh, for Pete's sake, Peter.

"Look, I get you're doing your job, but this is nothing. My friend stopped by to bring me ice cream. That's the scoop, here."

"Who's your friend?"

"One with two eyes, a nose, and a full head of hair," I say, snapping an unspoken sarcastic warning: *I know you and the Flash lady are up to something.*

He straightens, his chin thrust out, jaw tight. The typical mansplaining stance, identical to the condescending Detective Klink I encountered in the initial days following Nick's disappearance. How ironic the *Flash* lady and her rent-a-cop boyfriend suddenly want to help me when they think enough time has passed.

They must know about the money.

"Aren't you the guy who pulled my sister-in-law in for questioning?"

"I'm not authorized to discuss other investigative matters…"

"That's code for yes."

"I didn't say…"

"The mayor's wife can trespass all over people's marriages and she doesn't get an inquisition, but one sloppy comment by someone else after a few too many, and it's a capital offense."

Officer Peter Graham gives me a long, hard stare, and then hits the button on his vest radio, calling in his location, and the time.

"I'm going to walk around the property. If everything checks out, I'll be out of *your* hair."

He turns away from me and I slam the door, slouching against the frame, snapping the lock into place. I spin to face Melvin, who lingers in the adjacent hallway by the powder room.

"Grab the tape roll. We need to reseal this."

He blinks, uncertain what to say so I say it for him.

"We can't trust the police, Melvin."

36
CLAUDIA
September 4

Why didn't I think of it before? The original tip was straightforward.

"I think they are on to me."

Seymour is afraid. And if Seymour is afraid and wants my help, he or she isn't the same person trespassing on my property and sending me a scary video.

Tugging my rain boots on over the bottoms of my jeans, I grab a baseball cap to cover my head. It will be dark soon. No need for a wig. The idea of leaving my house without a hairpiece was inconceivable to me a month ago, but this week of milestones marks a victory to celebrate at another time. The new message confirms Seymour is still in play, but afraid to answer my question, at least in writing. It doesn't matter. A scavenger hunt always has more than one clue, and I want to live in the moment. I'm not going to let the video message frighten me back into a cocoon.

Time for a return trip to the cemetery.

Grabbing a flashlight, plastic gloves, a canvas bag, and my car keys, I slip my seatbelt into place as my cell phone lets out a familiar ring, the one set for when Peter is on the line. I shift the gear into reverse, while the call broadcasts from the car's speakers.

"Hi, Peter."

"Hey! Everything okay?"

Do I tell him about the video and my trespasser? Or is it better to get the next clue from the cemetery and then reassess the situation? I still don't know how he feels about my speech at the regatta. Maybe I should gauge that first.

"Um, sure, but I can't talk now. Something came up for work, but ah, about Saturday night…"

He listens while I pause.

"So, I've been thinking…"

"Uh-oh."

Damn. Out with it.

"Yeah, I don't think Saturday is such a good idea."

He's prepared, anticipating my protest, familiar with my insecureities. Only this time, he's wrong.

"Is this because of the regatta? By the way… your new friend called in a wild goose chase, today. Copped quite an attitude."

My new friend? His sarcasm confuses me, but the insinuation smacks like a palm to the cheek. Helping Lindsay Sutton at the regatta wasn't a replacement or a substitution for Stella. Or is this a dig for ditching my wig?

DO NOT TRUST LINDSAY SUTTON.

The video message came right after I sent Lindsay Sutton an email. Is that some sort of freaky coincidence, or was my computer hacked?

I blink.

What if my computer wasn't hacked, but is currently under surveillance by the police? *Peter knows I'm working on a tip about Wozilfin, and he knows I'm suspicious of Nick Sutton's death.*

He also knows I lent Lindsay Sutton my wig, and based on his comment, he's not a fan of hers.

I blink, again. What if *Peter* sent me the video?

"You saw Lindsay Sutton?"

"Yep. Don't worry. She's fine."

My mind does mental math.

"What time did you see her?"

"Just left her place. Called you first thing. Why?"

"Um, no reason. Hey, don't get the wrong idea. I want to see you, but the ethics police would cite me for accepting dinner from the mayor, especially given his candidacy."

"My badge is bigger than their badge."

His joke sweeps away my speckles of doubt, leaving a dusting of sexual innuendo in its wake and we laugh, the flirty kind of laugh language of mutual understanding. I feel foolish for doubting him.

"I have an interview lined up with the mayor tomorrow. Hope to interview his wife for a profile later in the week. I'll explain to him why I'm bowing out. Maybe, we can still grab dinner somewhere else instead?"

"Roger asked me to work security during his campaign events. I'm mulling it over."

His statement startles me, stimulating an extra pressure response on the gas pedal. Roger Desmond is a small-town mayor. Most members of Congress don't have protection details, even after assassination attempts. What does he fear?

Maybe, his wife.

"Can you do that? What does your chief say?"

"Haven't asked yet. The mayor sprung it on me after I handled the Brenda Sutton matter the other night. He said we can talk more at dinner."

So, you're going, I think to myself, disappointed he didn't change his mind. My fingers hit the blinker, turning from the less populated end of Main Street on to Route 150, a coil of a road transitioning urban life into rural. Dusk is falling, a visual equivalent for our conversation.

"Give me a rain check?" he asks.

"Sure, but the 9/11 anniversary is a week from today, so if you're thinking about honoring Stella..."

"I told you. I *do not* want to talk about Stella."

The cemetery is less than a mile down the road, and as perplexing as Peter's response is, dwelling on it must wait. "Got it. Let's catch up soon."

"Deal."

The call ends, and I'm left stewing about Peter's association with the Desmonds. If the clue awaiting me at Seymour's grave implicates Diane Desmond, my moral dilemma will be shrouded by an ominous shadow. Do I compromise my sources and methods by telling Peter what I suspect before developing solid proof? It's a potentially slanderous allegation, one that could cost me everything I built here. But, if I say nothing and someone else is killed, can I live with myself?

The answer swells in me. My health is the victim of the most massive murder plot ever carried out on American soil. Staying silent is the equivalent of complicity. I can't *not* do something.

The ornate iron fence work of Lakeview Cemetery snakes against the growing darkness, umbrellaed by the looming canopy of the cedar trees. My tires slow as I enter the burial grounds, passing the imposing vault, before winding to where the cement ceases, and pea gravel begins. The pathway to Seymour's grave.

Cutting the motor and headlights, I am paralyzed by the truth Peter revealed. His comments are as concerning as his job offer.

You know where to find my answer.

The Seymour email alert, the one signaling a new message from my anonymous tipster, chirped at the same time Lindsay Sutton was otherwise occupied, copping an attitude with Peter. The email with the video was sent not long before that, from a separate email account, suggesting I have two distinct, anonymous messengers.

I swallow, placing my hand on the door handle.

Whatever awaits me at the gravestone of a Revolutionary soldier, I am confident of one thing: If Peter was talking with Lindsay Sutton about a trespasser, she can't be the graveyard snitch. She wouldn't have had the chance to send me the email.

But, if the video of my room of disguises was recorded on a cell phone, it could be attached to an email and sent in a matter of seconds *from* a cell phone. Did Peter send it from his phone right before he knocked on Lindsay's door? Or did Lindsay?

Another thought suddenly occurs to me.

What if Lindsay's trespasser is the same one who paid a visit to me?

37
LINDSAY
September 4

Melvin scrapes the bottom of his ice cream bowl with his spoon, the clink of stainless steel against glass broadcasting his procrastination.

It's his second bowl of ice cream. He doesn't want to leave me. And I don't want him to go.

A happy coincidence.

Mother doesn't need to know.

I promised her, with the whiny pill-deprived, wine-induced hysteria of a daughter coming unglued, that I'd stick to self-isolation while sanitizing the house for other hidden secrets. She made me pinky-promise. In a sock puppet-like lecture fit for a preschooler, she explained how my sister-in-law's comments about leaving the house are just one of those things that don't belong. And she was quick to point out Claudia Marton's along-came-a-spider-act too, her helping-hand a devious entanglement, snaring me in her web.

But, nowhere in Mother's mind-your-own-business-and-sit-on-your-tuffet speech did she forecast a Grocery Galleria greeter showing up on the back porch, loaded with a gallon of mint chocolate chip and a knick-knack, paddy-whack tune of murder to boot.

Melvin may be the pied piper luring me out of seclusion.

"What happened to Gwendolyn?"

His shoulders slouch, rounding forward, the weight of grief bearing down. He shakes his head, raising his index finger into the air, spinning it in a tornadic rotation. His motion hypnotizes me and as I watch, his hand smacks the table with force, causing me to jump.

"She went from being a feisty jackrabbit to a tortoise in a shell. She was spry, cantankerous. Great periods of clarity." Melvin holds his hand up and flaps it dismissively, with a hogwash gesture, before snapping his fingers and adding, "She changed overnight."

161

His description is a finger poke at the far corners of my memory, jabbing with familiarity, pressing recollection of a conversation from a day not long ago.

"...when Franny goes zombie-like-silent is when you worry. There's a spark left. Don't kill it."

Marlene Flynn tried to warn me about Fran. I remember, now. It was the day my mother-in-law dug her fingertips into my throat... the same day I fished out Nick's fortune.

"Changed how?"

"Never spoke again. Catatonic. Her soul trapped, stuck in the shell of her body. I couldn't get her to speak. Her eyes became these empty pools. She died before I could get them to make the switch."

"Switch?"

"The medication they put her on, after she started getting feisty. It was only supposed to mellow her out, but it killed her. They killed her on purpose, and I think I know why!"

Melvin slams his hand on the kitchen table again. The mail flutters to the floor, occupying new territory for the foreseeable future.

"Why?" I ask, barely able to breathe.

Melvin's voice drops to a whisper.

"I was told it would make her more comfortable, less agitated. Fewer outbursts."

Scrunching my face, I study him, trying to untangle the jumble of his words. Seeing my confusion, he takes my hand, seizing his chance to further my understanding.

"Same reason they killed your husband, dear. To shut them up."

My thoughts spin like a record on a turntable, but they skip over a new scratch.

"You think Dr. Desmond killed your wife with different medication and her husband is covering for her?" I ask, slowly piecing his statements and my interpretation together.

Melvin massages his temples and readjusts his glasses. Leaning forward, his eyes radiate sympathy as he says, "Yep, I do. And I think your husband was on to their scheme."

38
CLAUDIA
September 4

The symphony of insects casts a peculiar backdrop, loud among the silence of the dead. Cicada nymphs trumpet their return, an engine trill of harmony in a sea of darkening night. A few crickets chirp from the weedy corners of crumbling gravestones, content in the cool, damp recesses of overgrowth, and the last of the seasonal mosquitos haunt the air, buzzing about with frenzied delight. They congregate around my hand holding the flashlight, an illuminated pathway for siphoning my blood.

The trek from the car to Seymour's grave marker is two hundred yards at most, but a chessboard of monuments sits between us, the tall kings the easiest to spot in the trickle of light. The lower stones, the knights and rooks of the lot, intensify my trepidation. In their crouched shadows lurk the nocturnal predators, with sharp teeth, beady eyes, and hungry appetites. I hear the rustling movements of raccoons or foxes sensing the presence of a pawn, vulnerable and weak. I pass one square monument at a time, eyes trained on the destination ahead, while questioning the sounds from behind the stone silhouettes.

My imagination magnifies the dangers, assuming the angel of death is here watching, ready to swoop down like a mean, flesh-tearing owl, feasting on the meat of my curiosity. And if not the angel of death, maybe the video trespasser. Television host Rod Serling was right. Under the umbrella canopy of early fall foliage and against the thick needle walls of evergreen branches, my mind creates a zone of terror, boxing me in tighter as my destination nears.

Seymour's monument rests a few yards beyond the reach of my flashlight beam, but the pace of my approach doesn't sync with the worry racing in my head. No one knows I'm here. Not Peter or Felicia. I pause, peering back at my car, a dark blob of safety. Or is it? Did I lock it? The campfire story of yesteryear pops in my head, the one where the bright lights of a tailing car flicker, amplifying brightness and creating a misunderstood distraction in the rearview mirror. This quandary presents the same sensation, a gooey marshmallow stretching with suspense, tugging my focus, making me question myself and where true danger lies. The moral of the fable.

The tailing car with glaring headlights illuminated the true menace, the one slouched in the back seat holding a knife. And here, in a dark, isolated cemetery, chasing a clue I'm not sure exists, a new truth comes to light.

Somehow, the toxins morphed my vision, making me fear baseball stadium flyovers and crowded skyscrapers, but not lone cemetery stakeouts and cyber stalkers. My hair loss blinded me to the dangers of self-isolation. I rejected those trying to understand my new normal, while I idled in test-drive mode with a learner's permit. Afraid to shift, reading sarcasm and slights in innocuous questions. It's not enough living in the moment, carefree and spontaneous, trailing stories like fallen leaves blowing in the wind.

My roots matter, too.

Felicia's annoyance at my obstinance and isolation would crumble into inexplicable disbelief if she knew I was here, alone in the dark, chasing a story about murder. And if she knew I was here by myself after an anonymous trespasser crept onto my property and videotaped my most sacred space, she would blow a gasket. My struggle with self-acceptance doesn't justify self-endangerment. It's unfair to my family, whose love didn't change even though my appearance did.

Think about Felicia and the girls. Find the clue and go home.

The beam of light from the flashlight bounces off the weathered fronts of stones. I squint, scouring the gleam until my pupils register the sight up ahead. Amid slivers of fractional light, red petals bleed for attention, propped at the base of Seymour's gravestone.

The tipster was here.

Trotting between monuments, I reach the bundle of flowers and crouch low. Slipping on gloves, the flashlight lay on the ground, illuminating the marker and the soil around it with a noticeable indentation.

A footprint!

The outline stretches wide and long, with a distinct tread. With my phone, I photograph the print, the flash lighting up the night, signaling my presence.

Big feet, man-sized, and bloody red roses…

My heart beats in tempo with the melody of the insects, a fast, pulsing urgency. Lifting the flowers, a Ziplock bag lays beneath the petals on a bed of damp sod. My fingers pinch the plastic, raising it to eye level. One item, flat and rectangular, fills the bag.

A glossy brochure touts "The best care in the world," and my mind flashes to the bulletin board list of destination points on Nick Sutton's delivery route.

Willow Bend Long-Term Care Home—a place where the administration of Wozilfin could be lethal.

Dr. Diane Desmond's stomping grounds.

39

LINDSAY

September 5

The Uber driver drops me off two blocks from Willow Bend, on the corner next to the no-parking sign. I'm disobeying Mother's edict, ditching self-isolation and leaving the house unoccupied. A calculated risk. The cash crates are still locked in my car, hidden in the double-door garage with the alarm siren set. After my meeting with Melvin, getting to Fran while she's still communicative is the goal. The hands of time are ticking; both with her memory, and in terms of her safety. Someone may try to shut her up, too.

Mother will understand. The memory of her deceptive check-in method at the various hotels we visited free floats in my frontal lobe, as my feet make quick business of the jaunt to Willow Bend. The repeated ruse of requesting an extra key for when "Daddy" arrived in every city we visited. My eyes observed, my ears listened. I played along and understood.

Everything can be made to look like something it's not.

Including me.

My hand sweeps away a stray tendril of hair drooping in front of my eyes, as the pedestrian walking sign lights up and I cross the street. The circular driveway of Willow Bend Long-Term Care Home winds through a porte-cochere, offering shelter for drop-off visitors and residents returning from day trips. Nearing the building, my presence triggers the motion detectors mounted above the sliding glass door entrance, which opens into the guest lobby. A large foyer table adorned with late summer gladiolas is situated in the center of the space, and I grab the counter pen, scribbling in the entrance logbook. The elevator sign points toward the information desk on the left, but I turn right, heading for the stairwell leading to the third floor.

166

Taking the stairs two at a time, I hustle, amped with purpose. Only nine weeks ago, both the police and *The Finger Lakes Flash* stiff-armed me with their "talk-to-the-hand" attitudes, which in my mind, included a middle finger salute. But now, right after I discovered the frozen cash register in my basement, ding, ding, ding… they're crawling up my ass, ringing my doorbell, and saving me from a gross bathroom floor.

It's no coinky-dink Claudia Marton sent me an invitation to meet with her at the exact time her cop-shop boy-toy showed up at my house. They're working together, covering up Nick's murder, which makes today's meeting with Fran crucial.

She's in danger here. Melvin thinks so, too.

A quick peek into the third-floor hallway reveals its emptiness, a welcoming sight under the glow of fluorescent light bulbs. I tiptoe along the familiar blue line painted on the tile flooring, past an open door where a sitcom laugh-track pipes from the speakers of a flatscreen television. The door to Room 319 sits cracked, opening into the modest space my mother-in-law calls home.

Knocking on her door, Fran calls out to me.

"Who's there?"

I step into the room. From her rocking chair, Fran stares at me, a magazine propped in her hands.

"Can I help you?"

"Hi Fran. It's Lindsay. How are you?"

Scrunching her face, she studies me. Her gaze travels over the pores of my skin like coordinates on a map, trying to pinpoint a location in her memory.

"You're not Lindsay."

Unfazed by her comment, my hand slides into my jacket pocket, fetching my damaged cell phone. My index finger points at the screensaver with Nick's beaming smile reflected on it.

"Look, Fran, isn't this a great picture of Nick?"

I extend my arm so she can view the picture of her son beneath the cracked glass on the phone. Her eyes alight with recognition, creases of delight forming around her mouth as her smile blossoms. She nods, and says, "That's Nicky. He left his lunchbox here."

She points to her kitchenette counterspace, where I see an insulated lunch bag resting at the far end. Nick used to pack lunch and eat with Fran at least once a week. The memory of him preparing London broil for steak sandwiches saddens me, but I don't have the heart to take the lunch bag back from Fran. I'm surprised I didn't notice it here before, but maybe Fran squirrelled it away, keeping a piece of Nick all for herself.

"Yes, he's so handsome in this picture," I say, not mentioning the bag. Turning the phone away from her while tapping the video recording button, I add, "I'm happy you are having a good day today, Fran. It's a nice day, like the day Nick and I got married. Do you remember our wedding?"

"Nick didn't marry you. He married Lindsay."

"Yes, Fran. I'm Lindsay."

"No, no. I'm quite sure."

"The wedding was a long time ago. You're expecting to see Dr. Desmond, right?"

Her brow furrows.

"The doctor?"

"Yes, Dr. Desmond, your doctor."

"No, no. My son…" The magazine drops from her hand, flustering her.

"I'll get it for you. The doctor wouldn't want you bending over so quickly. You could fall."

Retrieving the magazine, I give it back to her, noticing a slight increase in agitation.

"The doctor isn't here now."

"Yes. She's not here now."

"Good. She makes the boys fight."

Her comment fills me with apprehension. My motivation changed after talking with Melvin. Forget the whispers about me. This recording benefits Fran now. If Dr. Desmond is prescribing medication to tranquilize the elderly so they can't rage and complain while she accelerates their deaths, Fran is in grave danger.

"What do they fight about?"

My breath catches as her mouth forms the words.

"One of the boys loved her, and the other one hated her! Like when they were little, and one detested fish, and the other despised meatloaf. They never agreed." Fran laughs, oblivious to the value of her memory.

Nick and Oliver *were* complete opposites, each navigating life in their own lane. Neither one seemed interested in bridging the gap, although if Brenda is right about Oliver using other people's cars, it's possible Nick softened his stance. But why? And what fight does Fran know about? Did Nick tell her something he never told me?

If Nick loved Diane and they schemed up a plan to run off and start a new life, my husband was a stranger to me all along. Roger Desmond may have killed him out of jealousy. Brenda or Oliver could have killed him for putting the business and Fran at risk. But, if *Oliver* loved Diane and switched cars like Brenda said he does, Roger might have made the same jump I did and assumed Nick was the guilty party. Maybe Roger offed him by mistake, or maybe Nick figured out something wasn't right with Dr. Desmond's prescriptions, and the mayor shut him up. Deliberately.

"Which one loved her, Fran?"

She stares at me, studying my face.

"Who are you?"

"I'm Lindsay, Nick's wife."

"No. No, you're not."

"Who loved Dr. Desmond? Which boy, Fran?"

She shakes her head, not understanding.

"You're not… they don't… I'm…"

"You said something like this once before to me, Fran. You said, 'Nicky is in love with my doctor.' Do you remember?"

Her original statement, combined with Nick's truck parked outside the remote cabin, solidified my belief about an affair. But now, the assumption doesn't gel like it used to. *One of the boys loved her, and the other one hated her!* What if Nick wasn't the one who loved her?

The magazine falls to the floor again. Fran starts reaching down, but I pick it up for her.

"Who *are* you?" Fran's voice rises, her agitation escalating at an alarming rate.

"I'm Lindsay. I understand why you're confused. I… I can't come see you anymore. It's too dangerous. Don't take any new medication. Fran, do you hear me? Don't trust them if they try to change your medication!" Her brow scrunches, trying to compute my words. "Melvin will check on you since I can't. Do you remember who Melvin is? Shit. Probably not. I'm going to figure this out, Fran. For you, for Nick, for me… For everybody."

She watches me as I pause near the door, her face clouded, confused by me and my words.

"Don't be frustrated. You made total sense today. I love you, Fran."

I duck into the hallway, away from her room as she starts to yell. Her screams of "Who are you?" ricochet off the scuffed floor, traveling the length of the painted blue line.

Opening the door to the stairwell, I glance over my shoulder, between the strands of hair falling across my face. Marlene Flynn sits in her wheelchair near the nurses' station at the far end of the hallway, talking to Ken Preston and pointing in my direction. As he begins walking toward me, his face displays a myriad mixture of concern and suspicion.

My feet hit the treads of the stairwell, scampering as I flee the scene.

THE FINGER LAKES FLASH

Your online snapshot capturing the local news you need to know.
September 5

ROMULUS MAYOR ANNOUNCES CANDIDACY

Roger Desmond (I) will seek the 54th District State Senate seat in November. Desmond is challenging incumbent John Jefferies (R) and Paula Holden (D). Jefferies has held the seat since 2012.

Traditional party candidates are required to file entry paperwork by the first Tuesday in April of the election year. Independent candidates for state office must file paperwork at least twelve weeks prior to election day. A Focus Feature profile is coming later this week in the Community News Section.

THE FINGER LAKES REGATTA

SHATTERS FUNDRAISING RECORDS

Total Raised: $43,760

This year's event raised $4,000 more than last year's total.
Proceeds benefit The Finger Lakes Food Pantry & Homeless Shelter.
Coordinator Dr. Diane Desmond sets $50,000 goal for next year.

40
CLAUDIA
September 5

Roger Desmond's administrative assistant leads me into his office, a wide expanse of workspace asserting power, with built-in bookshelves trimmed with federal crown molding and floor-to-ceiling windows offset by walls painted an elegant Bullfinch pink. A trove of trinkets, photographs, and books crowd the shelves, hooking the eye with curiosity bait, begging the visitor to pause and appreciate the multifaceted experiences and taste of the occupant dwelling here. The mayor rises from his seat behind a solid oak desk, his tie swaying in tandem with his movement.

"Claudia! How nice to see you again! People are still talking about your statement the other night. Profoundly moving."

The mayor extends his hand offering a firm handshake, as his assistant exits the office, closing the door behind her.

"Thank you. I hope I didn't steal your thunder…"

Roger Desmond shakes his head, gesturing to a sitting area with a couch and two wingback chairs. "No, Brenda Sutton deserves the blame. Her sister-in-law, too. Please, come sit."

As we cross the room and situate ourselves on the furniture, his comment creates a natural segue for a necessary discussion.

"Yes, both Breanda and Lindsay Sutton interrupted my evening, as well. And, while I appreciate your dinner invitation for this weekend, I'm afraid it would be unethical for me to accept. *The Finger Lakes Flash* will be publishing feature profiles on each candidate for state office, and, of course, covering the election in November. It's important I maintain an appearance of impartiality."

The mayor appears surprised but raises his hand in a "say no more" gesture.

"Understood, although my wife will be disappointed. She wanted to speak to you about the medical issues 9/11 responders are facing since she'll potentially encounter them at Willow Bend."

I appreciate his lack of protest, while welcoming this perfect excuse to drop by Willow Bend to snoop around.

"Yes, my comments the other night piqued *a lot* of interest among the local medical community. It's encouraging. Please tell your wife I will stop by Willow Bend. I'll be running articles on the *Flash* next week as well, to correspond with the 9/11 anniversary."

Pivoting, I flip open my reporter's notebook.

"So, why does a successful *Democratic* mayor gather signatures and enter the State Senate race as an independent candidate the day before the deadline?"

Roger Desmond cocks his head and steeples his hands, crafting an image of ponderance and patience, which strikes me as both pretentious and phony. This softball opening question shouldn't require deep thought.

"Because I can," he says chuckling, turning to a side table where a pitcher of water with floating lemon slices rests. Seeing my pen isn't moving, he elaborates as he pours himself a glass of water. "My experience as mayor helped me recognize the need for a bridge between blue and red party voters. We've never been so divided, as a state, as a nation. When my wife and I began discussing the possibility of my candidacy, we put out subtle feelers in the community, trying to get a read. Overall, support came from both sides. So, here I am."

"You and your wife are a high-profile couple with demanding careers. What are the pros and cons of navigating dual power professions, and how does it help and/or hinder you as a candidate?"

My question catches Roger Desmond off-guard, casting his rehearsed responses about education, taxes, and infrastructure aside for a moment. When he counters, it's with the poise of an experienced politician.

"Public service and helping others come naturally to both of us, so having a partner who understands the commitment, the sacrifice, is a pro." He smiles, pleased with his response.

"And the cons?" I prompt, jotting in my notebook.

"Long hours, time away." His expression darkens as he considers his word choice. "Peter's offer to head my security detail is welcoming."

The pen freezes in my hand, my mind replaying his words, not sure how to interpret his comment.

"Why do you need security?"

He hesitates again.

"My wife is a successful and beautiful woman. The other night, you saw the animosity…"

"You feel you need protection from Brenda Sutton? Or Lindsay Sutton? What did she mean when she said, 'You got the wrong guy?'"

"No, no, look, I mean… those women are grieving, and perhaps had a bit too much to drink. But it goes without saying that men want my wife."

My Sandra brows perk with surprise, startled at his response. This is a non-answer to my question, and to the insinuations both women put on blast. The mayor senses he didn't satisfy me with his comment.

"With me campaigning, I think a guy like Peter can help, in case other situations arise…"

"I'm sorry, I'm confused. Is the protection for you or for your wife?"

"Peter and I plan to discuss this Saturday night at dinner. You sure you don't want to reconsider joining us?" He snickers, enjoying my befuddlement.

My mind sweats his spin, turning his words over, analyzing what is said versus what he implies. There are only two logical reasons for Peter to "offer" security assistance: Either he suspects the Desmonds are up to no good, or Lindsay Sutton was right… the cops *are* covering for them. Before I can respond to the mayor's question, he asks me two more.

"What's the matter? Don't you trust your boyfriend?"

41

LINDSAY

September 6

Twisting the lightbulb out from the overhead socket mounted on the basement rafter, I extinguish any chance of my nerves short circuiting again over a window well surprise. Melvin promised to park in front from now on, but removing the cellar spotlight protects me when I'm down here, allowing for free movement, away from the curious eyes of any other creepers and peepers.

Absent the overhead bulb, the glow-in-the-dark plastic bobbers and nightcrawlers hooked on Nick's fishing poles float in the darkness like colorful spheres and wiggly eels of yellow and green light. I hop off the step ladder, surveying the organized clutter of sporting equipment. It's acceptable now, compared to the shamble created on the night the money turned up in the freezer. A functional jumble of sports gear and hobby toys, a normal variety one would expect in the back recesses of a man cave.

Mother will agree.

She arrives tonight, on the red eye flight. We debated if I should pick her up curbside outside of baggage claim, leaving the house unoccupied, or if she should grab an Uber. We decided I'd swing by. She doesn't know about my field trip yesterday.

And I'm not telling her about the other one I'm making today.

The step ladder folds with ease, and I carry it and the light bulb upstairs to the kitchen pantry, depositing both for future use. The mess of mail amassing on the kitchen table got sent to the filing cabinet in the spare bedroom, and now, everything shines with a germ-free gleam. The house is ready for Mother. So am I. I need her help cracking the code on Nick's phone.

There's only one more thing I need to do before she arrives.

Grabbing my cellphone from the counter, my fingertips tap away, composing an invitation.

Claudia, Let's meet for a drink. Corks & Company 5:00 pm. ~Lindsay

175

42

CLAUDIA

September 6

After the uncomfortable meeting yesterday with Mayor Desmond, today's appointment with Stella's attorney fills me with another heavy dose of trepidation. Stella's presence lingers between us, amid a mountain of paperwork and options, a somber reminder of what binds our introduction. We don't speak of her but she's here none-the-less, lurking over my shoulder like a nagging ghost pleased her spooking worked. She'd be half-right. I'm here for reasons beyond preparing for my demise.

This potential murder victim/journalist needs to understand the motivations of the angel of death.

Don Weaverman's law office occupies the first floor of a converted bi-level home, split from a local accountant's office on the upper level. His reading glasses sit perched at the tip of his nose, his eyes peering over the frame of the lenses.

"Any questions for me before we start your paperwork?"

My body wiggles on the chair, the hard, wooden seat an apt parallel to this discussion. Smooth, efficient, but not comforting.

"As you know, my, um, situation, is perhaps, ah, a bit different…"

He squints at me, uncertainty reflected in the depths of his pupils.

"You plan to live forever?"

My nervous laughter breaks his squint, his face softening as he removes the glasses from his nose and leans forward on his desk.

"Estate planning can be stressful. I've been doing this for thirty-five years and can't say anybody enjoys the process. But I have witnessed relief and comfort, once we get it done."

My head nods in response to his kind smile, but I can't control the bubbling words, which burst from my mouth like molten ash, hot and fiery and deadly serious.

"I want to control my death. It's important to me."

176

"The paperwork spells out your wishes…"

"No, I mean, I want the flexibility to choose how and when I die."

His face shifts, somewhat recoiling from the shock of my words. He slumps back in his chair studying me, trying to register the temperature of my intent, as a lava flow of emotion spews from my mouth.

"I'm a 9/11 responder case, and you saw what happened with Stella. She had her face ripped off to get her tumor out. They sliced her facial nerve, disfiguring her. Brain cancer still got her. And there's more. *Every day, there's more.* New cancers, unprecedented abnormalities, unexplained musculoskeletal disorders… My friend Angela's hip joints disintegrated before she was fifty, plus a disk in her back…"

Don Weaverman holds his hand up, hitting an imaginary pause button.

"Let's slow down, here. There are diseases and conditions you die 'with,' which is different than 'dying from' a terminal condition. From a legal standpoint, some states have death with dignity laws. One of the conditions is a terminal illness, where death is anticipated within six months."

My ears burn as his tone grows more serious.

"This is a controversial, often taboo, subject. We talk about euthanasia in veterinary medicine, but with humans, the term euthanasia is considered 'wrong' by death with dignity advocates. To them, this is a humane end-of-life option for mentally sound people with a terminal illness *confirmed* by at least two physicians." He taps his ball-point pen on the desk blotter, creating a triangular pattern of tiny ink flecks. "On the flip side, opponents cite moral and religious objections. They advocate palliative care and treatment for 'living with dignity' upon diagnosis, and hospice care when treatment has ended." His fingers make air quotations, while somehow still managing to hold the pen. "Most families can't agree on politics—imagine the discussions taking place about this."

The image of Felicia sitting in an auditorium watching Nadia play her violin reverberates in my memory, plucking a haunting chord. This decision and the corresponding planning are somewhat like an opus, a large-scale work of magnitude, the execution requiring significant coordination.

"Well, yes… um, my sister and I disagree a lot. I recognize my potential for, ah, complications in the future…"

"Have you spoken with her about this?"

I shake my head.

"You should. Where would you live? This isn't legal everywhere. And, as I said, you need a doctor willing to administer medication to hasten death, for a patient *of sound mind* with a confirmed *terminal* condition."

Full circle… *you need a doctor.*

"But we should still prepare your estate now, in case of an accidental death…"

"Um, so I'm clear… what if a doctor did this in a state where there isn't a death with dignity act?"

"Well, I'm not a prosecutor or the police but absent a change in state law, if the doctor and the patient conspire, I believe it would constitute second-degree murder." He rubs the bridge of his nose with his fingers, before repositioning his glasses, and adding, "Without patient consent, first-degree murder."

Absent a change in state law…

Roger Desmond's State Senate candidacy makes sense now. If elected, he can introduce death with dignity legislation.

I'm not a prosecutor or the police…

No, but Peter is.

Peter, the officer "offering" protection, to both the candidate *and* his wife. The cop in silent mourning, not copping to his grief over witnessing the slow, prolonged death of his beloved girlfriend.

"I told you. I do not want to talk about Stella."

Motivations align with my suspicion, now. Roger Desmond and Peter have a common interest, death with dignity legislation. And until a change in the law takes place, Dr. Desmond can prescribe Wozilfin to the elderly patients at Willow Bend, accelerating their deaths under the guise of helping them.

DO NOT TRUST LINDSAY SUTTON.

It makes sense! Nick Sutton delivered medications to Willow Bend, and his widow put a warning out to the masses on my media platform, insisting he had made enemies. Did Nick Sutton discover Dr. Desmond is mercy killing her patients?

"The cops don't want you to know."

The panic attack strikes like a shotput to the chest, pounding my windpipe. Somewhere in the hazy tunnel that follows, Don Weaverman's voice begs for an ambulance, and a realization floats within the wafts of looming darkness.

Lindsay Sutton was right.

Forty-five minutes later, the EMT crew agreed my panic attack was over, and that a gurney transport to the closest emergency room wasn't necessary. They unstrapped the oxygen mask and sat me up, but a clunky awkwardness remained, coloring my complexion with embarrassment.

My building blocks toppled.

Don Weaverman insisted on a follow-up appointment, one we could schedule later after I "processed" what we discussed.

His fingers made air quotes again, and he still never dropped the pen. No doubt, he'll want an ambulance on standby for our next meeting. This setback is a gut check but I'm not calling Greta. Not yet.

Drinks with Lindsay Sutton are at five. She's my portal to the Sutton family, and I want her to talk. A lot. If we can build trust, maybe she'll share her theory with me about who killed her husband and why. I'll print out her post, the one on Nick Sutton's In Memoriam page and bring it with me. It's a coded clue, and though I'm convinced she's not Seymour, maybe her suspicions will mesh with the signals he left for me at the cemetery. Does she know about the Wozilfin prescriptions? Or the line drawn through her husband's name on the delivery route schedule? What about Willow Bend and the Desmonds? Her sister-in-law has beef with Dr. Desmond. After Lindsay's outburst toward Mayor Desmond at the regatta, does she have animosity with his wife, too?

My eyes glance in the rearview mirror as I sink into the driver's side seat of my car. What a mess, I think, as I reapply lipstick and adjust Chloe on top of my head. Today doesn't have to end the way it started. My panic attack in Don Weaverman's office busted the forward momentum of my recent progress, but it's a minor setback.

Breathe. Everyone has complications. Dieters, addicts, over-achievers, me. I'm a journalist with a job to do.

Lindsay Sutton is a lot of things, too. A potential informant, a building block for a blockbuster news story. An anxiety sufferer, a person struggling with the unpredictability of grief…

And, possibly, a new friend in grave danger.

43

LINDSAY

September 6

Time to play sympathy mulligans.

My ass perches on a counter stool at Corks & Company, my snakeskin heels dangling by the footrest. The wine bar oozes a sexy vibe, a mixture of mood and attitude amplified by vast contrasts of light. Overall, the joint resembles a dark, stone cave, with backlit wine glasses aligned on shelving behind the bar. Scattered bistro tables sit under mounted wall sconces, and halfmoon footlights illuminate the pathway to the restrooms in back. Strapping my purse on the hook mounted below the bar counter, I grab my cell phone while I wait for the *Flash* lady to show up.

The server places a wine list in front of me, a bevy roster sporting the best local vintages. I select a semi-dry Gewürztraminer and he nods at me, before spinning around toward the wine coolers, searching for the correct bottle. My attention turns to the phone, firing off a quick text to Brenda.

Hey Bren! Can't wait to see you tomorrow! I'll pull out some trout. You can thank me by floating a couple of pills. XoXo

First mulligan stroke played and above par, in my opinion. This text resets the clock, recreating the same catch and release scenario from two weeks ago. Brenda wanted trout. I wanted pills. She'll think nothing's changed. And, if she's angling at access into my freezer, serving her the smoky fish she likes so much will make her bite. My mouth crooks into a pleased smirk. Mother and I have a little test rigged for tomorrow. Brenda's not expecting Mother, which once again proves why I'm the alpha and she's the beta. If my sister-in-law thinks she can drop anchor and fish around in my house, I'm going to snag her with the best safety net in the world. My mother.

The server places a long stem white wine glass on the counter, rewarding me with a healthy pour. Thanking him, I let the wine aerate for a minute, prepping for sympathy mulligan number two.

180

Claudia Marton and her boyfriend want me to ignore police corruption. That's what the hairdo handoff at the regatta was all about. She also wants me to forget that she erased my post. They don't want a snoopy wife raising red flags about her husband's mysterious death.

I sip my wine, a smug smile returning to my lips as Mother's words echo in my mind.

Women are not your friends! Don't trust them.

Chuckling out loud, I think about what I have planned. *We can be friends, Claudia. And, since you're so committed to earning my trust, I'm going to be a friend in return and remind you of the one thing you're forgetting.*

I glance toward the hostess counter near the front entrance. Speak of the devil.

The unflappable *Flash* lady looks flustered. She enters the wine bar, her hands brushing a wisp of hair from her face, the wig choice a ho-hummer. As her eyes adjust to the darkness, she scans the room, spotting me at the far end of the bar.

Show time.

She grins, and begins heading in my direction, pausing for a server with a platter full of wine flights. She saddles up on the stool next to me, extending her hand, all business.

"Hi, I'm Claudia. It's nice to see you again. Thanks for meeting me."

I shake her hand, playing along.

"I'm Lindsay. And I should be thanking you."

She smiles as she sets her phone on the counter and pulls her wallet from her purse, extracting her credit card.

"What are you drinking? I'm afraid my day got off to a rocky start and I haven't eaten, so I'm going to order some food. Split a cheese board with me?"

"Sure."

She hands her card to the bartender, ordering the charcuterie for two, and a glass of sparkling water.

"This is Gewürztraminer, very dry. No wine for you?"

She shakes the ho-hummer, plopping her wallet back in her bag and plucks out a pill bottle, rattling it in her hand.

"Nope. As I said, rough morning. Had an attack. The first one in a while. As soon as the food comes, I'm taking my meds."

She shakes the pill bottle and sets it between us on the counter, the label facing me.

Anti-anxiety medication.

Power play.

I've underestimated her. She's strategic. Pretending to be flustered, dangling what I crave most right under my nose, like a creepy predator at a neighborhood park with a box of chocolate candy. Well, goody-goody gumdrops. This is getting interesting.

"Sorry you're having a bad day. Does it, um, have anything to do with, ah, your hair situation?" My index finger points to my own head, before grasping a tendril and twirling it, pasting a look of curiosity on my face. If she's going to wave pills at me, I'm going to play with my hair.

"Yep, my attacks started at the same time as the alopecia. My medical doctors say my hair loss is an auto-immune disease possibly triggered by 9/11 toxic exposure, and my therapist says post-traumatic stress disorder set it off, but nobody will say one way for sure. There's a lot of crisscross finger-pointing."

"That sucks."

"Pretty much, yeah. And when I lost my hair, I gained a whole lot of anxiety."

Claudia can act. This is an award-winning performance. She's believable. I almost do feel sorry for her. Almost.

"Well, look, um, I don't know the etiquette on wig sharing, but I mean, thank you, for helping me the other night."

She smiles a weak smile, a buddy-bonding moment in her game plan, I'm sure.

"I took your wig to Wigwash Wonders, you know, so I could give it back clean." I take a sip of wine. "I had no idea there are, like, cleaning services for wigs."

Her shoulders relax, and if I didn't think she was out to trick me, I would say she appreciates my confession.

"Thanks, that's nice of you. Wigwash Wonders does everything… washes, cuts, highlights. They style any type of wig. I take mine there all the time. It was a learning curve in the beginning, for sure."

She reaches into her purse, pulling out a plastic bag containing my scarf.

"I had your scarf cleaned, too."

The charcuterie board arrives, with a wedge of brie, slices of smoked

Wisconsin cheddar, and a blue cheese spread arranged between pitted olives, tapenade, and artisan bread. As we unroll cloth napkins and place them on our laps, I extend an offer, ready to take control of this parley.

"My tab is open. Please, let me pay for this, as a thank you."

She chews on a slice of cheddar and shakes her head, swallowing before she speaks.

"No, please. It wouldn't be ethical. As the owner and operator of *The Finger Lakes Flash*, I'd like to ask you a few questions in my official capacity as a journalist. I can't accept gifts… even yummy cheeseboards."

It wouldn't be ethical.

Is covering up the murder of my husband *ethical*? Was taking down my post *ethical*? Her phony-baloney morality clause stinks more than the blue cheese spread she's shoveling in her mouth. This is a full-on cat-and-mouse game, and she thinks I'm the mouse, easily baited with a wedge of cheese and a bottle of pills.

"Aren't you going to take your medication?"

She nods her head, wiping her mouth with the cloth napkin.

"Uh huh. Sorry, didn't realize I was so hungry." She unlocks the childproof cap, jostling a pill tablet out of the vial and into her mouth, before taking a long sip of sparkling water. I toss a couple of olives into my own mouth, wishing they were anxiety pills, as she returns the water glass to its wet imprint on the cocktail napkin. Her fingers snap her purse open, and she drops the vial back in before removing a piece of paper. Leaning back on her stool, she spots the double hook underneath the bar countertop and hangs her bag next to mine.

"Can I ask you about the post you made on your husband's In Memoriam page?"

"Why don't we start with you telling me why you took it down?"

She nods, anticipating my question.

"Your brother-in-law, Oliver, is my client. He requested it, and I agreed."

"Why?"

"Professional courtesy, I guess. It was business for me. I didn't see any harm in taking it down."

Don't trust other women. No wonder Mother called this rule a gem. My hunky hubby is found in a creek and this "journalist" doesn't think *any* harm comes from removing his wife's post about a police cover-up? Her performance is starting to slip.

"Seems to me an *ethical* reporter would want to pursue a story about murder and police corruption—especially when you accepted my phone call in June and wanted me to go on the record."

"I do."

Her cell phone alights atop the smooth granite surface of the bar counter, with the name "Peter" displayed on the screen. Claudia's face contorts with displeasure.

Peter, a.k.a. the cop, a.k.a. her backup.

How fitting, her knight in shining armor calling precisely when she's starting to flounder.

"You can take that. I'm going to run to the restroom."

My hand reaches for the bag hooked under the counter while she nods her head, answering the phone. Turning my back to her, my feet skip along the halfmoon lighted walkway to the ladies' room where I scurry into a stall, knocking the bolt lock into place.

Score.

Her vial of pills rests on top of her wallet, next to a pack of breath mints. With jelly fingers, I fumble with the childproof cap, nearly dropping the vial in the toilet bowl. Oh, for heaven's sake. I can't end up on another bathroom floor with this woman around. My fingers twist again, this time releasing the protective cap into the palm of my hand. I've earned this. One for now, more for later.

A Cheshire cat grin spreads across my face.

The mouse just ran away with the cheese.

44
CLAUDIA
September 6

Peter's timing stinks.

Lindsay Sutton believes her husband was murdered and the cops are involved in covering it up. She doesn't know that I also suspect Peter knows more than he is letting on. What if *he* sent me the video email message? And worse still, if Lindsay tells me a plausible story, I either need to confront Peter with it or stay away from him, neither of which appeals to me. I want more than anything to give him the benefit of the doubt.

"Hey, Peter."

"Hello… wanted to check on you. My buddy on day shift patrol told me he responded to Weaverman Law today with an EMT crew. Said you couldn't breathe. Are you okay?"

His inquiry stirs my anxiety. He's a career law enforcement officer, who loved *my best friend*, who died a martyr. Now, he's checking on me, while I'm with a potential informant who questions his integrity and wants to bring him and his department down.

"I'm doing better, now, thanks. Listen, I spoke to the mayor. He understands why I'm bowing out Saturday night for dinner, but I owe you a rain check. Want to grab a bite with me tomorrow night? Maybe a Friday night fish fry at The Thirsty Minnow?"

I'm the thirsty one. All this talking about maintaining journalistic ethics and here I am pretending this is sorta/kinda/maybe a date, except I'm strategically scheduling it after meeting with the mayor, Lindsay Sutton, and hopefully, Dr. Diane Desmond at Willow Bend tomorrow. Part of me wants a date, but a bigger part wants the missing pieces to the Wozilfin story.

"Deal."

"Great. I'll call and reserve a lakeside table. Does six-thirty sound good?"

"Fantastic. See you then, Claudia… And hey, I'm glad you feel better."

My heart sinks, thinking how nice these words are to hear, and yet, they are the same words he could never say to Stella. Lindsay Sutton settles back on her bar stool, hooking her bag under the countertop as I say goodbye, ending the call.

"Sorry about that. Um, where were we?"

She sips her wine, less agitated than she was before the telephone call interrupted us. She signals to the server for another round, selects a piece of cheese from the platter and says, "You wanted to know why I think your boyfriend is a dirty cop."

45
LINDSAY
September 6

Claudia blinks rapidly, processing my words and their weighty implications. The server brings me a fresh glass of wine, which is a show prop more than anything. Thanking him, I also indicate that I'm ready to close out my tab. I take a small sip of wine, enjoying the crisp flavor. Mixed with the anxiety medication, I'm playing a dangerous game of happy hour roulette, but I won't drink much more. The pill is helping to take the edge off my frayed nerves until backup arrives. Mother's plane lands in a few hours. Claudia has picked up on my signal that I'm ready to go. There's only one thing left for me to do as she asks another question.

"Why do you think your husband was murdered, and why would the police cover it up? What did you mean when you yelled at Mayor Desmond at the regatta?"

She's rushing now, fearing I'll slip away.

"You're not from here, are you, Claudia?"

She shakes her head, studying me. The corners of my mouth turn up. If Claudia Marton wants facts, here they come.

"You know in the morning, when the lakes look like glass, and you can hear the calls of the loons?"

She nods, listening.

"People listen for the loon calls, Claudia. They're a signal." My hand raises the wine glass to my lips, pausing my story, toying with her apt attention. One slow, long sip.

"The loons are part of the package, nature's way of welcoming the wine drinkers on the pricey pontoon tours, as they hop off and on at the docks of the tasting rooms. And, of course, the minivan families, all those exhausted parents with two kids and a dog? They wait all year for their morning cup of coffee at the lake with their feet dangling off the side of a pier, counting the callouts from the loons."

She squirms in her seat, anxious for me to get to the point as I continue to taunt her.

"The calls are like a symbol of location. Who's here, or there. A status ranking. Small towns are full of small minds with deep pockets and long memories. A power structure exists, and if the structure stays unified, it survives. No one wants dead bodies floating in the lake or decomposing in a creek. Everybody wins when business booms."

Her forehead creases with deep folds, contemplating the visuals my explanation paints in her head.

"Murders kill business. So do scandals. Combined, they upset the power structure."

"Are you saying your husband was killed because he wanted to break the mold?"

"Yes. I think my husband knew too much, planned to expose it, and they shut him up for good."

"Who's they? What did he know?"

"The people in power, of course. And now, you're in the same situation as Nick."

She startles, her body jerking upright, her shoulders tensing. The server places my bill in front of me, which I sign, not looking at the total.

"What do you mean?" she asks, as I rise from my seat.

"You're swimming against the current, dodging loon calls, Claudia."

Her eyes question me, as I take a final sip of wine.

"Let me give you a friendly reminder. Power structures have hier-archies. Conspiracies are built on the greed of the powerful. The lower the rank, the more disposable you are. They're only keeping you close to keep an eye on you. Like a loon call. They don't want any more posts like mine on your pages."

She glances at the sheet of paper she pulled from her purse.

"What did your post mean? What do you know?"

"I know your cop boyfriend is using you. You're the hairless head of *The Finger Lakes Flash*. And he wants to control the story."

46
CLAUDIA
September 6

The anti-anxiety medication isn't helping. I'm regressing, my forward progression falling away like strands of silky hair. My truth entangles with others' motivations in a sticky, fibrous web, trapping me in a weave of deception.

As Lindsay Sutton exits through the front door of the wine bar, her statements bob up and down in my mind like a kayak hitting a turbulent wake. It doesn't matter if fake eyebrows paste to my face, or if my lash strips flutter with the weightlessness of a colorful butterfly. Lindsay Sutton's belief is what people think but don't have the courage to say. I am the hairless head of *The Finger Lakes Flash*. Someone *damaged and disposable*.

How foolish of me to believe Peter saw me as something more.

I am not a distraction, or a desire, or even a substitution.

I am a living reminder.

A reminder of what he lost, of what happens when the damage gets too bad and there's no way to control its death grip.

I'm a toxic threat, in more ways than one.

I sensed Peter's hesitation when I mentioned Nick Sutton's death on the phone, asking him about Wozilfin. He knows I know about Wozilfin.

"You're in the same situation as Nick."

Lindsay's right. Peter wants to help one woman, and it's not me. The Wozilfin traces back to Dr. Diane Desmond. The beautiful, living angel Peter wants to protect. The woman who wants to spare guys like him the painful agony of watching a girlfriend slowly die from cancer.

I think they are on to me…

They… a conspiracy… two or more. Peter and the Desmonds.

DO NOT TRUST LINDSAY SUTTON.

189

"They don't want any more posts like mine on your pages."
I *do* trust Lindsay Sutton.
Reaching for my phone, I compose a necessary text.
"Peter, Cancelling dinner tomorrow night. Something came up. ~ Claudia"

47
LINDSAY
September 6

I'm so glad I listened to Mother about not trusting other women.

The look of panic on Claudia Marton's face when I called her bluff was classic. It was almost like she hadn't considered how she's just a low-level pawn in the big scheme of things. How her boyfriend doesn't really want her. He wants Dr. Desmond, like every other hot-blooded male in this town. He's using her to find out what I know. *To find the money.* Because somehow, the money is the key to Nick's death. My eyes glance in the rearview mirror, at the crates stacked in the rear seat.

For the second time tonight, I almost feel sorry for Claudia Marton. Almost.

It's not my problem that she never learned not to trust people. I'm surprised though. You would think as a hot-shot reporter she would understand the relationship between greed and territory, and how they blend. There's only so much room at the top, where everything is bigger. The egos, the wallets, the lies. Things get crowded. People are elbowed out. Like Nick. Who will Diane elbow out next? Her husband? The cop? Oliver?

The rubber edges of my tires scrape the curbside outside the big glass doorway leading to the terminal. She's standing next to a rolling bag, her body wrapped in a trench coat, belted at the waist. She takes a long, slow drag of her cigarette, absorbing the nicotine rush, before stomping on it with the tip of her shoe. I pop the lever for the hatch, and she places her bag on top of one of the money crates. With a slam, the hatch closes.

She enters and sits, her perfume tickling my nostrils, familiar and pungent.

She looks at me and grins.

Help has arrived.

"Hello, Mother."

48

CLAUDIA

September 7

My pity party for one was short-lived.

Scribbling my name into the guest book resting next to a beautiful vase of flowers, the ambience in the Willow Bend Long-Term Care Home lobby resonates with a welcoming tone. The place is tidy, the décor a tad outdated, but comfortable. An information desk sits to the left, near a bank of elevators. The woman working at the desk greets me with a pleasant smile.

"Can I help you?"

"Yes. Claudia Marton from *The Finger Lakes Flash*," I say, sliding my business card across the top of the desk. "I am here to speak with Dr. Diane Desmond."

"Do you have an appointment?"

Not exactly.

"I am writing a feature story on her husband's candidacy for State Senate. He informed her I would be stopping by."

All true. But that's not why I'm here.

When my head hit the pillow last night, Stella haunted my slumber.

"I think I deal with my guilt by creating a new situation to feel guilty about."

The prophetic words confessed to Greta at my last therapy session reverberated in my head. How selfish of me to pity myself while I'm alive, free to choose, free to live. Free to do all the things Stella was denied. I caved to the insecurity seeds Lindsay Sutton planted in my head, a projection of her own grief. Greta said it best: I self-sabotage because it's easier than celebrating my truth.

I am not defined by my hair or lack of it. I am a successful journalist, a business owner, a friend, and a sister. I am every bit as attractive as Dr. Diane Desmond. I *am* the hairless head of *The Finger Lakes Flash*.

192

And I owe Peter a truthful conversation. About Stella, my insecurities, and my doubts about him, professionally. Either Peter is working with the Desmonds to gather evidence against them, or he is a man so consumed by grief, he is lost and needs my help.

Stella would approve.

"Floor three, dear. Follow the blue line on the floor to the nurses' station. They can help you from there."

Thanking the woman at the information desk, my finger pushes the up button at the elevator bank. The door to the lift opens and I step inside, hitting button number three.

Emerging on the third floor, my eyes are greeted with blandness, a sea of gray sliced by a thin blue line on the scuffed, tile floor. The stark contrast to the lobby arouses a wariness in me, a similar sensation to the one I experienced the night before last at Lakeview Cemetery. The nurses' station sits a few yards to my left. Dr. Diane Desmond is huddled in deep conversation with a male employee, her back to me. My presence catches his attention, causing the doctor to turn around.

"Claudia, welcome! Roger told me you would be stopping by. I'm sorry I missed you the other day when you were here."

Her comment catches me off guard, but she doesn't give me the chance to correct her.

"This is Ken Preston, our nurse practitioner here at Willow Bend."

"Hello, again," he says, confusing me further.

"Have we met before?" I ask, extending my hand.

"We were so impressed by your bravery at the regatta," Dr. Desmond chirps, dominating the conversation. "Ken, we're going to step into my office for a few minutes, and then I'm heading over to the hospital to check on Mrs. Rossiter."

He nods his head, both to her and to me.

"Nice to see you, again," he says, before turning his attention to the clipboard in his hand.

I nod at him, assuming he's referring to my impromptu speech at the regatta.

"Follow me, Claudia."

Dr. Desmond leads the way down the drab hallway, past a series of open doorways to patient rooms. Her heels click an inpatient tempo, quick and steady, like a woman with places to go. She unlocks her office door, gesturing to step inside. The walls remind me of Oliver Sutton's workspace, adorned with diplomas and licenses encased in fancy frames, but absent a security camera. I glance at the far corners of the room, just to be sure.

"Please, take a seat. I'm sorry I only have a few minutes."

Despite her husband's claims, I didn't expect Dr. Desmond was seriously interested in talking about 9/11 responder deaths. My concern is using these minutes to obtain insight into her relationship, and her motivations.

"I'll make this quick. I need to ask you a couple of questions to round out my feature story on your husband's candidacy."

She smiles, folding her hands, projecting an air of calm and sophistication. Her confidence is reminiscent of the woman I observed at the regatta. Secure in who she is, and her place in life. But does she have a God complex too, the kind justifying shortening people's lives by mercy killing?

"What do you think your husband can offer the constituents of this district that the other candidates cannot?"

She considers my question, poised in her response.

"Roger's track record proves he brings innovation to the masses, always thinking on a broad scale. He did it in biotech, and he has done it as mayor of Romulus. He's worked hard to change mindsets, to adapt with the times, and to encourage people stuck in their ways to embrace technology and modernization for cost efficiency."

My hands scribble her words down in my note pad verbatim, the possible double entendre of their meaning carving an indelible impression.

"What change would you most like to see your husband accomplish?"

My question is her opening. Will she mention death with dignity legislation?

"Well, the same thing everyone in the medical community wants. Health care for all."

"Isn't that more of a federal issue?"

"Access to quality health care is everyone's concern."

"But I asked, specifically, what will your husband change if elected?"

"My role as his wife is to champion the person he is, the kind, caring man who wants to serve on a larger scale. As the candidate, he can answer your question himself."

Dr. Desmond is no fool. She's not going to jeopardize her husband's candidacy by spelling out a controversial agenda. Instead, she'll say a whole lot of nothing.

"How does a couple of your stature balance the power?"

"I beg your pardon?"

"You're both successful, with demanding professions. Does someone become a supporting cast member? Can a relationship sustain two high-powered careers?"

Her eyes narrow into slivers, her patience withering, as her desk phone rings.

"It's a *marriage*. Give and take. I'm afraid I'll have to say thank you and take this call. I also have a patient to check on."

"One final question. I noticed an uptick in the obituaries I post on *The Finger Lakes Flash*. There have been seven patient deaths here at Willow Bend this summer. From a health perspective, is something causing a spike in geriatric fatalities?"

"A larger elderly population. Geriatric medicine is about caring for the unique health needs of the aging, but we all die at some point."

She stands, extending her hand and concluding the interview, exuding control. Shaking her hand, I am unconvinced this meeting accomplished anything of relevance.

As I step toward the door, Dr. Desmond answers her phone, stating her name and title with panache. "Dr. Diane Desmond, how can I help you?" Clutching my notepad, I exit her office. My feet trace the blue line along the floor, and I'm thankful I won't be faking my way through dinner with her tomorrow night.

Maybe I was rash cancelling my dinner plans with Peter tonight. He sent a sad-face emoji response but didn't ask me what came up. Is it too late to cancel my cancellation? As I ponder my dilemma, someone signals for my attention.

"*Psst!*"

The noise filters from behind a semi-closed door to patient room 332. My feet slow down.

"Psst! Hurry! In here!"

I peer at the name plate mounted on the door. Marlene Flynn. Peeking into the room, a woman is seated in a wheelchair, her leg elevated and in a cast.

"Shut the door!"

"Can I help…"

"Sssh! Shut the door! Did you get my message?"

"Ah, should I call a nurse? You have me confused with someone else."

"No, no. There isn't time! Why didn't you stay the other day when you were here?"

"I… I wasn't here."

"I saw you, dear. I've been waiting for you."

"For me? I'm sorry, let me go find a nurse…"

"No! Here, take this!"

The woman leans forward in her wheelchair, extending her arm. She hands me a crumpled piece of paper.

"My grandson left to go back to college. He can't go to the cemetery for me anymore."

The cemetery.

"Take this and go. You'll find the instructions. Hurry! We're running out of time!"

I'm riveted by this revelation.

"You're Seymour?" I whisper.

Marlene cracks a small smile.

"Yes."

49

LINDSAY

September 7

"Are you ready, darling?"

Having Mother around again is great. We rehearsed our plan for tonight. The typical good cop/bad cop interrogation scenario, only with some anxiety medication and chilled wine mixed in. And the smoked trout, of course.

Mother exhales a long puff, flicking the ember ash on her cigarette into the ashtray next to the platter of fish. She's dressed in her black leather pants, a silky, low-cut blouse, and heels. Fancy, considering only Brenda is coming over, but also uncomfortable for a get-away driver escaping with a carload of money.

"Are you sure you want to wear those pants? You've got to go at least a few hundred miles tonight."

"Sweetheart, presentation is *everything*. When I stop for gas, do you want some lonely trucker thinking about getting in the hatch where the money is, or thinking about getting in my pants?"

Point made.

"Okay, you promise to call me when you reach a hotel?"

"Unless I'm otherwise engaged."

"Mother!"

"Darling, relax. Take a joke."

"Not funny."

"You worry too much. Follow the plan. You play the weepy sister-in-law, and I'll press Brenda's buttons. Keep pouring her wine, loosening her up. Once we have what we need, I'm out. Got it?"

Despite myself, a tiny pang of regret gnaws. I may never see Delaney or Melvin again after tonight.

"Lindsay, I mean it. I'm not dilly-dallying around. Make Brenda

197

talk, so I can hit the road. You pack up what you need, and head out tomorrow in Nick's truck. Go to Vegas, or Nashville, someplace fun. Stay away from Florida until we know the coast is clear."

That's the plan. It's a good one. Mother knows men in Florida who are whizzes at setting up secret offshore bank accounts in phony names. The kind where we can hide the money so I can use it for an embryo transfer or to adopt a baby. Mother knows men who can help with that, too. Mother knows a lot of men.

"I won't get to say good-bye to Delaney, and if Brenda is right about Oliver having the affair, and not Nick…"

"*Stop it.* Of course, Nick wasn't cheating on *you*. The affair, the disappearance, his death… none of it ever made sense to me. We'll get Brenda to cough up what she knows, and you can put all this ugliness behind you and start fresh."

"But I'll be leaving him, too. Alone. In the cemetery. Without a goodbye," I say, stepping away from the table and reaching for my purse, which dangles from a hook by the back door. Nick's phone rests in the bag.

"Before you leave, Mother, we need to crack Nick's code," I say, holding up the cellular device. "I'm down to two more chances, and if I'm wrong, we're locked out for good."

Mother gives me a sly smile, blowing a slithery cloud of smoke in my direction.

"Darling, you need to think like men do. Don't use your head."

She chuckles at my deadpan gaze.

"Sweetie, men don't think with their *brains*. They think with another part of their anatomy."

Oh, for the love of God.

"Mother, we don't have much time. What are you trying to say?"

She bites her lip teasingly, and purrs, "Pick a fuck date. Your first, the best, the kinkiest. Whatever. But Nick's code will link to sex."

The doorbell chimes, interrupting my dither.

Mother blows another puff of smoke in my face, stabbing out her cigarette in the ashtray as I stash Nick's phone back in my purse.

"Here we go, baby. Show time."

50
CLAUDIA
September 7

Slamming the car door, my finger presses the automatic lock button, my eyes peering into the side mirror. Seeing no one, I glance in the rearview mirror, double checking for anyone tailing me.

Nothing. Only me, sitting in the parking lot with the crumpled note. A note from Seymour.

Marlene Flynn was insistent that I get out fast, so no one would see us talking. Her words are jumbled in my memory, confusing me. Something about instructions, and her grandson going to the cemetery, and something about seeing me earlier in the week. What did she mean?

Unfolding the note in my hand, I smooth the paper and its deep creases out on top of my leg. Her words are written with an elegant form of penmanship, crafting a pleasant image on the page. It's a striking contrast to the deadly message they contain.

Nick Sutton warned me. He thought they are deliberately killing people, too.

Talk to John Corry at Sutton's Apothecary. He knows about me.

He'll talk to you. Be careful.

Don't let anyone know you're on to them.

My mind races. John Corry. I recognize the name. It was on the employee roster hanging in Oliver Sutton's office! I won't talk to Peter until I find out what John Corry and Nick Sutton discovered at Sutton's Apothecary.

Folding the note into a careful square, I open my purse. The printed posts from Nick Sutton's In Memoriam page are still there. I unfold them, ignoring Lindsay Sutton's statements, and zone in on a different dedication.

> *~No one made me laugh harder. My brother*
> *from another mother. Luv ya buddy!*
> **John Corry,**
> **lifelong friend, employee at Sutton's Apothecary**

A post from Nick's friend and work colleague. His name was on the *Flash* all along. The realization is electrifying, like fireworks illuminating the night sky with bursts of powerful brilliance.

Tomorrow, I will find my new informant, John Corry.

51
LINDSAY
September 7

"Look who's back!"

Mother's greeting as she swings open the front door catches Brenda by surprise. Her mouth falls open, stunned to see Sylvia Kelly in her hot-to-trot black leather pants serving as the welcoming committee.

"Come in, Brenda. Don't let my fabulousness scare you!"

Mother stands back, allowing Brenda entry through the door. Her disdain for Mother's unexpected presence is evident by the way she resets her jaw. She shoves a plateful of appetizers at Mother, regaining her beta bravado.

"Sylvia! Look at your tan! Be careful. Sun damage will age you."

Brenda breezes past Mother, heading in my direction with a magnum of wine. She sets the bottle down and gives me a giant bear hug, squeezing a bit too hard.

"Missed you, Lindsay," she says, and when she pulls back, her eyes alight. "Oh, look at the smoked fish!"

"Yep, last one in the freezer," I say, glancing at Mother.

Brenda plops down at the kitchen table, snagging a cracker and an appetizer fork, the freezer comment failing to register. "Well, liquid happy hour started for me a couple of hours ago. You girls need to catch up." She eyes my mother. "So, Sylvia, we need to talk about your hermit daughter." She digs into the trout, stabbing at it with ferocity. "I think she's ignoring *me*."

Mother slithers into a chair next to Brenda.

"Of course, she is. *I'm* here. Naturally, she's going to spend her time *with me*." Mother puts Brenda in her place without missing a beat. "Lindsay is still in mourning, so I came for a surprise visit. Here girls, let's have some wine and I'll make a toast." She reaches for the corkscrew, tackling the massive bottle of wine. The passive-aggressive war of verbal table tennis between the two assaults my psyche, worrying me a bit. Brenda is a formidable opponent for Mother's acerbic tongue. Time to start playing my part as the good cop.

"I'm sorry, Brenda, but the regatta was a dumpster fire. You got the whole town buzzing. Let's talk about what went down there."

Mother takes her cue.

"Lindsay says you think Oliver has a side dish," she coos, popping the wine cork.

Brenda doesn't flinch.

"No one understands the damage a side dish can cause better than you, right Sylvia?"

Mother smirks, as she pours three glasses of sparkling wine into flutes, unfazed by the zinger. "Who is she? And what could she possibly see in Oliver?"

Brenda's face sags and I wonder if we are playing this wrong. She's in battle mode with Mother, trying to out-sting her, but we need her to talk. I step up my good cop act again.

"Delaney was so upset, Mother. We can't forget about her."

My comment triggers a somberness in the room, resetting the mood. Mother seizes the opportunity, raising her glass and offering a toast.

"Fuck men. Take that however you want to."

Brenda and I burst out laughing, clinking our glasses together. Sensing an opening, I take it.

"What *is* going on with Oliver?"

Brenda sighs, before taking another hefty swig of wine. She sets her glass down, and unloads.

"He's been secretive for months. Even before Nick's death, but now, he's worse. I thought he was throwing himself into work to avoid dealing with his grief," she says, slugging more wine. "But he lied, more than once. He said he was working late. I drove by and either no one was there, or his car was still at the apothecary, but he was gone!"

"How do you know?" Mother asks.

"I spied on him, checking the security cameras. Sometimes, he wasn't there, but his car was in the parking lot."

The question nagging at my core slips out, faster than I intend it to.

"At the regatta, is that why you said he was using other people's cars?"

Brenda plops a cracker loaded with trout into her mouth, shaking her head as she chews. The wait is excruciating for me.

"I cornered a delivery driver in the stock room one day and asked him—what the hell is going on? He said Oliver uses delivery vehicles after hours, and sometimes, there's little gas left in the tank the next day. This started after Nick died." She turns to face me. "But when Nick was alive, Oliver would sneak away during the day, using Nick's truck."

My mind tries to compute the logic behind this arrangement. Taking a company vehicle during the day would interrupt deliveries, and snagging a lift via a ride service could leave a paper trail of clues to whatever Oliver is hiding.

"Where was he going? And why would Nick help him?"

Brenda scrunches her face. "I went back months on the security camera footage. I overheard calls between Ollie and Diane Desmond, setting up meetings. On one of the calls, he assured her he would be careful. There was a pause in the conversation, and then Oliver said Nick would stay quiet—as long as he ponied up cash so you two could try again for a baby."

My gasp causes Brenda to cast her eyes downward, and Mother crosses her arms. The money stashed in the freezer. I have my answer.

Fifty-one thousand dollars to borrow Nick's truck is *beyond* excessive. I gulp, thinking how Nick aided his brother with his infidelity, like I aided Mother, only he negotiated an arrangement where *we* benefitted! Nick was committed… to me, to us, to our dream of having a family. So much so, he helped his brother on the sly but cashed in, ensuring his assistance would guarantee us enough money for another round of IVF. I shudder, wondering if Oliver regretted the deal. Did Nick threaten to expose him? Or did Roger Desmond suspect his wife's cheating and retaliate? Nick wouldn't put me in a position to choose between a baby and worrying about how Oliver's infidelity affected Brenda and Delaney. His secret makes sense, now.

I glance at Mother. Brenda just admitted she found out Nick was helping Oliver betray her. What if *she* confronted Nick?

"That's my money, Lindsay. And Delaney's. It's communal marital assets."

Brenda's legal mumbo jumbo accusation stabs at me, but my backup is ready with a shield.

"You let her think Nick was having an affair, and all this time you knew the truth!" Mother fumes, lighting a cigarette in disgust.

Don't trust other women.

Mother is right. My sister-in-law deceived me for months. She let me marinate in a bath of bewilderment and betrayal. Beta Brenda pulled the ultimate alpha move right under my nose.

"Stuff it, Sylvia. I told her I didn't believe Nick was having an affair."

"It's not Lindsay's fault you can't keep Oliver happy…"

"Did *you* keep your husband happy, Sylvia? He didn't die on top of you!"

"Okay, both of you… stop!" I hiss.

Mother looks like she's ready to leap across the table and strangle Brenda, which won't help me. Brenda is mad about the money. And I knew all along if I could figure out the source of the frozen money packs, it would lead me to Nick's killer.

Brenda sent me to the freezer. I've been suspicious of her since the night I found the cash. But it's significant what she is *not* saying—she didn't discover the car switch because of a large cash discrepancy in the accounting records for the apothecary. So, if Oliver took money from the till to pay Nick for using his truck, he replenished the cash with other funds. Or he paid Nick directly with dirty funds and never touched the cash register. If so, Brenda isn't entitled to a refund.

"Mother, I would like a few minutes alone with Brenda, please."

Mother rises from her seat, her cigarette held at ear level with a glass of wine in the other hand. She glares at Brenda.

"I'll be out back. Scream if she tries to hurt you."

Brenda rolls her eyes and tops off her wine glass and mine, as Mother slams the back door behind her in a huff.

"Lindsay, I am…"

"Did you bring me some pills?"

My question catches her off guard, but she seems relieved, perhaps by the possibility of an exchange. Drugs for cash.

"Yes! I've got my script! You can have as many as you want!"

"Give them to me."

She twists in her seat, fumbling with her purse to retrieve the pills.

"Here. Keep it. Take it all."

I open the cap on the vial, jiggling the pills around. Tipping four into my palm, I pass her two tablets, and say, "Take these with me for old times' sake."

She gulps as I pass her the pills. We each put the medication in our mouths, locking eyes while washing the pills down with more fruity wine. One more double dose won't hurt me. It's just a crutch while I try to figure out if I'm sitting next to my husband's killer.

"Why didn't you tell me the truth about Nick? I was always good to Delaney."

"Yes, Delaney loves you! It's her I'm thinking about. That money belongs to us. If Oliver leaves me…"

I laugh, a guttural outburst, mocking and menacing. Alpha Lindsay is back.

"Oh, c'mon, Brenda! Diane Desmond isn't going to leave her husband for Oliver! And how do I know this money is from legitimate income at the apothecary? What if Oliver is mixed up in something else and he used shady proceeds to pay Nick?"

Her eyes narrow, and her voice drops to a whisper. My suggestion hit its mark.

"I'm not sure Oliver was having an affair. A lot of the drug suppliers are calling the house, asking for him. They say he's not responding to the messages they have left at the apothecary. Something's not right. They said our supply is inconsistent with other pharmacies our size."

She takes another big slug of wine, finishing off her second glass. She pours another, and this time when she speaks, her tone is panicked.

"Even if it's not an affair, something's off. I feel it. What if whatever it is makes Oliver split? I *need* the money, Lindsay. I'm scared."

Brenda's spiraling, as she guzzles more wine. What if she snapped, thinking she would lose everything? Did she kill Nick? What if she discovered Oliver was using Nick's truck before she talked to the delivery driver? She could be lying about when it was that she found out about the vehicle switch. And now she wants the money! I've got to get Mother and the cash cargo on the road. It's too dangerous for her to be here.

As if sensing my thoughts, the backdoor swings open, and Mother returns from the back porch, empty wine glass in hand.

"I heard laughter. Don't leave me out of the party."

"I was telling Brenda, Mother, how ridiculous it is to think a woman like Diane Desmond would leave her husband for Oliver."

Brenda's eyes glare over the rim of her wine glass, an ample dose of fight left in her.

"What's ridiculous is you two pretending lonely women don't screw other women's husbands. Everyone in town knows you're the champion bed bug, Sylvia."

I wince, the truth of the statement biting me more than Mother. She sets her empty wine glass down and places a defiant hand on her hip.

"Lindsay, honey, this party is getting lame. Give me your car keys. I'm going to the yacht club for a drink. Maybe, I'll run into an old friend or two!" She winks at Brenda, before walking to the dining room and grabbing her purse. I follow Mother to the door, our orchestrated paint-by-number ruse working with masterful precision. She'll leave now with the money, and I'll follow tomorrow. Handing her my car keys from the foyer table, I nod, assuring her I'll be okay. Alpha Lindsay has a plan for dealing with beta Brenda.

"Drive safely, Mother."

She grins, blows me a kiss, and walks out the front door.

Brenda pours more wine, her hand trembling on the stem of the wine glass. The alcohol and pills are kicking in.

"Where do we go from here, Lindsay? Are you going to pay me back, so we can be friends again?"

"Were we ever friends? Maybe, if you believe 'the enemy of my enemy is my friend,' cliché. We *both* mistrust other women—*that* sums up the bond between us. You *scolded* me for my post on *The Finger Lakes Flash*, and when I told you about the tracking device, you pretended it didn't matter. Now I know why! You suspected it was Oliver having an affair."

Brenda's eyes look away from me, but I'm not finished.

"Nick died! It doesn't make sense. If he was secretly saving for more IVF, why would he kill himself?" I cry. "He switched cars, and it got him killed! I'm not what or who you should be worrying about. Diane Desmond may not ditch her husband, but she *was* draped all over Oliver at the regatta. What does she want with him?"

Brenda's eyes alight like tiki torches.

"I don't know, but if *she* killed Nick, she might kill Oliver too!"

I blink, several times in succession, my mind tossing around her statement. She's right. Dr. Desmond and her husband have prominent plans, with his last-minute candidacy for State Senate. Melvin mentioned his wife's medication switch. Is it related to the phone calls Brenda received at the house from the pharmaceutical suppliers? What if Nick figured out the Desmonds were involved in something else? Something illegal with Oliver? It would explain why he was paid such an excessive amount. The money is still the key. Nick got paid to keep quiet.

Swallowing the rest of the wine in my glass, the mellow tannins meld with the relaxing effect of the pills I swallowed.

"I don't have your money, Brenda. You can look around for yourself. I'll even show you my bank records."

Lying to her is easy. Mother's plan delivered. My husband loved me. He wanted us to have our own baby. He didn't cheat. The money came from Oliver for a service Nick provided. As far as I'm concerned, the funds are clean or never went through the apothecary cash register in the first place.

If Brenda wants to look around, she can. The phony fish packages in the freezer are wrapped with the paper that had Nick's handwriting on them. I can say I thought they were fish. Put the pedal to the metal, Mother. I'm leaving, too, just as soon as I get Brenda out of here.

"You need to confront Oliver. Tonight. Something's not right. If he wasn't having an affair, some other major secret is going on with Dr. Desmond, especially since he was willing to pay Nick so much money to borrow his truck. If that's what got Nick murdered, you and Delaney might be in danger, too."

Her eyes grow wide as she slams her wine glass down.

"That bitch better not go near my daughter!"

"You should go. Can you drive or should I call an Uber?"

"I'm not waiting for an Uber. You're right, Lindsay! I'm sorry…"

"Don't. You're not sorry. You lied by omission. Your marriage is the failure—*not mine.*"

Mother told me not to trust women, but a teeny-weeny part of me did trust Brenda. She *was* more than my sister-in-law. This wouldn't hurt if that wasn't true. I lost Nick, and now I'm losing her, too.

"Please go."

I turn away, clearing Mother's ashtray from the kitchen table. I stand at the sink, collecting the stubs, my back to Brenda. There's only one thing left to do. Glancing out the kitchen window, the porch light illuminates Nick's truck, parked in the back on one of the cement slabs. My memory flashes to the day we toured this property, remembering Nick's joy seeing the back entrance and the extra parking spaces.

Nick was right.

This is *perfect.*

Mother's words echo in my head.

"Nick's code will link to sex."

The date was April tenth—we became proud owners of this house and received the key. We made love feverishly for days, christening every room. Our very own love shack.

As Brenda exits through the front door, I pull Nick's cell phone from my purse. I press four numbers on the glass face, entering a passcode, hoping I'm not wrong.

THE FINGER LAKES FLASH

Your online snapshot capturing the local news you need to know.
September 8

Breaking News: The Romulus Police Department is responding to reports of a woman's body found floating early this morning in Cayuga Lake. Fishermen reported the discovery near Weston's Boat Launch. Access to the lake via this launch site is suspended. The woman's identity has not been released, pending notification of family members. *Story developing...*

PART III
The Reveal

52

LINDSAY
September 8

The kiss of early morning sunshine breathes sweaty and hot through the windshield of Nick's truck. Squinting between the crusty clumps of yesterday's mascara, I sit up, leaning back against the headrest. A stitch in my neck shoots a pain signal to my throbbing head, compounding the pangs of my hangover, which pierce like a dart.

Rubbing my eyes with the heels of my palms, the lacerations in my flesh sting.

Small cuts and smeared, dried blood settle into the crooks of the jagged life-line creases on each hand. My tongue sweeps across my teeth, a chalky film coating my gums, while an empty wine bottle rests on the floorboard by the passenger seat. I stare at my damaged palms, confused about my surroundings and the state of my body.

A panoramic view of gravestones sits on the other side of the windshield, under a gorgeous canopy of blue sky. The Sutton family plots occupy enviable landscape within Lakeview Cemetery. This is where Nick is now, and somehow, I got here, too.

My body aches as I twist in my seat, stretching uncomfortably. I don't remember driving here, and I don't understand why my hands are scraped and cut. I glance in the rearview mirror, my reflection a sobering wake-up call. Tear-stained cheeks with dried rivulets of yesterday's makeup offset a deep red indentation where my forehead camped against the steering wheel for the night. Based upon the looks of it, passing out maybe saved me from myself. My body did not respond well to the dangerous mix of booze, Benzos, and Brenda's betrayal. If I didn't die from an accidental overdose, driving in such an intoxicated state could have easily taken care of business, too. I grip the steering wheel, steadying myself, trying to grasp the sequence of events.

The window. I remember staring out of the kitchen window, wanting Brenda to leave, so I could punch a code into Nick's phone and come here to say goodbye to him. I entered the date that we bought the house on the cellular keypad, thinking it would unlock. It didn't.

Brenda! She was going to confront Oliver. Has she called? What about Mother? Oh God, what if Mother called and I didn't answer? She'll worry, maybe even turn around and come back. How far out of town did she make it last night?

My purse sits on the passenger seat, and I snag it, fumbling for my cell phone. It's dead. Damn. I start the truck, and plug the phone into the charger, waiting for some juice and signal bars. If I'm this messed up, Brenda's probably worse off. She sucked wine down last night like a turkey basting itself, wallowing in a salty brine of her own making. All this time, she lied by omission, corrupting my memory of Nick with deliberate purpose. She was never my friend.

And now, more than ever, I want one. I want another woman I can cry to, someone to hug me and tell me all the feelings and thoughts I'm having about missing Nick are normal. My husband loved me. Only me. He wanted our happily-ever-after, with another embryo transfer and the possibility of a baby. *A future.* With my stinging scrapes, swollen eyes, and pounding headache, I want what Mother said I would never need. I want a girlfriend, one who understands lost loves and fractured dreams and unborn babies. Not an alpha or a beta, but an equal.

Women are not your friends.

My entire adult life I followed Mother's edict, believing she had my best interests at heart, but it left me feeling abandoned, like the night of the regatta when I lay crumpled on a dirty bathroom floor. What if the *Flash* lady did mean well when she lent me her wig? I wasn't nice to her at the wine bar, and not just because I snagged her bottle of anxiety meds. My insinuations about her boyfriend's true motivations were harsh, slicing at her insecurities on a day she confessed had been challenging for her. What if she does believe in me and wants the real story? In a sick way, she's almost worse off than I am, because even if I'm wrong about the cop boyfriend using her, he's still dirty for covering up Nick's murder. A bad guy is worse than no guy. What if she is my equal, another single woman struggling with panic attacks and anxiety, in desperate need of a friend?

My phone screen still bears the shattered cracks from tumbling to the cement floor in the basement when sweet Melvin surprised me with an ice cream treat visit. I promised him I'd look for paperwork about Fran, but with Mother coming and all the cleaning I had to do, I didn't do it. He'll think I bailed on him, that our new friendship didn't matter. Distrusting women has made me ill-prepared for maintaining friendships of any kind, poisoning me against the world. But now, with Mother on the road and Nick buried deep in the ground, life's loneliness is a different kind of enemy.

I am not Mother. I don't want to string my days with nights filled next to empty cocktail glasses and random men. I'm still the girl that ate gummy bears from a wayside vending machine while smushed in a bucket seat, dreaming of a big soap opera romance—one combining the innocence of a nursery rhyme with the grandeur of a fairytale, and ending with the happily-ever-after of true love and a baby carriage. Only now, I want friends along for the ride, too.

Staring at Nick's gravestone, I don't remember what I said to him last night. How did my hands get like this? So many questions.

My phone makes a dinging noise, registering a signal and a charge. Hot damn, back in business. Tapping in my code, the icons for the various applications light up the screen. The voicemail box is empty. No calls.

I scroll to the left, to the text message box. A red, number one on the app indicates a single message awaits me. I tap on the icon.

"Change of plans, darling."

Slumping against the headrest, I curse my stupidity.

During my slumber in the graveyard, Mother and her leather leggings ditched the highway and the hotel.

Damn.

Mother is the one with the pants problem.

53
CLAUDIA
September 8

Felicia's calendar reminder for giving me a ring is right on schedule. I anticipated the call with the anniversary of the 9/11 attacks this week. Despite my preoccupation with locating John Corry, hearing my sister's voice is welcoming.

"How are you doing, Claudia?"

Speak the truth.

"I had a panic attack the other day at the attorney's office, the one Stella sent me to."

Felicia's sharp intake of breath radiates through the telephone, pinging her predictable knee jerk reaction.

"See, you should come here, be around family…"

"No."

My abruptness startles her, but I'm quick to elaborate.

"I met with the attorney to discuss preparing my estate. I'm researching death with dignity legislation, and I want you and Bruce to understand this may influence where I live in the future and how things… um… are handled."

"Death with dignity? Are you dying?" Her voice teeters between a wail and a scoff.

"We're all dying, Felicia. And, given my exposure to the toxins, I need to plan, and I need you to *listen*."

She grows quiet.

"Look, every year at this time, people hang their flags, and they post their social media platitudes with thoughts and prayers and colorful hearts, but the truth is more and more of us exposed are getting sick. We're dying. *This is happening*."

The stillness of the silence on the other end of the phone empowers me.

"I know you love me and think a weekend at the ballgame with the girls will make me feel better, but it's not like that, Felicia."

The familiar clutch in my chest tugs, prompting me to spit out my thoughts while I'm still able to breathe.

"This is something we need to plan for. This isn't going away. And, I'm going to have some bad days, and they're not all going to fall around September. This has *changed* me. I'm learning to accept it. I need you to do the same."

A beat passes before her voice comes out in a quiet whisper.

"What can I do?"

The sound of those four little words is better than any hug. For once, my sister lets go of her linear thoughts, her predictable routines, and stops trying to fix a problem she knows nothing about with a preconceived, generic solution. The relief of not having to fight her again and not being on the receiving end of a snippy comment crumbles the unspoken barrier in our communication, opening an avenue for truth.

"Thank you for asking. I'm planning a follow-up visit in a few weeks with the attorney, and once I learn all my options, I want us to talk. Maybe in a neutral location, like a girls' weekend at the beach or something."

"I'd love to go to the beach together. Just you and me."

Her voice sounds a little weepy and my tear ducts are firing, so it's best to stop while we're ahead.

"I'll research it, and we'll talk again."

"Sounds good."

"Love to Bruce and the girls."

My hand swipes at my eyes, and I inhale a few deep breaths, before refocusing my thoughts on my computer screen. Finding my potential new informant John Corry is key to understanding the Wozilfin and the dangers at Willow Bend Long-Term Care Home.

As I stare at an online photograph of John Corry's home, the *Flash's* press release email box pings with a message from the Romulus Police Department. I shuttle my cursor to the email box, enlarging the new notification full screen. As my eyes read the words, a startled cry escapes my lips.

I gulp, absorbing the news contained in the press release.

This changes everything.

Well, almost everything. Finding John Corry is more crucial than ever.

THE FINGER LAKES FLASH

Your online snapshot capturing the local news you need to know.
September 8

Breaking News: A woman's body pulled from Cayuga Lake this morning near Weston's Boat Launch has been identified as Dr. Diane Desmond, age 44, of Romulus, according to police. Desmond is survived by her husband, Roger Desmond, mayor of Romulus. An autopsy is pending. The Romulus Police Department is expected to hold a press conference tomorrow, once the autopsy results are complete.

The mayor's office has not responded to requests for a statement.
Story developing...

Romulus Police Interview Transcript
Subject: Roger Desmond

Date: 09/08

Detective Klink: State your name for the record please.

Roger Desmond: Roger Desmond.

Detective Klink: What is your association with the victim?

Roger Desmond: She was my wife.

Detective Klink: How long were you married?

Roger Desmond:16 years.

Detective Klink: When did you last see your wife?

Roger Desmond: Friday morning, before we each left for work.

Detective Klink: Anything abnormal that morning?

Roger Desmond: Not really. She had early rounds at the hospital, then planned to go to Willow Bend to see her patients there. The editor of *The Finger Lakes Flash* stopped by to interview her for a feature story about my candidacy for State Senate. She was nervous about that.

Detective Klink: Why?

Roger Desmond: This editor, Claudia Marton, interviewed me earlier in the week. She wanted to know the pros and cons of a marriage involving two people with successful careers. She asked a lot of questions about our security details, too. Her friend, Officer Peter Graham, was considering working for me in that capacity. Peter was supposed to join us for dinner at our home tonight. Ms. Marton was invited, too, but she declined, citing a professional conflict of interest.

Detective Klink: Did you have any security for your wife?

Roger Desmond: We were in early discussions about it, but there was not a security detail in place, obviously, or she wouldn't have been murdered!

Detective Klink: Why were you considering security?

Roger Desmond: We were a prominent couple. People either loved us or hated us.

Detective Klink: Why?

Roger Desmond: Jealousy, I guess. My wife was an accomplished woman, attractive, intelligent. The whole package.

Detective Klink: Any idea who would want to stab your wife multiple times and throw her body in the lake?

Roger Desmond: At the regatta, Brenda Sutton made threatening statements toward my wife. You have the complaint I filed against her. There were hundreds of witnesses to her behavior.

Detective Klink: Why did Brenda Sutton threaten your wife?

Roger Desmond: She thought my wife was too chummy with her husband, Oliver Sutton. Diane and Oliver did business together at Willow Bend. Sutton's Apothecary has the contract to fill all the prescriptions for patients at the facility.

Detective Klink: Any possibility their relationship went beyond the business framework?

Roger Desmond: What are you asking?

Detective Klink: Was your wife having an affair?

Roger Desmond: Maybe. I don't know.

Detective Klink: With Oliver Sutton?

Roger Desmond: Possibly, but there may be others.

Detective Klink: Who else?

Roger Desmond: I don't have proof...
Detective Klink: Your wife is dead.
Roger Desmond: I am painfully aware of that.
Detective Klink: An affair would generate a
        lot of bad publicity, wouldn't it?
Roger Desmond: What are you implying?
Detective Klink: Bad publicity could sink a poli-
        tical campaign. Especially one built on
        family values.
Roger Desmond: What is your question?
Detective Klink: Where were you last night
        after eight?
Roger Desmond: Having a drink at the yacht club
        with an old friend.
Detective Klink: Who's the friend? And what did
        you do after you left the yacht club?
Roger Desmond: I don't understand. Am I under
        suspicion?
Detective Klink: Were you having an affair,
        Mr. Mayor?
Roger Desmond: Why so many personal questions?
Detective Klink: You're being evasive. Did you
        kill your wife because she was having
        an affair? Or because *you* are having
        an affair?
Roger Desmond: I would like to speak to my
        attorney.

THE FINGER LAKES FLASH

Your online snapshot capturing the local news you need to know.
September 9

Prominent Physician Murdered

Breaking News: An autopsy conducted by the Seneca County medical examiner has determined Dr. Diane Desmond died due to excessive loss of blood, a result of multiple stab wounds to her upper torso and neck. Local fishermen discovered her body early Saturday morning in Cayuga Lake. The Romulus Police Department is asking anyone with information to contact the department.

Dr. Desmond was married to Romulus Mayor Roger Desmond at the time of her death. The following statement has been released by the mayor's office:

"It is with tremendous sadness that we mourn the loss of such a generous and bright light. Dr. Diane Desmond was many things: wife, physician, philanthropist, friend. She always looked for new ways to help people. In lieu of flowers, donations in her memory may be made to The Finger Lakes Food Pantry & Homeless Shelter."

Mayor Roger Desmond announced his independent candidacy for the 54th State Senate District seat last week. The mayor's spokesperson advises the mayor has suspended his campaign.

54
LINDSAY
September 9

She's dead.

The carcass of trout lay splayed on the platter in the center of the kitchen table, dry and stinky from sitting out all night. Small, white herringbones protrude from the flesh-colored fish, a macabre parallel to the breaking news on *The Finger Lakes Flash*.

This is a killer mindfuck.

I reread the article on the cracked face of my cell phone, caught in a spiral of surreal disbelief. For months, my valves pumped venom through my veins anytime I thought of sexy Diane, remembering her hair blowing in the breeze as she climbed the front steps to the remote cabin in the woods. The image of her, pasted in memory, next to the one of Nick's truck. My anger fused the two, melding them, with hot contempt and hatred. But now, knowing what I now know, a chill curdles through my bloodstream, popping goose flesh on my arms and causing tremors in my hands—the same hands with unexplained cuts and scrapes.

What did I do?

The black hole of time resulting from my wine and pill inebriation, coupled with my injuries, scares me to death, but mulling it over only makes me want another double dose of medication. I'm still jump-out-of-my-skin-edgy and one dosage isn't strong enough. That's a big problem, on top of all my other problems. Mother is still missing in action, too. What did she mean by a change of plans? Where is she? Why won't she answer my calls?

Diane Desmond's murder changes everything. I can't vanish now, for heaven's sake. Disappearing from town immediately after a murder is like a face tattoo—noticeable, not pretty, and indelibly, a big mistake.

No, the best way to duck this is to make-like-a-duck. Paddle like

223

hell when no one is looking but stay calm on the surface when they are. The police can't ignore this murder. They'll be sniffing around soon, especially after Brenda's behavior at the regatta. My eyes blink, remembering the words she spewed here at the kitchen table:

"That bitch better not go near my daughter!"

The police will retrace her steps, building a timeline, like they do on *Dateline*. They'll learn she came here, drank with me, and Mother. They'll ask why Mother was here. Brenda will tell them I took her anxiety pills. The police will ask about my hands.

Oh, God.

Paddle, paddle, paddle. I promised Melvin I would look for paperwork about Fran. Maybe there's something there we can use. Whatever Oliver did with Diane at the cabin cost Nick his life, and somehow, I think the answer rests in fine print rather than on the sheets.

Unless the answer is in his phone. There must be *something* important there. What code did Nick use? I have one chance left. If I'm wrong, the device will disable—a consequence laced with a shitty stench, more for the potential loss of helpful information than because the phone was rescued from a toilet tank.

The filing cabinet in the corner of the spare bedroom stands shoulder height, with a hidden dent on the side flanking the wall. I tug at the top drawer. It creaks as it slides along the tracking. Nick created file folders for everything. Every instruction manual, every bill, every rebate. The thought normally would make me sad, remembering how I used to joke about marrying a warranty king. But with his term of service cut short, probably by the same desperate killer who attacked Diane, I can't waste time. The killer may come for me, too.

My fingers strum the file tabs, looking for anything related to Fran's long-term care at Willow Bend. Seeing nothing but house-related items, I close the drawer and move to the next one. About a third of the way back, my efforts are rewarded. The clear plastic tab on a file folder contains Nick's chicken scratched label: MOM'S EOB.

Fran's Explanation of Benefits insurance papers. Bingo. Pulling the thick folder from the drawer, I glance at my cell phone.

Still no word from Mother.

An explanation from her about her whereabouts last night would benefit me now, too.

Romulus Police Interview Transcript

Subject: Kenneth "Ken" Preston

Date: 09/09

Detective Klink: State your name for the record, please.

Kenneth Preston: Kenneth Preston.

Detective Klink: What is your association with the victim?

Kenneth Preston: She was the medical director at Willow Bend Long-Term Care Home. I work as a nurse practitioner there. We've worked together for several years.

Detective Klink: When did you last see the victim?

Kenneth Preston: Friday afternoon. She left work around 3:00 p.m. She said she was going to the hospital to check on a patient, Beverly Rossiter.

Detective Klink: Do you know if she made it to the hospital?

Kenneth Preston: No.

Detective Klink: Anything unusual about the victim's behavior on Friday?

Kenneth Preston: She seemed irritated by Claudia Marton, the lady who runs *The Finger Lakes Flash*. Dr. Desmond agreed to give an interview, to support her husband's candidacy for State Senate, but she said Ms. Marton attacked her marriage.

Detective Klink: How so?

Kenneth Preston: She didn't elaborate. Dr. Desmond and I were more confused as to why Ms. Marton was lying.

Detective Klink: Lying about what?

Kenneth Preston: Claudia Marton came to Willow Bend earlier in the week. I saw her and so did a patient by the name of Marlene Flynn. She exited another patient's room. I said to Ms. Marton on Friday. "Hello, again." She pretended like she hadn't been to Willow Bend earlier in the week. But I brought you the entrance logbook. She signed in on Wednesday and on Friday. You can see it there for yourself.

Detective Klink: Let the record reflect that Mr. Preston has provided an entrance logbook as evidence, which I am labeling as KP #1. Mr. Preston, which patient room did you see Ms. Marton exit from earlier in the week?

Kenneth Preston: I saw her leave Francine Sutton's room. Mrs. Flynn saw it too, as I mentioned to you before.

Detective Klink: Why would Ms. Marton visit Francine Sutton's room and deny it?

Kenneth Preston: I don't know. Maybe because of Mrs. Sutton's daughter-in-law?

Detective Klink: Brenda Sutton?

Kenneth Preston: No, the other one. Lindsay Sutton.

Detective Klink: What does Lindsay Sutton have to do with this?

Kenneth Preston: She thinks her husband was having an affair with Dr. Desmond before he died a few months ago. She told me Dr. Desmond's bedside manner extended beyond Willow Bend. Oh, and she made those comments on *The Finger Lakes Flash*, too.

Detective Klink: What comments?

Kenneth Preston: On her husband's In Memoriam page. Everybody in town was talking about it. You'll want to check those out.

55

CLAUDIA

September 9

Popping a salty French fry into my mouth, its greasy goodness activates my taste buds. I'm camped in the McDonald's parking lot on surveillance, munching on my food while spying on the comings and goings across the street.

Waiting for John Corry's emergence from Sutton's Apothecary.

My visor is flipped down, the windshield lined with protective tinting. Perfect for semi-concealment. Corry's workday should end soon. I'll follow him home, away from the apothecary and prying eyes. I wonder if he's as spooked as I am.

Diane Desmond's death is a game changer. I texted Peter and left voice mail messages, but he's gone radio silent. Dead air, as we used to say when I worked on television. All comments to the press come from the Romulus police chief, a standard and predictable control over the information released, designed to protect the integrity of the investigation and the eventual prosecution of a murderer. This is not the silence troubling me.

Peter knew I planned to meet with Diane Desmond for an interview. He knows I'm suspicious of Nick Sutton's death and the drug Wozilfin. The Desmonds invited us to eat at their home Saturday night and he still planned to go, the offer of security detail employment now ominous in the wake of Dr. Desmond's death. Whom did she need protection from?

Reaching into the food bag for a napkin, I scan the cars in the parking lot across the street. A fleet of delivery vehicles are parked at the side of the building, each car adorned with the Sutton's Apothecary's logo. It strikes me as curious that the apothecary does not have a drive-thru window like most chain pharmacies do. A woman dressed in a white technician's smock emerges from the apothecary, her purse strap hitched over her shoulder. She enters a compact car, and a moment later, backs

227

out of the parking space, exiting the premises. Another woman leaves the building with a shopping bag in her hand. She, in turn, enters another car parked in the lot.

Unable to find a napkin, I scourge in my purse for a tissue to wipe my oily fingers. Wallet, sunglasses, breath mints, brush, and lipstick. No tissues. But, more alarming, no anxiety medication.

Where are my pills?

My mind mentally retraces my steps over the past few days. I took a pill on Thursday, at the wine bar, and put the bottle in my purse when I pulled out the sheet with Lindsay's memorial posting. But on Friday, I don't remember seeing the bottle when I stashed Marlene's note and reviewed the posts again for John Corry's statement, my focus consumed by the Seymour reveal.

DO NOT TRUST LINDSAY SUTTON.

Either I'm loony, or Lindsay Sutton used her loon call story as a decoy and stole my anxiety medication. What if my video stalker *is* right about her? I swear under my breath, as two men exit the front door of Sutton's Apothecary. The taller of the two locks the front entrance door, and they bid each other good-bye.

Oliver Sutton and John Corry.

I refocus my gaze on surveillance, forgetting temporarily about the missing medication. The pair walk to their cars. Suddenly, Oliver motions back toward the apothecary building and waves at Corry. Corry nods his head and enters his car.

My hand cranks the ignition, prepared to follow John Corry home. As he puts his car in reverse, Oliver glances over his shoulder, watching him. He's waiting for him to leave, I muse. Why? What doesn't he want him to see?

My internet printouts of John Corry's home lay on the passenger seat. I can still do a knock-and-talk with him later. But now, Oliver Sutton's furtive actions pique my interest.

He's the one I want to follow.

Oliver walks back to the front entrance and stands there, fumbling with his keys. He eyes Corry's car as it departs the lot. Once the vehicle is gone, he strides from the doorway to the side of the building, plucking Sutton's Apothecary's placard from one of the delivery vehicles. Oliver tosses it into the trunk of the car and enters the driver's side, starting the ignition. The car begins backing out of the parking space.

My memory flashes to the phone call with Peter, when he mentioned the placard found miles from Nick Sutton's delivery vehicle. Why isn't Oliver driving his own car?

I ease out of the McDonald's lot on to the roadway, a healthy two-car distance behind Oliver Sutton. He drives at the speed limit, breaking for a yellow light when most would gun the engine. When the light changes, he resumes his pace, showing no indication he's aware of his tail. We pass multiple retail businesses and fast-food restaurants with prominent marquees before his rear right taillight signals a turn.

Slowing, he proceeds down the new street, while another car sandwiched between us turns as well, ensuring a one-car buffer. My hands grip the steering wheel, an idea dawning on me.

I know where he's going—a place he doesn't want to advertise his presence. Removing the placard makes sense now.

Three blocks later, Oliver Sutton pulls into the parking lot of the Romulus Police Department, next to a squad car.

Peter is leaning against the driver's side door, waiting for him.

Romulus Police Interview Transcript
Subject: Brenda Sutton

Date: 09/09

Detective Klink: State your name for the record, please.

Brenda Sutton: Brenda Hawthorne Sutton.

Detective Klink: What is your association with the victim?

Brenda Sutton: I don't have one.

Detective Klink: You were questioned the night of the regatta for making threatening statements directed at Dr. Diane Desmond, correct?

Brenda Sutton: The whole thing was blown out of proportion.

Detective Klink: I have the report here. Let the record reflect that I am referring to RPD Report #3489. Multiple witnesses at the yacht club reported hearing you say, "If she comes near you again, she'll pay for it."

Brenda Sutton: I don't remember.

Detective Klink: You don't remember?

Brenda Sutton: I had a lot to drink. Every winery in the Finger Lakes shows up with sample pours so people bid on their auction items and buy tickets for the raffle baskets. It's a fundraiser sponsored by local businesses, and most are wineries! Half this town gets sloshed the night of the regatta.

Detective Klink: Was Diane Desmond having an affair?

Brenda Sutton: That's what people are saying.

Detective Klink: People like you?

Brenda Sutton: She had her hands and arms draped all over my husband at the regatta and a room full of witnesses saw that, too. I didn't like it. I asked her to stop and when she didn't, the alcohol got the best of me. `

Detective Klink: So, you don't know if she was having an affair?

Brenda Sutton: I didn't say that.

Detective Klink: What are you saying?

Brenda Sutton: My husband supplies pharmaceuticals for Willow Bend Long-Term Care Home. Dr. Desmond was the medical director there. They worked together, but no wife wants a business associate putting their hands on her husband. Why don't you ask my sister-in-law, Lindsay Sutton, this question?

Detective Klink: Should I?

Brenda Sutton: She thought her husband, Nick, was having an affair with Diane Desmond. She even posted about it on the In Memoriam page of *The Finger Lakes Flash*. And what do you know? Nick Sutton is dead now, too.

Detective Klink: What are you implying?

Brenda Sutton: You heard me. `

Detective Klink: Ms. Sutton, where were you on Friday night?

Brenda Sutton: At Lindsay Sutton's house.

Detective Klink: Who else was there?

Brenda Sutton: My sister-in-law, Lindsay Sutton, and her mother, Sylvia Kelly.

Detective Klink: What time did you arrive and what time did you leave?

Brenda Sutton: I arrived around 6:30 p.m., and left, maybe an hour later.

Detective Klink: You left around 7:30 p.m., then?

Brenda Sutton: Approximately, yes. We had a

disagreement, and I left. I went home and waited for my daughter and husband to return. They were at the high school football game.

Detective Klink: What was the disagreement about?

Brenda Sutton: The subject of Nick Sutton having an affair came up. Lindsay's mother got all huffy and left before I did. What a hypocrite.

Detective Klink: Why do you say that?

Brenda Sutton: Look, if you burn a bridge in this town, people will still smell smoke twenty years later.

Detective Klink: I'm not sure I follow…

Brenda Sutton: Ask around. Sylvia Kelly slept with every stray cat in this town. And nobody has forgotten the damage she caused to the O'Reilly family.

Detective Klink: What do you mean?

Brenda Sutton: Seamus O'Reilly was a drunk, with a wandering eye and a temper. But he was sweet on Sylvia, and everyone in town knew it. They carried on in front of everyone, not caring one bit about Seamus' wife, Eileen, or his six red-headed kids. Well, there's a limit to how much public humiliation and shame a woman can take. Eileen O'Reilly tied an anchor to her neck and jumped from the bridge at the south end of Seneca Lake, near the entrance channel to Montour Falls. Now, Seamus had to look those children in the eye for the rest of his life, a punishment in a way. But Sylvia Kelly? Ha. There was no punishment for her. She just moved on to the next straying cat.

Detective Klink: I don't see how this is relevant…

Brenda Sutton: Oh, good grief. No wonder people

think their tax dollars aren't working for them. Let me spell it out for you, Sherlock. Lindsay Sutton lived in the shadow of her mother's shameful reputation all her life. That's a lot for a kid to take on. Add to that she thought her husband was having an affair with Dr. Diane Desmond. `

Detective Klink: Are you saying...

Brenda Sutton: I'm saying a woman can only take so much public embarrassment and shame. Lindsay yelled at Mayor Desmond at the regatta, "You got the wrong guy!" That was designed to deflect and distract. Nick Sutton ended up dead at Buttermilk Creek. Diane Desmond's body was pulled from Cayuga Lake. Do the math.

56
LINDSAY
September 9

"Where are you?"

The question flies from my mouth, laced with a heavy, accusatory tone. I don't even say hello. It's about time Mother returned my calls.

"Darling, relax. I'm *fine*. The money is *fine*. I thought, why come all this way here and not stop in at the yacht club for old times' sake?"

I want to scream, like a frustrated parent who catches their teenager sneaking out of the house at night and won't say where they're going or who they're planning to see. Mother never left town, and she didn't clue me in.

"Mother, there are fifty-one thousand reasons why not packed in my car. There's the plan *you* dreamed up and *I* agreed to, which you nixed without telling me, and, on top of everything else, Dr. Desmond was murdered!"

"Shocking, isn't it, darling? I saw the story on *The Finger Lakes Flash*."

"Mother, why didn't you stick to the plan?"

"I told you…"

"I don't have time for bullshit! This murder changes everything. I can't leave now. It would look too suspicious!"

For once, she takes a pause, my statement sinking in.

"I didn't think of that."

Her words thud, striking my psyche with the possibility of a sinister meaning.

"What are you saying? Mother, what did you *do* on Friday night?"

"I went for a drink at the yacht club. Dr. Desmond's husband was there, as a matter of fact. He bought me a cocktail."

A yelp escapes my mouth.

"You were drinking with *the murder victim's husband?*" I say, flabbergasted.

"Darling, you underestimate my charms. *Of course*, I took the opportunity to talk with him, to try to smooth things out after you yelled at him at the regatta. I wanted to find out if he had any relevant information. And let's face it, sweetie, no one can read men like I can. It's amazing what a little cleavage, a throaty laugh or two, and some direct eye contact…"

"Wait—what? What did you say? What did you do? *Did you sleep with him?*"

"What are *you* saying, darling? Look, if Diane was screwing Oliver, the mayor should be allowed to have a little fun in the sack, too. And who better to have a fantastic time with, than moi?"

"He might have killed Nick!" I snap, furious with her.

"It was two hours out of his life, and I thought pillow talk might reveal something that could help us. He went home. I stayed at the motel until morning to be discreet. I always have your best interests in mind…"

"No! No, you don't."

The words bubble up, uncorked and uncontained, after a lifetime of fermentation. I suffered because of Mother's lack of scruples and her warped views on people and relationships. The whispers, the guarded looks. "That's Sylvia Kelly's daughter" carried a river of insinuation and a guilt-by-association attachment in its wake, every time it was uttered. And, instead of complaining, I complied—complicit to Mother's duplicity, because hers was the only love I knew until I had Nick. But it's wrong. It's all so wrong.

"Mother, I don't have any friends because of you. Because of your rules, your little 'gems.' Your reputation. Your affairs. And now, I'm all alone, and it's no fun."

"You're not alone, darling. You have me…"

"No, Mother. I don't. You have your life in Florida. This is payback time. Take the money and do what I say. When things settle down, I'm leaving here. Going away, somewhere I can have my own identity, where I'm not so-and-so's daughter or wife. I want friends, Mother, and a baby. I want playdates with other families, and someday, another man to love. I don't want to follow your rules anymore. I love you, but I need you to play by *my* rules, now. Take the money and put it somewhere safe, so I can use it later for a baby. *Please.*"

A silence hangs between us, a temporary stonewall manipulation until she ends the call, without responding to me at all. For the first time in our relationship, I have the last word. Did she listen? I hope so.

The next step is up to Mother.

Romulus Police Interview Transcript
Subject: Oliver Sutton

Date: 09/09

Detective Klink: State your name for the record, please.

Oliver Sutton: My name is Oliver Sutton.

Detective Klink: What is your association with the victim?

Oliver Sutton: We were business associates. Dr. Desmond was the Medical Director at Willow Bend Long-Term Care Home. I am the owner and pharmacist-in-charge at my family's business, Sutton's Apothecary. We have a contract with Willow Bend to supply pharmaceuticals to the facility and to its patients.

Detective Klink: Can you elaborate on the terms of the contract?

Oliver Sutton: Sure. It's a binding, five-year contract as the sole supplier of pharmaceuticals to the facility, as well as to its patients. There are some pharmaceuticals the facility keeps on hand for emergent situations, and we fill the individual patients' prescriptions.

Detective Klink: What if the patient doesn't want Sutton's Apothecary to fill his or her prescriptions? What if the patient wants to use another pharmacy or apothecary?

Oliver Sutton: That's prohibited. When the patient signs a contract entering Willow Bend Long-Term Care Home, they agree to have all prescriptions filled by Sutton's

> Apothecary. Exclusive pharmaceutical contracts for patients in long-term care facilities or pain management programs are becoming quite common. It helps mitigate the chance of the patient filling multiple prescriptions for drugs with highly addictive properties, such as painkillers or stimulants, at multiple pharmacies at the same time.

Detective Klink: How would you describe your working relationship with Dr. Desmond?

Oliver Sutton: Cordial.

Detective Klink: Did you have a personal relationship, as well?

Oliver Sutton: We were friendly.

Detective Klink: Did you socialize outside of work?

Oliver Sutton: We attended many of the same charity events.

Detective Klink: Anything beyond that?

Oliver Sutton: What are you implying?

Detective Klink: Your wife put on quite a show at the regatta, so I need to ask… Were you engaged in an extramarital affair with Dr. Desmond?

Oliver Sutton: That's quite a jump to make over some drunken comments.

Detective Klink: I'm investigating the murder of the mayor's wife. I'm not leaving any stone unturned, so if you were having an affair, I will find out about it. And, if you lie to me today, I promise you Mr. Sutton, I will request the district attorney charge you with obstruction of justice.

Oliver Sutton: Ah, yes. Okay. Um, yes, yes, I was. We would meet about once a week at rental cabins.

Detective Klink: Very well, but Mr. Sutton, let me

caution you. I have little patience for the 'magic question game.' This is a homicide investigation. You need to be forthcoming and provide me with everything you know about Dr. Desmond. I am not here to pull teeth. You have a civic obligation to volunteer any information that may be pertinent regarding the activities and whereabouts of Dr. Desmond in the recent days preceding her death. There is a murderer in our community. Do you understand?

Oliver Sutton: Yes.

Detective Klink: Now, who knew about your affair?

Oliver Sutton: My brother knew before his death. My wife suspects it. So does Dr. Desmond's husband.

Detective Klink: How do you know Roger Desmond knew about it?

Oliver Sutton: Diane told me her husband suspected our affair, and he was hiring a security detail to keep tabs on her while he ramped up his campaign for State Senate. She resented it.

Detective Klink: Are you saying the mayor may have killed his wife out of jealousy?

Oliver Sutton: I didn't say anything of the sort.

Detective Klink: Where were you last Friday evening?

Oliver Sutton: I was at the high school football game with my daughter, Delaney. I was working at the Booster's fundraising booth.

Detective Klink: I have a report that was filed recently against your wife, Brenda Sutton, by Romulus Mayor Roger Desmond. Let the record reflect that I am referring to RPD Report #3489. Are you familiar with this report?

Oliver Sutton: I am.
Detective Klink: As I said, your wife made a scene
          at the regatta. Multiple witnesses heard
          her say, "At least she's focused on *her* hus-
          band, now" and "If she comes near you
          again, she'll pay for it." Was your wife
          calling Dr. Desmond out for the affair?
Oliver Sutton: You need to ask her.
Detective Klink: You are unhappily married,
          Mr. Sutton?
Oliver Sutton: All marriages have their ups
          and downs.
Detective Klink: That's not what I asked.
Oliver Sutton: I am married. Do we fight? Yes.
          All couples do. Including the Desmonds.
          Dr. Desmond and I were consenting adults.
          It doesn't mean we intended to run off
          together or get divorced.
Detective Klink: Is your wife a jealous person?
Oliver Sutton: My wife is insecure. She struggles
          with her weight and perhaps drinks too much
          wine, which amplifies her insecurities.
Detective Klink: Was she jealous of your brother,
          Nicholas Sutton?
Oliver Sutton: My brother? I don't think so, no.
Detective Klink: Your brother's death came as
          a shock?
Oliver Sutton: Yes, it did.
Detective Klink: Do you suspect suicide?
Oliver Sutton: The medical examiner listed the
          manner of death as undetermined.
Detective Klink: Was he depressed?
Oliver Sutton: He and his wife were struggling
          with infertility issues. That saddened
          him.
Detective Klink: Enough to take his own life?
Oliver Sutton: In my opinion, yes.
Detective Klink: How close were you with your
          brother?

Oliver Sutton: He worked at the family business with me when he wasn't deployed with the military. Our business gave him the opportunity to do both. He helped with receiving deliveries of stock, both the pharmaceuticals and the retail items we sell at the front of the store. He also had delivery routes.

Detective Klink: What do you mean, delivery routes?

Oliver Sutton: He would deliver prescriptions. We don't have a drive-through window, so deliveries help make us competitive with the chain pharmacies offering drive-up service.

Detective Klink: How would you describe your personal relationship with your brother?

Oliver Sutton: Nick and I made a good team. He was the friendly face of the operation, and I was the brains. Everybody loved Nick.

Detective Klink: What about outside of the business?

Oliver Sutton: Beg your pardon?

Detective Klink: What was your relationship with your brother like outside of work?

Oliver Sutton: We had different interests. Nick was athletic, outdoorsy. I am more cerebral, a big reader and thinker. As I mentioned, I also have a daughter, and I am active in the high school athletic department's Booster Club.

Detective Klink: Mr. Sutton, was your brother engaged in an extramarital affair with Dr. Diane Desmond, too?

Oliver Sutton: My sister-in-law thinks so.

Detective Klink: Are you referring to Lindsay Sutton?

Oliver Sutton: Yes. Nick's wife.

Detective Klink: How do you know she believes

> your brother was having an affair with
> Dr. Desmond?

Oliver Sutton: She yelled "You got the wrong guy" at the mayor at the regatta. She thinks he killed Nick. That's why she made comments on *The Finger Lakes Flash* following Nick's death, and she intimated to my wife she suspected as much. My business advertises on the *Flash*. I called the owner and requested that she take Lindsay's comments down.

Detective Klink: And you are referring to Claudia Marton?

Oliver Sutton: Yes. Claudia Marton.

Detective Klink: Did she comply with your request?

Oliver Sutton: At first…

Detective Klink: What do you mean?

Oliver Sutton: I don't trust Claudia Marton.

Detective Klink: Why not?

Oliver Sutton: Several reasons. For starters, I'd like to give you this. It's security camera footage from my personal office at Sutton's Apothecary. It shows Claudia Marton snooping around my office and taking photographs of work documents, some of which contain protected health information, like patients' prescriptions. That's an invasion of privacy.

Detective Klink: Let the record reflect Mr. Sutton has provided me with a thumb drive, blue in color, which I am labeling OS #1. Did you file a police report about this incident?

Oliver Sutton: I plan to today, after we finish this discussion.

Detective Klink: When did this incident occur?

Oliver Sutton: About two weeks ago, but I only recently learned about this evidence.

Detective Klink: Why would Claudia Marton photograph your office without your knowledge?

Oliver Sutton: I don't know. She's shown an extraordinary fascination with my family as of late.

Detective Klink: What do you mean?

Oliver Sutton: At the regatta, my sister-in-law, Lindsay, left the ladies' restroom wearing Ms. Marton's wig.

Detective Klink: Ms. Marton had a spare wig at the regatta?

Oliver Sutton: It was the wig from her head. My wife and I were escorted out of the yacht club minutes after Lindsay left, but according to many of my employees, Ms. Marton came out of the restroom with Lindsay's scarf tied around her head and marched to the front of the room. She gave a speech about 9/11 responder illnesses. Lindsay left the regatta wearing Ms. Marton's wig.

Detective Klink: Why do you think Ms. Marton gave her wig to Lindsay Sutton?

Oliver Sutton: No idea, but Ms. Marton hasn't stopped her snooping. She passed by the front of the station as I was parking. She's following me.

Detective Klink: How do you know what her car looks like?

Oliver Sutton: I pulled footage from my exterior surveillance cameras at the apothecary once I saw her actions in my office. She drives a Ford Fusion. Navy blue.

Detective Klink: Why do you think Ms. Marton is following you?

Oliver Sutton: I think my sister-in-law got to her.

Detective Klink: What do you mean?

Oliver Sutton: Lindsay thought my brother was having an affair with Dr. Desmond. She was a scorned woman.

Detective Klink: I'm not following...

Oliver Sutton: Lindsay has used *The Finger Lakes Flash* since the initial days following Nick's death to spin her narrative about the police covering up his 'murder.'

Detective Klink: You think that Ms. Marton believes your sister-in-law?

Oliver Sutton: Yes, I do. I think Ms. Marton is sympathetic to my sister-in-law. Ms. Marton craves attention—look at her behavior at the regatta. She ran countless articles on *The Finger Lakes Flash* about my brother. This is a boon for her business. And now, this situation is hitting close to home for her, too.

Detective Klink: How so?

Oliver Sutton: Your officer, Peter Graham, the one waiting for me tonight out in the parking lot? He swooped in, coming to Diane Desmond's defense at the regatta when my wife had a bit too much to drink. Guess who got forgotten when he rushed over, offering to help Diane Desmond? His date, Claudia Marton.

Detective Klink: What does this have to do with you?

Oliver Sutton: Women don't like to be scorned. I think she's working with my sister-in-law, trying to frame me for the murder of my brother and Dr. Desmond.

Detective Klink: Why would they frame you?

Oliver Sutton: For the money. My sister-in-law wants a life insurance payout for Nick's death. She can't get that with an undetermined cause of death. She needs the police to say Nick's death was a murder. Killing Dr. Desmond helps both of their causes.

Detective Klink: How?

Oliver Sutton: Brother killing brother makes quite the headline, very Cain and Abel. But if he also kills the brother's lover, the wife of the local mayor, the one person both women consider a threat? Do you know what you get when that happens? A blockbuster news story.

THE FINGER LAKES FLASH

Your online snapshot capturing the local news you need to know.
September 10

To commemorate the anniversary of 9/11, every day this week The Finger Lakes Flash will profile one 9/11 responder who is ill or lost their life from an illness incurred due to their response at a 9/11 crime scene.

Hero Profile: Stella Wesson, federal police officer

9/11 Crime Scene: The Pentagon

Duties: Officer Wesson served for nine weeks on the grounds of the Pentagon, assisting with evidence collection and the recovery of human remains. It was determined the air quality in the immediate vicinity of the Pentagon was toxic until at least November 19, 2001.

Interests: Officer Wesson loved to kayak, hike, bake banana bread, and spoil her nieces and nephews. She was an avid reader, never missed *Law & Order,* and had many close friends.

Illness: Officer Wesson was diagnosed with a malignant tumor in her parotid gland, requiring surgeons to cut her facial nerve upon removal of the tumor. This caused permanent disfigurement. Eight months after this surgery, Officer Wesson learned she had inoperable brain cancer.

Death: Officer Wesson died of brain cancer at the age of 57.

57

CLAUDIA

September 10

The sight of Peter's squad car outside my front window does not surprise me. In the wake of Dr. Diane Desmond's murder, it's understandable he's been swamped with work and keeping his lips sealed, especially to a local journalist. But I knew he couldn't ignore the tribute to Stella on *The Finger Lakes Flash*. She deserved the honor, and had he returned any of my telephone calls, he would have known to anticipate it.

As I gain confidence with my alopecia, the insecurities I covered up like scars are now prepped for exposure. Accepting myself means looking beyond my hairlessness, embracing the whole, and not defining who I am by any one dimension or detail. My baldness is a single aspect, as is my career. I'm not only a journalist. Stella was my best friend. One I loved and one I grieve, like Peter does. It is time for a real conversation with him about where we stand. Our jobs depend on confidentiality and source protection, but our hearts do not. If we can't talk about the investigation into Diane Desmond's murder, at least we can talk about us and the person we mutually loved.

Opening the screen door, I watch as he ambles up the driveway to the front walk, his head hung low. He climbs the front steps like a weary mountain climber, each leg-lift deliberate and pained. When he reaches the top, he grabs hold of the porch posts on each side of the steps for support. He doesn't raise his head.

"Hey, you look beat."

His head turns away from me. He says nothing.

"What's wrong? Is it the profile I published about Stella? I tried calling you. I'm missing her, too."

"I'm not here about Stella."

"We can't *not* talk about her…"

"That's *all* you ever want to talk about!" He snaps at me, his rugged face pinched tight with anger. "Every time you mention her, it takes me back. To all those damn doctors' appointments, to all the nights I didn't sleep because you don't get to sleep when the person you love is dying! They might not be alive when you wake up in the morning. I didn't sleep! And yeah, I'm trying to forget. Do you understand that? She's not coming back. Sometimes, I just want to forget."

His words stun me, distorting my perception of him like a fun-house mirror. All this time, I stretched his truth into a framework fitting my beliefs and accommodating my insecurities. But he's right. *He's right.* I do bring up Stella and I second guess everything he says or does, both professionally and personally, with a Stella filter attached. I don't want my alopecia to define me, yet with Peter, I've pigeonholed him as simply my best friend's boyfriend. And while I acknowledged to Greta the possibility neither of us had fully dealt with our grief over Stella's death, I assumed my struggle to live in the moment, to fully embrace the here and now, was parallel to his grief process. Peter's grieving differently than I am, immersing himself in the *present,* avoiding any mention of the *past*. We are an inversion of each other. I was wrong.

"I'm sorry. I… I didn't realize I was treating you the same way my sister treats me. With the unending questions and assumptions, and a tunnel view of all of it. I wasn't a good friend."

Peter's anger dissipates as suddenly as it appeared, and his head drops again. When he finally looks at me, his eyes are filled with a forlorn sadness.

"I'm not here as a friend. We can't see each other anymore, or call. I'm sorry, but no more communication."

"We *can* still be friends and talk. I don't want…"

"I'm not here as a friend!"

I gasp, the insistence of his words striking with a cold sting. He turns his head, his lips pinched. My mind spins, trying to read him, a sudden thought seeping into my conscience. Peter's not here in a personal capacity. He's here as a cop.

"Why did you come to see me?"

He sighs.

"You are a person of interest in the murder investigation of Dr. Diane Desmond."

58
LINDSAY
September 10

Fran's insurance paperwork muddles numbers and abbreviations with codes and procedures, stacking thick, like pages of a boring science textbook. This isn't my jam. My head doesn't compute what all these mumbo jumbo payments mean, or why Nick saved them. They must be important. He circled some of the insurance charges in bright red ink.

Today's brain fog eclipses yesterday's hangover headache, my confusion dense as paste. I refill my coffee cup with an extra jolt of brew. Maybe Melvin can act as my quasi-tutor, pinpointing why Nick drew target circles on these pages. We can compare them to Gwendolyn's EOB's. It's worth a shot.

He answers my call on the second ring.

"Hello, my dear. Hoping another ice cream visit soon will cheer you up. I've been concerned. Have you recovered from your fall?"

My fall. The mystery mapped out on my hands takes a surprising detour.

"Um, don't remember much. What did I do? How do you know I fell?"

"You called me."

Stunned, I swipe to the call history on my phone. There it is. 12:38 a.m. I placed an eleven-minute and thirteen-second telephone call to Melvin the night before last.

"Oh."

"Like I said, I was worried. You kept saying 'I'll miss you.' You wouldn't tell me where you were or where you were going."

Mother's plan was still a go at that point. I was saying my goodbyes. To Nick at the cemetery, and to Melvin on the phone.

"I'm sorry. I guess I had too much wine."

"Guess so."

"I don't remember falling."

He coughs and I wait, while he drinks a sip of something, quenching his throat. When he regains his voice, he scolds me with a gentle warning.

"You called me and kept saying goodbye. You said that you fell. I asked where you were, but you were rambling, not making any sense. Said your hands were bleeding. You shouldn't drink and drive."

The Dad lecture I never got as a teen. I soak in its sweetness for the few seconds it lasts, until Melvin adds a bitter ending.

"I take it the police didn't find you?"

Oh, shitty shit on shit.

"Um, no. Did you call them?"

"Of course, I did. I was worried about you."

The big red circles Nick drew on the insurance papers are ominous now. My search for answers as to what they mean needs to shift. Maybe Ken Preston can help me instead. Melvin was well-intentioned, but I can't trust him. Not anymore. Not after he called the police on the night Diane Desmond was murdered and put a great big target on my back.

Romulus Police Interview Transcript
Subject: Claudia Marton

Date: 09/10

Detective Klink: State your name for the record, please.

Claudia Marton: My name is Claudia Marton.

Detective Klink: What is your association with the victim?

Claudia Marton: Professional. I met with her on the Friday afternoon before her death.

Detective Klink: Where did you meet with her?

Claudia Marton: At Willow Bend Long-Term Care Home. I went to interview her for a profile piece on her husband's candidacy for the 54th District State Senate seat. I am the owner and operator of *The Finger Lakes Flash*.

Detective Klink: Did you sign the entrance log at Willow Bend Long-Term Care Home?

Claudia Marton: Yes, I did.

Detective Klink: Tell me about your visit to Willow Bend.

Claudia Marton: Well, like I said, I went there to interview the doctor for a profile piece about her husband. I arrived around 2:00 p.m. We went into her office, and I asked her a few questions. She ended the interview when she received a telephone call. She also said she was going to the hospital to check on a patient.

Detective Klink: What kind of questions did you ask her?

Claudia Marton: Mostly about the dynamic with

her husband as a dual-career couple. Readers want balance. They want the candidate to explain ideologies and articulate stances on issues, but they want to know the personal side, too. The spouse provides the family portrait, the 'flavor,' if you will, of who the candidate is as a person.

Detective Klink: Were you tough on Dr. Desmond during the interview?

Claudia Marton: I'm not sure what you mean by tough. I asked fair questions I believe readers want to know the answers to.

Detective Klink: So, you already interviewed Dr. Desmond's husband?

Claudia Marton: Yes, earlier in the week.

Detective Klink: And then, you came to Willow Bend to see Dr. Desmond on two separate occasions?

Claudia Marton: No, I only went to Willow Bend once, on Friday, like I said.

Detective Klink: Isn't it true you were invited to dinner with Dr. Desmond and her husband at their home on Saturday evening and declined?

Claudia Marton: Yes, that is true. I didn't think it was ethical for me as a journalist to accept dinner from an interview subject and political candidate whom I would be writing about on *The Finger Lakes Flash*.

Detective Klink: Do you consider yourself to be an ethical person, Ms. Marton?

Claudia Marton: I do.

Detective Klink: Let the record reflect I am now showing Ms. Marton evidence exhibit OS #1. Ms. Marton, I direct your attention to the monitor. Can you tell me what you see?

Claudia Marton: Um, that's me.

Detective Klink: And, for the record, can you tell me what you are doing?

Claudia Marton: I'm taking photographs in Oliver Sutton's office at Sutton's Apothecary.

Detective Klink: Do you always take photographs of people's private offices where they keep protected health and proprietary information?

Claudia Marton: No, I...

Detective Klink: Is it ethical to lie, Ms. Marton?

Claudia Marton: No.

Detective Klink: Let's talk about your other visit to Willow Bend. Not the one on Friday, but the one earlier in the week.

Claudia Marton: I told you, I went to Willow Bend once, on Friday.

Detective Klink: We have a bit of a problem, Ms. Marton, because an eyewitness saw you there earlier in the week.

Claudia Marton: I don't understand. I was only there on Friday! A couple of people did make comments I found confusing, like "Hello, again" or that sort of thing. It didn't make sense to me.

Detective Klink: Ah, and you're remembering these comments, now?

Claudia Marton: I didn't have a context for them. Were they referring to seeing me at the regatta, or around town?

Detective Klink: What if I told you I have evidence you were at Willow Bend earlier in the week?

Claudia Marton: That's not possible.

Detective Klink: Let the record reflect I am showing Ms. Marton evidence exhibit KP #1, the entrance logbook for Willow Bend Long-Term Care Home. I direct your attention to page six of the book, dated Friday, September 7, line number twelve. Can you tell me what you see there?

Claudia Marton: I see my signature.

Detective Klink: Now, let's go back to page four of
        the same entrance logbook, dated Wednes-
        day, September 5. Look at line number nine.
        What is written on line nine?

Claudia Marton: My name is written, but this
        is not my signature. It looks similar,
        but you can see how I add a curl on
        the letter 'C.' This other signature
        does not do that.

Detective Klink: So, you're telling me someone
        forged your signature into this log-
        book, and that my eyewitness, who pro-
        vided the name of an additional eye-
        witness, is wrong about seeing you at
        Willow Bend on Wednesday afternoon?

Claudia Marton: Yes! I was interviewing Mayor
        Roger Desmond on Wednesday afternoon,
        which can be confirmed by his appoint-
        ment secretary and by him. Aren't there
        surveillance cameras at Willow Bend?
        Did you check them?

Detective Klink: I did. Let the record reflect
        I am now showing Ms. Marton evidence ex-
        hibit WB #1. Please direct your atten-
        tion to the monitor. This is video camera
        surveillance footage from Willow Bend
        Long-Term Care Home, floor three. Will
        you please state for the record the time
        stamp on the video you are watching?

Claudia Marton: September 5, 2:14 p.m.

Detective Klink: I want you to watch this video, and
        I am going to freeze the frame in a bit.

Claudia Marton: Okay.

Detective Klink: Do you see this woman emerging
        from a patient room and entering the
        stairwell?

Claudia Marton: Yes.

Detective Klink: I'm freezing the frame, so you can
        clearly see part of the woman's face. For

the record, are you stating this woman is not you?

Claudia Marton: I'm positive it is not me. As I said, I was interviewing the mayor in his office across town, but I do know who that woman is.

Detective Klink: Who is it?

Claudia Marton: Lindsay Sutton. She's wearing my Nicole wig.

Detective Klink: Your what?

Claudia Marton: My Nicole wig. Wigs have names, detective, and I lent Nicole to her.

Detective Klink: You lent Lindsay Sutton a wig so she could scout Willow Bend two days before Dr. Desmond was murdered?

Claudia Marton: I didn't say that.

Detective Klink: Why does Lindsay Sutton have your wig?

Claudia Marton: I found her on the floor of the bathroom at the yacht club, having a panic attack. It was the night of the regatta. Her sister-in-law was causing a commotion over Dr. Desmond, and Lindsay was panicking.

Detective Klink: Why was she panicking?

Claudia Marton: I'm not sure it was one thing, but more of a combination of factors. Her husband died under strange circumstances. She thinks your department is covering up his murder. She called me shortly before her husband's body was discovered and posted comments about it on *The Finger Lakes Flash*. Oliver Sutton was angry, and asked me to take the comments down, which I did. They sat together at the regatta, and Oliver's wife caused a scene. People were watching, whispering. I think it all got to her.

Detective Klink: I still don't understand why you gave her your wig.

Claudia Marton: I suffer from anxiety and panic attacks and recognized what was happening. I understood her pain. She was afraid to return to the dining room. We both wore black dresses, so I gave her my wig to help her escape unnoticed. It was also a breakthrough for me.

Detective Klink: I'm not following…

Claudia Marton: I worked as a television reporter covering the crash of Flight 93 in Pennsylvania on 9/11. I inhaled the toxins in the air for days. My doctors think the toxin exposure may have triggered my hair loss. I have alopecia, which is an auto-immune disease. Before the regatta, I had never spoken publicly about my experience. Giving Lindsay Sutton my wig forced me to show the public what isn't being talked about. 9/11 responders from all three crash sites are *dying* from their exposure. There's also a whole bunch of people, like me, *living* with serious on-going health issues, too.

Detective Klink: You mentioned several things I would like to follow up on. First, the wig. You never asked for it back?

Claudia Marton: I met Lindsay Sutton Thursday night at Corks & Company, for that purpose. She told me she had taken it to Wigwash Wonders for cleaning. She never said she wore it again after the regatta.

Detective Klink: You met with her on Thursday?

Claudia Marton: Yes.

Detective Klink: What was her demeanor like?

Claudia Marton: Odd. I am acquainted with Officer Peter Graham. She thinks that he and this department are covering up her husband's murder. She talked about power structures

> in small towns, and how a good economy
> keeps powerful people in charge. She said,
> "No one wants dead bodies floating in the
> lake or decomposing in a creek. Everybody
> wins when business booms." And I think she
> stole my bottle of anxiety medication.

Detective Klink: Lindsay Sutton mentioned dead bodies floating in the lake on Thursday? The Thursday before Dr. Desmond's murder?

Claudia Marton: Yes, she did. I also noticed my bottle of medication was missing after I met with her. I took a pill while we ate. I remember putting the bottle in my purse. We hooked our bags next to one another. I think she swiped them while I took a phone call.

Detective Klink: And the posts you mentioned...

Claudia Marton: Would you like to read them? I have a copy in my purse. When I met Lindsay Sutton at Corks & Company, I wanted to ask her about them.

Detective Klink: Please show them to me. So, you were planning to question her, too?

Claudia Marton: Yes. I'm researching another tip I received that may or may not be related, so I wanted to ask her a few questions.

Detective Klink: Let the record reflect I am receiving a piece of paper from Ms. Marton containing postings previously published on *The Finger Lakes Flash*. This will be marked as evidence exhibit CM#1. Who did you receive another tip from and how does it relate to Nick Sutton's death?

Claudia Marton: I'm not at liberty to disclose my source, and as I said, I am not certain if it connects to his death or not. I will only say it involves the drug

Wozilfin and Willow Bend Long-Term Care Home.

Detective Klink: Let me get this straight: You are alleging that you are investigating a story about a drug being prescribed at the place where the murder victim worked as the prescribing physician... the same place where Lindsay Sutton forges your name into the logbook and dresses up like you to enter a patient's room, all while simultaneously stealing your medi-cation and accusing this department of corruption?

Claudia Marton: Yes. I know it sounds crazy, but you can check my alibi, detective. I've only spoken to Lindsay Sutton three times, but I do believe she's scared. Her husband is dead. And, while I can't explain why she dressed up as me, I'm worried about her safety and mine.

Detective Klink: Why is that?

Claudia Marton: I received another anonymous tip with a video attached to it. The message said *DO NOT TRUST LINDSAY SUTTON* and the video contained footage of the room where I store my wigs. Someone entered my prop-erty to make the video.

Detective Klink: Did you report this trespasser?

Claudia Marton: No, I did not.

Detective Klink: You didn't mention it to Officer Graham, either?

Claudia Marton: No... but, um...

Detective Klink: Why not?

Claudia Marton: Something the mayor said to me Wednesday afternoon concerns me, too.

Detective Klink: What did he say, Ms. Marton?

Claudia Marton: He said, "Men want my wife."

Detective Klink: Did you think he was referring to Officer Graham?

Claudia Marton: I'm not sure...

Detective Klink: Why is that important?

Claudia Marton: It was the way he said it. When a wife dies, the husband is always the first suspect, right detective? Well, Dr. Desmond gave her husband a reason to be jealous. Everyone sitting in the yacht club dining room heard Brenda Sutton yell at her at the regatta.

Detective Klink: What are you implying?

Claudia Marton: The mayor knew his wife was attractive to other men, and the mayor knew his wife made other wives nervous. If they were happily married, would there be any questions about her loyalty? I don't know, I guess what I'm saying is that sometimes the husband *should* be your top suspect.

59
LINDSAY
September 10

Taking a spin with Ken Preston in his mid-life crisis BMW is a small sacrifice considering how much he can potentially help me out. I don't have time to waste. Melvin's telephone call to the police about my missing whereabouts Friday night practically lights up the sky with warning beacons. The cops will come knocking and they'll ask questions.

Questions I can't answer.

On the night of Dr. Diane Desmond's murder, I don't remember driving to the cemetery. I don't remember falling or cutting and scraping my hands.

What if I fell lunging at Diane with a knife? What if I blocked out killing her?

No. My clothes weren't bloody. Or wet. Don't imagine problems. Focus on what's real.

Nick's phone is real. A real conundrum. Mother said the code must have to do with sex, but she has a one-track mind.

A one-track mind...

I'm jolted by a sudden realization. Why didn't I think of this before? Having a baby dominated my thoughts until I mistakenly suspected Nick was cheating on me. He was consumed, too—secretly lending Oliver his truck so he could pay for our next embryo transfer.

We scheduled the procedure for June fifteenth. I cancelled the appointment after Nick died.

Sprinting through the kitchen to where my purse hangs from a hook, I grab Nick's phone from the bag. My hand trembles, as I depress number keys. Zero. Six. One. Five.

Nick's phone screen comes to life.

"Oh my God, Nick. Oh, baby," I cry, overcome by how much my

259

husband wanted our little family as much as I did, and feeling ashamed that I ever doubted him. Swiping the back of my hand against a tear dribbling down my cheek, I navigate to What's App and scour Nick's contacts. A few military friends stationed overseas are listed, but only one name besides my own stands out: John Corry. Nick's childhood buddy and a pharmacy technician at the apothecary. I tap on this contact and find one remaining text string between John and Nick.

"Bro, can't figure it out. Scripts are legit, so Ollie is solid. But I agree, the math ain't mathing."

"Keep looking, Johnny. Too much money. Think he wants to bail on Bren and Lainey? Scared for Mom. Checking her papers. If scripts are kosher, what's the doc's agenda? Booty calls alone don't fly."

"Don't know, bud. I'm on it."

"Thx."

Nick didn't trust Diane Desmond! But, based on this text chain, the prescriptions were legitimate, and Nick was worried that Diane was manipulating Oliver. But how? And now that she's dead, is Oliver in danger, too?

Nick hid his phone in the toilet for a specific reason. Something on this phone was worth safekeeping. Opening his cache of photographs, I swipe left, toggling through a dozen or so pictures before I hit paydirt. Photographs of daily delivery invoices for Willow Bend Long-Term Care Home date back to March. Each record contains a listing of patients and their corresponding medications. My pulse quickens as I swipe, spying Gwendolyn Anderson's name on a roster next to a prescription for Wozilfin.

Wozilfin must be the drug Melvin was referring to when he said a new medication made Gwendolyn catatonic—but based on my review of Fran's paperwork, she wasn't taking this pharmaceutical, at least not while Nick was alive. If I can figure out how Wozilfin corresponds with the ink circles on Fran's insurance forms, maybe I can point the police in the right direction. Hell, any direction, away from me. I can't internet search my way through this—online databases only tell me what the codes stand for, but they don't help me understand what's out of sync or unnecessary.

Ken Preston understands this stuff. All the medical codes and claim charges, while I understand male egos, boys' toys, and their need to show them off. An easy-peasy trade-off, and a solid plan B, given Melvin's loose lips.

Ken sounded super excited when I called and asked him to come over after work today. I'm dying to hear what he knows about Dr. Desmond's murder investigation. Maybe the police searched her computer at the office, or she confided some deep dark secret to him. Someone hated her, that's for sure. Stab wounds aren't subtle. Unfortunately, neither are the marks on my hands.

Brenda must be shitting bricks after the fuss she caused at the regatta. Oliver is probably a fidgety mess, too. He was up to something at those weekend cabin rendezvouses. What did Brenda say about the drug suppliers? I don't remember. There's only one thing I am certain about.

Mother may be a problem.

The cops will question Brenda, and she'll probably tell them that Mother was back in town. They'll ask me why and I'll need a good answer, a solid cover story, like all those weekend camps Mother sent me to when she wanted to camouflage her away game meetups.

The doorbell chime interrupts my thoughts. Ken is here. Show time.

Inhaling a deep breath, I rip off the sealing tape and open the front door.

Damn. It's *him*.

"Mrs. Sutton, remember me? I'm Officer Peter Graham, Romulus Police Department. We'd like to talk to you about the death of Dr. Diane Desmond."

"I don't know anything about it."

"Well, maybe you can help us. We've found a knife, a possible murder weapon."

A knife? My mind jumps to the night of the regatta. When I arrived home, I grabbed a knife before I searched the basement. I put the knife back in the utensil drawer. At least, I think I did.

"What does that have to do with me?"

"Your husband's fingerprints are all over it."

60
CLAUDIA
September 10

The lobby of Wigwash Wonders looks like a twin to my room of disguises. Stunning wigs adorn an array of porcelain mannequin heads, propped like pieces of art behind the gold marble counter. A flat screen marquee lists prices for services, hairpieces for sale, and specialty bottles of wig shampoo, conditioner, and argan oil treatment, along with vignettes explaining the difference in caring for synthetic versus human hair wigs. Glossy brochures advertising hair donation and contact information for the National Alopecia Areata Foundation, The Bald Truth, and the International Alliance of Hair Restoration Surgeons stack in a triple tier holder.

Maude Miller, the store owner, greets me with a worried expression.

"Claudia, I thought of you the other day, watching the news about the firefighters in California. The report mentioned all the toxins they are inhaling while trying to contain the infernos. It's awful."

I nod, commiserating with her comment.

"Yes. The world is waking up and starting to understand the dangers. I read an article last week about the lead dust pollution caused by the fire at the Notre Dame Cathedral. Anywhere there's a fire, people are vulnerable."

Maude sympathetically pats my shoulder, before shifting subjects.

"What can I help you with today?"

"I lent my Nicole wig to an acquaintance who said she dropped it off here for cleaning. I decided to save her the trouble and pick it up myself."

"Sure. Who brought it in?"

"Lindsay Sutton."

"Let me take a look."

Maude types on her keyboard, her focus fixed on the computer monitor. A small crinkle emerges between her eyebrows, as her right hand hits the enter key repeatedly. Each finger tap corresponds with the deepening of the crinkle, transforming it into a line of worry.

"Claudia, I'm sorry. I have no record of it in our system."

She lied.

DO NOT TRUST LINDSAY SUTTON.

Lindsay Sutton is setting me up. I helped her in her time of need, and she thanked me by forging my signature, impersonating me, stealing my medication, and now flat-out lying. The heat of anger radiating through my body irritates my scalp under my Chloe wig, as my anxiety escalates with each throbbing beat of my pulse. Lindsay still has Nicole. She's keeping her, and for a reason. She wants to impersonate me again.

I know what I must do.

"Maude, I'm going to need to order a new Nicole wig, and can I see the synthetic piece up there on mannequin number three, please?" My finger points to a long, blonde hairpiece displayed behind the counter. Maude turns, reaching for the wig.

Two can play this game.

Romulus Police Interview Transcript
Subject: Lindsay Sutton

Date: 09/10

Detective Klink: Please state your name for the record.

Lindsay Sutton: Lindsay Sutton.

Detective Klink: What is your association with the victim?

Lindsay Sutton: My husband's fingerprints are on a potential murder weapon.

Detective Klink: Let's not get ahead of ourselves. Did you know Dr. Diane Desmond?

Lindsay Sutton: Yes. She was my mother-in-law's physician at Willow Bend Long-Term Care Home.

Detective Klink: How would you describe your relationship with her?

Lindsay Sutton: I didn't have a relationship with her.

Detective Klink: You sound angry.

Lindsay Sutton: Not a fan, what can I say?

Detective Klink: You told me a couple months ago you thought Dr. Desmond was having an affair with your husband, correct?

Lindsay Sutton: My husband did not cheat on me.

Detective Klink: That's not what I asked.

Lindsay Sutton: I am a grieving widow. Cut me some slack. My sister-in-law is the one you should speak with about an extra-marital affair. Weren't you at the regatta?

Detective Klink: We'll talk about your sister-in-law in a moment. First, tell me about the posts you made on *The Finger Lakes Flash*. The ones you made after I told you that we didn't have evidence of a crime connected to your husband's disappearance and death.

Lindsay Sutton: I came here to talk about the knife you found.

Detective Klink: You don't trust the police… right, Mrs. Sutton?

Lindsay Sutton: Someone killed my husband and now Dr. Desmond. The body count on your watch is rising.

Detective Klink: Where were you last Friday evening?

Lindsay Sutton: At home.

Detective Klink: Anyone with you?

Lindsay Sutton: Yes.

Detective Klink: Who?

Lindsay Sutton: My sister-in-law, Brenda Sutton, and my mother, Sylvia Kelly.

Detective Klink: How long were they there with you?

Lindsay Sutton: I didn't look at the clock.

Detective Klink: So, they left?

Lindsay Sutton: Yes.

Detective Klink: Did you go anywhere Friday night after they left?

Lindsay Sutton: Yes, Lakeview Cemetery, to visit my husband's grave.

Detective Klink: We received a call from Melvin Anderson in the early hours of Saturday morning. He expressed concern about your whereabouts and your welfare.

Lindsay Sutton: False alarm. I'm fine.

Detective Klink: Did you dress in disguise?

Lindsay Sutton: What are you talking about?

Detective Klink: Mrs. Sutton, I direct your attention to the monitor, where I am playing a videotape marked as evidence exhibit WB #1. Can you tell me what you see?

Lindsay Sutton: I see a woman in a hallway.

Detective Klink: Is that woman you, exiting your mother-in-law's room at Willow Bend Long-Term Care Home?

Lindsay Sutton: I'm blonde.

Detective Klink: Are you wearing the same wig multiple witnesses saw you leave the regatta in? The one Claudia Marton lent to you?

Lindsay Sutton: Okay, yes, I am, but I agreed to come here to talk to you about the knife you found. I don't understand how my husband's fingerprints can be on a knife when he died months ago!

Detective Klink: Yes. I'm sure that's quite upsetting. We're getting to that, but I would like to direct your attention to a recent transcript of a 911 call you made.

Lindsay Sutton: I told the operator to cancel the call. It was a non-emergency. How is this relevant?

Detective Klink: Let the record reflect I am reading from 911 Dispatch transcript #11745: *"Lindsay? Are you there? Lindsay, can you hear me?"*

"Sssh... please! Send someone!"

"A patrol unit in your area is en route. Lindsay, stay on the line with me, okay? Is anyone else besides you in the house?"

"No, my tape seals aren't broken. But someone is out there!"

Tell me, Mrs. Sutton, why did you tape seal your home?

Lindsay Sutton: I told you last June and I told you today. Someone killed my husband. I'm scared.

Detective Klink: Were the tape seals broken by the trespasser?

Lindsay Sutton: No, but...

Detective Klink: Were they ever broken?

Lindsay Sutton: No.

Detective Klink: I'm now going to direct your attention to a police report filed by Officer Peter Graham, after he responded to the 911 trespass call at your residence. Let the record reflect I am about to read from RPD #3684:

"At approximately 18:44, I responded to 745 Hemlock Street, Romulus. The owner of the residence, Lindsay Sutton, indicated her call to 911 operations was a false alarm, and the individual she originally thought was a trespasser was instead a friend delivering ice cream."

Lindsay Sutton: I repeat, how is this relevant?

Detective Klink: Who was the friend bringing ice cream to you?

Lindsay Sutton: Oh, come on. It was Melvin Anderson. He's in his mid-seventies.

Detective Klink: RPD #3684 continues, stating the following:

"Mrs. Sutton asked me about another investigation involving her sister-in-law, Brenda Sutton. She stated 'The mayor's wife can trespass all over people's marriages and she doesn't get an inquisition, but one sloppy comment by someone else after a few too many, and it's a capital offense.' Did you say that?

Lindsay Sutton: I was being sarcastic.

Detective Klink: Anyone else visit your home recently, Mrs. Sutton?

Lindsay Sutton: No! Now, would you please tell me about the knife with my husband's fingerprints on it?

Detective Klink: Latent prints can remain on an object, like a knife, for quite some time, and since your husband is dead, we need to establish who else had recent access to your home and to your knives. You've been kind enough to confirm that your sister-in-law, your mother, and Melvin Anderson were at your home recently, and you, of course. Determining who had access to the weapon is a key part of any murder investigation. So is the motive.

Lindsay Sutton: Are you saying one of us killed Dr. Desmond?

Detective Klink: We've got the written statements you posted on *The Finger Lakes Flash*. We've got verbal statements you made to Ken Preston and to Officer Graham, specifically about the murder victim. I have a video tape showing you dressed in disguise at the workplace of Dr. Desmond, two days before her murder. Claudia Marton filed a police report, accusing you of stealing her prescription medication on the Thursday before the murder, the same day you made comments about bodies floating in a lake. I have volunteered credit card receipts from Corks & Company confirming you were there with Ms. Marton and had access to her medication. The receipts contain recent signature exemplars from both of you and are being compared to the Willow Bend entrance logbook by handwriting examiners. Melvin Anderson also filed a police report, stating you were highly distressed and intoxicated during the window of time the murder took place, and your whereabouts were unknown. And, we haven't even talked about the condition of your hands, Mrs. Sutton. So, yes, we do think one of you did it, and you top our list. Anything you'd like to confess, or say to me?

Lindsay Sutton: I'd like to speak to an attorney.

61
CLAUDIA
September 10

John Corry's house nestles behind a circular driveway, the curvature wrapping around a flagpole displaying the Stars and Stripes. Dusk looms, nature's way of yawning, as day cedes to night. The streetlights illuminate, signaling bath time for the young children playing dodge ball in the roadway and drawing on the sidewalks with colored chalk. The dog walkers are returning home, settling in for the night. It's also about time for John Corry to step out his front door, cross the circular driveway, and lower his American flag.

Walking along the sidewalk, I place advertising brochures for *The Finger Lakes Flash* in mailboxes, watching the flag billow in the evening breeze. I sidestep two girls cruising on their scooters, their ponytails bouncing as they race to the end of the block. The image makes me miss my nieces, who started yet another new school year last week. Soon, they'll be grown up, off at college. The sweet days of their youth are slipping away. I owe it to them and to myself to visit more, and I will once things simmer down.

The murder of Dr. Diane Desmond set the local community abuzz, with many parents sitting on porch swings and front stoops, keeping a watchful eye on their children. I can't say I blame them, with such a violent murderer lurking in our midst. Still, her death screams overkill, a deliberate rage exerted against her. Who did she cross, deceive, or lie to, to elicit such a brutal attack? After my interview with the Romulus Police Department detective, Peter sent me a text, apologizing for snapping at me. I am sure his text message broke department protocol, and the no-contact rules he laid out to me. He's not allowed to associate with me now, not when I am a potential suspect in the Desmond murder investigation. Our pattern of circling around one another, grasping at what we are, or what we want to be, is insignificant now.

I am not a murderer.

I didn't answer Peter. I'm not talking to the police again, not any of them, until I talk with John Corry.

The fluttering flag begins to droop, a pully lowering it against a cloudy night sky. John Corry methodically tugs on the cord, his arm muscles taut and defined. I skirt across the street to the curtilage of his front yard.

"Mr. Corry? May I speak with you? I'm Claudia Marton from *The Finger Lakes Flash*. Marlene Flynn sent me."

He stares at me, my comment interrupting his nightly ritual. The flag hangs at half-staff, momentarily forgotten as he steps away from the pole and approaches me.

"My buddy is dead and now that doctor is, too."

His tone reflects his fear as he folds his arms across his chest, projecting a guarded stance.

"Please, Marlene is afraid more people will die. Help me understand Wozilfin. Was Dr. Desmond using it to mercy kill the elderly patients with dementia?"

John Corry scans the block, as if looking to see who might be observing our conversation. He thrusts his hands into the pockets of his golf shorts, attempting to appear casual, while his tone is anything but.

"Something has been off with the stock at the apothecary, and I mentioned it to Nick. The computer program we use is tracking an unusually high number of Wozilfin prescriptions this year. The numbers caught my eye. And... I noticed something else. The same people receiving the Wozilfin prescriptions also had simultaneous insurance claims submitted for other medications, stuff for diabetes, restless leg syndrome, high blood pressure, you name it. Things didn't add up."

"What didn't add up?"

"We only received enough stock supply of the Wozilfin pills from the distributors. But for other medications, the supply of pills we received didn't match the prescriptions. There's no way we could have filled them. I asked Nick about it since he delivered prescriptions to Willow Bend. He knew who got what. There were missing scripts. The situation didn't make sense to him, either."

My mind plays catch-up, trying to understand his explanation, but when it clicks, the truth materializes.

"So, the patients with dementia were prescribed Wozilfin and supplied it, but the other prescriptions for these patients weren't filled, because there wasn't enough stock supply of those drugs? Am I right?"

John Corry nods his head.

"Yes. Wozilfin can accelerate death in the elderly population. There are warnings about it. If you shut the patients up with Wozilfin, they can't say to their family members they're not getting their medicine for their other conditions, like diabetes, restless leg syndrome or anything else. The apothecary can bill insurance for all those meds and pocket the change and before anyone catches on, the patient dies—either from the acceleration caused by the Wozilfin, the lack of necessary medications for other conditions, or a combination of both."

Only you caught on, and you clued your buddy Nick in on the scheme.

"Nick warned Marlene. Why her?" I ask. "And did he confront Oliver?"

"I don't know. Nick and I used encrypted text messaging on What's App so his brother wouldn't get suspicious. Anytime I suspected fraud, I texted him. It was a big allegation, because doctors can prescribe any medication, even off-label. Dr. Desmond could justify the Wozilfin scripts a lot easier than we could prove she was intentionally mercy killing patients. Our hook was the other prescriptions, but Nick wanted to be sure about it. Marlene Flynn was friendly with Nick's mother and her mental faculties were sharp. Nick felt he could trust her. I don't know if he confronted Oliver or Dr. Desmond. But she's dead now, too."

"Have you told the police this?"

"I called the pharmaceutical suppliers, tipped them off. They work with federal investigators on stock discrepancy cases all the time. The feds will contact the insurance companies and obtain claim data and compare it to the pill stock supply." John Corry glances down the block again and whispers, "I'm scared, lady. Someone killed Nick. His wife tried posting about it on your site and the cops did nothing. He was piecing everything together when he died."

"What do you think happened to him?"

"Dr. Desmond's husband wanted big bucks to fund his political campaign. TV ads cost a bundle. She could write the prescriptions and split the profits on the unfilled ones with Oliver, then fudge the patient files and make everything look legit. I think Nick was worried about his mom and asked one question too many. The doctor was a charmer.

Maybe she called Nick and lured him to the bluffs with some bullshit story, and her husband showed up instead."

Lindsay Sutton's words about "the powerful people" echo in my mind, like the call of a lake loon.

"...if they stay unified, they survive."

If Dr. Desmond and Oliver Sutton had a prescription insurance fraud scam cooking, silencing Nick Sutton was necessary for survival. But someone wanted the doctor muzzled, too. It doesn't make sense to me.

"Marlene Flynn knows all this?"

"Nick warned her about the danger she might be in, too. Marlene told Nick she wanted to help and offered to keep an eye on Nick's mother. He gave her an empty pill vial with a Wozilfin label, so she would remember the name of the drug. Marlene was his spy."

Like she is for me.

"She could be in danger at Willow Bend!"

John Corry squints against the impending darkness and leans forward, whispering again in my ear.

"We're in danger, too. We all know too much."

62
LINDSAY
September 10

The crunch of pea gravel under Nick's truck tires grates on my nerves. It won't be long now. The police believe I killed Nick and Diane Desmond. They want me to confess to something I didn't do, to make their lives easier, since they can't investigate their way to the truth. Or maybe they don't want to. The mayor's wife was murdered and he's a viable suspect—one any competent police department wouldn't ignore. I watch enough *Dateline* to know the husband is *always* a suspect unless there's a cover-up, which, hello, there is. I've been saying it for months. No one will listen. And I know what's coming next.

The police are going to meet with the district attorney, some studious-looking dude or dudette with solid framed glasses and deep worry lines. They'll insist, "We need a warrant." The district attorney will rub his or her eyes under those big, goofy glasses and whine, "It's a circumstantial case, handwriting experts are wonky witnesses. We don't have enough for an arrest. Let's do a search warrant, see what we turn up. Go find that wig."

Only they won't find "that wig" because I'm going to dig it out of the freezer again, grab Fran's insurance paperwork, and hit the road. The Canadian border is less than three hours away. Once I'm there, I can dump Nick's truck and hop on a flight to one of those countries with sandy beaches and tiki huts. A tropical paradise kind of place with roadside fruit stands, foreign bank accounts, and loosey-goosey extradition laws.

Nick's truck bumps along the utility road as it slithers deeper through the wooded hillside, the headlights cutting the darkness as a thick blanket of clouds float in front of the moon. A raccoon scampers across the road, caught in the glare. I ease up on the gas pedal a bit, allowing the

273

animal to cross, its masked face a symbolic serendipity. With Claudia Marton's wig, I'll be the bandit sneaking away in the night. I wonder how much lead time I'll get before anyone notices I skipped town. The truck rounds the bend at the top of the hill, turning on the rear access road to my property. A mere fifty yards ahead, the high beam lights shine on a surprise.

My car. Mother is here! She should be halfway to Florida by now. Why is she parked out here, behind my house, with the crates of cash in the car? Why didn't she pull into the garage through the double door? Is she here to apologize to me? I curse under my breath, shifting the gear into park. Hopping down from the cab, I march straight to my car, grasping the handle. Unlocked. Damn.

In the darkness, I pull out my cell phone, activating the flashlight feature. The charge is anemic, the red warning bar popping up in the corner. With my mind preoccupied by the police interrogation and the knife found with Nick's fingerprints on it, I forgot to charge my phone. My fingers snap the lid open on one of the crates, and I see an array of pink boxes. I tug the crate, harder than necessary, and bump my elbow on the rim of the door frame. I curse again, my fingers opening a pink box and plucking tampons out. A thick roll of cash lay undisturbed at the bottom, squirreled away for a rainy day. Considering all the storm clouds in my life, that day is now.

Stuffing the box back in the crate, I shut the door, stomping up the back walkway to the rear porch. The house is dark and quiet. Mother's probably catching some shut-eye. God knows, her extra-curricular activities don't leave much time for actual sleep. Time for a wake-up call. We need to skedaddle.

"Mother!" I yell, into a void of darkness. I don't want to turn on the lights. Against the backdrop of late-night blackness, any illumination will highlight my movements throughout the house. If the police are watching, they'll figure out I'm prepping to flee. My mind flashes to a scene in *Wait Until Dark*, where Audrey Hepburn's character plots to outsmart her tormentor. Between watching Audrey stun the bad guys and my weekly dose of *Dateline*, the importance of having a plan isn't lost on me.

The utensil drawer sits at the end of the counter. I pull it open, debating if I should take the knives with me. I could swear I returned the knife to the drawer the night of the regatta. Someone with access to my kitchen knives killed Dr. Desmond, and given Mother's unpredictability the past few days, she's making me worry. In her own twisted way, she loves me with a feral fierceness. But why would she kill for me, after learning Nick didn't cheat? It doesn't make sense.

Reflecting on the conversation Friday night, *Brenda* had the biggest beef with Diane. *"That bitch better not go near my daughter!"* Brenda had access to the knives in the drawer when I walked Mother to the front door, and she put her motive on blast, turning her center table seat at the regatta into a three-ring circus. What if her fingerprints are on some of the knives in the drawer? That's a big clue. If I take them with me and my car is searched at the border, a wig and a knife collection might cause problems. I don't want to give them to Mother. She forgot to lock up the cash in the car. I'll leave them. If the police find Brenda's prints, it will take the heat off me.

Melvin's phone call to the police about me fired them up, too. Days ago, he sat here at my kitchen table, spoon feeding me a tale about the medication switch and the detrimental deterioration it caused his wife, Gwendolyn, melting my defenses with a sap story and some mint-chocolate chip. Melvin has motive to kill. Dr. Desmond was the prescribing physician for the patients at Willow Bend. And, if he wanted access to my utensil drawer, stopping by with a pint of ice cream was a slick move. While I argued with pesky police officer Peter Graham at my front door, did Melvin slip back into the kitchen and stuff a knife in his jacket? Why wear a jacket in early September? It's still relatively warm outside. And how did he know there is a back entrance to my property? Have I been wrong trusting him, blinded by loneliness and my lack of a father figure?

The police didn't say what kind of knife they found, only that it had Nick's fingerprints on it. I can't risk turning on the light over the sink, but I want to know which knife is missing. A set of yellow dishwashing gloves rests in the drying rack. I put them on, passing my gloved fingers over the knife handles, searching blindly for the empty cutlery slot in the drawer caddy. My mind translates what I touch. The big handle is the cleaver, followed by the chef's knife, a boning knife, a serrated bread knife, a utility knife, and a paring knife. Six handles, all there. My hand moves to the right, to the eight-piece steak knife set, counting under my breath. Between knives five and seven, my fingers dip into an empty slot. Steak knife number six is missing.

With a full drawer of larger knives, why would Dr. Desmond's killer choose a steak knife? A steak knife can be lethal, especially if it hits an artery, but the choice is strange. I toss the yellow gloves back into the drying rack, stymied at the thought, but time is slipping away. Mother picked the wrong time to catch up on sleep. I peer through the window by the sink, wondering if the police are squatting in the woods, dressed in ghillie suits, using night vision to spy on me. Being a military wife, I learned a lot about tactics. Seeing only a faint outline of the trees against the darkness, I move away from the window.

I cross the kitchen, opening the door to the basement, anxious to fish out the wig and get going. "Mother, wake up!" I holler again, as the heavy tread of my feet rumble down the stairwell until they reach the bottom, entering Nick's man cave. A neon beer sign hangs above the bar, casting a sheen on the glossy scales of the taxidermy trophies mounted on the walls. The beady eyes of the dead fish reflect the colorful glow from the light, creating an image of devilish possession. I turn away, imagining the freakish fisheyes watching me, and step toward the accordion door leading to the back room. It's pushed open, which surprises me.

I always shut this door, I think, trying to remember when I last came down here. The trout. I took the trout out to thaw. Did I forget to pull the door closed? My hand grasps the handle, testing it. The accordion door slides along its track, clicking shut as the magnetic connections meet. My eyes glance at a window well, faint moonlight trickling in through the glass pane. As I step forward, I stumble, tripped up by some unknown object. I fall into a pile of life jackets next to the kayaks. They collapse under my weight and my elbow hits the cement floor, the recipient of a second hard bump in less than ten minutes. Sitting up, I rub my sore arm. An eerie stillness haunts the room.

What did I trip on?

My hand reaches for my cell phone in my back pocket. No charge. So much for using the flashlight. I unscrewed the light bulb out of the overhead socket after Melvin's unexpected visit by the window well, unwilling to announce my basement presence to the outside world again. Not the brightest move.

Something is wrong. There's something on the floor. Something that doesn't belong there.

My hands pat the cement, feeling around in the darkness since I can't see.

I inch forward, my hand reaching, searching for the unknown, fearing what I might touch. After a half-dozen or more pats, my palm connects with a hard, plastic object. Nick's tackle box. My momentary relief evaporates. This doesn't make sense. I set Nick's tackle boxes along the wall when I straightened up this area after packaging the money. This box was over there when I came downstairs to get the trout.

My eyes dart to the window wells again. Any hint of moonlight has disappeared, hidden behind cloud cover, rendering me blind in a sea of darkness. The last thing I need is to fall again and knock myself out. I torque my body around, crawling inch by inch in the direction of the freezer, my hands reaching forward, bracing for another obstruction, some element not where it belongs. The cement hurts my knees.

Only a few more feet to go.

My fingertips brush the smooth, front surface of the freezer. I rise from the floor, grateful the interior freezer light will offer me a view of the room, and any other displaced sporting equipment. Gripping the rim of the lid, I lift, cool vapors and light assaulting my senses until I grasp what I see. The grayness of Mother's face, her open mouth and purple lips, with a thick anchor rope cinched around her neck, squeezing the life from her crumpled body entombed in the freezer.

I recoil, as a tortured wail escapes my mouth, shocked by the horror illuminated by the freezer light. A panic like I have never experienced seizes my breath and I turn, only to find my escape route blocked. A figure dressed in black emerges from behind the furnace, gripping Nick's ice axe with gloved hands.

63

CLAUDIA

September 10

Visitation hours at Willow Bend Long-Term Care Home ended more than two hours ago. By now, the second-shift crew has finished assisting patients with the standard rituals of undressing, personal hygiene, and the administration of nightly medications. I squat next to a dumpster behind the building, watching as a few windows blink with flashes of light from plasma television screens in various patient rooms. The dumpster stinks, emanating a foul odor of spoiled milk.

I must find a way into the building.

Shift change is coming up within the hour, a time of vulnerability and opportunity—charts are reviewed, supplies are restocked, and stories are swapped. The perfect distraction for hustling a patient out a side stairwell. Marlene and I need to go to the police. John Corry's warning about the escalating danger is spot on. Marlene knows too much, and with Dr. Desmond's killer still at large, I can't risk anything happening to her or to any other patients.

But first, I must figure out a way in. The front entrance is sealed tight and locked up for the night. Crouched in the dark, I wait for the inevitable health care worker who hasn't quit smoking, despite knowing the risks.

I'm wearing the Lindsay Sutton imposter wig, the anger-impulse purchase from Wigwash Wonders. On some level, sneaking in disguised as her feels like petty payback. Long tendrils of blonde hair flow past my shoulder blades and are topped with a baseball hat. If I get in, I'll pull it low, blocking my face from the ever-present security cameras. *If* I can get in.

My eyes narrow, staring at the back door, waiting for a chance to tailgate into the building. The cloud cover obliterates the moonlight, and the hum of the boxy air-conditioning unit is marred by a strange, mechanical clicking noise. I reposition from a squat to bended knee, like a ring-bearing suitor offering a proposal, and wait some more.

The backdoor cracks open with a thud. A scrub-attired worker emerges from the building with a large trash bag and a door stop in his hands. He slips the wedge into place and walks toward the dumpster. I remain motionless, holding my breath. He launches the bag into the container, and it lands with a smack. From the pocket of his scrubs, he pulls out a cell phone, a lighter, and a cigarette. He lights up, savoring the first drag, before walking into the unlighted section of the rear parking lot, his attention focused on his phone screen. With his back to me, I make my move, tiptoeing from behind the dumpster into the building.

Taking the stairs two at a time, I climb to the third-floor landing. Pressing my ear to the door, I listen. Silence. The nurses' station is at the far end of the hallway, with Marlene's room half the distance. Pulling the stairwell door open, I peek into the hallway. Empty. A nurse sits at the desk, her shoulders hunched. I wait, hoping the employee who dumped the trash grabs another cigarette and doesn't return to this stairwell. The nurse reads for another minute before rising from her seat, with what looks like a medical file in her hand. When she steps away, I shimmy into the hallway. Sidestepping past the semi-closed doors to patient rooms, I enter room number 332. She's awake.

"Sssh!" I say, putting my index finger to my lips. "It's me, Marlene. Claudia Marton from *The Finger Lakes Flash*. Don't scream."

Marlene Flynn sits in a recliner chair, her leg elevated and encased in a walking boot.

"What's happening?" She whispers, lowering the footrest on the chair.

"I'm scared. I talked with John Corry. He's scared, too. We need to go to the police and tell them what we know about the Wozilfin. It's not safe for you here."

"Tonight? Now? Did something else happen?"

"The police called me in for questioning, but that was before I talked with John tonight. We need to tell them what we know. Whoever stabbed Dr. Desmond is still out there. I don't think you are safe here. Come with me, we can go to the police together."

"I can't leave Fran Sutton alone. I promised her son Nick I would keep an eye on her. Her other son was here earlier tonight. First time he's visited her in ages."

Oliver Sutton was here. This can't be a coincidence.

"Why was he here? Did you talk to him?"

"Yes—for a minute. He said he wanted to speak privately with his mother. I think he plans to move her out of here tomorrow."

"Move her out? Did he say why?"

"He said it was too dangerous to leave her here after Dr. Desmond's murder. He had moving boxes with him and asked me to leave the room."

If Oliver Sutton is worried about his own safety, is that why he's making such a drastic move to relocate his mother? It makes sense. Dr. Desmond wrote the prescriptions. He filled them. It was a symbiotic relationship, and now half of that equation is dead.

"Are you sure Fran Sutton is still here?"

"Yep. The orderly with the John Lennon moppet haircut filled me in. Said Oliver was upset he had to wait until morning to sign the discharge papers. She's in room 319. Go check on her while I change from my dressing gown. I'll call the police and ask them to come speak with us."

"We can't! They'll know I snuck in here after hours."

"They'll figure that out anyway if we show up at the police station at this late hour. You broke an administrative rule, not a law. And if it helps solve Dr. Desmond's murder, they'll overlook a minor infraction."

Technically, I could be charged with trespassing, but I don't argue the point.

"I'll check on Fran and come back. Do you need help changing?"

"No. I'm plodding along well with my new boot. Just hurry back."

"I will."

As I turn toward the door, Marlene utters a final warning.

"Be careful, Claudia."

Opening the door a crack, the coast is clear. Trailing the blue line on the floor, my feet stride toward room 319. Fran Sutton's door is shut. Twisting the knob, I ease into the room. The door closes behind me with a distinctive click and I exhale, unaware I was holding my breath.

The room is dark, with curtains pulled tight. Ambient light from a clock radio illuminates a figure lying on a hospital bed. The form is covered with bedding and doesn't move. I stare at it, still standing at the door, uncertain if I should go farther. I don't want to wake Fran Sutton up, but the lack of movement concerns me. I can't tell if she's breathing.

I hold my own breath again and listen. Nothing. No sound. I can't see a normal rise and fall of her chest in the darkness. What if she's not breathing? Did Oliver upset her so much with news of the move that she needed a sedative? Or worse, maybe the stress of sudden relocation was too much, too fast. What if she's had a stroke or a heart attack?

Sliding my hand into the side pocket of my pants, I reach for my cell phone. My thumbprint illuminates the screensaver, adding enough light to see a duvet shrouded body on the bed. My eyes study the form again. I can't see movement or breath. If I use the flashlight feature, it might cause too much light to fill the small room and wake her. I don't want Fran to become upset, but I don't want to get caught, either. I'll tiptoe up, close enough to make sure she's breathing, and head back to Marlene's room.

My approach is silent, one foot in front of the other. With the light of my screen saver, I spot cardboard moving boxes littering the floor. Stepping to the right, I maneuver around a box, passing the entrance to Fran's bathroom. I take two more steps when I hear it.

Shallow, raspy breaths.

Only they are not coming from the form lying on the hospital bed.

The sound is closer, over my shoulder. Right behind me.

I spin, facing a tall figure holding a needle and a syringe.

64
LINDSAY
September 10

The hooded figure walks toward me, the ice axe slicing the air. My breath clogs in my throat. I back away toward the freezer, overcome with terror, my eyes never drifting from the weapon. I'm trapped, sandwiched between a madman and my mother's corpse.

I watch with horror as the light from the freezer illuminates a face under the hood.

"Thanks for inviting me over tonight, Lindsay. You made this easy for me."

Ken Preston grins with devilish delight, amused at my confusion. My former classmate's social awkwardness has eroded, his true self emerging from the phantom-shaped shadow of the furnace. He is the captor, and I am his prey.

"You… you killed my mother?" I whisper.

"Collateral damage," he shrugs. "I drove up the utility road toward the Tifton's hunting cabin to hide my car. But, as I passed the turnoff to your property, your mother was out back, smoking. She saw my BMW."

The macabre disposal of my mother's corpse, with the anchor rope still cinched around her neck, trumpets how much danger I am in. Ken is psychotic. He'll never let me go, not after I found him down here with Mother's body.

"Like I said, you made this easy."

"What do you mean?"

A laugh escapes his lips.

"The phone records will show *you* called me. I'm just the concerned high school classmate, checking up on a friend after receiving her distressing telephone call." His lip pouts, mocking my pain. "The same crazy Lindsay who forged a signature in the Willow Bend logbook and

282

dressed up in disguise. The cops think you're paranoid, after you posted those comments about them on *The Finger Lakes Flash*."

His deep voice offsets the methodic hum of the freezer, equal parts jarring and confident. Armed with the axe and his knowledge that it was me in Fran's room last Wednesday, he revels in his power play.

"I would never kill Mother!" I cry, watching the axe swing above his feet like a pendulum clock, ticking down the moments until he kills me, too.

"They'll believe me if I say you found out Nick was screwing your mother. You killed the wrong mistress. It wasn't Diane Desmond sleeping with Nick. Your mother fucked everyone."

The false accusation makes me gasp. What if he's right? No one will believe Mother is a victim, in any sense. She was the woman who tolerated her husband's infidelities, justifying the sexual prowess it manifested in herself as a salve, a way to cover up the deep wounds of insecurity his betrayal caused her. People *will* believe she would sleep with Nick. She'll always be remembered as the town predator. A woman with no friends. Like me.

"Here's how the story will go, Lindsay. First, you killed your cheating husband in a fit of rage because he fucked his mistress in *your* bed. Then, you stalked Dr. Desmond at Willow Bend, faking your entry while disguised as Claudia Marton. You wanted to eliminate Nick's lover, so you stabbed her using a steak knife from your own kitchen, one with Nick's fingerprints on the handle."

"No, no… I didn't. Nick never cheated on me!"

"You implied he did when we talked a few weeks ago in the Willow Bend parking lot. And what you didn't know was I had already found the steak knife in the lunch box Nick left in his mother's room. Pretty careless, don't you think, leaving a sharp object in a room with a dementia patient?" he chuckles. "No one knows I found the knife. I can say you killed Diane Desmond with it because you thought she was Nick's mistress. Are you following me, Lindsay?"

My mouth goes dry, remembering the lunchbox sitting on Fran's countertop when I visited Willow Bend. Nick's London broil sandwiches. Of course, he would take a knife to cut Fran's meat into smaller bites. A role reversal, a son caring for his ailing mother. The missing knife makes sense now.

"After you killed Dr. Desmond, your mother confessed *she* was the one fucking Nick whenever she visited town. You two had a fight, a big one. The kind where the unstable daughter wraps an anchor rope around her slutty mother's neck, to shut her up. *To make her pay.* Very prophetic, given how half the town blames your mother for Eileen O'Reilly's suicide."

He pauses, leaning forward on the axe like a walking cane. His voice grows somber. "You called me, despondent and rambling... saying you were going to kill yourself with an overdose of anxiety medication." He straightens, swinging the axe again. Tick-tock, tick-tock.

Oh God, if he makes me swallow pills, the police might buy this entire fake story! I have Brenda's pill vial in my room, and the bottle I stole from Claudia Marton is in my purse. *The police will believe him.*

"No!" I shake my head, glancing at Nick's sporting equipment, searching for any possible weapon. "*You're* the killer. Why? Why are you destroying my life?"

Ken stops swinging the axe, his face hardening.

"Your hero husband tried to destroy *me*! Everything and everyone I worked so hard for! Guess how many patients go weeks at a time without a visit from a single family member? Do you know who changes their diapers, or who calms them down when they rage in frustration because they don't remember where they are? I do. Me! I care for the forgotten souls all you pretty people are too busy to be bothered with. You treat them like you always treated me. As an afterthought, a bother. *A nuisance.*"

His words pummel me. I take a step backward, closer to the freezer.

"Every day, I went to Willow Bend and watched patient after patient suffer. Losing cognition, words, memories, trapped in shells of bodies with minds no longer capable of sustaining any quality of life. It's hard work, watching people deteriorate. A thankless job. *I* gave them mercy, prescribing the medication to calm their rage and hasten their deaths. I am their angel. I ended their misery."

Retreating another step away from him, my body abuts my mother's coffin. My hands brace against the rim, the cool air hitting my bent elbows. I can back away no further. The tightening wrench in my chest burns, sickening me. If I vomit, he'll attack. *Think.*

"But Dr. Desmond was the prescribing physician. Not you. I still don't understand."

"That bitch was too busy with her charity work and party planning to monitor the patients. She was never there! And then, she added her husband's campaign to her list of distractions. Why should she get the big bucks while I did all her work?"

Ken's retelling of the simmering resentment he felt toward Diane Desmond is only escalating his anger, but I still don't understand why he killed her. If I can't distract him, I need to stall him. Say something, anything.

Make every man feel like they are the most important person in the world.

"You were always there, Ken. I can vouch for that."

"Dr. Desmond didn't care about the patients—she cared about prestige. And I came up with a solution. I used *her* prescription authority number, not mine, when placing orders at Sutton's Apothecary. Your brother-in-law, Oliver, wanted to leave that frumpy wife of his. This was his way out. We made a lot of money off prescriptions that will track back to Dr. Desmond's prescriber number. The Wozilfin quieted the patients, and within a few months, they were dead."

Quiet. An idea comes to me. Wait for it. Wait for the right time.

"Oliver billed insurance for ancillary scripts for every patient on Wozilfin, and I doctored the charts. The anticonvulsants, the statins—all the other medications pay big time. A few months of insurance fraud. Each patient died before any of their families caught on. Hell, we saved those families *thousands* of dollars on residency fees at Willow Bend! And they weren't burdened facing their elderly family members who no longer recognized them. I cared about giving the patients a dignified death."

My heart races at his admission. Melvin was right! Ken and Oliver administered medication with lethal intent. Marlene Flynn noticed it, too, the zombie apocalypse taking over her floor at Willow Bend, as patients succumbed to the sedative effects of the drug. She warned me about it with Fran. Oh God, have they hurt her, too?

"Oliver helped kill Fran's friends?" I ask, incredulous.

Ken sneers.

"Oliver met with Dr. Desmond away from the office. They were screwing, and their pillow talk secured our plan. He reassured her. She didn't need to worry if her outside commitments took up so much of her time. The exclusive prescription contract with Willow Bend gave him oversight on every prescription. He told her he would let her know if anything was off. He lied, because our plan did benefit everyone, including the insurance companies in the long run. We split the profits from the ancillary prescriptions—chump change, considering how long those poor people may have lingered, otherwise."

The money stashed in the freezer was peanuts compared to the funds Oliver's scam bled from insurance companies. I missed the clues. Ken's swanky mid-life crisis BMW, his spiffy clothes, and the fancy cufflinks he wore at the regatta. Shopping is easy when you're stealing someone else's dime.

"Why would Diane Desmond sleep with Oliver?"

Ken lets out a chortle, mocking me.

"She felt ignored and used by her husband. Oliver told her what she wanted to hear. And the affair boosted his confidence. He could be more than the nerd trapped in a loveless marriage, outshined by his brother, and chained to his father's legacy. It was going smoothly, until your husband figured out the patients' insurance plans were paying for medications he never delivered."

Bile rises in my throat, triggering my gag reflex. The circles on Fran's Explanation of Benefits forms. Nick was tracking Fran's medications, checking to see if her insurance company paid claims for prescriptions Sutton's Apothecary never supplied. Circumstantial proof that he caught on to Ken and Oliver's scheme. Even Fran recognized the conflict, saying one of her sons loved Dr. Desmond, and the other hated her. But now, it's all too little, too late.

"How did my husband die? Who killed him? You or Oliver?"

"He had to be silenced, Lindsay."

Ken grins again, enjoying my horrified dismay.

"Who killed my husband?" I scream.

"I will ask the questions!" Ken snarls, his hands tightening around the axe handle. "Someone tipped off the pharmaceutical suppliers, and they called Dr. Desmond last Friday, asking her to explain the prescriptions. It's like a restaurant charging a customer for an omelet they never cooked, because they don't stock eggs in the refrigerator. Sutton's Apothecary didn't order a sufficient supply of drugs to match the insurance claims. *You* snitched on us, didn't you, Lindsay?"

Shaking my head, I protest.

"I didn't call anyone. I swear I didn't."

"You're lying. Haven't you learned by now that I don't let women in denial live? Look at Dr. Desmond! She can't deny writing the scripts because she's dead."

"You're not making any sense. Why would you kill her if you were framing her?"

His hands tighten their grip on the ice axe.

"She confronted me, wanting to know why I used her prescription authority number instead of my own. I told her to meet me after work by the lake, saying we could talk about her affair with Oliver. Everyone was hiding something."

"But why stab her?"

"I *told* you… We used *her* prescription authority number, but the gig is up. The pharmaceutical suppliers are on to us. But I've got it all worked out. Oliver will go down for this, not me. Dr. Desmond is the prescriber of record—if she's dead, she can't deny ordering the prescriptions. There's no proof against me. It will be my word against Oliver's, and he's got problems. He filled *every* prescription of Wozilfin. He was *screwing* Dr. Desmond. And he *killed* his own brother."

I gasp, the shock of his admission numbing me.

"A power structure exists, and if the structure stays unified, it survives."

Oliver killed Nick to keep his money-making scheme alive! I told Claudia Marton how conspiracies work—I understood the strategy, but I had the wrong players. My mind was stuck, circling around thoughts of police corruption, a jealous husband, and a backstabbing sister-in-law. But now, with the body count rising, the real players are getting boxed in, and they aren't in sync anymore. Their ruse is unraveling, and it's every man for himself.

Ken takes a step closer, the blade of the axe gleaming in the paltry light emanating from the freezer.

"You and your crazy behavior have created the perfect cover for me, Lindsay. Oliver told me how much you crave anxiety medication. You're going to swallow the whole bottle I brought with me. The overdose will kill you."

Everything can be made to look like something it's not. Mother's away games, Claudia Marton's patchy bald head, and my impending death.

Time is up.

Spinning around, I slam the freezer lid shut on top of Mother, extinguishing the interior light, blinding both me and my captor.

Quiet comes in a subterranean abyss of darkness.

<h1 style="text-align:center">65</h1>
<h1 style="text-align:center">CLAUDIA</h1>
September 10

I stumble backward, away from the piercing tip of the needle. The moving boxes block my escape path like track hurdles, causing me to fall to the floor. The figure approaches, each step silent yet calculated. The body on the hospital bed fails to move, despite the commotion in the room. As I scramble to regain my footing, the light from the alarm clock casts an eerie glow on the intruder's face.

"Lindsay, there's nowhere to hide. You're too late."

With the lack of light, the blonde wig fools Oliver Sutton. He thinks I'm his sister-in-law, Lindsay Sutton. And given the lack of movement on the hospital bed, his statement terrifies me. Did he kill his mother? I push a moving box between us as a shield, rising to my feet.

"This is your fault, Lindsay. You wouldn't shut your trap. Agents from the Drug Enforcement Administration paid a visit to the apothecary today and to my home, armed with search warrants. They know what Ken and I did. I won't go to prison. I'm taking off once I slip out of here. This ends tonight."

Ken Preston! Search warrants… the clever veil is exposed. But if Oliver sinks the needle into my skin, I won't be able to tell the police he confessed and plans to flee.

"Help!" I scream, pushing another moving box between us and backing toward the hospital bed.

My voice confuses him, and he hesitates before stepping around the box.

"You're like Nick. Poking around, asking questions, putting your nose where it doesn't belong. I paid him off, letting him think it was just an affair I was hiding. But he wouldn't give up." Oliver's voice is low, as he takes another step in my direction. "Do you know what he was doing? Checking

288

the prescription claims against the supply orders and then comparing them with his delivery records. He was trying to expose me."

John Corry was right! Oliver Sutton committed fratricide. He killed his own brother, and now, maybe his mother, too. She hasn't moved.

"I fooled him, Lindsay. He fell into my trap. I told him he busted me, and I said I was going to kill myself. Too much guilt over the affair and my shady business. He came to the bluffs above Buttermilk Creek, found me kneeling at the edge, afraid I would jump. I positioned myself to knock him off balance. He never saw it coming. Down he went, with all my secrets."

I back away with an arm outstretched, ready to fend him off at any cost. He steps around another moving box, as I lunge for the call button on Fran Sutton's bed.

He tackles me, dislodging my thumb from the plunger on the bedside call button. I jam my elbow into his arm, the weight of his body pressing down on me. We bump against the unresponsive body on the bed. The syringe drops to the floor. Oliver's hands encircle my throat. I flail underneath him, his fingertips squeezing on my windpipe. With the heel of my shoe, I kick backwards into his shin, knocking him off balance. The pressure on my throat releases long enough for me to turn to my side, as his fists start flying. A punch connects with my mouth, the sour tang of blood coating my tongue. He grabs at the blonde wisps of hair dangling beneath my ballcap, and the wig gives, releasing into his palm.

"Someone, help me!" I croak, squirming free from his clutch. He drops the wig to the floor and dives at me, throwing my body on top of one of the moving boxes. Falling to the floor, my head strikes the hard, cold tile. Oliver straddles my waist and reaches for something at my side.

His body is silhouetted against the dim illumination from the alarm clock. As I struggle underneath him, his hand raises, the syringe posed to strike.

"You!" he seethes, my hairless head revealing my identity. "You were sneaky, too! Taking photos in my office and lending your wig to my sister-in-law. I should have shut you up for good when I was in your home, videotaping your masquerade room. I'm tired of your disguises!"

From the hallway, voices echo, along with a clopping sound. My hands grasp his wrist inches below the syringe. His strength overpowers me, and I shut my eyes as the needle closes in.

66
LINDSAY
September 10

The thud of the axe tip hitting the lid of my freezer echoes in the dark basement. I lunge toward Nick's sporting equipment, the glow-in-the-dark worms and bobbers serving as valuable points of reference. My feet trip over boat cushions and lanterns, as Ken shouts at me.

"You'll never get away, Lindsay!"

His voice booms near the freezer. I push the kayaks between myself and Ken, tossing a small cooler in his direction, before turning toward the accordion door. My arms stretch in front of me, bracing for a collision with the furnace or the undercarriage of the stairwell. Panic carries me, as Ken trips in pursuit.

A trickle of light from the neon bar sign skirts through a sliver of space on the door frame, where the magnetic closure mounts. I yank the folding door to the side, round the corner, and scramble on to the stairs.

My chest burns, a boulder-sized pressure cramping the space between my stomach and lungs. Opening the accordion door illuminated the exit for Ken, and he's gaining on me. About halfway up the flight, I trip on a riser, my body crashing on the steps as a hand grasps my ankle, tugging hard.

"No!" I scream, kicking with my free foot. I connect with his body twice, around his shoulder. On my third attempt, I aim higher, my foot thrusting against Ken's face. He yelps, letting go of my ankle. Clawing to the top of the stairwell, terror is reflected in the wheezy cries escaping my mouth. The basement door slams behind me, as my feet plant in the center of the mud room. The backdoor to the kitchen is ajar, cool gusts of night air blowing through its companion screen door. It swings on its hinges, creaking in the night.

I never shut the main door.

When Ken sees this, he'll think I escaped out back! I slip from the mudroom into the garage, as thundering footsteps ascend the stairs. Crouching against the garage wall, I listen.

The basement door slams into the stop mount, a springing recoil announcing his presence on the landing in the mudroom. After a brief pause, he stomps across the kitchen to the screen door, which lets out a squeak before clattering shut.

Ken's outside, thinking I'm out there. The windowless garage is darker than the basement. I debate tiptoeing to the tool shelf to arm myself with a hammer, but if I bump into the shelf and anything falls to the floor, he'll know where I'm hiding. Better not.

Straining to listen, the beating thumps of my heart pound in my chest. He's calling my name.

"Lindsay! I know you're out here!"

His voice mocks my terror, a killer enjoying the thrill of his hunt. Listening, clues echo in the night. My ears tune to a familiar noise. A car door opening, the ting-tong chiming inside. He's looking in my car, thinking I hid in there! He'll check Nick's truck next.

But now… quiet. No rustling. No door slamming. No movement. Only the sound of my own breath.

Where is he? Did I hurt him with my kick?

I listen again.

The whistle of the wind rustles tree leaves. Somewhere, a frog croaks, amid a static buzz of insects. Ken hasn't shut the car door yet, and I don't think he's opened Nick's truck to look for me. Other than nature's night music, the quiet is haunting.

What is he doing?

The absence of the backdoor creaking and the lack of feet plodding across the kitchen floor reassures me. Ken must still be outside. Did he leave, fleeing up the utility road to the Tifton hunting cottage, where he stashed his car?

I step away from the wall, moving to the middle of the garage, where I stop and wait, listening again.

Nothing. Only nature.

I exhale, my shoulders relaxing, when suddenly, darkness evaporates.

The light on the automatic garage door opener illuminates above my head, bathing me in an incandescent glow. The rear garage door begins gliding up its track, one inch at a time.

Ken found the garage door opener on the visor in my car!

Panicked, I scramble toward the wall mount control for the front garage door. My palm slams against it as I drop to my knees. I glance behind me and see Ken and the axe trying to shimmy under the rising rear garage door.

The front door opens incrementally inch by inch, at the same pace as the back door, only a few seconds or so separating the electronic signals. I flatten myself against the cement floor and turn my head away from him, toward the long, front driveway to my property. A car's headlights beam as they turn in my direction. If Ken hits the tandem button on the garage door opener, it will stop the front door from opening.

"Help me!" I scream, scooching out from under the door, just as Ken's fingertips skim my ankle. I launch forward like a runner starting a race, sprinting down the driveway toward the approaching car, waving my arms.

The headlights blind me. I can't see the driver. As the car approaches, I point behind me while veering onto the lawn. Ken is clear of the garage door and stands, brandishing the ice axe. The garage light illuminates the crazed look on his face.

The car accelerates past me with a thrust of power, the driver flooring the gas pedal. I turn, watching as the car strikes Ken with lethal force, propelling his body backward into the garage. It thumps on the cement. The car doesn't stop, running over his tangled limbs and head, roaring all the way through the double-door garage. It crashes into my Tahoe, coming to rest with a loud, crunching sound upon impact. The car horn beeps, the interior light illuminating poppy red hair.

Brenda!

Running toward the car, I pass Ken's mangled corpse on the floor of my garage. Brenda is moaning in the front seat, resting against the deployed airbag, still strapped in by her seatbelt.

"Brenda!"

Frantic over the possibility she might be injured, I tug the door handle. Brenda's face radiates panic.

"I… I… did it, Lindsay. I c… ca… called one of those pill suppliers back. 'Member? I told you they were ca… ca… calling the house?" Her voice cracks. "I… I didn't tell you the other pa… part. I don't know what I would have done if I didn't get here in time."

"Bren, are you okay? How did you know that I was in trouble? What other part?"

"Ol… Oliver made me fill out all the supply orders for the pharmacy. He had the software on our laptop at home." Brenda sucks in her breath, trying not to hyperventilate. "He told me what to order and I did it. I did it without thinking! But then, when the suppliers were calling, I got scared. What if he was setting me up?"

My mind races, thinking back to how Ken said Oliver wanted to leave Brenda. I'm about to speak, but Brenda doesn't give me the chance.

"When the drug suppliers called again, I… I told them I didn't know what he was up to, but I said I would cooperate in any way I co… could."

Brenda climbs out of the car, and I lunge forward, hugging her tight. She returns the hug, but then pulls back, her hands gripping my forearms.

"Oliver… and Ken…" Her voice shakes. "Federal agents searched the house and the apothecary today. Lindsay, the agents asked me about Ken Preston. They said they called Dr. Desmond before she was killed! There were a bunch of prescriptions they had questions about, but she denied ordering them. Ken was the only person with access to her prescriber number who could have ordered the prescriptions. They suspect Ken and Oliver killed Dr. Desmond and Nick over this, and I was worried they would kill you, too!"

"They murdered all of them, Bren! Nick, Diane, my mother… Ken killed Mother! And he almost killed me!" Tears stream down my cheeks, the enormity of my loss mixing with gratitude for my sister-in-law's rescue. "Wait!" I say, with renewed alarm. "Where's Delaney?"

"She's at a friend's house. The agents were still searching at the house when school let out. I didn't want her to see what was happening. Where's Oliver?" she asks, her tone panicked.

"I don't know! Ken was in my house when I got home. He put… Mother… in…" Sobs choke me, as Brenda grabs my arm again.

"Oliver's not here?"

I shake my head, the crippling grip of shock overtaking my body, as I struggle to form words.

"Bren, remember how Oliver wanted to change Fran's medication? What if he's trying to kill her too, in case she remembers something? She still has good days…"

The whistling wind carries Brenda's scream.

"Fran!"

67
CLAUDIA
September 10

The door to room 319 opens, and someone switches on the overhead light. Oliver Sutton blinks, trying to adapt to the brightness. The long needle is posed to strike, mere inches above my eye. My arms are tiring, caving under the weight of his force.

"Get off her! Someone, help us!" Marlene Flynn's piercing voice dissects the silence, distracting my attacker. I wiggle, turning my head away from the pointy tip of the needle. An overturned moving box lays on its side to my left, next to an array of paperback books and a brassy, L-shaped bookend.

"I'll stick you with insulin!" Oliver screams at Marlene.

Insulin! Moving boxes are nothing but a prop. Oliver wants to run and is making sure his mother never learns what he's done to her other son and to her friends. If he injected Fran, her blood glucose levels will plummet, killing her in short order. She hasn't moved on the bed, and I am his next target.

"Help!" Marlene screams again, the walking boot hampering her advance. Her presence is the distraction I need, as my hand reaches for the brassy object. My fingertips touch the cool surface, and I swing, the brass making a stomach-turning clunking sound as it collides with Oliver's temple. He falls forward, his body trapping mine, blood trickling from his face and dribbling on my chin.

Marlene bends at the waist, helping roll his unconscious body off me. A nurse appears in the doorway and gasps, the bloody indentation on Oliver's face distorting his skull formation. The syringe and needle lay on the floor, next to the blonde wig, inches from Fran Sutton's hospital bed.

She does not move.

THE FINGER LAKES FLASH

Your online snapshot capturing the local news you need to know.
September 11
We will never forget.

A note to the readers of The Finger Lakes Flash:

On this solemn anniversary of the 9/11 terrorist attacks, The Finger Lakes Flash honors the 2,977 people who lost their lives and the more than 6,000 people injured. The attacks were the deadliest terrorist act in world history and the largest foreign attack on United States soil since Pearl Harbor on December 7, 1941. More than 90 countries lost citizens in the attacks.

In 2007, the New York City medical examiner's office began adding people who died of illnesses caused by exposure to dust from the plane crash sites to the official death toll. The number of 9/11 responders who have died due to their exposure to the toxins will soon surpass the number killed on 9/11. In 2019, funding for the 9/11 Victims Compensation Fund was extended through 2090.

I am a 9/11 responder experiencing health complications due to my response at the Flight 93 crash site in Shanksville, Pennsylvania.

Last evening, I again became a victim of a violent crime. To assist the Romulus Police Department and the Seneca County District Attorney's Office, I am suspending publication of The Finger Lakes Flash temporarily, while the police investigation and prosecution ensues.

To my loyal readers of The Finger Lakes Flash, I will live on and return!
~Claudia Marton

68
CLAUDIA
October 2

There's a new message in the tipster email box.

Despite all that has happened, the dangle of new information still excites me. I don't fear what's in the box. Oliver Sutton sent me the creepy video email, but I will not let him get the last word. I'm not letting the bad guys win.

I click on the new message, wondering what it could be.

Dear Ms. Marton,

I am sorry it has taken me a few weeks to reach out to you. Thank you for the flowers you sent to Lindsay. We held a private service for her mother, and once the burial was completed, we flew to my condominium in Sedona. My wife and I used to come here as snowbirds every winter before she became a patient at Willow Bend. I may stay permanently. We'll see.

Lindsay is not well. I thought the change of scenery would help, but she's had ongoing nightmares since the attack. Mixing alcohol with her prescription medication was frequent. We had a long talk, and I told her we needed to get her some help.

There is a facility here where the doctors and counselors monitor her, making sure she gets the proper levels of medication to help with the post-traumatic stress. She'll seem fine but then cries when a door slams or when a cool gust of air blows on her from a wall vent. The doctors call these her fear triggers... regular, everyday things that remind her of Nick and Sylvia's murders, and the terror she experienced in the basement and the garage. I'm an old man, so I don't fully understand all this Sigmund Freud stuff, but when I hear the song 'Moon River,' it makes me miss my wife, so I guess this is kind of like that in a small way.

I bring ice cream shakes to Lindsay when I visit her. She cried the other day when I told her I was going to write to you. She just nodded and cried. I think she feels terrible about what Oliver did to Fran and what he almost did to you.

Please take care of yourself and my friend, Marlene Flynn. I'm very thankful neither of you were killed. I'll keep watching for when The Finger Lakes Flash resumes operation.

Until then, be well.

~Melvin Anderson

Tears fill my eyes.

"*...but when I hear the song Moon River, it makes me miss my wife...*"

Oh, Melvin, you sweet man.

"*...I guess this is kind of like that in a small way.*"

Yes, it is, I think sadly. None of us can outrun triggers. They're impervious to state lines, time of day, or calendar years. They fill random air with loud noises, beautiful songs, and planes set against city skylines. They tickle your nose like the smell of an egg salad sandwich from a corner deli, or they smack you in the face with a blast of cool vapor.

Triggers are everywhere, and we all have them.

It's the one thing we all try to disguise.

THE FINGER LAKES FLASH

Your online snapshot capturing the local news you need to know.
November 3

Local Pharmacist Pleads Guilty

Local pharmacist Oliver Sutton, 47, pleaded guilty yesterday to two counts of first-degree murder, for the killings of his brother, Nicholas "Nick" Sutton, and his mother, Francine "Fran" Sutton, both of Romulus. Sutton, the owner and operator of Sutton's Apothecary, confessed to killing his brother last June, when his sibling discovered an elaborate insurance fraud scheme Sutton engaged in with local nurse practitioner, Kenneth Preston. Additionally, Sutton pleaded guilty to one count of attempted murder, for a September attack on Claudia Marton, the owner of *The Finger Lakes Flash*, and to numerous counts of insurance fraud. Marton was attacked after she discovered Sutton had killed his mother at Willow Bend Long-Term Care Home.

The Seneca County District Attorney says Sutton and Preston conspired to prescribe elderly dementia patients at Willow Bend Long-Term Care Home with antipsychotic medication that accelerated death, while also billing insurance companies for medications Sutton's Apothecary never supplied to these patients. Preston murdered local physician Dr. Diane Desmond and former Romulus resident Sylvia Kelly. He was killed by Oliver Sutton's wife, Brenda Sutton, while he attempted to murder Lindsay Sutton, the widow of Nick Sutton and the daughter of Sylvia Kelly.

Family members of eleven deceased patients have filed civil lawsuits against Sutton's Apothecary and Willow Bend Long-Term Care Home. Both entities are currently closed.

Sutton has a sentencing hearing in Seneca County Circuit Court on January 5. Prosecutors are recommending two life sentences without the possibility of parole.

69

LINDSAY

November 18

"No more ice cream."

Melvin eyes me with suspicion.

"Since when don't you like ice cream?"

"Oh, I like it. That's the problem. I like it too much."

He sits next to me on a bench outside, near the edge of the pine forest abutting my treatment center. The red-rock canyons are visible in the distance, bright streaks of crimson set against the desert horizon backdrop. Melvin hands the milkshake to me and I take it, letting him win.

"You need a little meat on your bones."

"I've gained six pounds!"

"That's okay. The doctors say you're doing better."

My gaze stretches, eyeing the rock formations.

"Yeah, I am. I'm not as edgy as those canyons, anymore," I say, pointing in the distance. "The doctors figured out the right level for my meds. Looks like I'll be getting out soon."

He nods, playing with the straw in his milkshake cup, before speaking again.

"Dr. Janson said it's okay for me to talk to you about a few things. If you start to feel upset, just tell me and I'll stop, okay?"

"Okay," I say, looking down at my feet. "She's teaching me this technique called 'grounding.' If I get that vacuum feeling, where all the air kind of gets sucked out of me, I'm supposed to look around and find five things I can name. Tree, rock, car… things like that."

"Does it help?"

"Well, sometimes I need to go on to the next step, which is four things I can touch. After that, three things I can hear, two things I can smell, and then, one emotion I can feel. Dr. Janson says learning to handle my anxiety triggers with cognitive behavior therapy is like strapping on a tool belt. She's big on this 'grounding' thing."

"We could all use a little 'grounding' now and then," Melvin says, before shifting slightly on the bench. He taps his straw a few times on the rim of the cup, and says quietly, "The life insurance payout was approved. They're wiring the money to your bank account."

Biting my lip, his words settle in. There's an unsatisfying victory sensation washing over me, where I win the game that I never wanted to play in the first place. All the buckets of money in the world can't equal what Nick meant to me. I look around. Cactus. Pebble. Shoelace. Flower. Sun.

"Then, the realtor in Florida scheduled the closing on your mother's condo for the end of the month. Once the mortgage, taxes, and fees are paid, you're going to net about fifty or so grand."

The calculator in my brain dings. Baby money is rolling in everywhere. The cops let me keep the money I found in the freezer. They couldn't prove it was the same money Oliver defrauded from the insurance companies. My understanding of comingling dirty money with clean money was spot on, which benefitted me, but unfortunately, won't help Brenda. Sutton's Apothecary is facing a bunch of civil lawsuits, and her lawyers are urging her to keep her personal financial affairs separate from Oliver's business. The good news is that she cooperated with federal agents, and they believe she didn't know what Oliver was up to. She won't be charged criminally. And fortunately, neither will I, since Claudia Marton convinced the police that I shouldn't be prosecuted for swiping her anxiety pills.

"That's good," I say, aware Melvin is watching me closely.

"And I booked the flights for Brenda and Delaney. They'll be here next week for Thanksgiving."

I bounce on the bench, my mood inflating with joy.

"Yeah! Oh, I'm so excited! I've been worried about them." I wrap my arms around Melvin and squeeze, giving him an appreciative side hug.

"Sounds like they need to get away, too. Brenda says Delaney misses a school setting. Homeschooling is depressing them, and with the lawsuits…"

His voice trails off, but my mind is racing.

"Do you think they will move here, by us?" I say excitedly, hopeful I can be close to them again.

"Brenda might be leaning that way, but there is a problem."

"What?" I ask, hoping he's not reconsidering his decision not to sue Sutton's Apothecary.

"My cooking. I tried watching that Contessa lady, Ina what's-her-name, but who am I kidding? We don't want to scare them off. We'll go out to eat on Thanksgiving, okay?"

I slap his arm playfully, as he smirks at me.

"That's probably the smartest thing you've said all day," I say, taking another sip of my milkshake. "You are my family now, Melvin. You know that, right?"

He nods, his blue eyes twinkling.

"Good. Because one of these days, I'm going through with the embryo transfer. My baby is going to need a grandfather."

He squeezes my hand, overcome with emotion. We sit for a minute in silence, taking comfort in our bond. Melvin pulls a handkerchief from his pocket, dabbing his eyes, before speaking again.

"Lindsay, there's one more thing."

His voice is quiet.

Uh-oh.

My fingers scratch my cotton sweatpants, before moving along the decorative hem of the pocket. Sixteen stitches. My index finger rubs the hangnail on my thumb. One more thing. Touch something else. I play with the straw, again.

"I spoke with your attorney. He got a call from your neighbor, Joe Tifton, asking about the property. They want the land, and would bulldoze the house so it doesn't become a lookie-loo draw…"

"Yes," I say quickly, interrupting him. "Whatever they offer, take it. Get it in writing they will raze the house."

Water in the fountain. A car door slam. A clicky-sounding insect.

"You okay, dear? This is a lot."

Peering at the canyons again, I inhale a long, slow breath through my nose. I reach into my pocket.

"Just one more thing, Melvin." I say, sliding an envelope into his hand.

"Mail this. Please."

70
CLAUDIA
November 22

The folding chairs are arranged in a circle, under outdated fluorescent lights. On a side table, a large coffee urn spits out a medium roast brew into Styrofoam cups. Angela and Patrice are here, welcoming me back to our weekly Tuesday night meeting, the one where I met Stella. It's healing to reconnect with them.

Marlene Flynn sits to my left, eager to discuss her grief over Francine Sutton's murder. She's got it, a horrible case of survivor's guilt. It haunts her days with thoughts of "what-ifs"—what if she had called the police sooner, what if she had spoken up immediately instead of sending me on a scavenger hunt for clues at the cemetery, what if she refused to leave Fran's room when Oliver arrived… what if. At night, the dreams come, too. While toxic dust clouds are the phantom ghosts appearing during my REM phases, Marlene sees the syringe and the needle. She wakes, shaking in fear, thinking of the fatal prick under Fran Sutton's thumbnail. In an age where "see something, say something" dominates, Marlene's old-school, second guessing of what her gut was telling her is a heavy burden. In some ways, she acted like a responsible journalist. Smelling the smoke of a story but not running with it without confirmation, or solid proof. Her torment is real.

Glancing at the cup of diluted coffee in my left hand, I notice new freckles dotting my knuckles. My recent trip to Hilton Head Island with Felicia was a much-needed respite, and rebirth. A little sun, a few tears, new understandings. Don Weaverman drafted my estate plans. Felicia is the named executor. Stella was right when she told me to get it done so I can get on with living. That's what I plan to do, the clarity of this importance as stark as the bald patches on my scalp.

I set the coffee cup on the floor, pulling out an envelope from my pocket. It came today in the mail. The return address is Sedona, Arizona. It seemed wise to wait until I was here to open it, in case the news isn't good.

A single sheet of paper is neatly folded in the envelope. I smooth out the creases and begin reading.

Dear Claudia,

I'm not sure where to start, because I owe you so much. Thank you for the flowers you sent for my mother's service. I don't remember much from those first days after... but thank you.

I'm sorry I didn't trust you. It wasn't really because of you or anything you did. I can see that now. I was raised not to trust women, and Nick was my everything. As you figured out at the regatta, my anxiety was off the hook, but that's not an excuse for how I treated you. I'm sorry I said those things about you and your boyfriend at the wine bar, and I'm sorry I took your pills.

I owe you a new wig. I haven't forgotten. Pick out anything you want at Wigwash Wonders. They will bill me.

This is the part, though, that's hardest for me to write. There are two more things I need to say:

Thank you for trying to save Fran. If Nick were here, he would say it, too.

The last time I talked with my mother, I told her I wanted to have friends. I'm tired of not trusting. You made me realize that other women don't have to be the enemy. And I'm happy I got the chance to tell my mother about the kind of person I wanted to become.

I hope you can forgive me, and someday, we can be friends.
~ Lindsay

I sniffle a bit, contemplating how my own journey learning to trust again helped a stranger do the same.

Everyone's clever veils have been lifted now, with truth shimmering like morning sunlight on tranquil lake water. Even the special kinds of truth, the ones that fall under the professional privilege umbrella.

Federal agents, tipped off by drug distributors about the supply discrepancies at Sutton's Apothecary, contacted the Romulus Police Department in preparation for the execution of their search warrants.

Peter knew Sutton's Apothecary was under investigation but couldn't tell me. I'm not harboring a grudge, because that would focus on the past, and I'm committed to living in the present.

I brush a few wisps of hair from my new Phoebe wig off my face, before reaching to my right and giving Peter's hand a squeeze. He squeezes back, stroking my knuckle with his thumb.

Peter belongs here at circle group, too.

Acknowledgements

I believe the best stories are always the ones that end with unexpected enlightenment. When I set out to write my first novel, many encouraged me to write about a female FBI agent, because "write what you know" is what writers do best. While there were many exciting aspects to my twenty-two-year career as an FBI agent, that wasn't the focus of the first story I wanted to tell. Simply put, the most fascinating aspect of my job wasn't me. It was the lessons I learned from the victims I met.

No two were exactly alike, and many experienced the worst tragedy imaginable at a time when they were already dealing with serious illnesses, unemployment, divorce, financial hardship, harassment, or the loss of a child. The complexities of life created general mistrust for many victims long *before* the crime occurred. Despite the admirable bravery, compassion, strength, and vulnerability I witnessed, many victims also simultaneously battled internal fears, underlying frustrations, desperation, and anger. For each person who struggled to regain trust because of criminal victimization, there was someone else who learned or was *taught* never to trust others in the first place.

The dichotomy between trust and mistrust permeated every case I worked on. And then, I wrestled with my own conflicted emotions when I became a potential crime victim myself.

9/11 responders who have died due to a designated health condition caused by the terror attacks are now included in the official 9/11 death count. I was a 9/11 responder at the Pentagon, and I have experienced many complex health issues in the years that followed 9/11. A parotid tumor was removed, my two hips were replaced, and I underwent extensive spinal fusion all within four years before I turned fifty. My various surgeons couldn't explain why parts of my skeleton disintegrated or why my tumor formed, but exposure to toxins at the Pentagon is believed to be the likely culprit. I fall into the same category as my character Claudia, where strange things have happened that no one can explain. I am a member of the World Trade Center Health Program, and I am monitored so the medical community can learn more about the potential health risks caused by toxin exposure.

Around the time of my surgeries, I started experiencing unexplained hair loss, and I found I worried as much about losing my hair as I did about survival, malignancy, facial disfigurement, and the ability to walk again. I also grappled with shame for worrying about potential scars, limps, thinning hair or bald spots when a lot of my fellow 9/11 responders were dying. And, like so many of the victims I worked with, I was angry, frustrated, and afraid. Many victims conveyed wisdoms to me through the years about how they had regained or maintained trust in an increasingly hostile world. These sage insights were prescient gifts I am forever grateful for receiving.

The Bald-Faced Deception depicts a suspenseful mystery, centered around two women afraid to trust, each for entirely different reasons. Their journeys of self-actualization are the subplot to this caper, but I hope this story will make you ponder some of the same questions they do. A list of topics for Book Club discussions is included in subsequent pages.

There are many people I need to thank for their tremendous support while I was writing this book. To my developmental editor, Kristen Weber, who embraced this novel and its story so enthusiastically, and encouraged me to flesh out the complicated relationship between Lindsay and her mother. Kristen, you have such a gift for analyzing story construction and character arc. I am so lucky to work with you!

To my beta-readers: Michelle Machado, thank you for always being my biggest cheerleader and helping spot all the big and little mistakes I make in draft after draft. I can't ever thank you enough for the time you have dedicated toward helping me become a published author. Thank you, Monique Comeau, for your keen eye and your appreciation of my humor! Author Rebecca Drake, thank you so much for your suggestions! I strived to incorporate many of them into the plot. In addition to Rebecca, thank you to my other writing friends, particularly Jolene McIlwain, Nancy Martin, Annette Dashofy, Susan Thibadeau, and Meredith Mileti. Your input on jacket copy, cover design, formatting, marketing, mystery writing and all the nuances of publishing were very helpful. And I *so* enjoy our frequent long lunches and Zooms!

To my great friends Lexie Craven Bryan, Vanessa Petersen, and Julie Halferty, thank you for always being in my corner, and for supporting this book.

A shout-out to all my friends and fans in the podcast world. Your support for my Patreon true crime podcast *Caught In My Web* has been incredible, and so many of you have been equally enthused about this book. Thank you!

Thank you to my parents, Tom and Paulette Weber, for reading early drafts of this novel and for championing me throughout my life. Your love and support mean the world to me, and I am fortunate to have you as parents.

And finally, to my children, Max and Madison, for bringing immeasurable joy and delight to my life. I am so proud to be your mother.

A Reading Group Discussion Guide

1. The character Lindsay suspects her husband is committing adultery yet never confronts him. Why do spouses avoid confrontation about infidelity, and is it possible to fully trust a cheating spouse again? Does losing trust with a spouse cause a person to trust other people less?

2. The character Claudia is very self-conscious about her hair loss. How much does your hair contribute to your sense of confidence and attractiveness?

3. Lindsay struggles with familial conflict, both with her mother and with her brother-in-law and sister-in-law. She questions if she holds her own family members to the same standards as the family members she gained through marriage. Are people more apt to forgive blood relatives than others for the same mistreatment or bad conduct?

4. Claudia feels guilty for exploring a potential relationship with Peter. When is it okay to engage in a relationship with someone that a close friend was previously romantically linked to, either through dating or marriage? Should women be distrustful of other women, like Sylvia suggests? Have you met women who avoid female friendships? If so, why do you think they do not want or value friendships with other women?

5. Lindsay is extremely paranoid about town gossip and rumors. What subjects are off limits for gossip? Do children with parents like Sylvia inherit unfair stigmatization?

6. Claudia and her sister Felicia have different ideas about what environments produce stability. Does living near family necessarily create stability, or does it create more friction and frustration?

7. Both Lindsay and Claudia struggle with anxiety. Numerous coping mechanisms (both healthy and unhealthy) are featured in the plot. Which of the anxiety triggers in the book did you relate to? How do you handle anxiety?

8. Should death with dignity legislation be available everywhere?

9. Claudia and Peter are grieving differently. Do you think men and women grieve differently for a reason?

10. A big theme in this book involves focusing on the past and/or fearing the future. How difficult is it to focus on the present, and does the inability to focus on the present affect overall happiness?

11. Diane and Roger Desmond are depicted as a power-couple, each with successful careers. Can spouses have equally successful professional accomplishments, or does one inevitably play second fiddle to the other?

12. Sylvia Kelly agrees to an "arrangement" with Lindsay's father. She tells Lindsay that "arrangements" can work as long as no one asks questions or voices complaints. Do you think "arrangements" can work?